THE LIES I'VE TOLD

Charles Serio

Published by: St. DeSales 2015

Published by St. DeSales 2015
978-0-9576873-8-7/978-0-9576873-9-4
Copyright: Charles Serio

CONTENTS

THE LIES I'VE TOLD

The Internet ruined everything.
Once upon a time, a teller of tales, like myself, could simply say
what he wanted and no one would be any the wiser.
But not anymore.

If I told a story, for example, about the time I had lunch with Sugar
Ray Leonard and Dan Rather at Governor Edward's mansion in
Baton Rouge in 1978, people can go on the Internet and find out if
that is true or not.
Maybe Dan Rather was no where near Louisiana in 1978 or Sugar
Ray was training for some big fight in Africa that year and there is
no way that he could have been breaking bread with me in the Deep
South.

So these days a storyteller has to be extra careful.
Because without belief in the story, you have no story.

This is why I blame the Internet for putting an unfair burden on all of
us who like to spin a good yarn. Exaggerating details and incidents
for effect is laden with danger.
Your cover can be blown and your story right along with it.

Most of my stories I've told many times in many circumstances.
I suppose, over time, some of the facts may have been shifted around
and some of the players changed too.
But until the Internet came along, I never had to worry about such
things.

All right, sometimes perhaps, my motivations in telling my tales may
have been slightly self-serving.

It is possible that I told some stories, because they might make me
sound interesting to someone I fancied.
It just might be the case that I made myself appear cool and collected
in a firestorm, when all around me were lost to panic and fright.

It could be argued, conceivably, that I wanted to pretend I had experience with some supernatural strangeness to impress some friends.
Maybe I hoped to come across as a reticent, unsung hero in a time of great danger to show off my bravery for the bedazzlement of the ladies.

I admit to that. I am not particularly proud of that fact, but it is the way it is.

But here you have it anyway. These are 'The Lies I've Told' most often in my life.
I cannot tell them aloud so much anymore, but more about that later.

So, go ahead. Start your infernal search engines, if you must.
And let the fries fall into the fat fryer as they may.

Ralph E. Waldo

STORY CHAPTER ONE

'SEAN HARBY WAS A ZOMBIE'

The incident described here launched my storytelling career. I first related it to other kids in my schooldays in the mid 60's. I thought it made me sound 'cool' or, rather, in the vernacular of the mid 60's, 'neat'.

These days, I'd probably tell it something like this:

By the early 21st Century, Vampires and Zombies were all the rage. I must admit that my knowledge of them is rather limited. I think Vampires are all about blood and sex now while Zombies are more about blood and gore.
I'm sure there is more to it than that, but that's how I distinguish them anyway.

Not that I believe in Vampires or Zombies.
Necessarily.

It's just that with Vampires and Zombies saturating the media so much recently, it reminded me of the first time I ever heard the word 'Zombie'. And the first time too that I ever saw someone 'Zombified'.

I was desperate to see my girlfriend. I was fourteen. You are desperate about a lot of things when you are fourteen. In fact, you are certain your desperation will kill you, if you cannot do what you simply must do.
And I simply had to see my girlfriend, Diane Tompkins. Whatever it took.

Diane Tompkins was the only girl on the planet to me.
Has there ever been anyone as beautiful? Has there ever been anyone so graceful and serene? Has there ever been anyone as hot as she was in her gym shorts?

3

No. That would be impossible.

And here it was the summer. No school. Long days of sunshine. Stolen kisses behind the groundskeeper's shed. Yes, the summer of 1966 promised to be hormone heaven.

But, no! No, Diane Tompkins had gone off to spend the summer as a counselor at a girls' summer camp. She would be at Padfoot Camping Grounds on the other side of the Maryland State Line. Out in the sticks.

I was not old enough to drive. No magic transit bus existed to take me there.

I was in misery.

I'd be mortified a brighter shade of ruby-red, if my older brother even knew I liked a girl. He'd never tire of teasing me. I couldn't tell my parents. There was no one I could ask for help in getting me there.

And it is in moments like those when you remember exactly how rotten it was to be a teenager. You do not control your own destiny and nobody 'understands'.

So I was miserable. I was 'snappy-unhappy'.

Even I hated me.

And then one afternoon, after playing with some friends, I went home for lunch.

There was a letter at my place at the table.

'That came for you this morning, Ralphy,' my mother said as casually as you like.

I looked at the return address. It was from Diane! The whole and entire address! I could write to her! I was so happy I forgot all about lunch. I grabbed the letter and floated upstairs to the room I shared with my brother.

Her letter was beautiful. Perfect penmanship. The occasional drawn and colored daisy in the margins. The row of gold stars across the bottom. Lovely! As lovely as Diane Tompkins. And that's a lot of lovely.

After soaking up the aesthetics for a while, I got into the content itself.

'Dear Ralphy', she began.

4

'I've made so many friends here at Padfoot already. Everyone's so nice! It's so much fun! We have campfires and sing-a-longs and all the little girls are so cute! And over on the other side of the lake is the Boys' camp and we meet with the boy counselors sometimes and this one boy, Max, showed me how to do archery. And I got good at it too!'

It went on like this for pages and pages. If it wasn't 'Max' teaching her how to sling her bow, it was 'Ricky' and how *'Everyone admires him, because he's just our age, but he's already one of the senior lifeguards!'*
I wasn't floating so much anymore.

And then about six pages in, her tone changed.

Diane said she met some girl named 'Charmaine' and Charmaine had 'psychic abilities' or so she wrote. And she went on about secret night visits to the Padfoot Headquarters House. She told me this was an old stone Manor House used now as offices and a meeting place for adult staff.
Diane said that Charmaine would take her and some of the other counselors there to hold 'séances' late at night.
'Charmaine told us that she can speak with the dead. And I saw her do it too!'
'I bet that Max is there too.' I fretted to myself.

Diane said the whole thing 'kind of scared' her, but she felt caught up in it now. *'Charmaine's really nice, but sometimes I want to hang out with the other girls and Charmaine kind of forces me to tag along in her stuff.'*
Stuff that frightened her.

Diane's dad had died only a few months ago. He was an ardent smoker.
Her father was a very popular guy in our neighborhood. People would bring their broken TVs and radios for him to repair. He had a workshop in his basement.
But he died slowly and painfully and Diane hadn't come to terms with that yet. If anyone can truly come to terms with losing someone they loved dearly.
She loved her dad and if she let herself think about him, she'd be in tears.

She certainly didn't need Charmaine's mystical musings to upset her more.

'She even forced my tent-mate to move out and moved in with me herself. And I really liked my old tent-mate too.'
She then concluded, *'If only you were here! You'd know just what to say so nobody would get upset. I wish you were here right now!'*
She signed her letter *'Miss Diane Tompkins, Bluebell Camp, Padfoot'* with all the letters in pretty curlicues.
That was it.

I had to get there. If it were possible to want to get there even more than I did before her letter arrived, then I did.
First, I would write to tell her that I was coming. Then I'd go.
But how?

Sean Harby was Tommy Harby's younger brother. I knew Sean from school. Tommy was in my class. Sean was in the year below us. He was the 'good boy' of the Harby clan. He was a straight 'A' student and an altar boy. He once won a bicycle for selling the most oatmeal cookies for the local Cub Scout Troop. But he was also naïve for his age. He was thirteen, but I don't think the puberty bug had infested him yet.
There were lots of Harbys. Five boys and four girls. I knew all of them well enough to say 'hi' or maybe play with, if there was some giant neighborhood snowball fight or something going on, as there was on occasion. But I was really only buddies with Tommy. Other than my friend, Fish, Tommy was my best friend.
My second best friend.

I went down to the Five and Dime to get paper and an envelope for my letter to Diane. Tommy was there too. He was buying his dad some aftershave for a Father's Day gift.
I told Tommy all about Diane and her letter and this Charmaine girl. And 'Max'.

'Let me talk to Mike,' Tommy said.
Mike was the oldest Harby boy.
'I'm blackmailing him, 'cause I heard him say he went road racing with his pals again last night. He has to do what I say for a while. So I won't tell Dad.'

Mike was always getting in trouble with the police for racing his car on back roads late at night. All the neighborhood kids thought he was a 'local hero' for that.

But I knew what Tommy meant. He meant he'd get Mike to drive us to Padfoot!
It was the prize in the Crackerjack box.
'That would be so neat, Tommy! If he only would! Come on, Mike! Come on, Mike!' I cheered. I was jumping up and down right next to where the Five and Dime sold the miniature turtles and the live, pink and blue-dyed Easter chicks.

Right after dinner, the phone rang. My dad was still not home from work. My mom answered.
'It's for you, Ralphy.'
It was Tommy.

'Yeah, Mike said he'd do it. He'll take us there on Friday. But I have to take Sean along, 'cause he heard me ask Mike and he'll squeal if we don't take him too.'
'Thanks, Tommy!' I shouted. And then I hung up.
And then I had to call him right back.
'What time?'
'Mike says right after dinner. Meet in front of Silber's so no one will see us.'
'OK'. And I hung up again.

I tried to appear calm. My brother was sitting right there too and I didn't want him poking his nose in. A fourteen year old's attempt at nonchalance.
'Who was that, Freckles?' he asked me. I could see he was suspicious.
'None of your beeswax, Bignose.'

Later, I told my mom that I was sleeping over at Tommy's on Friday night.
'Did his mother say it's OK?' she asked.
'Sure, Mom.'

I didn't like lying to her, but the truth was out of the question.

And while I was lying to my mom, Tommy was busy lying to his. He told his mother that he and Sean were staying for a sleep-over at my house on Friday.

That was our master plan.

Now all I had to do was sneak out of the house on Friday without my brother sticking his big beak into my business. Silber's bakery was in the opposite direction from where the Harby's lived, where I had lied that I was staying, so I didn't want him to see me walking down there instead.

At dinner on Friday, I tried to remain at my coolest. I ate properly and didn't wolf down my food as usual. My plan was to attract no attention to myself at all. Then, when dinner was done, I casually got up and headed upstairs to my room. Once there, I opened the window, slid down the eaves, hopped on to our Sears shed roof, then on to an adjoining tree branch, and jumped down to the ground. I hoped I was quiet about it. I guess I was.

I didn't run into my brother anyway.

When I got down to Silber's, Tommy, Mike, and Sean were already there waiting. Tommy jumped out of Mike's car.

'Mike's not talking to us. He thinks we're dirty little snitches, 'cause we have one over on him.'

I didn't care about that. I was going to see Diane and that's all that mattered.

Tommy and I got back in the car and away we went.

It took us about three hours to get to Padfoot Camping Ground. I think it would have taken longer if Mike hadn't been driving. His car was a souped-up Dodge Charger with dual exhaust and those racing stripes so popular at the time.

Mike had two speeds. Fast and faster. We'd cheer him when he overtook someone, but he just drove on with a stony face.

It was around 9pm by the time we got there. Mike pulled up at the Padfoot Camping Ground entry sign with the painted animal footprints on it.

'We're even,' Mike grunted at Tommy.

'When you picking us back up?' Tommy asked.

'Just be sure and be here in three hours,' Mike said. 'If you want a lift back, be here then. Midnight. I ain't waiting for ya.'
And Tommy, Sean, and I got out. Mike roared off to wherever he roared off to.

To reach the camp, we had to walk through the forest on the camp trail. Luckily, because it was summer it was still light out. We kept walking until we could see camp signs for different groups who were staying there.
Diane wrote that she was staying at the 'Bluebell' Camp, so when we saw a sign for that, we headed off in that direction.
We ran into a group of little girls. I asked one of them if they knew Diane. She said that she did and pointed to a tent just in front of us.
'Thanks,' I said.
As we walked away, I could hear them all giggling. They started chanting.
'Diane has a boyfriend. Diane has a boyfriend.'

We walked up to the tent the girls indicated and, just then, I saw Diane walking toward us from the opposite direction.
'Ralphy!' she squealed. 'You made it! You found me!' She gave me a squeeze of a hug.
'This is Sean,' I said. 'He's Tommy's brother.'
'I'm so happy you're here,' she sighed.
I was happy too.

Diane took us into her tent. It was pitched over a raised wooden slatted platform.
There seated on one of the two cots was Charmaine.
'Charmaine, this is Ralphy and his friends,' Dianne announced.
'Hello, Earthlings,' she said.
'Hello,' I replied.
I remember thinking she didn't look very 'psychic' to me.
Whatever 'psychic' is meant to look like.

'Is that the fortune teller witch?' Sean asked pointing at Charmaine.
'Plug your hole,' Tommy mumbled as he slapped down Sean's pointing hand.

Charmaine was a tiny, plain, and mousey haired girl. Her mouth was full of overly large white teeth or overly thin lips that made her teeth look larger as a result.

9

Her green eyes glowed like a cat's in the lamp light.

I don't know. Maybe I was expecting her to be wearing a turban or something. And covered in beads. She didn't look at all 'otherworldly'. OK, her eyes were a bit strange, but other than that she seemed pretty normal to me.
And those large teeth of hers signified nothing either. My Third Grade teacher, Mrs. Adams, had teeth just like that and if she was a psychic, she kept it pretty well hidden.

Ironically, I later had a girlfriend, Sheri Weinstein, who had similarly green Charmaine eyes. Sheri was an exotic dancer and had two Burmese cats that growled like wild beasts and a boa constrictor she used in her act. But why tell you that? You'll never believe me. And I digress.

'Diane, did you tell your friends we're visiting the dead tonight?' Charmaine asked.
She said this as casually as if she were announcing a camp sing-a-long that evening.
'We all will meet at the Manor House at half past ten precisely,' she proclaimed.
That was half an hour or so away.
'The kerosene lamp makes the air smell fumy,' she said loftily as she rose to leave the tent. 'I need to clear my 'channel' before we meet. Diane, bring your friends with you. Max and that other boy are going to meet us there too.'
Max.

We stayed in the tent for a while and Diane told me more about what was going on.
'You see how she is, Ralphy? It's impossible to say no to her. But really she's 'nice', I mean really, and I like her, but she does get bossy.'

Eventually, Diane led us over to the Manor House where we were meant to visit the dead,
'I hope it's not Gran,' Sean worried. 'Or Pop-Pop either.'
'Will you plug it?!' Tommy scowled.

We went into the Manor House via a backdoor. There were two boys already there.

10

'This is Max,' Diane said. 'He's the one who gets the keys to let us in at night.'

'Swiped them from Jelly Knees,' he said.

'Jelly Knees' was their nickname for one of the senior camp counselors, he explained.

The other boy was called Bradley, but he never said anything. He just stared and stared at Diane. I don't think his psychic interests were genuine.

'Stare at my girl again and you will be visiting the dead for real,' I thought to myself.

We made our way upstairs and entered a large conference room. Charmaine was there with another girl named Ingrid.

'Let us gather,' Charmaine instructed.

'Ingrid, turn off the lights.'

Charmaine then took out a candle, lit it, and placed it on the table in front of her. The dying light of a late summer evening spilled through the open windows.

Everyone started to sit down around the large mahogany table in the middle of the room.

Diane sat beside me and Tommy was on my other side. Sean was sitting next to Tommy.

'Let us all join hands,' Charmaine continued.

'Let us draw the spirits and let them speak!'

So we joined hands. Well, we kind of did. I certainly held Diane's hand, but Tommy and I were not so keen and we just held our hands in the proximity of one another. But Sean held Tommy's hand tightly.

And then Charmaine began her séance.

'Powers of the East, West, North, and South. Guardians of the Watchtower! Hail! Hear our call. Earth Mother open a channel between the living and the dead. Let the dead speak and their words come through me.'

She incanted all that in a 'mystical' type of voice.

OK, I am paraphrasing here. I cannot remember the exact words Charmaine used, but I do remember something about 'Guardians' and 'Watchtowers'.

But nothing happened.

'It always starts like this,' Diane whispered to me.
'Shhh!!' hushed Charmaine. 'The spirits are trying to contact us.'
But still nothing happened. We sat there together in an awkward
silence. Fifteen minutes must have passed.
Nothing.
If I weren't holding Diane's hand, I would have been bored.

And then, all of a sudden, Charmaine shook her limbs, shuddered,
and said, 'I see a new spirit! One who has just recently passed. One
who is known well to more than one of us.'
Diane squeezed my hand tighter and let out a little 'oh'.
'Speak, spirit! Tell us why you are here.'
But the 'spirit' did not speak. At least I didn't hear any spirit
speaking.

Charmaine was shaking and quaking. She'd utter little guttural noises
that did sound rather creepy. Then she took a deep breath and
shouted, 'He is here!'
She slumped forward as if in great exhaustion.

We all started looking around the room.
All I could see were the people gathered around the table. But, I must
admit, I did feel spooked.
Then the annoying Max shouted, 'Look behind you! Look at the
mirror!'

A large ornate mirror was fixed to the wall directly behind where
Diane, Tommy, and I were sitting.
I turned around to look.
There, in the mirror, I could see our reflections of course. But, just
above our reflections, appeared the shadowy figure of what looked
like a ghostly man.
Diane screamed.
'He is here!' Charmaine crowed triumphantly.

It was all too much. Everyone started to panic despite Charmaine's
attempts to keep us in the 'spirit realm'. We all got up. As we moved
away from the mirror, I looked back. I could still see that shadowy
figure.
And that was it.
We all ran out of the 'séance' room like it was a scene out of *The
Towering Inferno*.

Except for Charmaine.

'I must finish the ritual!' she shouted after us. 'With or without you!'

It was going to be 'without you'.

As we ran down the stairs, Tommy noticed Sean was not with us.

'Where is he?' Tommy asked as he rolled his eyes.

Against all my better instincts, I went back upstairs to help Tommy find Sean. We went back into the room. Charmaine was sitting there with her eyes closed and intoning something silently. I dared not look back in the mirror.

Sean was just sitting there and staring out into space. Tommy went over and punched him in the arm to get him moving. But he still would not move. We both had to grab him under his arms and drag him out of there.

He was as stiff as a shop window mannequin.

We went back to Diane's tent. I don't know where 'Super Max' or 'Staring Bradley' went. I guess back to their camp.

We put Sean down on one of the cots. He was like an ironing board. To me, it looked like he was literally 'scared stiff'.

We actually had to place him down flat with me holding his head and Tommy his feet.

As we did so, Diane said, 'That was the scariest one yet! I told you! She talks with the dead!'

Tommy was poking Sean and trying to get him to come around. But Sean did not respond. We even got a cup of water and threw it in his face, but he neither blinked nor moved.

'Stop farting around!' Tommy shouted. 'You're embarrassing me! This is why I don't take you nowhere!' and he continued to poke at him and shout at him, but it had no effect.

After some more attempts by Tommy to rouse Sean, Charmaine and Ingrid entered the tent. Charmaine looked drained as if all the energy had been siphoned from her. Ingrid helped her to sit on the other cot.

'That was a powerful apparition,' she gasped. 'That's the most powerful one I have ever summoned.'

Diane then pointed out Sean's 'frozen stiff' situation.

'He's not aware we're even here!' she said to Charmaine in a panic. 'He's been like that ever since we left the house!'

Charmaine struggled to her feet and walked over to where Sean was lying. She reached down and felt his forehead.

'Ice cold,' she said.

'His spirit has been captured. I have heard of such things before.'

And Tommy said, 'He's just goofing around.' And with that, he pinched Sean's arm for all he was worth. But Sean just lay there oblivious.

'We must return to the house. Everyone who was there must return,' Charmaine insisted. 'I must break the hold the spirit has on your brother.'

'Yeah, I'll break his hold!' Tommy said. And he pulled at Sean's hair so hard that no one could have faked not feeling it. But Sean did not feel it. He just stared into the distance like he was far away.

Diane looked at me with fear in her eyes. She didn't want to go back to that house. And I didn't much either.

'We must go back right away,' Charmaine commanded.

But we could not go back right away. I looked at my watch and saw we would have to make our way back to the Padfoot entry sign to meet Mike or we'd miss him.

I pointed this out to Tommy.

'Ralphy, you go there and tell Mike what's going on,' he said. 'Tell him Sean's acting kooky and he needs to come here and snap him out of it.'

So Diane and I walked back to the entry sign together. It was dark out now and Diane led the way with a flashlight. Under normal circumstances, it would have been a golden opportunity for a romantic flashlight-lit summer stroll with my girl, but these were not normal circumstances.

'This is all my fault!' she cried. 'That poor Sean! His spirit captured! Oh! How awful!'

I tried in vain to comfort her.

'Sean is acting just like Dad before he died. He didn't recognize anyone around him either,' she said with tears in her eyes.

'I shouldn't have asked you to come. You came to help and all I've done is help make your friend lose his soul!'

She went on like this all the way back to the sign.

We arrived maybe fifteen minutes after Mike's midnight time limit.

There was no sign of Mike. At that hour, there was no traffic at all. I couldn't even hear a car in the distance. It was completely silent and it had grown very dark. Diane and I stayed at that sign for nearly half an hour, but Mike either left, because we were late, or he was late himself or he forgot about us or he ditched us.

'He ditched us,' I said to Diane.

We hurried back to the tent. When we got there, Max and Bradley were there too. Tommy was starting to look really worried. Sean was still ramrod stiff and had started to drool. It looked like something out of a horror movie.

'Yeah, I saw this movie at a drive-in once with my brother,' Max said. 'It was about how these people lose their souls and become the living dead. They called them 'Zombies'. Zsa Zsa Gabor was in it too.'

(Zombies. That was the very first time I had ever heard that word.)

'Whose brother are you calling a Zombie?' Tommy challenged Max. You don't mess with Harby boys when one of their own is in trouble. I knew that, even if Max didn't. But luckily for Max, he had the good sense to back down.

'I'm just saying,' he said squirming.

'Well, don't,' Tommy glared.

Finally, when I found the chance, I told Tommy about Mike and that our ride was gone.

He was getting very fed up with everything now. When he gets like that, no one is his friend. Not even Yours Truly.

'I have to call home! I have to tell Mom everything,' Tommy despaired. 'We're stuck here. How could he just leave us here? He said midnight, didn't he? And then he's a no-show!'

I wanted to tell Tommy not to mention me to his mom, but I thought better of it.

'She thinks you're staying at my place tonight anyway,' I said. 'Call her in the morning. Maybe Mike will show up after all.'

Charmaine kept insisting that we needed to go back to the house and 'free' Sean's spirit.

'If we do not summon that spirit in the mirror back to us, Sean will be like this forever,' she said.

'Shut up! Shut your cuckoo trap!' Tommy snarled back.

Everyone looked shocked. Diane looked like she was going to start crying again.
'Look, Tommy, it can't hurt, can it?' I ventured. 'Let's just do it and see if it helps.'
And he looked at me like he could kill me along with everyone else there.
Grumpily, he eventually said, 'All right then. Let's go free the Zombie.'

We went back to the Manor House. Tommy and I carried Sean all the way there. I must admit that his skin felt very cold and clammy. It was sort of like carrying a very large dead fish. Max and Bradley helped us get him up the stairs to the conference room where Charmaine had performed her séance earlier.

'Everyone must sit in the exact same positions as before,' she told us. 'Everything must be just as it was the last time.'
We all sat down. It looked so weird to see Sean, ramrod stiff, propped up against the back of a chair. There's no way we could have folded him into a seated position. It was like he had no joints.

Ingrid turned off the lights just as she had done the first time.
Charmaine relit her candle and then said the same exact words that she had used before with the 'Guardians' and the 'Watchtower'.
And just like before, nothing happened at first.
Diane's hand was sweating as she held mine.

And then, suddenly, Charmaine started to quake again and utter those disturbing grunting noises. Like she was possessed.
We all stared at her. Well, I stared at her.
And then she said, 'I can feel his presence. He is among us again! Spirit! Show yourself!'
Max looked up at the mirror. 'There it is!' he shouted.

I turned around to have a look, even though I was scared myself. Diane just held her eyes firmly closed and whimpered. And sure enough, there in the mirror was the shadowy figure again.
It was so creepy.

'I command you, spirit!' Charmaine ordered. 'Leave Sean in peace. Let his spirit return to him. I banish you! I banish you! I banish you!' And after she said, 'I banish you' for the third time, we all heard a loud cracking noise.

I watched as that large ornate mirror started to split with fissures in front of my eyes and bits of it fell to the floor. Then, in one loud crack, the whole mirror just fell to pieces. I threw my hands over my head and ducked to avoid the shattering shards.
All of us, even Charmaine, ran for our lives. We were running so fast that no one noticed that Sean was running right there alongside us.

We all ran back to the tent. Everyone looked very shaken up.
'I don't want to go to another séance, Tommy,' Sean cried.
And Tommy just hugged and hugged him and patted his hair. There were tears in Tommy's eyes too.
'They're too scary, Tommy,' he blubbered.

Sean said he remembered nothing about being a 'Zombie' or that we went back to that room a second time. As far as he knew, he was still there at that first séance. And I believed him.
And everyone else did too.

Tommy and I stayed over at the boys' camp with Max and Bradley. Sean had fallen asleep in the girls' tent. We thought it best to leave him there in peace. I found out later that meant Diane had to sleep on the tent floor.

The next morning, Tommy and I walked back to the entry sign just in case Mike had left word about why he didn't show up. But there was nothing there.
'I have to call Mom,' Tommy said. 'First I'm going to ask to speak with Mike like there's nothing going on, but if he's not there, I'll have to tell her everything.'

Tommy and I walked over to the pay phone. We both emptied our pockets of whatever coins we had. I gave my coins to Tommy and he made his call.
I waited a little distance away while Tommy was on the phone.

I started to think about everything that had happened.

It was great to see Diane, but I didn't really help her with the Charmaine problem. I got swept up in her hocus-pocus just as much as Diane did.

But I got to see her which, I suppose, made the whole thing worthwhile.

Well, at least Max knew to steer clear. At least that was something. I just thought how some of my 'schemes' seem to get other people into trouble or difficulties. Like Tommy and Sean.

I told myself that I would take all the blame back home for any bad stuff that resulted, because of our adventure.

I was just thinking this, when I heard the most heart-wrenching sound I ever heard in my pre-adolescent life.

It was Tommy. He was wailing and wailing. The receiver was just dangling down from where he had dropped it.

Tommy rushed over to me. He grabbed me by the shoulders. His eyes were wild and staring. I thought he had gone mad.

'He's dead! He's dead! Oh my God! Mike!!'

He let me go and paced around in little circles. His tears were streaming down.

'Mike's dead! He's dead!'

Tommy told me that his mom was hysterical when he called her. She didn't know where he was. The police had called late last night to say that Mike had been found dead. It was a car crash. He'd been road racing and flew off an embankment on a back road somewhere up near Padfoot Camping Ground, they said.

When Tommy's mom called my mother to tell him about Mike and found out we weren't there, it threw both our families into a panic. They even had the police out looking for us.

There would be an almighty horror-show when I got home, but I couldn't worry about that now.

Mr. and Mrs. Harby were driving up to collect us and identify Mike's body and all the other gruesome things they'd have to do. Tommy and I went and got Sean and the three of us just waited in silence at that sign until the Harby's arrived.

I couldn't feel anything. I was just numb.

Like a Zombie.

None of us got into any trouble or woe when we returned home. Mike's death had changed all that. In Baltimore neighborhoods of the time, the death of some family's young son or daughter was mourned by all the community.

A quiet reverence would reign. And the Harby's would always be remembered as the family who lost their boy, Mike.

Now I'm sure you're thinking to yourself, well, OK, but Sean was a naïve thirteen year old boy. He just scared himself.

Or we all just imagined that shadowy figure in the mirror. After all, we were quasi pre-pubescent kids ourselves. We just wanted to believe we saw a shadow and so we did.

Or maybe you're thinking that I was a hormonally challenged kid myself at the time and so my perspective on what happened is questionable.

Maybe.

I can't really explain what happened to Sean or that shadowy figure who Charmaine described as 'one who is known well to more than one of us'.

All I can tell you is what I remember happening.

Mike Harby died on a summer night in a car crash near Padfoot Camping Ground. That fact cannot be disputed. I was at his funeral. I saw where they laid him in his grave.

The rationalists among you may scoff, but what happened at Padfoot Camping Ground in the summer of 1966 is exactly what I have related to you here.

I can't explain it, but that doesn't make it any less true.

And that's because it is true.

As best I can recall.

STORY CHAPTER TWO

'YANKEE BOYS'

This is one story I have repeated countless times, even to my own family, but long after it all happened of course. I am sure though that I never tell this story quite in the same way twice.

In 1970, I was in High School in Baltimore. My family had moved out to the suburbs while I was still a student there and to get to school I now had to take a very early transit bus. It got me to school an hour before I was meant to arrive.
But if I took the next bus, I was always ten minutes late for the start of class and that did not go down well.
My early morning 'Get up, Ralphy' call from my mom was earlier than ever before.

Stevie Fishmann was my very best friend when we were kids and in High School too. And we used to hang out, as you do, and get in minor trouble just to shake up the powers-that-be. In fact, it was Stevie who, when we were ten years old, first told me the 'Facts of Life'. It was that which taught me to keep an open mind on things, even when they sounded totally ridiculous. And to a ten year old kid, who didn't know the score, the 'Facts of Life' sounded very ridiculous indeed.
By the way, nobody called Stevie, Stevie. Except maybe his dad or some new teacher until they caught on. Everyone else just called him 'Fish'.
Even his mom.

Fish used to take that very early transit bus to school with me. He didn't really need to do that, because he still lived in my old neighborhood, but, as I say, we were blood brothers.

One day in late March, we arrived at school with that spare hour to kill, and we came across something out of the ordinary.

My High School had a flagpole in the middle of the campus. I cannot ever remember seeing an actual flag flying from it, but there definitely was a flagpole. When we turned up early that particular morning, we saw a fellow classmate running something up that pole.

That classmate was John Bogarde and he was what we used to call a 'Freak'.
In those days, that meant someone with long hair and poor personal hygiene. But not a 'cool guy' like a rock 'n roller or psychedelic guitarist. He just had long hair, smelled poorly, and kept to his own company. I had nothing against the guy myself, but he was not my friend. I knew him. I'd say 'Hi', if our paths crossed. But that was about as far as it went.
I had no feelings about him one way or the other.

But back to my story.

And so Fish and I both sauntered over together to where John, the 'Freak', was standing at that flagpole. And when we looked up, we saw the flag the Freak had flown.

It was an SDS Flag. That stands for 'Students for a Democratic Society', if you didn't know, and they were big on street protests and the occasional act of mindless violence at the time. I think their flag was white with a balled-up red fist in the center. John's flag had an orange fist, as I recall, but the point's the same.

So, there we were, three young guys staring up at John's handiwork, when all of a sudden we hear a booming voice behind us.

'What do you think you're doing, Waldo?!'
(I still don't know why I was singled out.)
It was Mr. Schmidt or 'Messerschmitt' as some of us used to call him. Well, not to his face, of course, nor in front of the 'weenies' neither.
'Messerschmitt' was the teacher in charge of student discipline. The one you had to sit with in a classroom after school, if you did something that they didn't like. Like talking back. Or sticking chalk in the erasers so one of the kookier teachers ended up putting more chalk on the board than removing what was already there. Or even filling paper bags with locusts and switching them with other students' lunch bags.

21

Anything like that might mean, if you were caught, that you ended up sitting in a classroom after school for hours, in silence, with 'Messerschmitt'.

But Messerschmitt was even more a daunting prospect than usual. His face went a passionate shade of purple like the color of his fury. He really went 'mental', as people used to say.
'What have you boys done?!' he bellowed. He was trembling in his anger.
'Take that down! Now!'

We could tell that this was not going to end happily. And after John took down his flag, and Messerschmitt saw what the flag was, he went ballistic. All three of us were marched straight into the Principal's office. I had the impression that he thought we had committed some major act of treason. To be honest, I never saw Messerschmitt other than angry throughout my entire High School career, but this was the angriest I ever recall seeing him.
He was literally spitting mad.

The upshot of our meeting with the Principal, Mrs. Waterford, or rather 'Snooty Boots', who'd parade around fiercely with a self-important air, was that all three of us were suspended for a week. Of course, neither Fish nor I said we were just innocent bystanders. We were never given the chance to mention that anyway, so what was the point? John said nothing either. Messerschmitt and Snooty Boots did all the talking. Loudly.
We were told to go home and stay home. Our parents would be informed and it would go on our 'Permanent School Record' which sounded really bad at the time.

Luckily, for me anyway, my parents were away on vacation. They had left that very morning. They were going to visit my brother who was in the army and stationed at Fort Knox, Kentucky. I was meant to stay with Fish and his family.
Ironically, the last thing my dad said to me before they left was, 'You will behave yourself, Ralphy, while you're staying with the Fishmann's, won't you?'

I don't think they ever really knew what happened. Unless they were privy to my 'Permanent School Record' where, I guess, all my transgressions were exposed.

The three of us skulked out of the Principal's office. Snooty Boot's stare and Messerschmitt's glare were burning holes in us as we did so.

As I say, I was meant to stay with Fish while my parents were with my brother, so I didn't have to face them yet.
And it wouldn't be too bad for Fish either. His parents were of the 'understanding' type.
I am sure they would know their son was just swept up in circumstances. I remember him telling me that it was 'NBD'- No Big Deal.
As for John, I did not really know him or his family. I didn't know if there would be any repercussions. And I didn't even bother to ask.

The three of us left the school grounds together and walked to the bus stop.

So we were suspended. For a week. And as that week was the week before 'Spring Break', it meant no school for the three of us for two weeks. And this idea suddenly just sprang into my head.
'Let's get away from here. Let's hitchhike down to New Orleans for Mardi Gras!'
Make the best out of a rotten deal.
That was my thinking.

I just included John in my proposed road trip, because he was there with us and in the same bowl of chowder. He made one of his 'Freak Faces' that some students would use as an excuse to mock him.
'So are you with us or not?' I asked him.
'I suppose so,' he mumbled.

So Fish, The Freak, and I planned to meet the next morning and begin our adventure to Dixie. 'Ralphy, I'll just tell my parents we're staying over at my cousin's while we're away. NBD.' Fish explained.
And that is exactly what he did. I don't know how John explained away his absence.

That next morning, we met bright and early. The sun was shining with nary a cloud in the sky. It was a balmy Baltimore day.
We all had our book bags stuffed with what we were certain were essentials, so we would be ready for anything. Or so we thought.

The gods of fortune were smiling down upon us and, as soon as we stuck out our thumbs, we caught a ride with a trucker all the way to Tennessee. He even bought us lunch. And a few more rides after that found us in New Orleans.
Easy Peasy to the 'Big Easy'.

We had very little spending money. We knew no one. But it was paradise. We had made it. We had arrived. No nasty stories about rednecks attacking John for having long hair. Nothing like that. In truth, it was smoother passage than we had any right to expect. Clueless naiveté sometimes works out quite well.

And what a time we had. It was like your birthday, Christmas, and Halloween were all rolled into one, big ball of fun. I still have some of the bead necklaces that the girls throw from cotillion floats as they parade by. It was also the very first time I ever saw more than one girl with her top off. And it did not matter at all that we had no money. People were giving us drinks and food and dancing in the streets. Strangers let us sleep in the back of their cars and invited us to barbecues. We forgot all about our troubles back home and simply took in the adventure. We stayed there for over a week partying, dancing, and basking in the festivities.
It was one of the most extraordinary experiences of my young life. But like all such pleasurable experiences, they come to an end far too quickly for our liking and we had to start thinking about how we might get back home.

And it is in getting back home where my story really begins.

It was nightmare. We did catch a ride out of New Orleans right away, but the hippie couple in the van, who gave us the lift, were only going as far as Arkansas. And once there, we waited by the side of the road with our thumbs sticking out for hours and hours. And then it started to rain. Buckets. Finally some chicken farmer picked us up. He said he was heading to Alabama. We were having so little luck making any progress that we just went with him. We'd try our luck by traveling through the Deep South. If nothing else, maybe the weather would be better.

But the weather was not better. And after we said goodbye to the chicken farmer, our luck in getting another ride was no better either.

There were just a few more days left before my parents returned from visiting my brother and I thought it prudent to get back to my home town before they did. They were definitely not as 'understanding' as Fish's folks were. Plus, we were meant to be back in school after our enforced absence and there would be 'unpleasant repercussions', if we did not turn up. We certainly didn't want to face a strafing by the Messerschmitt or a kicking from Snooty Boots either.
In fact, we had to be there. We had to show up.

We started to feel the pressure and, with little or no money, our options were thinner than a Kraft cheese single.
A Kraft cheese single! If we only had some! Our lack of food was constantly gnawing at us. John had a bag of soggy 'beignets', New Orleans doughnuts. Some girl had given them to him during Mardi Gras. We were surviving on those.
But there was plenty of water to drink. It never stopped raining.

Our plan, or what we considered a plan, was to go through Alabama and into Georgia where we could get on Interstate-95. Then, if we were lucky, we could get some trucker to take us all the way up the East Coast and back to Baltimore.
With, hopefully, no one the wiser about our great expedition.

But things did not go to plan. We just could not get a ride in Alabama. Fish thought we should cut John's hair a bit, because he was blaming him and his long locks for our lack of luck. But John was not agreeable. Understandably so.
We waited and waited in the pouring rain until nightfall. But there was nowhere to sleep and nowhere to seek shelter. Not that we had the time anyway. The clock was ticking.

You know how it is when you get caught in rain like that with no way to escape it? Eventually, you just surrender to it and accept your fate that you will be drenched. You are still soaked, but you don't moan about it so much. And that was how we were. We were not happy. We were stressed. But no sense whining about something you can do nothing about.

And then, when we least expected it, a result. A preacher, dressed in black with one of those 'black padre' flat-brimmed hats, slowed down as he passed us and stopped.

We ran like Flash Gordon to his car.

Fish used to get very manic when he was excited and he kept shouting, 'Thank you! Thank you. You saved us! You saved us!' to the preacher.

I am not sure if that was the kind of saving a Bible Belt preacher had in mind, but bless his heart, he surely did us a good turn.

Our rescuer told us his name was the Reverend Mr. Black which caused us all to raise our eyebrows, because that's the name of an old Kingston Trio song.

I think Johnny Cash did a cover of it too. I'm not sure about that, but we all knew the song, *The Reverend Mr. Black*, anyway.

We were just starting to make our way, when the Reverend began to sing at the top of his lungs.

'I gotta walk that lonesome valley. I gotta walk it by myself. Oh nobody else can walk it for me. I gotta walk it by myself.'

He would spontaneously sing that refrain throughout our ride with him.

'I do it when the Spirit moves me,' he informed us.

But I didn't feel in danger in his company. I think you can burst into song without being a homicidal maniac.

He was a big man for a preacher. He looked like Robert Mitchum from that film, *Cape Fear*.

'You boys looked like you were drownin' out there,' he observed. 'What you swimmin' with the fish for? Why you not safe and warm indoors?'

It was a good question. The three of us had been asking ourselves the very same thing while standing on the side of that road in the slashing rain.

The Reverend drove through the night and the pouring rain until we reached the border with Georgia where he was headed. And we got out. It was dawn, but it was hard to tell it was dawn. The rain was just sheeting down mercilessly

So we had reached Georgia. Now all we had to do was catch another lift across Georgia to the intersection of I-95, beg a trucker to take pity on us, and drive us north with him. And all would be well.

But all was not well.

We could not find one kind soul to pick us up and get us out of that weather. Truth be told, we were looking a bit on the rough side by then and even I would have thought twice about picking up our scraggly band. And no one did.

We stood there in the wet all that day. There was not even much traffic. It was a bad spot, but it was the only spot we had.
We were so drenched that our shoes squelched while we walked. Our equally soaked book bags grew heavier and heavier to drag along with us.
Those topless girls at Mardi Gras seemed a lifetime ago. Something out of a dream that keeps long-term prisoners going.

And we had to get back. We had just over a day and a half remaining now before school restarted and my parents returned and our crazed adventure would be rumbled. And we would be rumbled right along with it.

Then it happened. And in that happening is the real point of my story.

Night had come again. Call it dusk if you must. Our antics to attract a ride were growing ever more outrageous. Fish even ran out into the highway and waved his arms around like a lunatic as the few cars still on the road water-glided by. But all that did was nearly get him killed.
Meanwhile the Freak and I shouted profanities at any car that passed us and didn't stop. That also did not result in getting us out of the deluge.
We were miserable. We were losing hope. We were hungry. We were dead exhausted.
We felt stupid.

It grew darker and darker. And the few drivers that were out there, who passed us by, had now disappeared completely.
We stood there on the side of that road in the dead of night. Alone.

Then, while the rain continued to pelt down cruelly upon us, we spotted two pairs of headlights, one on each side of the road, and coming at us in the same direction. Fast.
Engines roaring, two road racers, side by side, flew past us, splashing heavy sprays of water all over us as they did so.

We watched as they zoomed off into the distance.

'There goes another Mike Harby,' I thought to myself, as Fish and Freak shouted obscenities at the racers who had just soaked us.

Mike Harby was the brother of a friend of mine who died attempting just such adrenaline fueled highway high jinks.

'Jesus, Ralphy!' Fish said. 'Can you believe those two assholes?!'

'No,' I quietly replied as I wiped the water from my face.

My sadness at Mike's memory transported me out of the rain momentarily.

And then, as I was lost in that sorrow, and as we stood there in our misery and without hope, it happened.

Out of nowhere, an old Ford Fairlane approached, slowed down, and stopped.

We all quickly scrambled into the backseat of the car.

'Where you boys headin'?' the driver asked.

And so we told him.

It was obvious the driver had been drinking. Quite a bit.

He was a short and stout guy with a severe 'flat top' haircut.

'Well, I am headin' home and you boys are welcome to stay with me and get out this wetness.'

The three of us looked at one another.

'What you think, Ralphy?' Fish muttered to me under his breath.

'How far away is home?' I finally asked the driver.

'Oh, just a five minute drive away or so. Just over that ridge.'

And so we all agreed. We'd get some rest. We'd get up really early and have better luck tomorrow. We weren't going to get anywhere that night anyway.

And so we went with him.

To his home.

Home turned out to be a mobile home, but it clearly hadn't been mobile for quite a spell. It was a permanently fixed mobile home I would call it.

Our drunken benefactor, Elwood, offered us a drink and some Hostess cupcakes. He let us dry our clothes in his dryer. We didn't take the drink, but to have dry clothes again was the equivalent of winning the lottery to us, so we gratefully accepted that kindness. We sat around in some bathrobes he gave us, ate our cupcakes, and talked with Elwood for a while. But when our clothes were finally dry, all we could think about was sleep. Sleep.

Elwood told us he had two spare bedrooms.
'Boys, I got a room with a single bed and another with a bunk bed. Sort it out between y'all.'
'I'll have the single,' I quickly said as Fish scowled at me.

He showed us to the rooms and I went into the single.

I was dry again. There was a bed there. This was good. Or so I thought at the time.
'Good night, boys,' Elwood called out as he walked down to his own room.

Maybe half an hour passed. Maybe more. Maybe less. All I really remember was that I had just thrown myself into bed and was thinking about the day while waiting to drop off.
Then it happened.

There was a knock at the door.
It was one of those moments.
I did not want to hear a knock at the door, so I pretended that I did not hear a knock at the door.
But again there's the knocking. I'm thinking, 'That can't be Fish. He wouldn't bother knocking. It can't be John... '
Knock knock knock.

I went over to my jacket. I had a Mexican 'stiletto knife'. My brother and I bought one each, when we were in Tijuana once with my parents when we were kids. The metal had the strength of chicken wire. I am sure it would have broken into bits, if I had tried to use it in earnest. But I carried it as a deterrent. It looked 'fierce' even if it was worthless.

I pocketed the knife and said, 'Who's there?', and Elwood let himself in. I smiled as he did so, but inside I was getting worried.

'What's up, Elwood?'
I thought I was sounding cool and not bothered. Anyway, that was the impression I hoped I was making.
'I'm gonna show you somethin'. Somethin' interestin',' he said.
'Oh yeah? What's that?'
'This you never seen before. Yankees never seen nothin' like this.'
'OK,' I said in my coolest, not bothered, best.

Elwood walked over to the other side of the room. There were built-in wardrobes. The kind you'd slide back to open. He went over to the wardrobes and slid them apart.
'Whatcha think of that?'

And he was right. I saw something there that Yankees do not see. There, in that wardrobe, were perhaps two dozen Ku Klux Klan uniforms.
All neat in a row.
Elwood took one out.

'This one's mine. See this insignia? That's showin' that my daddy was also Klan. Ever seen that before?'
And I assured him I had not in my most 'this is normal' tone of voice.
'I thought you'd find this interestin'. Now you got yourself a story to tell, dontcha?'

There was no menace in his voice. In fact, he was simply proud. I didn't even need to consider my Tijuana protection. Then Elwood bid me goodnight.
'Sweet dreams.' And he was gone.

I did not feel threatened by Elwood, as I say. But what about his compadres? What if they all decided to stop by for a powwow? What if they found our long-haired Freak sleeping here? What if they found out Fish was Jewish? What if they found out that I went to his Bar Mitzvah and decided I was guilty by association? Like Fish and I were guilty by association with Freak and his flag? The very thing that was responsible for getting us into this mess in the first place. Oh, that's right. I was responsible for getting us into this mess in the first place. Hitting the road was all my idea.
This was all my fault.

'Ralphy, this is worse than when you talked the Harby's into driving you to see your girlfriend,' I said to myself while shaking my head. That was another of my adventures that ended more than badly.

I sat there on the side of the bed for what was probably ten minutes, but felt like ten years. I wanted Elwood back in his room and hopefully asleep.

You know what it's like when you don't want to be heard? Like trying to sneak back home at what your mom is going to call an unacceptable hour? Every step sounds like you're making enough noise to wake the sleeping deaf. It was like that.

Ever so gingerly, I made my way out of my room and down the hall to where my two friends were. I was scared. I won't lie. I was scared and convinced I was shaking the foundations as I walked.
If permanently fixed mobile homes have a foundation.
I was shaking anyway.

I went into the room with the bunk beds. On tiptoe.
I put my hand over Fish's mouth so he wouldn't shout out.
'We got to get out of here,' I whispered.
As I said, Fish and I grew up together and so he knew something was seriously wrong without having to ask me what it was. We were close enough to communicate just with our tone of voice.
We grabbed John and the three of us crept out of that place slowly and carefully until we were out the front door.

It was just after dawn. When we were safely away, I told them what happened. And then we all ran across a field and scrambled over and sank down behind a low stone wall.
It had stopped raining. The sun was glowing huge and red just over the horizon.

We crouched behind that wall for I don't know how long. No one wanted to look to see if Elwood and maybe his white-sheeted cronies were looking for us.
Looking for us with ropes in their hands.

And then, 'Boys! Hey, Boys! Yankee Boys! You round? Boys! Boys!'
It was Elwood shouting from the door.

We froze.

'Boys! Yankee Boys!'

The next thing I knew John had stood straight up.

'Freak! Freak! What are you doing?' Fish exclaimed as he signaled rapidly with his hand to get him to sit back down.

'Get down! Don't you know those people don't like long-haired Freaks like you?' Fish shouted in a hoarse whisper.

'They don't like anybody,' I said.

But as we spoke, John just started to climb back over the wall and made his way toward Elwood.

Fish and I looked at one another. I had a feeling we both wanted to say something, but we didn't know what that something was. But we didn't need to speak to know what each of us was thinking.

'Freak!' Fish spit through his clenched teeth. 'Freak!'

I'm not sure how long we waited there, but I promise you we felt every single second.

Then suddenly we both looked up. There, calm as you like, were John and Elwood staring down at us. John was holding three paper bags.

Then Elwood said, 'John said you boys lost your keys climbin' over the wall. Did you find them?'

'Oh! Yeah yeah yeah!' Fish finally stammered.

'The keys! Yeah, we found them. Yes, we did.'

'Well, that's fine then. Y'all left so early I thought I'd missed you. Here, I made you some lunch for the road.'

John waved the paper bags at us.

'Thanks,' I said.

'Uh yeah,' said Fish.

And with that Elwood said, 'Good luck, boys.'

And we were alone.

'He could have offered us a lift,' John said matter-of-factly.

Fish was furious. 'Freak, you are crazy! You are one crazy, smelly Freak.'

'Why? Cause I decided I'm not scared of Elwood and some white sheets?' John replied.

'Ever hear of a gun?' Fish spit back at him.

But I was thinking maybe Freak was right. I said nothing.

We wolfed down Elwood's paper bag lunch as we made our way back to the highway. There was even a marshmallow pie in mine. The sun was out. It was actually pleasant for the first time in three days.
I was feeling better already.
But our problem was the same. We were running out of time and running out of it quickly. We absolutely had to catch a ride soon... Soon.

We were marching along back to the highway, as quickly as we could, to try to make some time.
And then, suddenly, John stopped in his tracks. Stone-dead.
It looked like he was in shock.
Fish and I looked at one another. I just shrugged.
Then Fish raced over to where John was standing.
'What's your story, Freak?' he asked him. 'Did you forget we're in a hurry?!'
John looked at him pleadingly and then he said,
'You don't suppose it was poisoned, do you?'

Fish just stared at John while this question washed over him.
A few seconds passed.
And then suddenly John burst out laughing and started running to the highway.
'Ahhh! We're poisoned!' he mocked as he ran.
We ran after him too.
Fish was screaming, 'Freak! Freak!', as he ran as fast as he could to try to catch him.
I started laughing till my sides hurt and so was John running up ahead of us.
Soon, Fish's fury faded away and we were all laughing as we ran back to the highway.

But, as was the case yesterday, there was little traffic and, what traffic there was, passed us by like we were invisible. It was not a good moment. Not for three teenagers.
Not for anyone.

And then right out of the mouths of angels, we heard it:
'Oh nobody else can walk it for you! You gotta walk it by yourself!'

It was Robert Mitchum, I mean, Reverend Black of course. He was singing so loudly we could hear him as his car approached. He was singing to high heaven.

To say we were overjoyed is not the right word. It was a much bigger joy than overjoyed. 'Superjoyed' perhaps. And when the Reverend saw it was us, he stopped.
'You boys about in the same spot where I left you yesterday. No luck, huh?'
He had that right. No luck indeed.

Fish and I took turns telling Reverend Black about what had happened.
'This is a world full of misunderstandin', young fellas,' he replied. 'The Lord is callin' for a lot of healin', 'cause there's a lot of healin' needed.'

He then proceeded to drive us all the way across Georgia near to the intersection with I-95 and our route home. As we got out, he handed me a card.
It read: '*Reverend Mr. Timothy Black, Healing Services*' and his phone number.
'Good luck getting yourself back where you're meant to be,' he said. And away he went.

We were near Waycross, Georgia and found a trucker's stop. Fish asked everyone there if they were heading north.
'If you could give us a ride,' he said, 'you'd be saving us. Saving us!'
And one trucker did.
I have always liked truckers since that day. They know what it's like to be far from home. And they know how important it is to help a stranger, because they might be a stranger in need themselves one day.

The trucker took us all the way up I-95. All the way to Baltimore. Freak, Fish, and I went straight to school. We even got there on time.

As for me, I was very lucky. My parents ended up staying an extra day in Kentucky with my brother, so they were never the wiser about my adventure.

At least I think they weren't, unless they saw my 'Permanent School Record'. And if they did, they never spoke about it.

I know some people ask me if John became best friends with Fish and me after our Mardi Gras road trip. But that wasn't the case. Teenagers can be funny like that. You get on with those you do and you don't with those you don't. Despite our sharing all that time together, John stayed the same silent loner. I guess if someone had been picking on him, I might have said something.
But we never became best buddies or anything like that. Nor did he develop a better relationship with soap and water.

But, to this day, I still think about him standing up and not hiding in fear.

As I say, I have told that story many times and I always end it the same way. I reach for my wallet and show them Reverend Black's little card. I always carry it with me. I show them his card so they will know my story is true.
After all, seeing is believing, isn't it?

But, as I may have warned you at the start, my story keeps changing in the telling. There might be some modifications in the telling here. I'm not sure.

STORY CHAPTER THREE

'GYPSUM'

How many times have I told this story? Dozens and dozens. More.
It was always one of Nora's favorites.

'Tell them the 'Kentucky' story, Ralphy!' Nora would shout out.
Then she'd turn to whatever social group we were with and say, 'It's
so good! But it's so sad too!'
And she'd hush the group and wave at them to settle down.
'Tell them, Ralphy!'
Nora was superb at setting up one of my stories. Of course, I have to
set them up for myself now that Nora is gone.

I usually began the 'Kentucky' story something like this:

Scott was the first friend I made at College. I knew no one there. I
was living away from home for the first time and I was on my own. I
had left my family and all my childhood and High School friends
behind me. There was no 'Fish' there, no Diane Tompkins, no
Tommy Harby. No one from my past. No one that I knew. My
childhood days were well and truly over.
I was on my own in the tiny Pennsylvania town of Biglerville.

In High School, I had to wait for an hour or so after classes before I
could catch the first transit bus home. I used that time to go to the
library, once in a while, and go through these fat books about all the
different colleges and universities in the world. And I read about this
little college, Biglerville, in Pennsylvania. There was just something
about it. It just clicked with me and I knew that was where I wanted
to go.
But, as I say, no one else from my High School or childhood days
went there.
I was alone.

Scott was a big-hearted, friendly, outgoing, and extremely likeable guy. He was big on the sciences and chemistry in particular. He knew lots of people at Biglerville College. One day at the dining hall, he sat down next to me, because all the other tables were full.
We just hit it off.
I hear he is a Professor of Chemistry at some famous university now. It doesn't surprise me in the slightest.

It was through Scott that I met and made many friends at Biglerville. He even introduced me to my college girlfriend and future wife. I could say something sarcastic about that, but I won't.

Through Scott's encouragement, we both did some amateur dramatics together there and sang in the college 'Pop Ensemble'. He jump-started my new social life and for that I am forever grateful. But Scott was determined to be a scientist and in that we differed. I was not sure what I was determined to be. But I was fairly confident that it wasn't a scientist.

In the summer of '73, after our freshman year, I got a call from Scott. 'I've just heard back from a Geology Professor, Ralphy, at the University of Kentucky,' he began. 'I contacted him about the cave systems in Kentucky and he sent me an invitation to a caving expedition. We're going to map an underground system that's never been fully explored. You want to come along too?'
This all came as a bit of a surprise, but it sounded interesting.
'OK,' I said.

So we made a plan. Scott was going to head down there on his own and I was going to meet him a few days later.
'Is it OK if I bring a couple of friends along?' I asked him.
'I don't see why not,' he replied.

I told my girlfriend, Nora, the one Scott had introduced me to, and my friend, Charlie, who did some drama shows with me and Scott. They were both keen. Nora was keen for anything out of the ordinary and Charlie would do anything for a laugh.
Charlie borrowed his dad's car and, when everything was settled, we were on our way to Kentucky.

I don't remember too much about what happened during the long drive there. I recall that Charlie only had one '8 track' tape, Jethro Tull's *War Child* with the song, *Bungle in the Jungle*. He repeatedly played that over and over throughout our journey.
But I don't remember much else.

When we finally got there, we made our way to the university campus and found Scott.
He introduced us to the Geology Professor who had invited him on the caving expedition. The plan was that we would camp near the cave system that night and start the exploring early in the morning. So, once again, we were back in the car and this time driving toward the hills and the caves.

It really was in the middle of nowhere. Charlie was driving his dad's car off-road and down pastures and up little, and not so little, craggy hills. Scott and the Professor led the way in their own, far more suitable, vehicle.
But we finally got to the spot in question and set up camp.

Now, if you do not know Kentucky country, and you may not, you should know that it is a very beautiful place. But it is also a bit wild and a bit eerie to be truthful. From our camp, you could look up at the surrounding hills and see the tops sort of collapsed in like someone had popped a bubble. I'd never seen such collapsed hilltops before.
I asked the Professor about them.
'There are cave systems all throughout this part of Kentucky,' the Professor informed me. 'Those 'bubbles', as you call them, are the result of the cave structures beneath.'

Scott told us that part of the cave system we would be exploring had been mapped just the week before. 'But we're going to go further and map the section that no one has explored yet,' he said in anticipation.
'As far as anyone knows, that is,' the Professor added with a chuckle.

We sat around a fire that Charlie laid and drank some beer from the cooler we had in his dad's car. Nora asked about equipment and other necessities we might need.
I hadn't thought of that.

The Professor walked over to his Jeep and grabbed some things out the back.

'Here are some safety helmets and some carbide lamps,' he said when he returned from his vehicle.

He fixed the lamps over the brim of the helmets. He then showed us how to light the carbide lamps by running the palm of our hand over a little generator wheel.

We practiced.

'They'll stay lit for a considerable spell,' he said. 'But just swipe your hand like I showed you, when they start to go out, and they'll light again.'

Seemed easy enough to me. Or 'NBD', No Big Deal, as my childhood friend Fish might say.

Very early the next morning we ate and washed and then started the trek to the cave system entrance. It wasn't far from where we camped.

Along the way, we came across an old, abandoned, and dilapidated stone bungalow.

'Before the war, there used to be lots of these miners' houses near cave entrances,' the Professor shared with us.

'They used to mine the caves for salt peter and gypsum and mineral salts and the like. There was lots of feuding over cave mining rights too. They say it was a bit like the Wild West,' he laughed.

'But then the cave mining business all went bust. The land's only used to graze cattle these days.'

Now I must be honest. I knew next to nothing about caving or 'spelunking' as they sometimes call it. And Nora and Charlie were equally clueless. Scott, on the other hand, had done all this before, if not in Kentucky. His only real advice was to try to 'keep moving'. He also gave us some safety advice which mainly consisted of being sure we were always together and always knew where one another were. At all times.

The Professor handed us some ropes and clamps to share out among us. He then gave each of us a little bag with some Rice Crispy bars.

'You might get hungry as we go along.'

We were all set now.

We found the entrance to the system. It was high enough to enter without having to stoop over. We all walked together into that dark world. Water was running down in little rivulets underfoot. It was wet in there and getting darker with each step we took. We stopped and swiped our lamps and they all came on and we continued our progress.

I was thinking that this was all fun and easy going and quite an adventure.

We continued to make our way down the wet entrance to the system until the Professor came to a sudden halt.
'OK. We're going to have to repel down from here.'

I walked over to where he was standing. When I looked ahead, all I could see was a shadowy darkness. The Professor indicated for me to look down. I did. And then I saw it. A sheer drop of a hundred feet or so. If you didn't know to look for it, you could have walked right off that ledge without a care in the world.
'Hmmm,' I thought. 'I better start concentrating.'

We got out the ropes and the clamps and Scott and the Professor tied the ends off and threw the long lines down into the darkness. And, in turn, we repelled down that rock face all the way to the pitch black bottom.

Once there, we found ourselves in a narrow, cramped space. I could see there were several little caves in the sides of the cavern walls all around. There was an empty water bottle at the entrance to one. The Professor had placed it there during his previous visit a week ago.
'There it is,' the Professor said. 'We go through there.'
He put the water bottle to one side and went in. Scott followed and the rest of us joined in behind.

I am guessing, but I'd say the tiny cave we crawled into was about as wide as a manhole cover. We were all flat on our bellies and dragging ourselves forward with hands and feet. The effect was like a very clumsy snake slithering.

We crawled. We crawled a hundred meters like that. Two hundred. Four hundred.
Nora was crawling ahead just before me.

'Watch out, Ralphy! It's really wet here!' she shouted back.
She kept up a meticulous and running report on what to expect five feet in front of me.

We slithered down and up and right and left through the three foot wide space.
Our forward progress could only be described as slow.

Let me be the first to warn you. If you have any claustrophobia issues, you should not try doing this.
Really. Don't.

I heard Scott's muffled and echoed voice ahead.
'Keep moving. Keep going. It's not much further.'
'Scott says to keep moving,' Nora translated.
And so we did. We dragged ourselves on and on.

Just after I had sworn to myself that I would never go caving ever again, I heard a lot of muffled, echoed chatter ahead.
'Oh! I can see it,' Nora informed me.

What Nora saw was that the cave had relented and, at last, opened up some more. Soon, all of us were on our feet. We were standing in a long, narrow crevice. You could touch either wall with your hands without stretching. There was a gap in the floor of the crevice like it was split in two. There was an inky blackness down the gap which varied from about a foot to a yard in different spots.

We stopped and gulped for air for a moment. I looked down at my clothes. They were in shreds. I was wearing a sweatshirt and it was cut to ribbons. The rest of our group were in similar disarray.
'Careful here, everyone,' the Professor warned. 'Watch your step and try to keep to the sides.'
His advice sounded wise.

We walked and hopped rock to rock through the narrow crevice. It was physically demanding, but not soul-sapping like the snake slithering section.

Oh! And those carbide lamps that 'last for a considerable spell'? Well, they don't. You have to keep relighting them. Every few minutes. And it isn't easy to swipe your hand over a little generator wheel when one, your hands are wet, and two, your hands are also rubbed raw. But you dare not take a step without your light being lit. It could be your last.

We kept moving forward. Suddenly, I heard Nora screaming something and Charlie laughing. 'Bats, Ralphy!' she squealed in echoed terror. 'Bats!'
I wasn't sure if it was better to be bringing up the rear and not stumble upon horrors first or be up ahead and face it and be done with it.
'Bats! Bats!'

I was just thinking to myself, 'Did she just say 'Bats'?', when I could see the problem. As I made my way to the others, I saw there were thousands of bats happily roosting on the walls like bat wallpaper. The walls we were meant to keep close to. For safety.

Nora's screams sent some of the bats off into a panic and, as we tried to go forward, several bats would swoop at us just to make things that little more impossible.
Charlie was laughing his head off. When things got 'stupid', as he would say, it always struck him as very funny. I guess he thought dodging bats while trying not to fall to your death was hilarious.

I must have been struck on my helmet by ten bats as I made my way through that crevice. But there was no 'Dracula moment' or anything like that. The bats were panicked. Nora was panicked. And Charlie and I were too, although we just wouldn't let on that we were.
But not Scott and the Professor. They had a 'seen it all before' type of attitude. They seemed actually to be enjoying all of this.
Perhaps that's what Charlie found stupid and got him laughing.

This scenario went on for another hour or so. Crawling on your belly for a mile or more, then hopping three feet to your left and then to your right to avoid falling to a certain death, followed by getting whacked in the head by flying bats in a panic, then putting your hands on the side walls to steady yourself and sending off yet more bats to plague you- this was 'Caving'.

But I was wrong. This was not caving. This was only the grueling awfulness you had to go through before you really got started. And then suddenly it was all worth it.

It was more than amazing. I have to admit it. I had never seen something quite like it before. As we came to the end of the narrow crevice, we all stopped stock-still.
'Look!' said Scott. 'Look!' Nora said astonished. .
There spread out before us was an enormous cavern.
It was wide. It was tall. It was semi-bat free.
All the environmental elements for which I had been craving.

We had to jump down from the end of the narrow crevice corridor to the cavern floor.
There, at one end of the cavern, was a mighty, thundering waterfall forming a pool below it. It was spectacular. We all walked over to it as if mesmerized. The sound was deafening. But what a sight. I felt special. I was seeing something the ordinary person would never see. Nor the sane for that matter.

There were enormous, glittering, crystal-like structures rising like pillars from the cavern floor. Even in the dim light of our carbide lamps, the colors were breathtaking.
'What are those?' Nora asked Scott.
'Gypsum pillars,' he replied.

The Professor had us all look into the waterfall pool.
'Do you see them?' he said. 'Can't you see them swimming?'
And we looked and we saw. There were these very tiny fish in there.
'They have no eyes,' the Professor told us.
'Because they don't need them.'

And all of a sudden, I am a very enthusiastic caver and taking an interest in everything.

We all stayed in that cavern together for a couple hours or so. We'd wander around and look for other features there. I didn't even want to think about the moment when we'd have to retrace our steps and get back above ground.

Then Scott came over to me and took me aside.
'The Professor and I are going to go on,' he said.

43

He showed me an entrance to another cave that I swear was even tinier than the first one we crawled through.

'All the section we just did was mapped last week. They stopped here and turned and went back. But we're going to go on and map this new area now. Do you want to come with us?'

I said I'd ask the others, but I needn't have bothered. There was no way we were going to go into another hole. Especially an uncharted one. I quickly went over to ask Nora and Charlie and just as quickly came back.

'I think we'll head back,' I said.

Scott and the Professor got their things together. Once they were ready, Scott came back over to me. He motioned for me to walk with him. He led me over to where we had dropped down to the cavern floor from the crevice corridor. He took out his canteen.

'I'm going to leave my canteen at the entrance here,' he said.

'Just leave it there when you start to go back. I'll collect it when I return.'

I asked him why.

'I'd just feel safer knowing you had a marker for the entrance.'

I was a little amused.

'You don't need to do that, Scotty! We just came out of there. We know where the entrance is,' I laughed.

But he was insistent.

'I'd just feel safer.'

Then Nora, Charlie, and I watched as Scott and the Professor squeezed themselves into the unexplored cave entrance.

We were not envious.

(Scott told me later that this new cave petered out after about 600 meters and they had to crawl back out ass first.)

The three of us went back to the pool beneath the fall and ate our Rice Crispy bars. They were delicious and I do not even like Rice Crispy bars. We sat there talking and laughing and making fun of each other.

'Eww! It's a bat! Eww! I'm gonna die!' Charlie would mock us.

Then Nora noticed something.

'What's that?' she asked. She was pointing down into the pool. The one with the little blind fish.

Seeing is at a premium when you are caving and it is not an easy thing to do. Everything is in shadow or ghosted around the edges. It is difficult to make things out. Even with a carbide lamp. And hearing is not much better. Sound echoes everywhere and what you thought was someone speaking behind you is actually someone forty feet away. Caves are sense tricksters.

We all peered down to where Nora was pointing her finger. I couldn't see anything there. And then Charlie scooped his hand into the water and picked something up.
'There we go,' he said.
In his hand was the head of a baby doll.

Now, I do not know about you, but as for me, if I am going to endure misery for the sake of seeing something pristine and unique, I do not want to know that someone else has not only been there before, but brought a baby doll along with them too.
If it had been an Indian arrowhead or a Tribal headdress from 'Running Brave', that I could have accepted. I could have imagined Running Brave leading his people, the Shawnee, into the caves to escape some hostile tribe or natural disaster.
That would have been fine.
But a baby doll head? No, that ruined everything.

Charlie was laughing at my upset.
'Baby Doll's eyes don't work here,' he joked. 'Because she doesn't need them.'
'It's like Scott of the Antarctic finding a Frisbee on his way to the South Pole,' I moaned.
Charlie laughed and laughed and his laughter echoed all around us.

Nora, Charlie, and I stayed in that cavern for at least another hour. It was, after all, a dark world of wonders, despite 'Baby Doll', and the prospect of the journey back was not something any of us were relishing.

But, eventually, we did decide to face the long slog back. We all got our things together. And made our way back toward the crevice entrance and the outside world.

I was leading the way.

Then Nora said, 'No, no, I think it's over here. You're going in the wrong direction.'

'She's right,' Charlie said. 'It's this way.'

So we walked across the cavern floor in the direction Nora suggested.

'No, this doesn't look right either,' Charlie said eventually. 'Where is it?'

'I think it's back the other way,' I said.

So we went back to where I first thought the entrance was, but there was no entrance to be found.

Next thing I know, we are all scrambling off in our own direction and hoping to find the entrance. But we could not find it or Scott's canteen which was marking the spot. And this went on for quite a while.

I was not panicking, yet. Yes, it does sound mad that we could not find the entrance, but caves are, as I've told you, disturbingly disorienting places. That's true whether you have a 'sense of direction' or not.

'We'll find it,' I thought to myself. 'It's just an inconvenience. We'll find it eventually.' And while I was thinking that, Nora let out a scream.

'Look at this! Ralphy! Look at this!' I could hear her voice echoing. 'Look!'

'Nora!' I called out. 'Where are you?'

'Over here! Look what I've found!' I think that is what she said. Her voice was bouncing everywhere. I scanned around the shadowy cavern and my light went out. I lowered my head to flick my hand across the light. When it came back on, Nora was standing right in front of me.

'Look what I found!'

She was holding something in her hands.

'Look at what?' I asked her as I tried to refocus my eyes.

'It's a little girl's dress! Look!'

And she held up a very soiled little girl's sundress

'Look!'

'You found the right spot?' Charlie asked as he rejoined Nora and me.

Nora held up the little girl's dress for Charlie to see too.

'What's that doing in here?' He asked with a puzzled frown.
And we didn't know.
Nora balled up the little dress and put it down the front of her jeans.
As she did so, she said, 'I'm taking this back with me. Something is
not right.'

But we were taking nothing back with us, because we couldn't find
the right entrance to take us back anywhere.
We looked and looked. We looked separately. We looked together.
And then finally…
'Here it is!!' Charlie laughed. 'Here's the canteen!'

I mumbled my thanks to Scott. I glanced at my watch. We had been
searching in vain for the best part of three hours.
I still think, to this day, that if Scott had not insisted that he place his
canteen at that entrance, we'd still be in that cavern.

We climbed up to the crevice corridor and started making our slow
progress back through the crawlway and the bats.

I won't bore you with the return journey above ground. Suffice it to
say that the bats had not moved from their roost, the snake belly
through the crawlway was just as miserable as before, and it took us
a few attempts to climb back up the ropes on the rock face toward the
cave system entrance.
Its best moment was the moment it was all over.

We emerged into the light of a hot, sunny afternoon.
We took some time to blink at the glare, catch our breath, and shake
out our limbs before we could walk properly. I looked at the
collapsed hilltops surrounding us.

There, as we noticed on our way into the cave, was the unoccupied,
weather-beaten stone bungalow in the field near the cave entrance.
On its porch was a rusty swinging bench. We all walked over and
parked ourselves on it and creakily rocked back and forth in our
exhaustion.

Charlie's car and the Professor's Jeep were parked nearby where we
had made camp earlier. Nora went over to Charlie's car and put the
girl's dress in the backseat right next to our Styrofoam beer cooler.

'I'll be putting that in the trunk later,' Charlie said to me. 'Creepy'.
'Too creepy,' I agreed.

Nora came back with a suggestion.
'Look! There's a pond just over here.'
She pointed at some muddy brown water adjacent to the bungalow.
'Let's go swimming!'
It was hot. We were dirty and our clothes were like rags hanging off
of us. There was some sense to her idea.
Nora was determined to go in. However I had some experience on
the wrong end of some of her 'suggestions' in the past. Nora's
schemes did not always work out as advertized. I gave it a miss.
Charlie was not so lucky.
'Let's go!' Nora said as she started stripping down to her underwear.
Charlie laughed as he followed suit. They both left their clothes on
the porch and went over to the 'pond'.
I just sat there on the swing and rocked back and forth.

I started thinking about being lost in that cavern. Nowadays, if I hear
a report about trapped miners like the ones in Chile or China, I just
shudder. Their fate was a million times worse than mine and mine
was scary enough. How anyone could keep going when trapped in
that darkness for weeks is miraculous. I'd never last. I am sure, if it
were me, I would kill and bite off the leg of the nearest miner just so
I didn't die hungry.
But those guys are made of sterner stuff than I am.

So I was thinking about being trapped forever in that cave, and lost
miners, and people buried alive or trapped in the air pockets of
buildings that collapsed in earthquakes.
And I was just thinking that when…
'Help!'
It was Nora. I snapped out of my reverie.
'Help! Help! Ralphy!'
It was Nora and Charlie.

I got up and ran over to the 'pond'. There, about five yards out, stood
Nora and Charlie.
'We're sinking!' Charlie shouted. He was laughing, of course, but
looking like he didn't know what to do either.
'We can't move!' Nora too was laughing as she said it, but I could
tell she was also deadly serious.

I didn't know what to do. They were knee-deep in red-brown muck. Sinking deeper apparently.

I looked around and saw a long branch on the ground. I grabbed it and shimmied on my stomach to the edge of the pond. I crawled out that way until they could reach the branch I held out in front of me. Then I tried to stand up. It was gooey underfoot, but I just about managed it. Charlie grabbed the branch with one hand and Nora with the other.
Then just as I got the branch into Charlie's hand, I heard them. Lots of them.
Then I saw them. Lots and lots of them.

All our yelling had attracted the attention of the local cattle herd back to their watering hole. For that was what our 'pond' really was. They were mooing and descending en masse from over a hill on the other side of the water.
I pointed this out to the others.

There was some heaving and slipping and some panicky angry words going on, but somehow Charlie leveraged his leg free and then pulled Nora out with him. They sort of crawled-walked their way back toward dry land. I tugged and tugged on that branch with the all of me until they were both clear.
The cattle blinked at us in their confusion.
'It was like suction all around you,' Nora said to me in amazement.
'Moo,' I replied.

They got themselves cleaned up as best they could. Meanwhile, I left our helmets, clamps, and lamps beside the Professor's Jeep for Scott and the Professor to collect on their return.
We decided maybe it was time to head back to civilization.

Charlie put the girl's sundress in the trunk and started the car. We tried to get back to the two lane blacktop from which we had descended to make camp the night before.
It was not easy. We were driving up through pasture and over rocky ledges and uneven dirt tracks. Twice, we had to get out and push ourselves out of some rut. I don't know how Charlie did it, but finally we got to the road above.

Now, I don't know why this is, but it seems to me that once you feel you are through with doing something very demanding, like caving or escaping muddy quagmires, you tend to drop your guard.
You're safe again, you think. You relax. You enjoy yourself.
I don't know if that was the reason or not, but we were laughing and joking and Charlie was not really obeying the rules of the road.

As I mentioned, it is very hilly in that part of Kentucky and Charlie took to putting both his bare feet on the dashboard, when we were driving downhill. And sometimes downhill went on for some fair distance. There was not another vehicle in sight. We did not think it was a dangerous thing to do.
I thought nothing of it in fact. Until we heard the siren.

We looked back and saw a black and white patrol car behind us. The red light on the patrol car's roof was flashing. Charlie pulled over and the cop stopped and got out.
Charlie realized he was not wearing any shoes, so he reached under his seat to grab them.
That was not a good idea.
The cop thought something bad was going down.
He drew his revolver.
'Get out of the car!' He shouted. 'Slowly! Get out! Show me your hands!' We did just what he asked. We got out. Slowly.

I do not know if you have ever had a gun aimed at you before or not. I hope not. It is not something I could really recommend. All I can tell you is that you just go along with whatever is suggested by the person who has the gun. And when someone who is nervous is holding that gun, like this cop was, you are sure to comply carefully with any instructions you receive. And we did.

He had us hold our hands above our heads. He pointed the gun at Charlie. 'Over here!' he commanded and he indicated that Charlie needed to move to the passenger side of his dad's car. The window was down. The cop asked for his license and registration. Charlie reached for the glove compartment.
'Stop!' the cop shouted. 'Face me and open that slowly.' Charlie did. He handed the cop his details. He then forced us to walk to the back of our car and keep our hands in the air while he checked Charlie's details in his patrol car. Eventually, he re-emerged.

'You know it is illegal to drive without your feet on the pedals, Mister?' the cop asked Charlie sternly.

'Do you know it is illegal to drive without wearing any shoes? You've got an 'Out of State' car here. We get a lot of drugs comin' into our town from 'Out of State' cars. You got any?'

And we all assured him that we did not. Of course, we did have two quarts of warm beer sloshing around in melted ice water in our Styrofoam cooler, but we did not bring that up. It is also illegal in that part of Kentucky to have alcoholic beverages.

And then Nora came to our rescue.

'Officer, we only came here to your beautiful State to visit your world famous caves. We heard so much about them that we really wanted to see them for ourselves.'

And she went on and on about how we were there with a Geology Professor from the State University and how we were helping to map a new cave system and how terribly exciting it all was and how thrilled we all were to have such an experience.

And it worked.

The cop changed his demeanor completely. All of a sudden we were just a group of nice young people. He holstered his weapon.

Nora told him all about the helmets and lamps we used.

He now decided that he liked us.

'Yes, Miss, this is the greatest spot on Earth for cavers. Mammoth Cave is the largest in the world. You really need to get over there and see that while you're in these here parts. I've done some caving myself. Me and my boys. The history behind some of these caves is fascinating.'

'Is it?' Nora asked full of feigned, intoxicated interest.

'Yes, Miss, there was even a time around here when we had something called the 'Cave Wars'. Business people used them for mining and such and feuds broke out over who had a right to the land where a particular cave was situated. There was a lot of nastiness going on.'

The cop, who introduced himself as Deputy Carvel, then told us all a story:

'There was once a local businessman named Collins,' he began as he sat back on the hood of his patrol car. 'He was trying to buy up the rights to mine a cave system for gypsum. That was worth a fortune in them days. They say he struck a deal with the land owner.'

'They both made a ton a' money. At first. But somehow their business deal went sour and each side lay blame on the other,' the deputy explained.

'And then, soon after, Collins' young daughter went missing. I'm talking about thirty, forty years ago now, I reckon. Masked men broke in and took her right while she was sleeping in the family home. Took some of her clothes and dollies too according to her mammy. Her folks raised the alarm and all the police and locals formed a search party. But they couldn't find a trace of her. They reckoned it was an act of revenge, but they couldn't prove nothing,' he said.

'There was no ransom note,' he continued. 'And no one ever found her. She just disappeared. Such was the goings-on back in them days.'

'What was the little girl's name?' Nora asked him fearfully.
'They named her after what made them their fortune,' he said. 'Gypsum'.
Nora, Charlie, and I all slowly looked at one another.
'Something wrong?' Deputy Carvel asked in puzzled confusion.

Nora got Charlie to open the trunk where he had put the little sundress Nora had found in the cave. She showed Deputy Carvel the dress and told him about 'Baby Doll'.
'We didn't know it, Officer, but we may have stumbled on where they took 'Gypsum',' Nora said with tears in her eyes.
'Someone needs to go back there, because we didn't find her body.' And she started getting weepy and flung her arms around me in a snuggle for comfort.

Deputy Carvel took the dress.
'Y' all better show me that cave,' he said. We told him again about the Professor and how he knew exactly where it was and we rode with the deputy in his patrol car back to the cave, so he'd know exactly where it was too.
We all gave him our phone numbers and addresses so we could be contacted, if the police needed us, and then he drove us back to our car.
'We'll be talking to that Professor and organize a search party. Y'all may have solved a terrible tragedy from a tragic time,' he said.
'Maybe I'll be seeing y'all again.'

He then reminded Charlie, 'You best mind your driving, Young Sir.'
And with that, Deputy Carvel got back into his patrol car and moved
off. He stuck his left arm out the driver window and waved goodbye
as he passed.

Not much of merit happened after that. We just headed back to
Pennsylvania. I remember stopping at a gas station and Charlie
buying an Elvis Presley Compilation 8-track tape with the song
Kentucky Rain.
That's easy to remember. He played it all the way home.

Now, I know, some people will ask me about what happened later
and about Scott and the Professor and what they discovered.
First of all, the Kentucky police never contacted us. Not that we had
anything to add to what we'd already told Deputy Carvel.
But I can tell you that Scott found out through the Professor that they
never found Gypsum's body. He did say they found the doll's head
there in the waterfall pool where Charlie had left it. They discovered
the items we found belonged to the kidnapped girl, so that's
something.
I try not to think about that little girl dragged down there though.
It makes me shudder still.

As for me and Scott, I suppose we grew apart after that. Not from
anything serious. I was with Nora and most of the things I was doing,
I was doing with her now.
That is just the way it is with young love sometimes. All of a sudden
the two of you have a new best friend. One another.

When I used to tell that story, Nora, my future wife-ex wife, would
jump in with support and dramatic effect. She'd add little details
about Gypsum and how 'really' she felt someone was looking at us
the entire time we were in the waterfall cavern.
She'd tell them, 'I could feel her presence.'
Sometimes, she would get up and act out the moment she first saw
Gypsum's dress. It was gripping.

But I can only tell you what I recall. We're both of us missing the
'Nora Factor' here though. And that really helped to seal the deal in
believing this story. Truly, it did.

But you should believe in its truth anyway, because it is…True.

STORY CHAPTER FOUR

'OLD BLUE EYES'

Sometimes, when I tell this story, people say it is a 'Shaggy Dog'.
I suppose there are many parts to it and perhaps that explains why.

Part of this is Nora's story. Not that it is about Nora as such. Rather,
part of this story is a story that Nora once told me.
But her story does also tell you some things about Nora.
Every story is about the teller just as much as it is about the story
itself. 'Shaggy Dog' saga or not.

Of course, Nora is not here to tell you her part of the story in her own
words. You will have to make do with what I can recall about it.
There are some facts that I do not know or may have forgotten, but I
will relate it as best I can remember.
Were she here, she could fill in the details much better than I.
But she is not here and there is nothing you and I can do about that.

It was 1972 and I was just starting my studies at a small college in
Pennsylvania. I knew not a soul there. It took me a few days or so
before I made my first friend. His name was Scott. I once went with
him to Kentucky on a caving expedition, but that's another tale and
has little to do with this one.

One day, as I was walking through campus, I saw a large crowd
congregating in front of the biology building. They were all
whooping and shouting in encouragement. I wandered over to see
what it was all about.
Scott was there too. I walked over to stand next to him.
'What's going on?' I asked him.
'Look!' he said as he pointed upwards.

There, on the roof of the biology building, was a naked woman
dancing to music. She was covered in blue body paint. That wasn't
something you'd see everyday, so you can understand why a crowd
might gather.

The woman could really dance. There was a guy up there with her. I guess it was her boyfriend. He was in charge of the music.
'Go! Go! Go!' the crowd yelled in encouragement.

I should say the crowd was made up of about 99% male students. The co-eds who passed by either looked away or tut-tutted to their female companions as they walked past.

The naked blue dancer finally stopped dancing and the crowd uttered a universal 'Awww' in disappointment.
And the crowd dispersed.

'Who was that?' I asked Scott. He seemed to know everyone.
'Her name's Nora,' he said. 'She's only a freshman, but she's already on the senior cheerleading team.'
'I can see why,' I nodded.

To be honest, I never really thought much about Nora after that. But later that year, I was in a student musical production of *You're a Good Man, Charlie Brown* and Nora was also in the show.
I could sing, dance, and act a little. I had been a child actor and once performed with Debbie Reynolds in the stage version of *The Sound of Music*.

I started to notice in rehearsals that every time I would sing or dance, Nora would be watching me from the wings.
Other cast members must have noticed this too. Some of the seniors would tease me.
'You've got a fan there! That's one cute groupie!'
I ignored them.

Then, one day, when I went to the dining hall for breakfast, Scott called me over to his table. Nora was sitting there too.
Scott was beaming.
'What are you so happy about?' I asked him as I sat down with my tray.
'Oh! Nothing!' he answered cryptically.

Nora kept going on and on about how 'talented' I was and that I should be on Broadway.

'You make everyone else look like an amateur,' she insisted.
'You're the best thing in the whole show!'
Scott just sat there with a face full of smiles.

Later that day, I had a history class with Scott. After the lecture, he approached me.
'Nora likes you,' he told me. 'She asked me if she could sit at my table this morning just in case you showed up.'
'OK'
'She's really nice!'
'She has a boyfriend,' I said. 'He was changing the music for her when she was dancing on that roof.'
'No, no! She's finished with him. She likes you!'

You might laugh, but I have never been particularly good at reading the signs that someone liked me. In fact, I am terrible at it. I practically need to be hit over the head with a heavy hammer before I catch on.
And Nora was so beautiful and so popular. All the senior boys were chasing after her.
'You should talk to her,' Scott insisted.
So I did.

The Sunday afternoon, after that meeting with Scott, was a dreadful day on campus. It rained so hard all the fields were soaked and the pavements ran with water. I was caught out in that mess and raced back to my dorm. As I did so, I saw Nora running ahead of me. Just then the skies opened in a mighty torrent and I caught up with Nora, grabbed her by the arm, and led us both to shelter on a train car parked on a siding. We talked throughout the deluge teeming outside our train car haven and when the squall at last relented, Nora and I walked back to the dorm together.
From then on, Nora and I were, what they used to call, an 'item'.

Now, I have had to tell you all of that so you can understand a few things. Nora and I were an item. But we were also both fiercely independent. I liked that about her. I don't like being fussed over like some former girlfriends would do.
Nora was completely happy to let me do my own thing and I was equally happy that she do hers.

And now that you are aware of that, I can begin our story.

One Friday evening, I was walking back to my dorm. I had to cross a road to get there and a pizza place was on the corner of the road I was crossing. As I walked by, I heard my name shouted. I turned around and there was Orion, one of the other actors in *'Charlie Brown'*. Orion was a senior. He was exiting from the pizza place with a big sandwich in his hands.

'I'm going down to Durham to see my brothers for the weekend,' he said with his mouthful. 'We're all going to the big rock concert at Charlotte Speedway. You want to come?'

'When?'

'Now!'

I thought about it for a moment and said, 'Why not?'

I grabbed some stuff from my dorm room, got into Orion's car, and we both headed south.

I could tell you a long and interesting story about that journey, but that would neither be this story nor Nora's story within it. It would be mine. So forgive me for not filling you in on the details about the mass brawl that broke out at the Speedway concert or how Orion would drive through tollgate booths without paying.

I never told Nora I was going away that weekend. I knew that she wouldn't mind.

I just returned, slightly worse for wear, to college on the following Monday morning.

When I saw Nora again, she was sitting in the dining hall with two guys.

They were laughing and acting like they were old friends. I walked over to where they were sitting.

'This is Donny and this is Bobby!' Nora told me.

I didn't know them, but I knew them by sight. They were both seniors in the music department.

'I tried to find you over the weekend, but I figured you had other plans,' Nora said. 'Bobby said he needed to get home and had no ride, so I said we should all hitchhike there together.'

Both Bobby and Donny were very shy. How Nora met them, I do not know. But I know Nora and I am sure the hitchhiking idea was entirely hers.

'We had such an adventure, didn't we?!' she asked them.

And both of them smiled bashfully as they nodded their heads.

Nora went on to tell me that Bobby hailed from Durham, North Carolina and his sister was getting married there. Donny was his best friend.

I didn't say that I was in Durham as well with Orion and his brothers.

'We just took off and started hitchhiking. But this one weird man, who gave us a lift, went west when he said he was going south and I had to make up an excuse to get us out of his car,' Nora explained with great suspense.

'There was something wrong about him,' Donny said. 'We ended up in West Virginia.'

'Right in the middle of nowhere!' Nora laughed.

And Nora told me how they were stuck there on the side of the road for the longest time before they could get another ride. That reminded me of a time when I went hitchhiking with some High School friends. We also spent a lot of time being 'stuck' on the side of some road.

'And finally this car stops,' Nora said excitedly, 'and it's full of people already and we just crammed in there with the rest of them. And the driver said he was going south, but really he wasn't. He was on the lamb from the law!'

Nora told me that the driver's name was Aboja and that he was a professional safe-cracker and bank robber. The others in his car were part of his posse.

'And Aboja would have to take all these side roads to avoid the police.'

Donny and Bobby just smiled along as she told her story.

'And eventually we knew that we couldn't get to Durham in time for the wedding, so we just hung out with Aboja and his friends. He took us to some really good redneck bars and there was country music and then we went to his place, so he could change his clothes, and he tried to get me into bed, but I told him no and he was so nice about it.'

I wasn't liking this story.

'And at Aboja's place other people just kept arriving and they all had instruments and started to play together. And they even let Donny and Bobby borrow their instruments so they could play too.'

'We were just jamming,' Bobby contributed.

'And then,' Nora said, 'they had this enormous barbecue and we all ate and drank and we ended up staying there for the night. And Aboja tried to get into bed with me again and told me that we should get married. He said that was the hillbilly way. He was so funny!'

I really was not liking this story.

Nora said that this Aboja character dropped them off the next day at the Interstate, so they could catch a lift more easily.

'He gave me his number and said that I should come back soon, because there was going to be a really big party and he was going to show me how hillbillies dance.'

So that's Nora's story about 'Aboja' as best I can remember it.

Very soon after that, Nora and I moved in together. I was taking a summer theatre course at the college and Nora stayed the summer there too and the next thing I knew she had moved all her things into where I was living.

And I was happy with that, even if we had never spoken about it. Nora was like that.

Our first summer together was paradise. The weather was gorgeous and we didn't have a care in the world. The only thing I had to do was rehearse plays for the summer season. The rest of the time was Nora's and mine.

One fine summer's day, we were walking in town and went down an alleyway that we used as a short cut. The alleyway ran past the back of a row of houses. And suddenly Nora stopped.

'What's that noise?' she asked with her ears pricked.

'What noise?'

'Shhh! Listen!'

I did and then I heard this pathetic squeaking sound coming from a trash can.

Nora went over to have a look.

'It's probably a rat, Nora! Be careful!'

But it wasn't a rat.

Nora took the lid off the trash receptacle. It was full of rubbish, but the squeaky sound was growing louder. I went over and knocked the trash can over with my foot.

Some of its contents spilled out on to the alleyway.

'Oh my God!' Nora shouted.

'It's a puppy!'

And there half-buried in orange peels and hair nets was a tiny little puppy.

'How could someone do this?!' Nora fumed.

'We have to save it, Ralphy!'

Nora picked up the puppy. It could only have been a few weeks old. She brushed off the coffee grounds and mess that had covered its little coat.

Nora was a fearless young woman. If there was injustice or intimidation, she would confront it. We had that in common. I don't put up with bullies either.

She was so incensed that she marched up to the backdoor of the house behind which we had found the puppy in the rubbish.

'Throwing out puppies!' she shouted at the door as she knocked and knocked.

'Heartless monsters!'

But no one answered.

'Come on, Nora,' I said. 'They're probably too ignorant to feel guilty anyway.'

We now had a dog. On closer inspection, we noticed our rubbish heap puppy had blue eyes. I had never seen a dog with blue eyes before. I have since, but this was the first blue-eyed dog I'd ever seen.

She appeared to be what they call a 'collie mix'. There was certainly some collie in her, but most of her was the 'mix' part.

'I'm going to call her, 'Boj', after Aboja,' Nora announced.

'Why don't we call her, 'Ol' Blooey'? She has blue eyes,' I suggested.

'Ol' Blooey! No! Her eyes are just the same shade of blue as Aboja's eyes!'

So Boj it was.

Boj. Named after a Hillbilly safe-cracker who tried to bed my girlfriend. Twice.

Once Nora had nursed our discarded puppy back to health, Boj was quite a little devil-dynamo. She would chew on anything, but her favorite chew toy would be either my or Nora's right shoes. How the dog knew it was the right shoe, I cannot fathom. But it was always the right one.
But over time, Boj grew into a more placid dog and was a core member of our trio.

Boj was a sleek and skinny black and tan mongrel. She had tan markings at exactly the spot where we humans have eyebrows. She also had incredibly long eyelashes for a dog.
The combined effect made Boj's expressions almost human-like. The look of concern she could make when something troubled her, like a thunderstorm, was priceless. One of our best friends, Charlie, nicknamed her 'Bette Davis.'

A year or so later, Nora and I were married. Nora insisted that Boj attend the ceremony.

I know that everyone's pet dog is special and loved and amazing too. I don't deny that. But I have had dogs all my life and I have never come across a dog like Boj before or since.
Boj was a true 'rare bird' dog.

Attending a wedding was no challenge to Boj. All you had to do was give her instructions and she would follow them to the letter.
'Just stay right here inside the church door, Boj,' Nora would say.
'And you mustn't make any noise or distract anyone.'
And that is precisely what Boj would do.

Boj grew to become famous on campus. Even Professors not known for being cuddly would just swoon at the sight of her. She was everyone's best friend. Years later, people would come up to me and tell me stories about something Boj had done that I never heard about. Like the time she saved a little boy from drowning in a wading pool by dragging him out by the back of his trunks. Dozens and dozens of stories like that made the rounds.

We never had to put her on a leash or make her wear a collar. We never 'trained' her. She was just a freak of the canine world. Better than Lassie.

I think Boj was about six or seven years old when she had her first professional booking. Nora and I had both graduated by then and were living in Baltimore.

I heard about a man who was selling luxury condominiums on the Potomac just outside of Washington DC. I had no job and was willing to take anything that came along. The Condo guy wanted someone to distribute flyers on the street to advertize his condos. I called to arrange an interview and then drove over to his office with Boj in the car with me. When we arrived, I let Boj out of the car. Before I went in for my meeting, I said, 'Boj, you stay right here by the entrance. And don't wander off and don't let anyone take you either.'
I think that was the command I gave her.

I went into the office block, met the Condo guy, and he hired me on the spot.
'We'll do it for a few days and see how it's going,' he said.
We both left his office together.

When we exited, I saw two young women making a fuss over Boj. They had brought her a bowl of water.
'Is this your dog?' one of the girls asked in rapture.
'What a cute dog! And so clever!' the other girl said.

When the Condo guy saw Boj sitting there, he joined the girls in stroking her.
'Well, say hello, Boj,' I told her.
And Boj craned back her neck and let out a little squeak of 'hello'.
The two girls practically swooned in delight.
The Condo guy was very impressed.
'Does your dog do any other tricks?'
'I don't know,' I answered. 'Ask her to do something.'

And the Condo guy told Boj to bark and she barked. He told her to stay, while he threw a stick, and she stayed. Then he told her to fetch the stick and she fetched it. He held his hands up and told her to stand up. And she stood up.

The girls erupted in squeals of glee.
'So clever! So cute!'
'Amazing!' Condo guy said. 'How did you teach her to do all that?'
'I don't know how she does it,' I said to him.
'We never taught her to do any of that.'

And the Condo guy insisted that both Boj and I would distribute his flyers.
'How much are you charging for the dog?' he asked me.
I just ventured, 'How about half my pay?'
'Done!'

The Condo guy wanted me to dress as a 'mime' and wear a bowler hat to distribute the condo flyers. I was supposed to 'mime' as I handed them out.
'You can mime, can't you?' he had asked me during the interview.
'Sure,' I lied.
'That way there's no need to talk!' Condo guy explained.
'Everything's on the flyer!'

Nora made Boj a little canine costume that matched the black and white striped top I planned to wear. She even made a tiny papier maché bowler hat for her that looked like the one I would don.

Mime. It was the curse of the late 70's and early 80's. Everyone seemed to be a mime. They were everywhere. And on this job for Condo guy, I was one too.

I had done some training in dance. I was flexible. I could do some physical things, like stretching, that the normal human being could not contemplate.
So, it was nothing for me to pretend I was a mime, even though I was not one.
I didn't even bother putting on 'White Face'. I would just draw a large, thin, curly moustache on my face. It made me look like Salvador Dali.
But I could act a trifle. I could bend myself into a pretzel shape and out again.
Everything else I just faked.

The first day on the job, Boj and I went to Dupont Circle in Washington DC. We stood at the entrance to the Metro and handed out the flyers.

Everyone took one. Boj drew the crowds and I tried to be as mime-like as I could.

Women especially went crazy. They would stop dead in their tracks and simply melt at the sight of Boj in her mime costume.

'Hello, Cutie!' or 'So cute! So adorable!!!' they'd swoon.

Several of them handed me slips of paper with their phone numbers. I did not mention this to Nora when I returned home.

Everywhere Boj and I went to hand out those flyers, the same thing would happen.

Then, about three days into our job together, a man approached me. 'I have a job you might be interested in,' he said. As I was pretending to be a mime, I could not say anything back to him.

'Here's my number. Call me,' he said.

He patted Boj on the head and walked off.

When Boj and I got back home, I called the number the man had given me.

'White House switchboard, what number please?' a woman responded.

'The White House?' I asked in shock.

'Yes, what number please?'

I told her the name of the man, Gary, who told me to call.

'Connecting you now.'

'Gary Young. Hello. How can I help?'

I told Gary that I was the mime he saw on the street earlier.

'Wonderful! Your dog is terrific! I want to book you for an event at the White House,' he said.

'What event?'

'For the 'South Lawn Easter Egg Hunt'. The kids will love it!'

This Easter Egg Hunt had become a tradition at the White House and young children were invited to search the South Lawn for decorated eggs.

Boj and I were hired.

I was the White House Mime and I wasn't even a real mime.

To be truthful, Boj was a better mime than I was. I would tell her, before we went out on our mime double-act, 'Boj, no matter what happens, you cannot make any noise. You have to be silent, you follow?' Then I'd add, 'You can move around and look at people, but you can't react vocally.'

OK. I didn't say 'react vocally'. I'd say, 'No talking, Girl.'
I knew she knew what that meant.

And she was superb. She never made a sound, unless I told her to do so. She'd even try to copy my 'mimey' movements much to the amusement of the crowd. Boj, uncannily, possessed the sense of balance of a reincarnated Taiwanese acrobat.

The Easter Egg Hunt job went down very well. The kids all adored Boj and I got away with murdering the mime profession. With Boj there, no one would challenge my mime credentials.

Gary was more than pleased with how it all panned out.
'I have another little job for the two of you,' he said. 'Nancy Reagan is launching her 'Foster Grandparents' campaign next week. There will be two hundred children here and some celebrities will be on hand too to give the launch some publicity. All you have to do is keep the kids entertained.'

So Boj and I were booked for yet another White House event.
The following week we both put on our matching mime costumes and went to entertain the kids at the launch of the 'Foster Grandparents' campaign.

We were ushered into an enormous marquee that had been erected on the South Lawn. It was packed. In addition to the children, there were White House staff and 'hospitality girls' everywhere. The media was in hyper-drive and there were dozens of photographers and news teams at every turn.

News quickly spread that there was going to be a 'very special guest' attending. It must be quite a special guest, I thought. President Reagan and his wife were both already there.

Boj and I got to work and started doing our little act for the kids.

I must tell you that Boj would do almost anything for a piece of cheese. I felt badly about taking advantage of her weakness.

If I held up a piece of cheese, and whispered in her ear, 'Stand up, Boj! Dance! Do your Conga Line!' she would. She'd get up on her hind legs and do a hoppy motion back and forth in a little dance. The kids would go wild.

And as there were mostly kids in that marquee, they'd squeal, 'Give Boj the cheese, Mister Mime! Give Boj the cheese!'

And when I would, everyone would cheer. Children and adults alike. Boj was powerless in the face of cheese.

We were carrying on like this when something happened that I had never before experienced.

As I've told you, there must have been two hundred children and nearly as many assorted adults there in that marquee. I was doing my mime 'fall down' routine, where I would walk forward, fall down into splits, and then draw myself back up on to my feet to carry on walking. Boj would 'mime' biting me on my posterior to encourage me to get up from the splits.

That usually brought the house down, but for some reason, I simply stopped in the midst of doing that and my eyes were drawn to the marquee entrance.

And everyone else's eyes were drawn there too.

As one, every head swiveled to look at the entrance.

And then I saw why.

It was Frank Sinatra.

I didn't know he would enter the marquee at that moment. Lots of people were coming and going through that entrance during the 'Boj and Me' mime show.

But some kind of 'Frank Force' was on display and its lure was irresistible.

I have never seen the like. Even Boj was interested.

It was unnerving to discover how easily we can all lose control of our own behavior.

Frank had a large group of his own people with him. The media went berserk. Camera flashes were everywhere and television news crews were tripping over one another to try to gain a better position to film him. I'd never before seen so many cameras flash in unison. They created an eerie, pulsating wave of intense bursts of light. It made Boj go all 'Bette Davis'. I stroked her head in calming reassurance.

Nancy Reagan left the President's side and went over to collect Frank. She paused for a moment while the two were filmed together. Then she led him back to where her husband was. Frank and Nancy seemed to be old chums. You could see they were relaxed in one another's company. President Reagan seemed less at ease with Frank, but perhaps being President makes it difficult to be at ease with anyone. He was simply his jocular self as he was with anyone else. Unlike Nancy, I did not get the impression that he and Frank were friends. But it was a Hollywood moment at the White House and set the whole place buzzing.

Nancy and Frank walked over to a raised stage platform. Boj and I had just been doing our act in front of it until Frank's arrival upstaged us.
She went to the microphone and introduced Frank to the crowd. Women of a certain age, who should have known better, threw all decorum to the hounds and flocked to be as close as possible to Frank.
They blocked the view of all the children. And I was no better really. I stood on tiptoe as close to Frank as I could get and did pointless little hops up and down to try to get a better view.

'Nancy is an old pal of mine!' Frank joked. 'When she told me about what she was doing here, I told her to count me in!'
And everyone cheered.
'Does anyone want a song?' he asked the crowd. The response was deafening.
Frank removed a crib sheet from his jacket pocket and then sang two numbers. A cappella.
I wish I could tell you what songs they were, but I was as bad as everyone else and just stared at him in dumb amazement.

Then Nancy Reagan gave a little speech about her program and how children need guidance and she wanted every grandparent who could spend the time to 'adopt' a child who had no grandparents.
The President also spoke briefly to lend his support.

And after the little speeches, food and drink were served to the kids. Gary walked over to me.
'Just go back up front and keep doing your thing. The kids love your dog!'

So we went back up in front of the stage and Boj and I did some more 'mime'.

Well, Boj did really. I took out another sliver of cheese and whispered, 'Boj, do your fashion show.'

And she got up again on her hind legs and 'walked' like she was on a catwalk. She'd go forward and hop about like a diva. She'd put her paws under her muzzle like she was posing for a glamour magazine. Then she'd turn herself around, look back at the kids, and roll her eyes.

'Give her the cheese, Mister Mime! Please give her the cheese!' the kids would scream in unison.

I guess Frank and his entourage were watching Boj's 'fashion show' too. I heard a gruff voice shout out near where he was standing. 'Make your dog sing!'

And quick as you like, I whispered to Boj, 'Sing your scales, Girl.' And on my cue, Boj sat down and, depending on how high or low I held the piece of cheese, she'd modulate her howl's pitch as best she could.

Everyone found this hilarious.

Poor Boj. Left to her own devices, Boj would rather be sleeping. It was her favorite pastime. And here I was making her do things she would never do given the choice.

She was a stoical mime-mongrel though and put up with it.

Boj did a few more star turns for the kids and then we went to have a little break.

I took Boj out to relieve herself and one of the hospitality girls brought her a bowl of water. 'Your dog is so cute! Her face is so expressive!' And she fell to her knees to hug Boj. That happened a lot with strangers new to Boj.

'So cute!' she squealed as she headed back inside the marquee.

I watched as Boj lapped up her water. Then I heard a voice calling out, 'Mime guy, that's quite a pooch you got.'

I turned around to look at who it was.

A big man in an expensive Italian suit was standing there.

He told me his name was Giacomo and he was Mr. Sinatra's 'Personal Assistant'.

Then he handed me a check. It was for $25,000.

'What's this?' I asked him.
'It's for the dog. Mr. Sinatra wants you to have it.'
'No, the White House agency pays me a fee for the dog.'
'No,' he replied, 'Not for the fee. For the dog.'
I didn't understand him.
'Frank wants your dog,' he explained.
'My dog? He wants my dog?'
'Yes'
I was stunned.
'He wants to buy my dog?'
'Yes'
'She's... not for sale,' I told him in a stammer.
'You won't sell? But Frank wants her!'
'I'm sorry,' I said. 'But I can't sell him my dog.'
Giacomo did not look pleased. He put the check back into his pocket.
'I'll be back,' he said mysteriously.

But he did not come back. Instead, a young woman soon came over
to where Boj and I were having our break. She was a Scandinavian
stunner who could only have been a Super Model or Movie Star.
But she was not.
She introduced herself as Viva and said she too was one of Frank's
'Personal Assistants'.

Viva was a far more formidable challenge then the beefy Giacomo.
She effortlessly oozed an easy sensuality in her Chanel ensemble.
She could best be described, I reckon, as a walking, talking
aphrodisiac. I got the impression that men were in real danger in her
presence.

'I've been watching you perform. You're very flexible, aren't you? I
find flexible men very sexy,' she pointed out. 'Did you know that?'
'Not really,' I responded stupefied.
'Uh huh,' she smiled. 'They can fit in all the right places.'
Viva readjusted the bowler hat on my head.
'Do you ever perform in Vegas? Perhaps we could get together.'
And she handed me her phone number.
'When you're in Vegas, you just give me a call, Flexy. I'll take good
care of you.'
She crouched down provocatively and began stroking Boj's neck.

I didn't know what to say, but I got away with it since I was a mime.

'Here,' she said, as she straightened up again even more provocatively.

'Frank wants you to have this.'

It was a check. This time for $50,000.

'It's for your dog.'

She had me stunned, but somehow I mastered myself.

I told her the same thing as I had told Giacomo before.

'I can't sell him my dog.'

'You want more money?' she asked me in surprise.

'No, the money's fine. It's just that I can't sell my dog.'

'But, why not?'

'It's my dog!'

She looked at me like I was the most pathetic loser that she'd ever come across.

And, I suppose, if you aren't a dog lover yourself, you might just be thinking the same thing.

Viva shook her gorgeous, Nordic mane and then she and her Chanel pencil skirt wiggled magnificently away.

Boj and I went back inside and did some more mime for the children. I brought half a dozen kids up in front of the group to help me with a trick.

I 'mimed' that they all had six-shooters. And, in turn, they should all 'shoot' Boj.

When they did, Boj would do an operatic death scene each time.

'Let me! Let me!' the other kids would shout.

The campaign launch was coming to an end and I started to put my things back into my bag to head home.

I let some of the kids come over to stroke Boj.

She was a star.

Then I heard a voice behind me.

'What's the problem, Mime guy? My money not good enough for you?'

I turned around.

It was Frank Sinatra.

He joined the kids in stroking Boj.

'How you doing there, Blue Eyes?' he chuckled to Boj.

Once Frank had arrived, Boj had to share star billing with him. A large crowd quickly gathered around.

'That's a pooch and a half you have there, Kiddo,' he said to me.

Frank picked Boj up in his arms and cuddled her.

'So my money's not good enough for you and Blue Eyes, huh?' he teased.

'No, Mr. Sinatra. Your money is plenty good.'

'So why are you refusing my checks? You want cash?'

'No, it's not that. I told your assistants. I can't sell you my dog.'

'Why not? You can get another dog.'

'That's true. But I can't get another wife. She'd leave me if I sold Boj.'

'Of course you can get another wife,' he joked. 'I've had eight of them myself!'

And he let out a throaty little laugh like he was poking fun at himself.

'I just can't do it, Mr. Sinatra.'

'You must love that dog,' he sighed.

"I love my wife too.'

But we agreed a plan. If Boj ever had puppies, I would let Frank know about it.

'You can have the pick of them, Mr. Sinatra. Free of charge.'

Frank had another of his assistants come over. He was even bigger and tougher looking than the broadly built Giacomo. He handed me a card.

'You can always reach Frank on this number. You are to show it to no one else.' He paused as he stared at me.

'You should be noddin' yes,' he said darkly.

I nodded.

I went home and told Nora all about what happened.

She was truly irate.

'Who do these people think they are?' she raged. 'They just think they can have anything they want and do anything they want to do too. They just flash their money around and get their flunkeys to do their bidding!' (I decided not to tell her the part about Viva.)

'And I couldn't call you to tell you what was going on,' I said in mitigation. 'I was at the White House. They don't have pay phones.'

Nora cuddled Boj close like she would never let her go.

'No one is going to take you away from us,' she said to Boj.
'No one!'
And, ever since that day, whenever Nora would hear Frank Sinatra's name mentioned or one of his many hits played, she'd say,
'That's the guy who tried to steal Boj!'

Of course, he did not try to steal her.
He offered a fortune for her.
But Nora did not honor such distinctions.

Boj and I did a few more jobs together here and there, but I eventually got a full time job at a box factory and ended my mock mime career.
I don't think Boj was too bothered about that.

A few months after the 'Frank Sinatra Episode', Boj started feeling very poorly. We had no idea what was wrong with her. She wouldn't eat. Not even cheese. She'd get up, if we called to her, but mostly she slept on her mat. Her breathing was heavy and labored.
She was not well.

We took her to the vet. She examined her and found a 'growth' under her leg.
She did some tests and we came back a couple days later for the results.
'It's cancer,' she said.
Nora's chin started quivering.
'I am afraid it is a problem with some blue-eyed dogs,' the vet said.
'They are prone to genetic disorders and cancers. It's spread quite a lot. We should think about putting her down.'

Nora may have been fearless, but when it came to Boj that was a different matter.
Her eyes welled up in tears.
'We'll take her home and talk about it,' I said.
I felt like it was someone else speaking the words that came out of my mouth.

A few weeks later, Boj had become so ill and listless that we had no choice but to put her down.

Nora would not go with me for that. I wished I didn't have to go and do that myself. I drove to the vet alone with Boj struggling for breath beside me in the front passenger seat.
I stroked Boj in comforting sadness as the vet put her to sleep.

I brought Boj's body back with me. I didn't want the vet to deal with it. I covered Boj with a blanket I had brought with me and drove back home alone with my mind firmly fixed on the traffic to stop up my rising tears.

Nora was crying and crying inconsolably when I got back with Boj. I thought she might start keening.
'We have to give her a proper burial,' she sobbed.
I tried my best to wear my 'brave mask'.
'I want to take her to West Virginia,' Nora said through her tears.
'Where I met Aboja. I want Boj to rest in the mountain forest there.'

So, we drove to West Virginia. Boj was wrapped in my raincoat. And when Nora was happy with the spot she found in the mountain forest, we buried Boj there.

Frank Sinatra never got his pick of Boj's litter. Free of charge or otherwise.
She was gone.

Many, many people knew Boj and experienced some of her amazing antics for themselves. Even now, if I'm with people who knew her, Boj will come up in the conversation at some point. And laughter at her past exploits is sure to follow.
Every time.

These days, we would have 'You Tube' videos of her and she would have won, *The World's Funniest Pets*, repeatedly had that program existed while she was with us.
But such things did not exist in Boj's day.

It's a shame too that Frank Sinatra has died. Were he still around, I could give you his personal phone number and he'd tell you all about Boj himself.

And then you'd have no doubt that my story is true.

STORY CHAPTER FIVE

'HELL'S ANGELS'

Of all the tales I've ever told, this is the one I have repeated most often.
Maybe not in its entirety, but certainly bits and pieces of it.

It all took place in the early 70's and I do not think it possible that some of the events that happened then could possibly happen now.
The world has changed and we along with it.
But the early 70's was a different world than the one we live in now.
With different possibilities.

Nora and I were innocents.
And this is an innocents' story.

Nora and I were just married.
We were still at Biglerville College and Nora and I had moved out of the dorms. We lived in a converted boat marina a few miles from campus.
While we were continuing with our studies, I worked as a waiter at an American Civil War 'theme' restaurant. All the waiting staff wore Civil War costumes and the clientele were mainly tourists.
Biglerville is not far from Gettysburg and its Battlefield Memorials.
There were plenty of tourists. Especially in the summer months.

The Civil War theme restaurant owner was a madman. He was meant to be the chef, but when things grew busy he would suddenly disappear and leave his kitchen assistant to fight the rush alone.
Sometime later, he would reappear dressed as Ulysses S. Grant and chat to the customers while they waited impatiently for their meals.
He did look like General Grant though, so I have to give him that.

That summer, Nora and I finally decided to take the honeymoon that we delayed, because of our studies.

Our idea was to drive along Old Route 30 from Philadelphia all the way to California. We'd stay there the entire summer before heading back East.

Nora and I had adopted a puppy, soon after we first met, that some idiot had thrown out with the trash. Nora was adamant that we take 'Boj' along with us on our honeymoon, but I convinced her it wasn't a good idea for a puppy to spend all that time on the road. We would leave Boj under the care of our friend, Charlie. Reluctantly, Nora agreed.

At the time we had a VW Fastback with a fuel-injected and air-cooled engine. It was the first commercial vehicle to have a 'computer' which controlled the fuel injectors.
Now I am sure Volkswagen has come a long way since then, but our VW always had something wrong with it. Usually it had something to do with those fuel injectors. I am handy, though not an expert with cars, but if something went wrong with what they called the 'black box computer', I was stumped. It had to go to the shop as it did many times. It spent many visits there.
To great expense.

Nora and I both worked for a few more weeks to gather money for our delayed honeymoon. I stuck with the Civil War place and she worked at a nursing home. And once we thought we had enough money to go, we did.

Old Route 30 is not a highway. It is, for the most part, a 'two lane blacktop' that winds its way across America from Philadelphia in the east to San Francisco in the west. It passes through every little town and hamlet along the way. It is not the route to take if you want to make time. But for seeing the 'Real America', it couldn't be topped. And it was the 'Real America' that we wanted to see.

Our VW struggled up and down the hills of western Pennsylvania, but did much better on the flats of Ohio and the Midwest.
If we came across a little town we liked on the way, we would just stop, get out of the car, and explore. We were free to do what we wanted.

Such freedom is harder to come by when we get older. Even if we had the time to explore, there would always be some nagging worry about the kids or work.

Freedom costs more as we age.

At first, Nora would keep asking, 'I wonder how Boj is doing?'
I missed the dog too, but it was getting a touch annoying. After all, it was our honeymoon.

But after a few days into our road trip, she stopped doing that so much. She started to let go and think of the adventures that might lie ahead.

And, indeed, adventures did lie ahead.

As it was the summer, there were many smaller towns and cities that had local fairs or festivals. Usually these centered around some agricultural item. Like mushrooms or broccoli. Nora and I would see some homemade banner on the roadside promoting one of these festivals and, if it took our fancy, we'd go, stay an hour or so there, and move on.

We didn't really stop for any serious length of time until we arrived in Chicago.

Chicago. Let me try to put this into some sort of context for you.
This was 1974. Nora and I had not yet been married a year. We were in love and fearless.

Issues like 'race' meant nothing to us. We treated everyone the same. But race certainly was a big issue at that time and there was racial tension and hostility in Chicago.

And elsewhere.

When we arrived in Chicago, Nora had a surprise planned for me.
We were talking about finding a hotel and staying a few days, but we had to watch our money. I kept going on about that, I do admit.
Once we were in California, we'd get jobs and be fine. But we had to get there first.

And then Nora said to me, 'I've been holding out on you.'
I didn't know how to respond.

And she started laughing, 'I have more money than I told you!'
And she took out a thick wad of bills.

'Where'd you get all that?' I asked in pleased shock

And she explained how she had been doing overtime, but didn't tell me.

'We can stay at a good hotel. With a hot bath!' she said gleefully.

So we found a good hotel with a hot bath and, after we cleaned ourselves up and had something to eat, we decided to go out on the town. Nora suggested we try a jazz or blues club. Chicago was rightly famous for music at the time.

We walked over to the 'El', the above-ground train system there. Nora asked at the ticket booth which train we should catch to the music club area. A young black woman behind the booth told us what train to take.

'Go all the way to the end of the line,' she replied without emotion. 'The clubs are all there.'

The train we were told to take finally arrived at the platform. We got on and sat down. I don't think we were paying much attention to what was going on around us. We were lost in each other and yakked away happily.

I suppose we were on the train about half an hour, before I looked around. All of a sudden, I saw that everyone else was looking rough, dirty, or both. A few stops later and all the other passengers were poor black people. Some lone wolves and some mothers with children. I thought nothing of it. I was happy the rough and dirty group had departed.

But just a few stops later, the passengers had changed again. Now it was mostly groups of young black men or boys. Some would scowl, if they caught my eye.

By the time we reached the end of the line, there were only a few people still on the train other than the two of us. They all looked very tough or very drunk or very drugged.

They did not look very friendly.

The train door opened and we got out. We found ourselves at the top of a set of wooden stairs that led down from the platform. There was one light just above the staircase landing. And no other. Nora and I looked down to the street below. There were very few street lights functioning. It was dark, gloomy, and unwelcoming.

We were on 43rd Street in Chicago's Southside.

43rd Street did not seem to receive any basic public services. Many of the buildings there were in ruins. Most of the others were boarded up and rife with graffiti.

We went down the stairs. We had seen a neon light reading 'bar' in one of the few buildings that had any sign of life.

'Maybe that's an authentic blues club,' Nora hazarded.

We made our way toward the neon 'bar' sign. As we approached, we could see there was a group of black men out front. They were singing in harmony. And really good they were too. But as we walked into their view, they suddenly stopped. They just stared and stared at us. They looked like they were in shock.

We could see the little bar was no music club without having to go inside. I think I mumbled a 'hello' to the singers as we walked by, but they just kept staring.

We kept walking. It was so dim. The entire neighborhood looked dreary, desolate, and cast in shadows. And we couldn't see anything up ahead where things were better lit or any indication of people making music.

We were stymied. Neither of us knew what to think.

'There are no clubs here,' Nora finally said.

And as she said that and we stood in place for a moment to think what to do, a white Cadillac Eldorado drew up alongside us.

The passenger window rolled down. There were about six young black guys inside. The guy at the window wore a funky 70's style hat and said to me,

'How much for that girl there?'

Now, I don't know about you, but when I am asked something out of nowhere and unexpected like that, it takes me a moment to get my bearings.

'What did you say?' I asked him confusedly.

Then the driver took his hands off the wheel and squeezed next to his pal at the passenger window. He also had a funky hat on.

'What did you say?' he growled.

He looked very aggressive. Nora and I just turned away and started walking.

Quickly.

They pulled up adjacent to us again.

'Hey, Boy! Where you going? How much for that baby girl?' One funky-hatted passenger shouted. And then they stopped the car. Nora and I just kept walking. We could hear the car doors slam behind us.

We were nearing a corner when, out of a puff of smoke, a police patrol car magically appeared. When the occupants saw us, they screeched the brakes and stopped. Inside were two Chicago cops. One jumped out and ran toward us while the other flung wide the back door of their cruiser. The cop that ran at us first grabbed Nora and lifted her up and ran back to his car. Then the second cop ran up and did the same with me.

They threw us bodily into the back of their car like we were sacks of potatoes.

And then they spun their wheels, siren blaring, and drove off in a real hurry.

'Can you believe these stupid college kids?' the driver breathlessly asked his partner.

'What the hell is wrong with them?' He spoke like we weren't even there.

The two cops were breathing heavily and kept talking about how stupid we were and crazy. But mostly stupid.

And then the cop, who grabbed me from the street, turned around and said, 'Do you know you made us get out there? We don't go out on the street. That's not our job. We stay in the car. That's what we do. Stupid college morons! You made us get out! You take a girl there? You're lucky you aren't dead.'

He was more disgusted at us than anything else.

They dropped us off at the 'Loop' in the heart of Chicago and sped away.

They were so furious at us that if I had said the 'thank you' they deserved, they would only have grown angrier.

Nora and I went back to our hotel. We agreed that we would leave Chicago in the morning. We were both still shaking at what had just happened.

Nora said, 'There's a 'bad vibe' here. We don't fit in.'

Sometimes, I think about the hatred that ticket booth woman must have had for us. When I think back about our interaction with her, when we asked for directions, I remember that she did not smile or look us in the eye. Even though we were as friendly to her as we would have been to anyone else. It was in our nature. I remember her looking down as she casually sent us into serious danger.
I learned that day that racism can come in any color.
And it does.

Or perhaps it was simply our happiness that she resented.

We continued our journey west. We reached Iowa and drove past mile upon mile of cornfields under a perfect azure sky. The corn was at the height of its glory. If anything was an antidote to the urban blight that was 1974 Chicago, it was Iowa's cornfields.
But we did not stop for any appreciable time until we arrived in Nebraska.

When we reached Lincoln, we saw banners everywhere promoting the Nebraska State Fair. We needed a break from the road anyway, so we decided to see what it was all about.
What it was all about was a giant step back into the past.

It was unrelentingly wholesome. There were booths advertizing Nebraskan agricultural products. There were contests for best cabbage or livestock. There was a beauty pageant for Miss Nebraska State Fair. There were side tents where children's seed collections were being judged. Blue, red, and gold ribbons hung from some of the exhibits.
And then there was the 'Midway' where all the fairground games were held like 'Ring Toss' and 'Guess your Weight'.
Games from the past.

The Midway was the province of the 'Carnies'. Somehow, I don't think they were from Nebraska. They certainly were not wholesome. I won a watch for Nora by knocking over some milk bottles with a battered ball, but the Carney would not pay up.
'You leaned, buster,' he scowled. He gave Nora a bumper sticker as a prize instead.
It read, 'Take a sandwich to lunch'.

Some of the Midway attractions would probably be illegal now. I can't see customers these days wanting to gape at the 'Baboon Lady' or 'The Pig-Faced Woman' or the 'Two-Headed Boy' for that matter. Even if the Two-Headed Boy was advertized as 'World Famous'.

We got back into our VW and kept heading west. As night fell, we felt we were no longer on Earth. Western Nebraska is flat and barren in every direction. It is more a moonscape than an earthly one. Tumbleweeds barreled across the road. It was also the end of the Great Plains. The Rocky Mountains themselves now beckoned before us.

And it was at this point when our car began to feel the strain. It did not enjoy the long uphill climbs. Some were so steep that we could barely get her moving over 10 miles an hour. And that's despite my foot to the floor.

We drove through the night. Or rather I did. Nora slept beside me as I tried to stay awake. There was no place to stop. We had no choice but to keep moving.

When Nora awoke, she was welcomed by the Rockies. We had climbed and climbed through the night. Finally, we stopped going up, but keeping track of old Route 30 was not an easy task there. I made several wrong turns and had to retrace our steps.

At one point, we ended up taking a road, I wrongly thought was Route 30, up a very steep hill. It started snowing even though it was summer. We ended up in a place called Ward, Colorado. It was a ghost town. I guess there used to be mining there, but that was long since finished. It reminded me of an old abandoned miner's bungalow we once came across while caving in Kentucky.

Long-left and long-forgotten buildings in disrepair lined both sides of the only street there. Loose wooden shutters banged in the wind. Old wooden signs had fallen into the road. Nora was fascinated. I was too concerned about being lost and the toll on our car to be fascinated. 'It must be a miners' ghost town,' Nora decided. 'I bet no one has been here for decades.'
'Except for ghosts,' I replied.

We finally found Route 30 again and once again it demanded that we drive further up into the stratosphere. I could tell the car was 'acting funny'. It was becoming harder and harder to steer.
It eventually decided it had put up with enough.

We were just outside a tiny town called Eagle, Colorado. There was not really much of a town there at all. I pulled the car over to the side of the road and stopped.
Then, believe it or not, I saw a sign across the road. It read 'Eagle Motor Repairs'. It was a shack on the side of the mountain. There were car parts and old broken down cars and trucks in the grounds surrounding it. We found the owner. He was a very friendly and welcoming guy. He introduced himself to us as Arby Farmer.
When he looked our VW over, he told us that we had a broken steering linkage.
'I'll have to order that in for you, buddy' he said. 'It might be a couple days before the part arrives.'

Nora and I slept in the car while waiting for the linkage to appear. During the day, we'd go out and walk in the Rockies. Nothing much happened apart from Nora almost stepping on a rattlesnake in a dry river basin and me almost getting us killed by taking us down a path that was intersected by about a thousand antelope stampeding past us.

Two days later, the car part arrived, and even though Arby did give us a great deal on the repair, we were still left in a bad way. After paying Arby, we only had enough money left for the fuel we'd need to get to California and some minimal food.
And that was it.

As Route 30 took us south toward Boulder, Colorado, I could see that our travels had begun to take a toll on Nora.
Nora was never a moaner. She always looked for the adventure in anything and hardly ever complained. But I could tell she was exhausted and unhappy.
'Don't worry,' I told her. 'I will figure something out in Boulder so we can sleep in a bed.'
'A bath would be so good,' she said hopefully.

It was in the middle of the night by the time we arrived in Boulder. I drove straight to the University there.

It was summer and the students were away. Nora and I cased the campus and found a student resident building with an unlocked window.

We scrambled through it and went in.

Nora used the shower and other facilities. Meanwhile, I found a carpeted common room and laid out our sleeping bags under a grand piano there. Nora came back happy and clean.

We settled down for the night. Or so we thought we did.

I was dreaming about The Old West, I think, when I was awoken by the sound of terrible singing off in the distance.

'Buffaloes! Buffaloes!' roughly sung off-key and punctuated by drunken laughter.

'Buffaloes!' I listened as the racket grew closer.

Nora peacefully slumbered through this discordant din, as the 'singers' grew nearer and nearer, until suddenly the lights were switched on our stolen sleep-over spot and the drunken singing just as suddenly stopped. The next thing I knew Nora and I were being dragged out from under our grand piano bed canopy by three huge guys in gym shorts.

'What you doing here?' 'How'd you get in here?' 'I'm calling the police!' they took turns shouting at us. 'Call the cops!'

I could smell the stink of stale beer on their breaths.

Unfortunately, we soon discovered, we had chosen to stay at the resident building of the Colorado University Buffaloes football team. These guys were as big as professional football players. They were being groomed to become professional football players.

And then things started taking an ugly twist.

'Look! He brought a girl for us, fellas!' one particularly nasty pig-eyed jock said.

'Come on, baby! We'll give you a bed to sleep in!'

I knew Nora was scared. She held my hand so tight, she cut off my circulation.

'Come on, baby, I'll hold your hand for you. I'll hold it real good,' one of the jocks drunkenly jeered.

I was more worried about these jocks than I was about those Southside Chicago 'gang bangers'. At least they thought that Nora was 'for sale'. That was only logical. Why else would a white guy bring a beautiful young woman into their 'hood'?
But these jocks were not logical. They were the sort that just took what they wanted. They were arrogant and self-serving with an opportunist's gleam in their eyes. I feared the worst.
Two of the jocks whispered something to each other, looked at Nora leeringly, and started reaching for her.
I put myself into 'Fight or Die' mode. Lost cause or not.

Just then, an even bigger guy came into the common room. He was a very tall and very broad black guy who made even the other three gigantic jocks look puny in comparison.
'Why you pussies wake me up?' He thundered as he rubbed the sleep from his eyes.

They all started telling him about what we did at the same time. It was obvious that he was the captain or something.
'Look, Cap!' one of them said to him.
'The nice little fella brought us a treat!'

I decided to talk to 'Cap'. I explained what had happened and that I was only trying to give my wife a break from sleeping in the car.
'This was supposed to be our honeymoon,' I ventured. 'We thought this place was empty.'

He looked me up and down. He was one tough looking guy.
Then he said, 'You can't stay here. Go your way.'
The others were still wild-eyed and aggressive, but he waved them all off.
'Let them go. You pussies don't know what it's like not to have no money.'

I don't know if 'Cap' ever made the grade in the NFL, but I hope he did.

84

We got ourselves out of there as quickly as we could. We were both badly shaken up by what had just nearly happened. We tried to rest for a while in the car, but soon gave up and then continued to make our way west.

Finally arriving in California gave us a great sense of accomplishment. We had overcome many obstacles to get there. But we really didn't have a destination anymore. We just kept driving until Nora suggested we stop in Fresno.
It was as good a spot as any.

Again, I thought to go to the university there. This time we would look for student accommodation notices. It was bound to advertize cheap places to stay as that would be all students could afford. We found one offering a room in a farmhouse and, after a quick call, we drove to that address.

It was a hacienda style house with grape vineyards surrounding it. We met the owner, Jeff, and his girlfriend, Cindy. I told them we had no money, but we would get jobs and pay them as soon as we did.

'Don't worry!' Nora said. 'We will get jobs. You'll see. We are good to live with. We do our dishes and we don't make a mess and we don't make a lot of noise either.'
She went on and on. Finally, Jeff looked at Cindy and said, 'Let them have the room next to ours. Anything to shut her up.'
And he slumped off in his sullen way.

Cindy showed us our room. She was very sweet as opposed to the sour Jeff. She told us she was the current USA roller skating champion. She then took us outside and showed us the built-in swimming pool and warned us about the grape vineyards.
'Stay out of there,' she cautioned us. 'They use heavy duty pesticides on those table grapes. No one eats them here. We all know they're full of poison.'

We met the others living there. Besides Jeff and Cindy, there were two minor league baseball players, Denny and Bill, who played for the Fresno Giants, Calvin, who sold vacuum cleaners door to door, and an ex-Marine, Stanley, who looked haunted by his past.

We made for quite a mixed bunch.

Jeff spent most of his time in the garage behind the house. I found out he was rebuilding a 1947 Harley-Davidson from parts. Throughout the day, other motor-heads would stop by and give advice and help refurbish a part. All of them were current or past members of 'Hells Angels'. At first, they didn't want much to do with me, but I wore them all down in time. I was always after them for advice on repairing my VW. All these guys could have done that in their sleep, but I was not as blessed as they were.

Jeff was clearly their leader. He was a big, hulking guy with long blonde hair.
Jeff didn't talk much and he did not put up with any 'nonsense' as he would call it either. But even though I was very foreign to him and his interests, he grew to accept me as did the rest of his 'crew'. They'd even let me use Cindy's Harley Roadster sometimes to ride with them.

I used to sport a goatee in those days and had long hair pulled back into a short pony tail. All the motorcycle guys started calling me 'The Russian'.
I imagine I must have looked like what they imagined a Russian might look like.

I know everyone thinks that 'Hells Angels' are these awful drugged and violent criminals. But that is not my experience of them. They were different than 'normal folk' perhaps, but they worked and they had a healthy lust for living and they cared about their women and their kids too.
They also had a great sense of humor. They found me very amusing anyway.

I was asking them advice on how to do a valve job on the VW. Of course, I had to borrow Jeff's tools to do that. I went back to his garage over and over again seeking further advice.
During what must have been my 'tenth advice visit', Jeff said, 'Russian, you are an idiot! But you're a funny idiot, so you're all right.'
He then ambled over to where my VW was parked, dragged his bulk under the car and with the turn of a ratchet fixed the problem immediately. I had been at it for over six hours. It took him all of two minutes.

Nora landed a job at the Fresno Holiday Inn cocktail bar. They gave her a costume to wear. It consisted of denim hot pants and a purple polka dot halter top. She had to shave her legs to work there.
She had to wear make-up too. That was not Nora's normal practice.
Basically, her job entailed serving drinks and being harassed by drunks and punks and dirty old men. In exchange, she earned tips.
I'd never seen Nora in make-up before. And it struck me how beautiful she truly was.
I often forgot that. How beautiful she was.

I, on the other hand, found myself a far better job.
(Please do take that ironically.)
I was the manager of the graveyard shift at 'Short Stop', the local competitor to 7-Eleven. I was also the only employee on the graveyard shift. I managed myself.
It was the most dangerous job I've ever done in my life.

Beneath the register, there was a cudgel for defensive purposes. Any bill larger than five dollars went straight into the floor safe to deter robbers. There was a sign on the counter which informed customers, and potential robbers, that we did not have the key to that safe. We sold everything from hard alcohol to beer to food and fuel and more. There were pinball machines too. Consequently we attracted every 'Night Crawler' out there.

When Nora and I would meet after our work shifts, we'd sometimes swap stories about anything unusual that may have happened.
One time, Nora told me about an incident with a Mexican mother who insisted Nora put coffee in the baby bottle from which the mother was feeding her infant.
'They bring babies to a cocktail bar!' Nora exclaimed.
'Leche? Leche?' Nora said she kept asking the mother. But the mother just grew angrier and kept shouting, 'Café negro! Café negro!'
Nora shook her head as she told me she then put coffee in the baby bottle and then the mother mixed it with some formula and gave it happily to her baby.
Nora spared me most of the stories about the lechers and gropers who must have made her cocktail serving life a misery.

I was only seriously threatened twice at Short Stop in the three months we were on our honeymoon in Fresno.

87

Once, a Mexican gang came in at four o'clock in the morning wanting to buy some beer. It was illegal, at the time, to purchase beer after 2am. They just walked back into the storeroom and emerged with several cases. I told them that I could not sell them beer.

A guy with gold caps on his teeth came over to me. He took out a big knife.

'There's a problem?' He asked with a glare.

I decided there wasn't.

He threw some money on the counter and they all left. It was more money than the beer would have cost.

Another time a very drugged looking couple came in. The woman was like a member of the 'Living Dead' from some 'B' movie. And the man's eyes looked dead too. I had never seen pupils like his before. They looked runny.

He had a handgun stuffed down the front of his jeans for all to see. He tried to buy some fuel with counterfeit bank notes that had a picture of George Washington and tens in all the corners.

I said, 'Hey! Look at this! It must be some sort of misprint! You should save these and sell them to a collector!'

There was a strained silence. He fumbled with the handgun, but I just kept talking amicably. 'Gimme Popsicle,' he finally uttered. He put some coins on the counter and left with his zombie.

I looked out the window and saw their pick-up truck was parked at the fuel pumps. He started his car, but instead of pulling away he reversed right into one of the pumps. It set off a geyser of fuel. They just stayed there in their pick-up with fuel flying up all around them. It looked to me like they had both passed out.

I had to call the fire department to come deal with that one.

Nora and I did not have to work every day. When we had time together, we explored the area. We took long moonlit walks in the grape vineyards, even if we had been told to steer clear. We saw the Redwoods. We hiked in the mountains. We visited San Francisco. We went down to L.A. and the Southern California beaches.

Fresno may be in a hot-as-blazes valley, but it is a good central spot from which to see the rest of California.

Our jobs were not inspiring, but our location was.

The 'Farmhouse', as we called the hacienda where we were staying, was a magnet for visitors. And not just 'Hells Angels'.
Cindy would invite her female roller-skating friends around in the mornings and they'd swim naked in the pool for much of the day.
I came to learn that Cindy did not like clothes very much. I guess she didn't. She hardly ever wore any. Often, I would come down for breakfast and run into Cindy completely naked, except for some skimpy panties, in the kitchen. One of her life's goals, she said, was to achieve the perfect tan. But she was very careful about her eyes. She always wore sunglasses, if not much else.

And then there were the parties. I might get home from my shift at 7:30 in the morning and there would be a full blown party going on. Nora would be chatting away with the baseball players or Calvin the Hoover salesman.
'I got home from work,' she told me. 'And the house was throbbing. I gave up on trying to sleep through it.'
She told me this with a beer in her hand.

The party-goers were a very mixed bag. There were motorcycle guys and their girlfriends, there were roller-skating friends of Cindy, some of Calvin's sales buddies, and there were baseball fans and teammates of Denny and Bill too. Plus other assorted weirdoes.
I guess Nora and I would fall into that category.

One time, I came home to one of these impromptu parties and saw a guy driving his motorcycle with sidecar inside the house. His girlfriend was in the sidecar and screaming her head off. People were diving over couches and chairs to escape being mown down. Eventually they drove straight through the living room's picture window and on to the porch.
Jeff grabbed the drunken biker by the throat and said, 'You'll be back later with a crew to fix that.'
It wasn't a request.

As I've told you, he did not put up with 'nonsense' unless it was his own.

Very late one Sunday night, when there was no house party, Nora and I woke with a start. There was a lot of loud banging and shouting from strange voices downstairs. We could hear things being broken and smashed. Then we could here footsteps coming up the stairs. I got up to see what it was. But just as I opened our bedroom door, Jeff, whose room was next to ours, came out of his room at the same time.

He stood there naked and holding a shotgun. He pointed it at the people coming up the stairs. Everyone froze. I looked down and could see it was Denny and Bill and what I guessed were other members of the Fresno Giants. They must have won a handsome victory and were drunkenly celebrating.
'Bill threw a shut-out!' Denny blared. And they all cheered and threw beer at Bill.

'Stay right there while you still have a head!' Jeff roared.
He could see who it was, but he didn't care.
The baseball players all held up their arms and shook and wiggled their hands at the wrist as a sign of surrender.
'Jeff! Jeff!' Denny pleaded. 'It's us!'
Jeff lowered the shotgun. 'You ever do that again. I'll shoot you.'
Denny and Bill kept apologizing and apologizing.
'Baseball! Idiots!' Jeff said as he turned and went back to his bedroom and Cindy.

I can honestly tell you that there was not one single day during our time at the 'Farmhouse' which passed without some surreal incident like that happening.

For instance, there was a running story about Stanley, the ex-Marine. He spoke to no one except for Cindy, Nora, and me. And only because we always tried to speak with him, if we ever saw him. Mostly, he would just stay in his room and join in with nothing. Including shared cleaning responsibilities.
As a result, Jeff wanted him out. But the soft-hearted Cindy always stayed Stanley's execution.
'He served his country, Jeff!' she might plead. 'My daddy was a Marine too!'
And, grumpily, Jeff would let the matter go.

Then, one day, Stanley came downstairs with a German Shepherd puppy in his arms.

He must have waited until the house was empty before going to get the puppy. And waited again until he could get the puppy back to his room without anyone noticing.

But he couldn't have kept his secret to himself for long.

'Puppy whines' would have given him away.

Like Nora, Cindy adored puppies. The two of them made such a fuss about it.

'So cute! Look at his little nose! Who's got a little nose?' Cindy said in baby-talk.

And Nora lamented, 'Now I miss my little Boj so much!'

But Stanley just said, 'I think there's something wrong with it.' He then held the puppy tightly to his chest and headed back to his room. And so the fate of Stanley's puppy became a big concern for the two girls.

None of us ever saw him take the dog outside. He must have used a litter box. If we saw him, he always had the puppy tightly pressed against his chest. I never saw the dog walk on its own.

One day, a few weeks later, I ran into Stanley heading up the stairs.

His puppy was not with him.

'Where's your dog?' I asked him.

'He died,' he said with his sad eyes. 'He died.'

And he continued up the stairs to his room.

When the girls heard of this, Nora stopped speaking to him and Cindy did too.

'People should have to get a license to own a dog!' Nora said to me.

I bit my tongue and said nothing.

I gave two week's notice at Short Stop, when our stay in Fresno was coming to an end. They stopped paying me from that point, even though I put in many shifts in those two weeks. The guy who hired me was the franchise owner and he must have pocketed my earnings. I called and called him. I needed that money for our return journey, but he either didn't answer or lied that my pay was coming. I had to make up for that shortfall with Short Stop products.

I filled the tank, took some motor oil, food, drinks, anything Nora and I might need for our journey back to Pennsylvania.

Our California Honeymoon was at an end.

Before we left, Jeff called out for me to come to the garage behind the house. When I entered, his crew grabbed me and then formed a silent circle around me. I stood in the middle blinking in confusion. 'Russian,' Jeff announced. 'We have something for you.'
And he gave me an official 'Hells Angels' membership pin.
'Now you can scare your people back East.'
They then rough-housed with me for a while in way of welcoming me to the club. (I am forbidden by club rules to go into any further initiation rite detail. Sorry.)

I still have the pin. It consists of two wings and a skull with the words 'Fresno Chapter'. I used to wear it on an old leather vest I had, but not now. I do take it out of the box where I keep it though and show it to people sometimes when I tell them this story.

Nora and I waved our goodbyes and we drove off.

We headed south. We'd take the expressways and Interstates back this time and not Route 30. It would be much quicker getting home that way.

I had spent a lot of time getting the VW up to scratch before setting off. We planned to drive through Death Valley and into Arizona and points east.
But when we drove into Death Valley, we hit the height of a heat wave. It was absolutely burning hot out there. I will try not to exaggerate. Maybe it was 130 degrees.
Maybe more.

The VW did not respond well to that. It had an air-cooled engine with no cool air coming in to cool it. At first it started to struggle and then started making bizarre noises. And as we drove through the Valley, it began to send up smoke signals to inform us that all was not well. We had no choice but to keep going. We could not break down in Death Valley.
That was not a survivable option.

I willed our VW on and on as the smoke billowed out more and more.

Soon, we could not see out the windshield. We were driving blind. Finally, the car sputtered and rolled to a stop. When the smoke had cleared, we saw we were in Needles, California.

And just there, where we rolled to a stop, was, much to our surprise, a Volkswagen repair center.

We couldn't believe our luck. I went into the garage and asked the mechanic to take a look at our car. He popped the trunk, where the motor was, and had a quick look.

'No, no, you've cracked the block,' he said. 'This car is totaled.'

He then said he'd give us $100 for our car for 'parts'.

Nora and I did not know what to do. I told the mechanic to give us a minute to think and we'd make a decision. Nora went off to call Charlie and tell him that we had a problem and would be delayed in retrieving Boj from his care.

When she went to do that, I went outside to clear my head and think about what we should do.

I was standing on the curb of the pavement just outside the car repair place. There was a hippie hitchhiking right at that spot.

He must have noticed that I was distressed.

'You don't look so good,' he said to me.

He was a tall guy with long black hair and a scruffy beard.

'What's wrong?' he asked me in a soothing voice.

I told him what happened.

'We'll be hitching rides alongside you,' I said to him after explaining our situation.

'That doesn't sound right to me,' the hitcher said.

'I'm a Volkswagen repairman. Do you mind if I have a look?'

(I know that sounds incredible, but it's true.)

And the next thing I knew, both of us walked back into the garage together.

The hippie hitchhiker walked over to our car. He made the mechanic pop the trunk again.

'No, the block's not cracked,' he said after a brief look.

He reached into the vehicle and adjusted something.

'It's just the timing,' he said. 'Turn it over,' he told me.
He helped himself to a timing gun from the mechanic and proceeded
to time our car.
It purred like a contented German kitten.

Even though I knew the garage mechanic was a lying thief, I just
pretended it was an honest mistake. I got the car back and went to
give Nora the good news. I told her about the hitchhiker.
'We should give him a ride,' she said.
But when we got to where I first found him, he was gone.

The return journey was uneventful. The only trouble we had was
getting fuel. There was an OPEC 'oil crisis' going on at the time. We
had to top up wherever we saw a station that was still open. I had to
bribe one car attendant with a jar of beef jerky and a pint of Jim
Beam that I had taken from Short Stop, so he'd fill our tank.
We made it back East in half the time it took to get to California.
And our long delayed honeymoon was finally over.

I'm sure that I have told that story countless times, as I say.
I'm sure too that I am overlooking an interesting Transcontinental or
Fresno event or two in the retelling here.
But one event cannot be overlooked.

Nora and I had lost much of our innocence as a result of our
adventures. We began to figure out when to be 'wary'. And with that
'wariness' came a loss of simply embracing life's adventures as they
unfold. We lost our trusting nature. When before our journey, we
always looked to the best side of someone else's nature, we now no
longer did. Our natural sunny dispositions were not so sunny
anymore.
I suppose some would say that it is a necessary loss.
But it is a loss all the same.

The only 'Farmhouse' person we ever saw again was Denny.
He never made it to the Big Leagues.
Years later, Nora and I went to his wedding in Tucson.

We were living in Dallas at the time.
But that's another story.

STORY CHAPTER SIX

'THE FALLACY OF THE HAT RACK'

Some friends tell me that this is one of their favorite stories. I usually only tell it under the influence of too many beers. After all, most of this story happened under the influence of too many beers. Come to think of it, perhaps this is one of my friends' favorite stories, because they listened to it under the influence of too many beers as well. If you wish to grab a quick tipple before I begin here, feel free.

It was a transitional time in my life. And Nora's too.
Nora had just graduated from Biglerville College with a Dance degree. She was a year behind me, because she hadn't enough credits and had to sit through another semester. I had been working as a waiter at a Civil War theme restaurant near the university while she completed her studies.
But after she graduated, and we were both ready to put ourselves out there in the 'real world', we suddenly realized we didn't have a clue about how to do that.

Life, so far, had been unfolding in an organized way. We went to school. We went to college. We fell in love. We passed our exams. We were married.
But after that, life becomes less preordained and you have to start to make your own way.

We ended up staying in Biglerville for a year or so.
It was easy living there. It was pleasant. It was cheap. We had our college friends readily at hand. We could just hide there from the 'real world' and mark our time.
There was no need to test yourself there.

Many ex-students never escaped this 'Siren Seduction'. They remained trapped in this land of pleasant living.
Nora and I didn't want to be among their number.
So after a while of this 'going through the motions', we knew we had to find our way in life. We had to make the next step. Somewhere.

95

We were considering this next step, when we decided to move to my hometown of Baltimore.

I had no real job at first. I'd do 'bits and pieces' when they came along. I even pretended to be a 'mime' for a short while. Nora found a job working part time at a care home. She wasn't earning much. We had found a place to rent in the city, but of course the rent had to be found.

My dad told me that he had a friend in Baltimore who owned a factory that made cardboard boxes. So I called my dad's friend, met him, and he offered me a job as 'Baler' at the Clippermill Box Works. My main job was to put all the cardboard scraps into bales for recycling.
And I gratefully took the position.

But, as I say, it was a transitional time.
And neither Nora nor I were sure what our next step would be.
Later, when we were stage performers, things took care of themselves.
But we did not yet know that we would pursue such a life.
We didn't know what sort of life we might pursue.

So, I was baler at a box factory.

It was not easy work. Everyday, I would return home covered in cardboard dust and paper cuts. Mr. Mooney, who ran the place, was involved in a program that encouraged hiring ex-offenders. I was the only one there who did not have a criminal record.
The other workers were trying to rebuild their lives and Mr. Mooney gave them the chance. But he was also a demanding boss and did not like 'slackers' as he'd call less than diligent workers.
I earned every penny I made there.

And after work, I'd go straight home, remove my filthy clothes, clean off the cardboard dust, and go to the local university and take ballet classes.
(Yes, ballet classes. Yes, you did hear that right.)

I used to take jazz classes with Nora and the other Dance majors at Biglerville, sometimes, and Nora had given me a gift of a course of ballet classes for my birthday that first year in Baltimore. Her gift puzzled me. I'd never studied ballet before.
It really surprised me though how much I liked it. I don't know why. I guess I have never been very good at self-analysis. If I enjoy something, I simply enjoy it. I didn't ask myself 'why' I enjoyed ballet.
Nonetheless, I could not get enough of it.

I didn't share that passion with my co-workers. We got along well, but I don't think they would have known what to make of one of their own doing pirouettes after work.
I spared them and myself that.

One evening at ballet class I met Larry. He and I were in the same bowl of bewilderment. Most of the others in class had a lot of experience. Larry and I were complete novices. We didn't even know how to put on a leotard properly. We stood by one another at the ballet barre and would whisper helpful suggestions when one or the other of us went wrong.

Larry wanted to be a male model. 'The first male super model,' he told me. Or so he hoped to be. He showed me a portfolio of photos from the few jobs he had done. He wanted to do ballet to improve his 'physique and gracefulness', so he claimed. I wasn't sure yet why I was doing it, but I found it a new world and was determined to learn more about it. Despite how truly awkward I was at the start.

Larry was a very handsome black guy. His dream was to be the very first top black male model. He was tall. He was good looking. He was kind and friendly and worked very hard at his dream.
We became fast friends.
We started to do things together after class. Nora and Larry also hit it off. He was our first new friend in Baltimore.

Nora was a 'Modern' dancer. She had taken ballet as a child, but she preferred contemporary dance much more than ballet. And after her shift at the nursing home, she'd go to a dance studio and take classes there.

And so that was our life in Baltimore. We both worked at tough, soul destroying jobs and then did the things we dreamed about after work. It made the situation bearable.

Or nearly so.

It must have been around March, when I first started to whine to Nora that I needed a break.

'We have to get away from here. I'm there six days a week, every week. It's driving me loopy.'

'What do you want to do?' she asked me.

'I don't care. Just get away for a little while. Just a change of scenery.'

'That sounds good to me too,' she said.

We had both recently lost our dog, 'Boj.' She had to be put down. This also contributed to my desire for a 'change in scenery'.

It would do Nora a world of good too. The loss of her beloved Boj had hit her hard.

But, I must admit, it was my own restlessness that was the greater motivation.

Nora was very good at springing surprises. Like that ballet class birthday gift. She was blessed with the ability to come up with the unexpected.

One day, after I came home from the factory and ballet class, Nora had prepared dinner. That was not like her. We tended to fend for ourselves.

After dinner, she said very casually, 'Oh, by the way, Ralphy, we're going to New Hampshire the week after next.'

'New Hampshire?' I asked as if I hadn't heard her correctly.

'Yes, we're going to New Hampshire and all our friends are going there too!'

'What do you mean?'

'I called Charlie and he said that his friend has a hunting lodge there. And he called his friend and he's invited all of us to go!'

She was very excited.

So was I.

'Charlie's going, and the two of us of course, and Charlie's new girlfriend, Sue, I really want to meet her, and Fred, he's the one whose family owns the lodge, and Pete and Bill, Charlie said they're friends of Fred's at Biglerville, and anyone else who cares to come along,' she said in a rush.

'Wow!' was all I could say in response.

'And Charlie said that Fred says the lodge is really nice and way out in the middle of nowhere. How about that?!'

'That's perfect, Nora. Perfect.'

Nora said that we were all going to meet that weekend at Charlie's house to plan things and who would bring what items we needed. I was so excited I started counting the days before we'd actually go to New Hampshire.

Our dream hunting lodge holiday was just a couple of weeks away.

The next evening, Larry and I were talking after class. I told him about the hunting lodge.

'Why don't you go too, Larry? It'll be fun!'

He didn't look impressed.

'It's in the middle of nowhere? There's no phone?'

'No! That's the whole point. You can commune with nature just like God intended.'

And after some more of this cheerleading, I convinced Larry to join us too, but he was smiling sheepishly as he accepted.

'You know, Ralphy, I've never been out of the city before. There's not going to be any bears or anything is there?' he asked.

'Of course not!'

That weekend, Larry, Nora, and I drove up to Charlie's house in Philly where we met up with the rest of the hunting lodge expedition. To be honest, Nora and Charlie's new girlfriend, Sue, did most of the practical planning. They even made lists of what goods we were all meant to bring.

The rest of us mainly drank beer and horsed around.

While we were there at Charlie's place, I noticed a change had come over him. Nora and I hadn't seen him for about a year. He was one of our best friends while we were at college. He used to be a wise-guy and always making with the jokes. He'd usually start laughing whenever something or someone around him was 'stupid', as he would say. We once went on a Kentucky adventure together and ended up lost, deep inside a cave, and even then he'd be laughing his head off.

But now that he was with his new girlfriend, Sue, he was no longer the joker in the pack. He had become 'serious and manly' now. His sense of humor had changed too. He was much more ironic and sarcastic.

I had never met Fred before. Or Pete and Bill. I thanked Fred for letting us use the lodge.

'Well, I haven't been there since I was a kid,' he told me. 'But my dad and uncle go up there all the time.'

Sue began to distribute the lists that she and Nora had made.
We were discussing who'd bring what items.
And then Fred said, 'The lodge has almost everything you could possibly want anyway. Other than food. It's has all the mod-cons now for sure. You don't really need to bring all that stuff!'
I could see Larry was pleased to hear that.

Pete and Bill were still at college, where Nora, Charlie, and I had graduated, and so was Fred.
As the beers began to have their effect, they started to tease Fred relentlessly.

'Tell them about your term paper, Freddie!' Bill begged.
'I pee'd myself when I heard this! This is so funny!' Pete shared with us.
Fred turned bright red in his embarrassment.
'Come on, Freddo!' Pete laughed.
And finally after much coaxing, Fred told his tale.

'It's not really funny!' he began.
Pete and Bill were already laughing.
'It's not! I should never have failed!'
And Pete and Bill laughed even louder.

'It was a term paper about feminism and the play, *A Doll's House*. I thought what I wrote was brilliant! It was just that professor's limited thinking that failed me.'

'Limited thinking is right,' Bill said wiping his eyes.

Pete was choking with laughter now.

'Tell them how you titled it!' Pete said with tears streaming down his face.

The Fallacy of the Hat Rack! Bill roared. 'That's what he called it!'

'You know, you really should have read the play first, Freddy!' Pete teasingly scolded him.

'I read the play!' Fred protested. 'I just wanted to say that women are not hat racks that you can stick in the corner and forget about!'

Pete and Bill both began to hammer their fists on the tabletop in glee.

'That prune-face of a professor said I had failed to grasp the central character's predicament. She was being treated like a hat rack! That's the whole point!'

'Maybe you can get it published, Fred,' Charlie said mock-seriously.

Pete went on to say, after he had caught his breath, that Fred had submitted this grand theory of the 'Hat Rack' on one sheet of paper. And then he laughed some more.

'Prune-face or not, Freddo, no professor is going to accept that!'

'It was a last moment inspiration!' Fred said in his own defense.

'A last moment rush job more like,' Charlie deadpanned.

Pete and Bill laughed so hard that I thought they'd do themselves an injury.

And then Bill drunkenly stood up and grabbed everyone's jackets and posed with them hanging over his arms and the top of his head.

'I'm a hat rack!'

We all agreed we'd meet at Charlie's again to drive up to the lodge the following weekend.

'I just hope the weather's good,' Fred said. 'It can get cold in the mountains this time of year.'

'But it's heated, isn't it?' Larry asked in concern.

'You'll be warm and toasty indoors,' Fred reassured him.

'Nothing to worry your mind.'

I gave notice at work that I was going to be away. Nora did the same. Now all we had to do was get through the next week and our dream lodge would be ours.

If only for one long weekend.

Work dragged on and on. I dropped a pallet holding flat-packed cardboard boxes from the forklift. My mind was already in the woods.

Mr. Mooney was not happy.

'That's my profit you're dropping, Ralphy!' he shouted at me.

He was right, but I could not wait to get away.

It was finally the morning of the start of our New Hampshire adventure.

Larry arrived very early at our house. He carried a garment bag, like one that might be used for suits, and a battered old suitcase with floral decals.

'I borrowed it from my mom,' Larry said indicating the suitcase. 'I have to be careful with it.'

Nora and I had packed what we needed into separate backpacks.

Larry did not look like he was ready for nature.

I was loading everything into the car when I looked down at Larry's feet. He was wearing expensive Italian loafers.

'What are those?' I asked him.

'Loafers,' he replied like I had gone nuts.

'Well, I don't think they'll last too long in the woods, Lar,' I explained to him.

I took him back inside the house and found an extra pair of boots.

'Try these on.'

They were brown. Larry tried them on. I could see he was contemplating something.

'Yes, I think I can make these work,' he said.

He had no hat either.

'If it gets cold, Larry, you might need one,' Nora told him.

She went over to a closet and, after hunting through the mess, found a hat for him. It was a fake fur Russian hat with flaps that could be unbuttoned and used to cover your ears.

Larry tried that one on too.

Nora attempted to button the flaps under his chin.

'No, no! I can get this to work, if the flaps just hang down loose,' he protested.

Larry was very careful to look 'right' at all times. Perhaps he was expecting to find a fashion model agency next to the hunting lodge. Even in the brown boots and the Russian hat though, he still looked good.

When we left Baltimore, it was a lovely spring day. Pleasant, I'd call it. Not too hot. Not cold. Porridge perfect.

We rendezvoused with the others in Philly, as we agreed, and drove in convoy up to New Hampshire. Charlie and Sue in one car, Pete, Bill, and Fred in another, and Larry, Nora, and I bringing up the rear.

We didn't stop, other than for gas, until just before we reached Boston. There was a roadside diner and we all pulled into the lot.

'When I was a kid, my dad and uncle would always stop here on the way to the lodge,' Fred shared with us. 'The food's great!'

We found two tables together. The waitress took our order.

'I never got my morning run in today,' Bill moaned. 'As soon as we get there, I'm going for a run!'

Pete told me Bill's dream was to make the Olympic team.

'All he does is run,' he said. 'He's been going on about his missed morning run all the way here, the whiny baby!'

Our food arrived, but Fred was wide of the mark in calling the food 'great.' The food was not great. The food was lousy. Everything was swimming in grease. Even the cutlery.

A greasy spoon. Literally.

I left my hamburger swimming in its slop. Nora's salad was drowned in a foul Thousand Island dressing. Larry's 'chicken in a basket' was a grizzled mess.

Only Fred ate happily.

Perhaps his childhood memories had seasoned his sandwich.

Before we got back into the cars, Sue and Nora re-checked supplies. Nora led this checklist scrutiny.

'First Aid kit?' Nora asked Sue.

'Got it,' she said.

'Breakfast things?'

'Check.'

This went on for some time.

'Beer?' Pete finally interjected.

'Check and double check,' said Fred.

In the end, they both decided we had everything we could possibly need.

'You're not going to need all that stuff!' Fred laughed.

We were not in the diner for very long, but the weather changed while we were.

It grew much colder and began to flurry.

Our convoy got back on the highway.

Now, it wasn't much to worry about at first. In fact, the snow flurries came and went in patches, but by the time we hit the New Hampshire State Line, it was really coming down. I could barely make out Charlie's car in front of me.

'We'll be doing no walking in this!' Larry lamented.

'I should have brought my loafers!'

The highway itself was not snow-covered to any real degree. We drove through Concord and then Lebanon without too much trouble. The snow was more in the air than on the ground. But that all started to change by the time we neared our destination.

Fred's hunting lodge was just outside Woodstock, New Hampshire, near the White Mountain National Forest. And as we got closer, the snow grew deeper and deeper.

And it grew colder too.

'It looks like they've had snow up here for weeks,' Nora said in shock.

Finally, I could see Charlie's car pulling over to the side of the road. I did likewise.

When I got out, I saw Fred's car had pulled over too just ahead. Fred walked back to us.

'OK! We're nearly there!' he announced. 'We just take this side track to our left and pull over there. We have to walk the rest of the way in.' We all got back in our cars.

The 'side track' was a rocky, unpaved path and covered in freshly fallen snow.

We made little progress before we had to pull over again.

We all got out.

'OK! We follow this path and the lodge is just over the top of that hill,' Fred told us.

'Get all your stuff and we'll be there in no time!'

We all grabbed our things.

Before we set out for the lodge, I looked at Fred. He was carrying a large hunting knife on his belt, what looked like a starting pistol, a flare gun, and a bow and arrow. He had a small knapsack on his back.

'He thinks he's Hemmingway on safari,' Charlie pointed out to me.

I must say it did look odd with Fred decked out like GI Joe and Nora walking beside him and carrying a shopping bag full of Doritos and Hostess Ho-Ho's.

'If he doesn't bag any Big Game, we can let him shoot some Twinkies,' Charlie suggested.

We followed behind Fred down the path to the lodge. It was not easy. There was a good foot of snow beneath our feet and the path was treacherous and slippery.

Larry's expression was priceless. He looked like he was off to the gallows.

'It's all right, Lar,' I told him. 'If we have to stay inside the lodge for a while, until the weather clears, it'll still be fun,' I assured him.

I tried not to laugh. With his Russian hat covered in snow, he looked like a white-wigged judge.

'OK! There it is!' shouted Fred up in front of us.

We made our way, as best we could, up to where he was.

There at the top of the hill we all had our first glimpse of the hunting lodge.

I will do my utmost not to exaggerate.

It was dreadful.

It was so bad that the words 'hunting lodge' should never be used in any description of it.

There was an ancient looking rope and plank bridge that had to be negotiated to get to it. This was over a deep ravine with a raging stream at its bottom. The bridge was now covered in snow and ice. It swung slowly in the chilling wind.

That alone was bad enough.

But to see the 'lodge' itself was far worse.

It was a shack at best. And that is being a bit unfair to shacks. It was even missing a part of the wall down low at its right front corner. We could see tarpaper flapping in the wind where the missing wall should have been. A wooden deck porch with weather-worn chairs surrounded the front of the lodge. And the rest of it looked in not much better condition.

It was certainly not a welcoming sight.

'Like I said, I haven't been here in a while,' Fred reminded us.

No one said anything. It was snowing and it was getting very cold. We all just wanted to get inside and be warm again.

'Grab your stuff!' Fred ordered. 'And keep moving! Just do what I do!'

He started to cross the bridge and we all watched how he did it and followed.

Somehow, we all struggled our way over that bridge. Some of the planks were either missing or half fixed to its sides. We held our balance as the bridge swayed and made our way very tentatively across it. Just as Fred had done.

Fred was acting as if this was all very normal and exactly what we should have expected. Larry was crossing the bridge right before me. As he struggled with his garment bag and his mother's suitcase, he turned to me and said,

'I think Fred uses his head as a hat rack too.'

We had all made it to the other side alive.

Fred lifted a rock near the 'lodge' door and grabbed a key. I am not sure why. The door was barely fixed to its frame. One little shove would have been anyone's key in opening it.

We went in.

No one must have been there for a very long time. The floorboards were broken or absent in spots. A lopsided, roughly hewn table commanded the center of the room. One of its legs was a good three inches shorter than its companions. A cold wind was coming through the tarpapered section of the wall that was missing. There was even a little pile of snow that had crept in through there.

I looked around the interior of the lodge.

There were deer antlers and other trophies fixed to the interior walls.

106

There were many plaques about hunting on the walls as well.
One was of a hunter trying to relieve himself from behind a tree. His two fellow hunters could not see him. They held their guns aloft and one said, 'Listen! I think I can hear a buck snort!'
Rubbish was everywhere.

There were simple wooden-framed bunk beads. There was one for each of us. But no bedding. We all just chose a bunk and threw our things on them.
'It's freezing!' Pete said. 'Where's the heater?'
'There should be propane gas tanks outside,' Fred told him. 'We'll just hook them up and it'll be warm in no time.'

He went out with Pete to deal with the tanks. A few minutes later they returned.
'There are no gas tanks!' Pete told us in panic. 'We're all going to freeze to death!'
Fred looked at the stove. He opened and closed it.
'We can build a fire in here,' Fred suggested.
'With what? Everything's covered in snow!' Pete said to him in exasperation.
'Where are the mod cons?' Larry asked me hopelessly.

I know. As soon as we saw things for what they were, we should have left immediately. Were I you, I would say the same thing. But around that time, in the late 70's-early 80's, people were yet to think like that. Most people wouldn't have sent back their meal at a restaurant, because it wasn't warm enough. You just took your experiences as you found them. Good or bad.
We were all at Fred's 'hunting lodge' for a long weekend with our friends.
We were there and so that's what we would do.
And make the best of it.
I can understand though why you might think that was silly now.

Charlie approached me.
'We have to get some heating, Ralphy. Let's go out and see if we can find some.'
And then he asked, 'Freddy, are there other hunting lodges nearby?'
Fred said that there were.
'There are lots of them all along the trail further down.'

'We'll be back with some heating,' Charlie told everyone.

Charlie and I went back out and crossed the bridge to the trail. Huge icicles hung from the trees. It had become seriously cold. The snow was getting deeper too and it made it difficult to make any progress. We just kept trudging our way down the trail until we saw another 'lodge'. This one was very nice and well built. It did look like it had all the creature comforts for which you could wish.
Unlike our ramshackle shack.
Charlie led the way as we went around to the back of the lodge we had found. We saw a gated enclosure there and in it were some propane tanks.
'Let's get one of these beauties back with us,' he said.

The tank was about five feet tall and heavy beyond belief.
Charlie and I struggled with it back to our lodge. It was anything but a stroll. We had to stop every few feet to regain our strength.
When we finally got it to the bridge, Charlie yelled out, 'Some help over here! Pete! Bill! Get out here!'
Somehow, the four of us managed to get that thing across the bridge to the lodge without it or us falling into the ravine below.
Charlie connected the tank and opened the valve. There was a very rewarding 'swooshing' sound.
'That should do the trick,' Charlie said.

We went back into our lodge. It was quite a sight. Everyone was still bundled up and eating the junk food we had brought with us.
Fred was still looking through doors and cabinets for anything useful.
'I found some candles,' he said, 'so we won't have to be in the dark.'
He also announced that he had found two cans of spam, three, unpredictably ancient, Mason jars of some sort of unidentified bottled berry, some matches, a First Aid kit, ('You see? I told you that you didn't need to bring one,' he said to Nora), a checkerboard, a nearly full deck of cards, and two threadbare blankets.
'Well then. We're all set for anything,' Charlie said tongue-in-cheek.

Bill and Pete went out to gather some firewood. They brought it back into the lodge.
'If we leave it for a while, it'll dry out eventually,' Pete said hopefully.

'We wanted to cook dinner for everyone,' Sue said disappointedly. 'Charlie and I were going to make pasta.'
'Nobody's cooking anything with wet wood. They'll have to wait until tomorrow to taste your special sauce,' Charlie manfully consoled her.

The tank that Charlie and I had stolen started to do its job. It was not exactly warm. It couldn't be with the elements gaining entrance through the hole in the wall.
But it was no longer freezing.
And that cheered everyone up no end.

'I'm going for a run,' Bill said.
He said this as much for himself as for our benefit.
It was getting darker out and the snow certainly had not let up, but Bill was determined.
I am not a runner myself, but I suppose once you get into the habit, you don't like to break it for anything.
'He runs come rain or come shine,' Pete said while rolling his eyes.
We all watched as Bill did up his coat, put on his hat, and went out into the snowy wilderness.

The rest of us just got as comfortable as was possible considering the situation. Mostly this involved eating yet more junk food and drinking from the supply of beer we had brought along with us.
Fred kept rummaging through the lodge in the hope, I guess, that he would find something useful or distracting. He was looking under bunk beds and the wood burning stove too.
'What's up, Freddo? Did you lose an earring?' Pete teased him.

Nora was the only one doing anything constructive. She started to clean the lodge and clear the rubbish off the floor.
She even found a broom with a broken handle and began to sweep, as best she could, the dirt out the door. She created a wedge from the rubbish and pinned it under the 'short leg' to straighten the wobbly table. She took the lodge's threadbare blankets and used them to cover up the hole in the wall.
No one helped her. I did not even think about helping her.
'Shut the door, Nora!' was all the assistance I gave to her efforts.
Mr. Mooney would not have been impressed with my work ethic.

Larry was telling Sue and Charlie about his fashion model dreams. If Bill was a determined runner, then Larry was a determined model.

'There are no famous male models,' he told them.

I had heard all this from him before.

'It's just the women who get all the fame and money. But men want to look good as well. Men buy clothing too, don't they?' Larry asked rhetorically.

'I never thought of it like that,' Sue said.

'The whole industry is changing and I want to be ready for it!'

Pete and I played some checkers. We used Doritos and peanuts as markers. I could not beat him no matter how many times we played. We switched to rummy, but the result was the same.

Maybe it was my losing streak. Maybe it was the many beers I had been downing. I am not sure, but the next thing I know I am encouraging everyone to go back outside and enjoy the mountain air.

'It'll be fun!'

I am sure they will carve that saying on my tombstone.

Only Pete, Nora, and I went outside. The others had better sense. Larry looked at me like I had cabin fever. He just ignored me and kept talking with Charlie and Sue.

The three of us went out and sat on the distressed chairs on the porch. The wind carried the falling snow into our faces. We sat there drinking our beers and looked out across the swinging bridge into the woods.

It was beautiful. Yes, I know, it was miserable, but it was truly beautiful there too. We were out alone in nature. Everything was pure white from the snow. Icicles, like giant diamonds, hung from all the surrounding trees.

'You said you wanted a change of scenery,' Nora reminded me.

While we were out there, the snow slackened. It was just flurrying again now as the light began to fade more and more. Nora went back inside and returned with some candles. She put them in some empty cans that she had picked up from the lodge floor.

It made for a kind of Christmas light effect.

'You should have grabbed some more beers while you were in there,' I told her.

It was so silent out there on the porch. There was no sound, save for the wind and our own voices, while we sat and drank. Every once in a while, Pete would say, 'Listen!' and we'd all stop to listen. Then he'd say, 'I thought I heard a buck snort!' And we'd laugh every time he did it.

Beer can do that to you.

And then our drunken merriment was interrupted.

We heard an echoed noise in the distance. It sounded like a human voice and it shocked us. Another echoed shout shortly followed.

'That's Bill!' Pete said.

He stood up and went over to the bridge.

'Bill! Bill! Is that you?' Pete hollered across the ravine.

'Bill!'

Nora got up and ran back inside the lodge to tell the others.

I went over to Pete at the bridge.

'Let's go find him,' I said.

We made our way across the bridge. Yet another echoed shout pointed out the direction we needed to go. The snow was over a foot deep and it was getting darker by the minute.

Pete and I went down the snow-covered trail as quickly as we could.

We must have only made it a few hundred yards when we saw Bill.

He was standing there in the middle of the trail. Completely still.

He was watching something, but he was standing between whatever he was looking at and us. We could only see Bill with his back to us.

We slowed down and crept closer.

And then we saw it.

Standing about ten yards from where Bill stood was a bobcat.

I did not know it was a bobcat when I saw it. I mean, I do now, but I didn't then.

I had never seen a bobcat before.

It just looked like a feral wildcat with serious teeth and claws.

Something you'd prefer to see on the other side of a cage.

'It came out of nowhere,' Bill told us in a whisper. 'I was running in the woods, because there was better footing there and when I came back on to the trail, there he was. I shouted out a couple times, but all he did was blink at me.'

111

The bobcat was staring at all of us. The cat itself was not very large, but he was not afraid of us either. I think he was more sizing up the situation than anything else. At least that was what I was hoping.

All three of us stood there staring. Well, all four, if you count the bobcat.

And then suddenly we heard a loud bang accompanied by a flash of light.

I turned around and saw that Fred had discharged his flare gun.

The bobcat beat a hasty exit.

Everyone had come out to search for Bill. After the bobcat had run off, Bill told them what happened.

Nora ran up and clung to me tightly and wouldn't let go. She was shaking.

'Is everyone all right? Did it bite you?'

'Don't make a fuss, Nora,' I said as I pulled away from her.

We all walked together back to the lodge. Nora held a flashlight to lead the way. It gets dark in the mountains in a hurry, I learned.

'What was that thing?' Larry asked me.

'Some kind of wildcat,' I told him.

'There are wild cats out here?' he asked me nervously.

'I guess there are, Lar,' I said.

Fred's heroics with his flare gun renewed his confidence after our disappointment at his 'mod-con' hunting lodge.

When we got back indoors, he started giving us a 'wilderness safety talk'.

He showed us how to use the flare gun and starting pistol.

'I should have done this as soon as we arrived,' he said.

'We should have left as soon as we arrived,' Charlie quipped.

No one got much sleep that night. Maybe it was all the junk food we had in lieu of dinner.

And every time I thought I could drop off to sleep, someone said something.

'Does anyone else smell gas?' Sue would venture.

'I smell something funny too,' Nora said after a long pause.

'It's supposed to smell like that!' Fred growled back. 'City slickers! That's how it is with propane!'

112

Pete kept up his 'Listen!' joke at random points throughout the night. It was nearly dawn before anyone fell asleep.
Before I did anyway.

I was awakened by the sound of loud 'thwacks' and laughter. I went outside to see what was going on. I was greeted by blue skies and sunshine.

There, on the porch, Fred was holding his hunting bow and firing arrows at the icicles hanging from the trees and on the banks of the raging stream under the bridge.
Pete and Bill were with him. When Fred hit a target, they'd all cheer loudly.
'Bull's-eye! Banzai!' they'd shout. They already were drinking again. I looked at my watch. It was not even 7 o'clock in the morning.
The unexpected sunshine had rekindled their spirits.
When they saw me, Pete said, 'Last one out has to go fetch the arrows. It's the rule!'
And they laughed some more in beer-fueled amusement.

I have played some drinking games in my life, I do declare, but this was a new one on me. When Fred missed, he had to take a drink. When he hit his target, the rest of us did. Fred was missing much more than he was hitting.
A drunken archer.

I was in the midst of this mad activity when Nora came running out of the lodge. Sue was right behind her.
'Come in and look at what we found!' Nora said breathlessly.
'Hurry!' Sue added.
Fred, Pete, Bill, and I staggeringly followed them back into the lodge.

Charlie was looking at something he had spread across the 'de-wobbled' table. Larry was sitting beside him.
'Do you think it's real?' he asked Charlie.
Fred went closer to have a look.

'That's it!' Fred said excitedly. 'You found it! That's what I've been looking for! Where'd you find it?'

'Behind the stove,' Sue told him.

'It's a treasure map,' Nora said as she tugged at me.
'Look! It's even marked where they think they buried their gold.'
I think the early morning beers had got the better of me.
'Who buried what gold?' I asked in a muddle.
'Look!' Nora said again.

There, spread across the table, was what looked like an old trail map.

'My grandfather bought an old book about the local Indian tribes when he was a young boy,' Fred said. 'My dad told me the whole story once. Granddad saw it in a bookshop and then he found this map pressed in the pages of the book. It's a map of where the Indians buried their gold when they were fleeing the colonists. It has all the old Indian trails used by the Abenaki. Legend has it that they buried their gold near this part of the White Mountains which they called the Crystal Hills.
My dad and uncle and I would go looking for it, but we never found it. We'd always try again whenever we came here though. It's a family tradition!'

It was immediately agreed that we would all go for a long hike and find this 'Indian Gold'.
Charlie did not seem very convinced.
'A hike would be good. Gold or no gold,' he shrugged.
But Fred was at his overly enthusiastic best. 'Maybe we'll find it this time! My dad thinks it's along this river bank,' he said pointing out a line on the map.

We quickly ate breakfast which consisted of Cheerios and yet more junk food. The wood Bill and Pete had dragged into the lodge the previous evening was still not dry.
Once we had eaten, we all got our things and started to head out for our treasure hunt.
Larry took his Russian hat down from one of the wall-mounted trophy antlers where he'd hung it up to dry the night before.
We were all good to go.

Fred took the lead. He had the map with him in his shirt pocket.
We ambled behind in pairs and trios. I was walking with Charlie and Larry.

'You don't seem too convinced about this, Charlie,' I said to him.
'You don't think it's a real map?' Larry asked him.
He sounded hopeful that it was.
'Well, I'd be more persuaded if it didn't say, 'New Hampshire
Gazette' in the bottom margin. I think it's just an old newspaper
souvenir.'
'His grandfather didn't find it in an old book?' Larry asked.
He sounded so disappointed.
'I think that Freddy's dad and uncle liked to tease him as much as
Pete and Bill do now,' Charlie suggested.

We walked and walked. The sun was shining, but there still was
enough snow beneath our feet to slow our progress.
Fred found the start to another trail on his right. He stopped until all
of us had caught up with him.
'OK! My dad told me this is called the 'Indian Head Trail'. We go
this way and the trail follows along the same stream that runs past the
lodge. After that, it's a bit of a climb, but then it gets easy.'

We took the new trail and, as Fred had told us, it followed along a
stream.
It was stunning scenery. We could see the 'Crystal Hills' in the
distance in front of us.
They glistened in the sunlight.

We simply followed the path even if the snow was a bit deeper there
than on the main trail we had taken from the lodge.
A herd of deer must have been spooked by our talking. They were
hopping and leaping through the snow just up ahead of us.
'Look at that one bounding!' Sue enthused.
'Oh! I love deer!' Nora sighed with pleasure.

We kept walking in our little groups of twos and threes. The trail had
been following the stream for some time before it swung away from
it to the right.
'OK! It gets a little steeper here for a while,' Fred shouted back to us
in warning.

He wasn't kidding. Once the trail veered away from the stream, we
started to climb. The canopy of the forest kept the snow under our
feet to a manageable depth. It was easier to walk, but the steep climb
had its own challenges.

We kept ascending higher and higher. We must have been climbing for over an hour before the trail leveled off. There was plenty of huffing and puffing.

Fred stopped to look at the map.
'It's along this river bank here,' he said to Nora as he pointed at the map. 'That's where my dad and uncle think it is too. It's a few more miles until we get there. I think we'll check the opposite bank to the one my dad and uncle explored with me.'
'If we find it, how are we going to get it back?' Nora asked him.
'Let's find it first!' he laughed.

The trail did not stay level for long and we again began to hike steeply uphill. The sun was melting the snow and little rivulets would run down the hill as we climbed it.

We had been walking for hours before Pete shouted out, 'I'm hungry!'
'And me!' Bill seconded.
'We'll stop when we get to the top of this hill!' Fred yelled back at them.
About half an hour later we had.
Everyone slumped down to the ground.

Nora found a grassy glade beneath some trees. There was not much snow on the ground there and a thick trunked, hollowed-out, conveniently fallen tree marked Nora's spot where we all could sit.
'We can eat over here,' she said beckoning us over.
It then dawned on me that no one had thought to bring anything to eat.
'Eat what, Nora?' I asked her.
And she opened her backpack and pulled out some sandwiches and fruit. She even had a supply of beer.
'Will this do?' she smiled.
It would.

We all sat down, began to eat and drink, and were feeling very good about our little adventure.
Charlie said nothing about his doubts.

Fred told us a little more about the Indians and their gold.

'The Abenaki were dying from all manner of European diseases after the colonists arrived. They had no resistance to them according to my dad. If they caught even the flu, they would die. They tried to flee north to Canada to be safe, but had to leave their gold behind. They hid it so they could reclaim it later. My dad said that the Abenaki were a peaceful tribe and even showed the settlers how to grow corn. They'd help them survive the bitterly cold winters.'
'A lot of good it did them,' Pete said.

We were all taking in this tale of Indian lore when Larry asked, 'Where's my apple? It was right here! I laid it on the ground and now it's gone!'
He was sitting at the end of the huge fallen tree we were all using as a bench.
He stood up and looked around. Then he knelt down and looked into the tree hollow.
'Maybe it rolled in there,' he mumbled to himself.

Fred kept up his Indian story.
'My dad said that the Abenaki were called the People of the Dawnland. Legend has it that a crow brought them the first kernel of corn. It was in its eye.
They always revered the crow as sacred and would never harm them even if they were eating their cornfields. They merely shooed them away.'
'Good thing they didn't revere bobcats,' Pete contributed.

And then we all heard a mighty scream.

It was Larry.
His hands were covering his face. He was rolling face down on the forest floor and in obvious great pain.
I ran over to him.
'What is it, Lar? What's wrong?'
But he wouldn't, or couldn't, talk.

I tried to pull his hands away from his face, so I could see what was going on.
'Yieee!!!' he screamed. 'Don't touch it! Don't touch it!'

Charlie came over and the two of us tried to roll Larry onto his back.

It was not an easy task. Larry was a very strong guy and he was squirming in resistance with all his strength.

'Larry!' I called out as we struggled. 'Take your hands away! Let me see what happened!'

Finally, he stopped and slowly lifted his hands.

Then we could all clearly see what the problem was.

About seven long quills were stuck in his face.

'Porcupine,' Fred said.

We helped Larry back up to sit on the tree trunk.

Fred examined the porcupine's work.

'They'll have to come out,' he decided.

Larry was not quick to agree. He knew they had to be taken out, but he didn't want to do it cold turkey.

Nora went to Larry and told him to be very still.

'I'll get them, Larry,' she said.

I went over to help, but I wasn't sure how.

'Try to breathe, Lar, like in ballet class,' I said to little effect.

And despite his protests and wails of pain, which scared the birds from their roosts, he finally settled down enough to let Nora begin to pull out the quills one by one.

We all watched them, as the snow in the air billowed down upon us, falling from the trees which the birds had vacated.

An agonized scream accompanied each de-quilling.

Larry was very shaken up, but after closer examination, the damage did not look too bad.

'You'll have some welts tomorrow,' Fred told him.

'You're lucky one of them didn't get in your eye.'

We decided to abandon our search for the Abenaki Gold. We wanted to get Larry back to the lodge and clean his wounds. No one had thought to bring the First Aid kit.

We started to make our way back. It was far easier retracing our steps. Most of the journey was downhill in that direction.

Larry was not in so much pain now. He'd rub snow on his face and kept asking me if the porcupine attack would leave scars. I lied to him that it wouldn't, even though I had no idea one way or the other.

When we reached the stream, Nora made us all stop so Larry could splash water on his face and clean it properly.
'That's much better,' he thanked her.

We were nearing the point where the Indian Head Trail we had taken intersected with the main trail that led back to the lodge.
And as we did, we heard the oddest sound.

It sounded like a low rolling thunder punctuated by thumping noises.
We all stopped to listen.
'What is that?' Sue asked in confusion.
And as soon as she asked that question, there was a massive explosion in the distance.

The next thing I knew, I was on the ground. And so was everyone else.
The sound echoed and echoed all around us.

Years later, I was walking in London when an IRA bomb let loose. I fell to the ground then too, even though the explosion was over a mile away.
It was as if the shock of it suddenly made me lose my balance. There in the woods, it was just the same.

We all got up in slow motion and looked at one another. I guess everyone was hoping someone would know what just happened.
But no one did know.

We shook off the snow and bits of twigs and muck from our falls to the ground.
'Probably loggers,' Fred ventured. 'They dynamite the stumps.'

We found the main trail, still deep with snow, and trudged our way back towards Fred's lodge.
When we reached the swinging bridge, we all stopped.

I am sure if someone had taken a snapshot of us at that precise moment; it would have shown all of us with our eyes as nearly wide open as our mouths.

The lodge was no more.

What used to be Fred's Hunting Lodge was reduced to splinters and smithereens.

Smoke wisped around the remains. Little fires were dotted here and there consuming what was left of the timber construction.

There was no sign of any wall or roof or anything that would have indicated there used to be a structure there at all.

It was completely gone.

We all stood there watching in amazed silence.

Charlie noticed that the far side of the bridge, nearest the lodge, was also burning. We crossed over, while we still could, and Charlie put snow on the smoking part of the bridge to put it out.

Bill and Larry ran up to where the lodge used to be.

'All our stuff's gone!' Bill yelled back to us.

'My running shoes!'

Larry walked over to where Bill was running his foot over the burnt remains.

'I can't find Mom's suitcase,' he said to Bill in a daze.

Pete joined them as they searched the burnt lodge rubble. He was looking for something.

After a while he shouted, 'Listen! Here it is!' holding something triumphantly aloft.

In his hand was roughly half of the 'Listen' hunting plaque from the wall. Its edges were burned black.

'I thought I heard a buck snort!'

Fred started to argue heatedly with Charlie.

'You didn't hook up the propane tank right!' he hollered.

'The gas line was probably blocked,' Charlie said. 'It probably hadn't been connected for years, Fred!'

'You should both just be glad we weren't in there when it happened,' Nora scolded them.

There was nothing else to do. We all had a look to see if any of our possessions were still in one piece. But everything was gone, except, luckily, for our car keys. Bill was right about the rest of our gear. What could be burnt was burnt.

Everyone helped to put out the little fires that remained.

We crossed the bridge again with just what we had on our backs.

We made our way down the path back to where we had abandoned our cars yesterday.

Our long weekend away was over.

We followed Fred to the Park Ranger Station. We all had to make statements about the 'incident'. One of the rangers treated Larry's wounds.

'Will I be scarred?' Larry asked him nervously.

'No,' the ranger said kindly. 'I don't think you'll emerge disfigured from your encounter with that porcupine. You're lucky you didn't end up with a quill in your eye though.'

Fred, looking on, gave a woodsman's nod in agreement.

I watched as Fred got back in his car with Pete and Bill. One of the rangers followed them in his Jeep back to the lodge.

The rest of us headed back home.

That was the very last time the group of us ever got together.

We'd talk about meeting on the phone and ask about how the others were doing, but we never went on an adventure like that again.

Perhaps we all thought we had cheated death together and didn't want to tempt fate.

Soon after the hunting lodge disaster, I was given a scholarship to study at Dallas Ballet. Nora and I moved to Texas.

We did go back to Baltimore, on one occasion, several years later. I was performing there in *The Nutcracker*. I made a point of trying to get in touch with Larry, but the number I had for him didn't work anymore.

I took a cab over to where he used to live with his mother, but they must have moved.

I didn't know the woman who answered 'their' door. I asked her about Larry, but she said she didn't know him.

I found a neighbor and asked if she knew where Larry was living. The way she looked at me filled me with dread.

'Larry passed last year from complication of Aids, bless his soul,'
she sadly told me.
'His poor momma went to live with her sister's family in Alabama.'

By the end of the 80's, Nora and I had lost twenty six friends and/or
family members to Aids.
Our friend Larry was one of them.

Looking back, maybe I should have heeded Fred's silly theory of *The
Fallacy of the Hat Rack.*
If I had, perhaps Nora and I would be together still.

But that's another story for another time.

STORY CHAPTER SEVEN

'THE PECOS PLAZA'

A few years ago, I met up with some friends at a London café not far from where I was living. I hadn't seen some of them for ages. There was the usual catching up to do and discovering where the bodies were buried and who had been doing what to whom.

My old college friend, Charlie, was there too. He was in London on business. I once had a 'near death' experience with him in a Kentucky cave and again in the New Hampshire mountains, but those are different stories.

Our conversations flowed along with the wine and beers we were drinking.
I hadn't seen Charlie for quite some time. We'd phone and exchange emails, but this was a chance for us to catch up properly.
I asked him about his girlfriend, Sue. She was also with us on that New Hampshire disaster.

'No, no, Ralphy, you're talking ancient history there,' he said. 'We were thinking of getting married when she started going all 'Femi-Nazi' on me. All of a sudden, I was 'controlling' and she said that she couldn't 'breathe' anymore. Next thing I know she starts calling herself 'Susan' instead of Sue. I guess she thought it made her sound 'stronger'. We just started arguing the whole time and decided we'd call it a day. I heard she married some Brit guy. She could be living over here now as far as I know. I haven't seen her for years.'

When he asked me about Nora, I didn't say very much.
'No, Charlie, we're not together anymore either.'
I left it like that and he didn't press me for more.

Charlie was telling us all that he worked for 'Apple'.
'I'm in London to shake up our UK offices,' he explained.
'Some of the senior managers are going to be looking for new jobs.'

Charlie told us he was now senior vice president. He was always a capable guy, but I was impressed anyway.

'I'm Apple's 'bad apple cop',' he joked.

He then started telling us a story about an Apple employee who was arrested and jailed for 'corporate espionage'.

When he finished his story, he added, ''It makes you ask yourself whether you can trust anyone anymore.'

And that reminded me of a story too. One Charlie had never heard, but one I had told many times before.

I think I began my story something like this:

I was with the Dallas Ballet. I was brought there on a scholarship. Nora and I were living in Baltimore, when she paid for some ballet classes as my birthday gift one year. I was a bit surprised by her gift, but went along and caught the 'ballet bug'. I couldn't get enough of it. And some months later we were in Dallas.

It was hard work. We would do four classes a day and then hit the gym. And Dallas can be a swelteringly hot town. Just going for a walk, in the long summer months, will bring on buckets of sweat. Dancing in that heat is madness itself. We had just one, solitary fan for the entire dance studio. It was like a symbol of coolness rather than having any real effect.

I also would work at the local theatres, when the Ballet season was over. Our dance contracts only ran for nine months of the year. The rest of the time we had to manage for ourselves. The local theatres were always on the lookout for dancers though, so it worked out quite well.

Once during the Ballet season break, I was cast in a production of *The Threepenny Opera*. The producers brought in a photographer to do the publicity photos. When the photos were developed and printed, I was amazed at the result.

The photographer was a genius. I do not use that term lightly. He was a photographic genius. Everyone looked both terrific and interesting in every single photo. And that was no easy trick. Everyone was not terrific looking and interesting at all. But the photographer made us all appear to be so.

I was still married to Nora then and when I showed her the photos, she was equally amazed.

'Who is this guy?' she asked in wonder.

He produced huge black and white prints full of 'character' with unusual, but expressive, lighting and shadowing.

I still have the ones he made of me to this very day.

I didn't know who the photographer was at the time, but when I next saw him I made a point of finding out.

One day I was in the theatre lobby, when I saw the photographer leaving the theatre. He was fumbling with his photography case and trying to fit some lenses back in their place. I walked over to him and asked him his name.

'Johnnie Walker,' he said. 'Like the whiskey'.

He was a small guy, distinctly average looking, but full of energy looking for an outlet. He was also wildly unconventional and making conversation with him was a struggle.

But I persevered and over time we became "talking" friends. As opposed to close friends. I mean, I didn't really know him. I would talk to him, unlike the other performers who tended to avoid him. But that was about it. His only close friend seemed to have been his girlfriend, Sally. He'd mainly talk about her.

'She has it all, man. I see Paris fashion photo shoots. Cover of 'Vogue'. The whole nine yards.'

At the final performance of *The Threepenny Opera*, Nora came to watch the show. Johnnie was there too.

Nora was extremely social and outgoing. As a result, she made friends very easily. And she immediately struck up a conversation with Johnnie and was swooning over his photographs and his wonderful 'eye'.

'You are gifted,' she said.

And Nora always had a soft spot for the 'gifted'.

Nora suggested that we all go out to dinner together. Johnnie called Sally and the four of us went for a Mexican meal.

Upon meeting Sally, the first thing that struck me was that she was simply stunning. She was a 'Texas Rose', if ever there was one. She'd be greeted with several Texas 'Yahoos' from passing cars wherever she went.

But Sally was also drinking from the same unconventionality cup as Johnnie. They did fit well together, even if she was a good head taller than he was.

We went to a place called 'Pilar's Buena Vista', which was the restaurant where Nora was working at the time. After dinner, Johnnie and Sally took to doing many shots of tequila in the restaurant bar. Nora and I were not persuaded, but we stayed to talk.

And Johnnie started to tell us all about a job he had coming up in Mexico.

'The Cuidad Juarez Chamber of Commerce wants to create a new image for the city,' he said between downing shots. 'They want me to come up with some photos to convince American tourists that Cuidad Juarez is historic and a chance to visit 'Old Mexico'.'

This gave Sally the giggles. I later discovered that almost everything gave Sally the giggles.

Cuidad Juarez does not have that 'image'. It's a very poor Mexican border town. Texans would go there to buy clichéd Mexican souvenirs or indulge their worst instincts on sex, cheap alcohol, and drugs. It was well known for being dangerous.

This was in the days before the mushrooming of the 'maquiladoras', the Mexican assembly plants, which attracted a spurt in population and skyrocketing crime.

But around this time, in the late 70's and early 80's, it was not yet a hot spot for murders and drug cartels. But even at that time, it had a lawless reputation, if not yet a worldwide homicidal one.

I had never been there myself, but that certainly was the 'image' I had about the place.

'I have to be there on Friday,' Johnnie said.

That was in two days time.

'I don't know how I can get there though. Maybe there's a bus?' he asked of no one in particular.

And then Nora asked, 'Are they paying your travel expenses?'

Johnnie said that they were. 'They're paying for everything. Even a souvenir sombrero, if I want it.'

126

Sally said that's all she wanted. She swore it.

'Then I can bring a piece of 'Old Mexico' home with me,' she grinned.

And then Nora dropped me right in it.

She blithely announced that now as I was 'free', since the run of the show was over, I could drive Johnnie there. Before I could even gulp, Johnnie said that was 'perfect'.

'And I can pay you for the drive, Ralphy,' he told me. 'Well, the client will. And you can see Cuidad Juarez for yourself!'

And with that Johnnie and Sally had another shot of tequila.

He said to Sally, 'We're going to Mexico!!' And they both hopped up and down a bit together in a drunken celebration.

'To Mexico!' Johnnie said. And he threw some money on the bar. 'I'll see you tomorrow,' he slurred.

And they both left.

This was typical Nora. She was always volunteering other people to lend assistance to someone else. Mostly she volunteered me.

I knew Nora had to work that weekend and wouldn't be able to come along with us. It would have been fine, if she were coming too. I wouldn't have minded. But without her, I faced a very long drive with people who I didn't really know very well at all.

'We won't be able to spend time together this weekend anyway, Ralphy,' she soothed.

Cuidad Juarez is a long way from Dallas. True, it is just over the Texan border, but Texas is one big, huge, enormous State. The drive there would take at least 12 hours, if not more. It's so far away that it's in a different time zone.

I'd be spending the best part of twenty four hours behind the wheel over the weekend there and back.

At the time, Nora and I owned a Dodge transit van. Her father and I had refitted the interior before we drove down to Dallas from Baltimore. We put in a sunroof and customized built-in compartments for tools. There was an air mattress in the back for passengers to sleep on during long drives.

On our way home, I stopped and filled the tank, checked the tire pressure, oil, and inflated the air mattress.

Early the next morning, there was a loud knocking on the door. I checked the bedside clock. It was 5am. Nora mumbled to me to answer it and, rubbing my eyes, I made my way to the door.
It was Johnnie and Sally. They were dressed exactly as they were when I last saw them.

'We partied at the 'Recovery Room' -*a local bar*- and Sally said, let's just hit the road!' Johnnie explained drunkenly.
'There's no time like the present,' Sally yawned.

They had not even bothered going to bed. They had no bags. They had nothing except for two half-consumed beers in their hands.
'I need to use the ladies' powder room,' Sally giggled.
I took them both inside and while Sally was in the bathroom, I quickly threw some of my things into a bag.
'We're going to Mexico!' Johnnie kept saying.
'Ole'.
Nora, blessed with this ability, slept right through it all.

I drove them over to where they were living and they both hopped out of the van.
'I just need a couple things,' Sally said. 'We'll be right back.'
'Don't go anywhere without us!' Johnnie warned me mockingly.
And they ran inside.

I must have sat there for the best part of an hour while they were doing whatever they were doing. At last, Sally emerged with two paper bags stuffed with clothes and Johnnie followed behind with all his camera stuff.
And, finally, we were all on our way.

Johnnie and Sally kept up their drunken conversation for about half an hour or so and then promptly fell asleep. I drove west and would continue driving west for quite some time.

I got on to Route 20, the main highway for points west of Dallas. As Johnnie and Sally slept, I drove through Fort Worth and headed toward Abilene. We were making excellent time. Texans are 'big' about everything and they certainly are big about putting their foot on the gas. I had to go well over the speed limit just to keep up with the flow of traffic.

I didn't hear a sound from the back of the van until we were nearly in Sweetwater. Sally broke the silence with one of her signature giggles, but before I could say something I realized her giggles were the result of Johnnie's affections. I sat there trying to distract myself from the sound of their love-making. I was not very successful nor were they helping me to be so.

"I'm hungry!' Sally said after they were done with their exertions. 'What you think, Cabbie?' Johnnie asked me. 'Time for a pit stop?' As we had just entered the Sweetwater city limits, I agreed it was.

We found a little Tex-Mex café and went in. Johnnie brought one of his cameras in with him. As Sally went to visit the 'little girl's room', as she put it, Johnnie and I sat at a table.
A large blond waitress quickly came over.
'Bring us three Dos Equis,' Johnnie told her.
'And some menus,' I added.

Johnnie loaded some film into his camera. He reached back into his camera case and took out a lens.
'This is a 'fish eye' lens,' he said. 'It lets me center on the subject while all the background is pulled far into the distance.'
He took several photos of me while I sat four feet across from him. The locals looked on in disapproving confusion as each flash went off.

'That bathroom is so funny!' Sally said when she rejoined us.
'The ladies room has 'Senoritas' on the door. It's the first time I ever had a pee in Spanish!'
And how she giggled.

The waitress came back with our Mexican beers and tossed the menus in the middle of the table.
'I'll be back presently to take your order,' she said.

My travelling companions made very short work of their beer.
'Two more!' Johnnie shouted out across the room. They drank and drank through lunch. In fact, the two of them ate almost nothing at all. Johnnie's chicken-fried steak went untouched and Sally's quesadilla was only picked at. I ate my burrito and refried beans as they ordered beer after beer. Their drinking carried on for a good couple of hours. I nursed a cup a coffee to keep them company.

And as they drank, their conversation grew louder and louder. Johnnie took yet more photos, this time of Sally, who would stand up and 'pose' in a mock fashion runway manner. Twice her drunken gyrations nearly resulted in waitresses dropping their trays.

When the bill came, I had a nasty surprise. Neither Johnnie nor Sally had brought any money with them. Or very little money anyway.
'You get this, Ralpholo,' Johnnie told me. 'And I'll pay you back when we hit Jerez.'
I had no choice but to agree.
The locals followed us with their eyes as we left. If eyes could talk, they would have said, 'Y'all aren't welcome back here.'

We were back on the highway with Midland the next main city on our westward route. Johnnie, thoroughly revived by the beer, was joking and laughing and setting Sally off too.
'Hey boss!' He shouted at me, 'What were the two Mexican firefighting brothers called? Hose A and Hose B!' And he continued in this way for quite some time.
'What do you call a Mexican with a rubber toe? Roberto!' And Sally would laugh until snot came out her nose.
I was thinking how much more pleasant the drive was when they were asleep.

We passed through Midland late in the afternoon. I pulled over into a service area and started refilling the tank. Sally ran off to the toilet. It was the first thing she thought to do whenever she stopped doing whatever she was doing.
Johnnie, for his part, scampered off to the 7-Eleven adjoining the gas station.
When I returned from paying for the gas, the two of them were already back in the van.
'Let's go!' Johnnie said. All of a sudden he was in a rush.
Go Johnnie Go.

When I got off the slip road and back on to Route 20, Johnnie had an announcement.
'OK!' he said. 'I got anything you want!' I could hear him rustling through something in the back of the van.
'Who wants some Fritos? Who wants some Mallo Cups?'

'Where'd that come from?' I asked him. 'Didn't you tell me you had no money?'

'Who needs money?!' Johnnie laughed. 'When you have a 7-Eleven?! Five finger discount!'

If I didn't really know Johnnie before this trip, I was certainly beginning to know him now.

'Turn on the radio, Ralphy!' Sally pleaded while munching away at some of Johnnie's ill-gotten swag.

My Dodge Transit van was equipped with whatever was the most basic dashboard radio they supplied at the time. It worked well enough, but was not what you'd call a 'sound system'.

I fiddled with the dial, but mostly there was only static. We were between Midland and Odessa and there weren't many radio signals aimed our way.

I finally tuned into a Country Western station, but the signal kept coming and going.

'How's that, Sally?' I asked. But there was no reply. Their false beer revival had waned and they were once again asleep in the back.

I kept the radio on for company. The drive between Midland and Odessa is flat and straight. It's mostly ranch-land with the occasional oil derrick to break up the landscape. It was not built up at all in those days. There were few places to stop. A driver faced a long and monotonous journey.

And as any driver in such circumstances will know, it gives you plenty of time to think. Too much time in fact.

Left to your own company, you might be alone in your thoughts for hours.

I had to keep retuning the radio. The signal would come and go. On the rare occasion when I found a song I liked, the signal would let me down halfway through and go back to static.

I was getting tired. There was no one to talk to. I kept messing around with the radio going up and down the dial until I could hear something clearly.

And then, eventually, I tuned into a strong signal coming from some station somewhere. It was the only station I could get.

It was a radio call-in show. Not my usual radio fare, but, as I say, my only option to distract me on the drive. And keep me awake.

After about fifteen minutes of listening to people complain about the local football coach and the 'goings on' at the University of Texas, the program was over.

There were a few commercials about a funeral parlor *('It's your last chance to say goodbye.')* and a feed store *('We meet all your feed needs to keep those doggies rollin'!')* and then the next talk-show host came on.

This one had his own theme tune. It went something like this:

'We're the Nightcaps, Nighty Nightcaps,
And we love to talk and play.
We love to hear each other laugh.
We love each glad 'hello'.
But most of all, we love to hear,
The voice of our own Herb Jepco!'

It carried on in this vein for another verse. Herb's listeners all appeared to be house-bound and elderly. Incredibly, Herb seemed to know every single caller. He'd ask after their health and how their husbands were recovering from their surgery and if they were entering the marrow competition at the State Fair again this year.

He knew every caller's back-story.

I guess he had a lot of repeat callers. It was as if all the callers were ringing their favorite uncle.

Herb kept me company all the way to Odessa. The show itself was not entertaining, but it was so peculiar that it held my interest. However, had there been other radio station options, I don't imagine I would have stayed with Herb.

Perhaps it was this experience that put me into a surreal state. Perhaps I was going stir crazy. Maybe it was the tiredness catching up with me. I don't know. But all of a sudden it hit me that I was in the middle of nowhere with two other people I wasn't sure if I wanted to be awake or not.

And just as that thought hit me, Johnnie stirred.

'What's that?' He mumbled.

'Nightcaps,' I said.

'Nightmare more like,' Johnnie snorted. And his grumblings woke Sally.

'We have to pull over,' Sally said.
'Nature calls.'

As we stopped for Sally, I watched as the huge West Texas sunset completed its final journey leaving twilight in its wake. West Texas boasts an enormous sky. Its uninterrupted flatness affords views to every horizon.
We got back in the van, after Johnnie had taken some photos of Sally looking to relieve herself in some privacy. Sally, with her pants down, frantically waved her hands and arms around in giggly embarrassment in a futile effort to make him stop.

It was growing darker by the minute. We were almost in Pecos, where I'd have to get off Route 20 and get on to Route 10 for the final approach to El Paso and the border with Mexico.

Johnnie had obviously shoplifted a bottle of wine from the 7-Eleven along with the junk food. The two of them started drinking from out of the bottle.

I was trying to keep an eye out for the signs for Route 10, when I started seeing flashes of light from the back of the van. It was Johnnie taking yet more photos of Sally. There was a lot of commotion in the back as Sally took instructions from Johnnie.
'Stand up! That's it! Let me get over here. Take off your top. Now you stand over me! Perfect! Now bend over!'
This was all accompanied by Sally's diabolical giggling and flashes of light from the camera.
They carried on like that for the next half hour or so. I was just about to say something about helping me look for the Route change, when I heard a police siren.

I pulled over, but Johnnie and Sally just proceeded with their photography session, as if nothing had happened.
A giant of a Texas State Trooper and his smaller colleague both approached the van.
'License and Registration, sir,' the Giant said to me.
I handed them over to him as camera flashes continued emanating from behind me.
'What's going on in the back of your van, sir?' the Giant inquired.
Before I could answer, the Smaller Trooper said, 'Y'all get out of the van.'

I got out, but my drunken passengers did not.

'We're taking photos!' Johnnie shouted out at them.

'You Fascists made taking photos illegal now too?'

'Pigs!' Sally screamed.

The two troopers made me open the back door of the van. They had to drag Johnnie and Sally out on to the side of the highway.

There was much swearing and struggling as this took place.

Johnnie held on to his camera in the struggle. As I tried to explain what we were doing to the police, Johnnie started taking close-up photos of them. The flashes were going off right in their faces.

'Please stop doing that, sir,' the Smaller Trooper said.

But Johnnie would not stop. Sally kept yelling, 'Pigs!' and 'Freedom to the people!'

As the policemen tried to reason with Johnnie, he kept scampering around them while taking more and more photos.

'We have proof now, Pigs!' Sally shrilled.

We were all handcuffed and frog-marched to their patrol car.

As we sat in the backseat with our hands behind our backs, Sally became hysterical with rage. 'Death to the military industrial complex! Fascists!'

Johnnie was more concerned about his camera than anything else.

'Be careful with that, you honky redneck!'

The Giant called in to his station.

'We have a situation here two miles outside city limits. Two white males and one white female. Out of State license. Suspected car theft.'

There was some response from the station, but I couldn't make out what they said.

When we arrived at the station, the three of us were separated.

Sally kept screaming abuse as two cops grabbed Johnnie under his arms. Then two more did the same to her. She howled and fought like a mother bear who'd lost her cub as they dragged them both away. Johnnie, meanwhile, was singing, *'We Shall Overcome'* as loudly and tunelessly as was humanly possible.

I was taken down a long corridor, in the opposite direction to where they'd dragged Johnnie and Sally, and then through two different sets of caged metal doors. I kept trying to explain what had happened to the policeman who was leading me, but he said nothing.

Finally, we stopped. There was a huge holding cell in front of me. There must have been a dozen men already in there.

The policeman opened the locked door and said, 'In you 'git''. They were the only words he said to me. And after he locked the door again, he walked away.

I had never been in jail before. I looked around without trying to make any eye contact with anyone, but none of the other prisoners paid any attention to me. Two of them were playing cards in the corner. Everyone else just sat there on the floor, except for the three biggest and toughest looking men. They sat together on the one long bench provided.

Kings of the Dung Hill.

About half an hour later, another policeman came over to the holding cell and signaled at me. 'At last,' I thought, 'someone can see this is all a big mistake.'

But after he called me over to him, he simply handed me a blanket through the bars. He was not interested in anything I had to say. He looked at all of us lazily for a moment and moseyed away.

'We'll all go up in front of the judge tomorrow,' an old man in soiled clothing said to me. He told me that he was picked up for vagrancy. 'I was just minding my own business, but they don't care.' I could smell stale cigarettes and alcohol on his breath.

'You ain't got a smoke on ya, do ya, amigo?' When I told him I did not he said, 'Best thing to do, pardner, is just settle in for the night.' As that was the only option available, it seemed a good idea.

Nights in West Texas can be very cold. I did not know that then, but as the night passed I learned that was true. People were trying to sleep on the floor. They held their thin blankets tightly to them.

I just sat on the floor and tried to be inconspicuous. Invisible would have been better, but that was not possible.

And tired as I was, I dare not sleep.

Then, in the middle of the night, while I was lost in my own thoughts
and trying to forget what had happened, a fellow prisoner came up to
me.

'Give me that blanket. You don't need no blanket. You give it here.'
He was aggressive. He was ready to fight for that blanket.
This caught the attention of the others.
A distraction from the boredom.

'You keep that blanket, Boy!' someone shouted out at me.
'Yeah, that's your blanket!' someone else laughed.
Then the guy, who wanted my blanket, grabbed it and started to pull
it from my hands.

Now, I do not know, even to this day, why I did what I did. Maybe I
was so tired that I simply couldn't take anymore. Maybe it was
Sally's infernal giggling that pushed me over the edge. Or Johnnie's
casual self-centeredness. Maybe it was sheer survival kicking in.
I don't know.
But as this man grabbed at my blanket, I just lost it. I let him have
the blanket by suddenly letting go of it. That took him by surprise
and he fell over backwards. I then jumped on top of him with the
blanket over his face and started swinging away.

'You want this blanket? You want this? Is that what you want? You
want my blanket?'
And I punched and punched him on each question.
There was cheering in the cell.
'Atta boy! Whip his ass!'

The guy beneath me stopped struggling. I took the blanket back and
when I did I saw his face was a bloody mess. Two policemen
shouted outside the cell door.

'What's going on?!' They saw the prisoner I had bloodied. 'Who did
this?'
But no one said anything.
I suppose even when you are in a hell-hole like that, the people you
are suffering with share a code. The Code of the Confined.
'Keep it down!' one of the cops said.
After they left, one of my cellmates said to me, 'Welcome to the
Pecos Plaza!'

No one bothered me after that. Even the aggressive guy knew to keep
his distance. I was feeling so charged up, I could feel my heart
pounding.

It was the longest night I ever knew and would ever care to know.

The next morning two policemen came and took us all down together to see the local magistrate. The small courtroom was in the same police station where we had spent the night. We all just sat there in the cramped courtroom and waited for our names to be called.

There was no sign of Johnnie and Sally.
I won't lie. I didn't give a damn about them.

'Ralph E. Waldo!' the clerk announced.
I stood up.
It was my turn to face the judge.

The court clerk read out the charges:
'Car Theft, Reckless Driving, Transporting a minor, age seventeen, for the purposes of prostitution, Creating and conspiring to distribute pornographic images, and Resisting Arrest.'
Then the clerk added, 'The minor's pregnant, Your Honor.'

He made me sound like some big-time villain. And I'd no idea Sally was only seventeen. Or pregnant for that matter. Not that anyone had done anything to her. Like put her in a brothel or anything.
But thinking back on her behavior, I must admit it made sense. She certainly looked older than seventeen, but she did act like she was seventeen. Or rather she acted like an immature seventeen year old might.

It was my turn to say something. I had no lawyer. No one acted like I should have a lawyer either. I told the judge what happened. He had a look on his face like he had heard it all before. But then, the Giant Trooper, who had arrested us, told the judge that the van was not stolen after all.
'But what about the pornographic photos they were taking?' asked the judge.
And the Trooper said that I was the driver and that they had the two pornographers in custody. I guess he meant Sally and Johnnie.
'They're due up to see you tomorrow, Judge,' he said.

The judge decided I was not guilty of resisting arrest. 'How's a skinny mosquito like you going to resist Bo? He could carry you under one arm.'

That's right. The Giant's name was 'Bo'.

The judge fined me $100 for reckless driving and another $100 for impounding my van. No one said anything about the prostitution charges.
And if $200 doesn't sound like a lot of money to you now, I promise you, back then, it was.

The clerk wouldn't take my check. I had to see Mr. Black, the bondsman. He was easy to find. He was breathing down my neck while I was trying to pay my fine to the clerk.
I figured it wasn't a coincidence.
I gave Mr. Black a check for $275 and then he paid the clerk the $200 I owed. The Pecos Court bondsman, Mr. Black, must have made a bundle in those days.

I had to hitchhike to the other side of town to the police impounding lot to collect my van.
After showing them the fine receipt, I got back in the van and headed east back home to Dallas. Alone.
With only the 'Nighty Nightcaps' for company.

Now, I know many of you will ask me what happened to Johnnie and Sally. I can honestly say that I don't know. I never saw either of them ever again. Neither did I ever discover the fate of Sally's 'baby'.

Once in a while, I will see a photograph in a magazine or a billboard and can tell that it's Johnnie's work.
He was that good. His photos were distinctive and in his own special style.
He was, as Nora said, 'gifted'.
But I never saw him again at that theatre where I first met him. Or anywhere else.
Nor Sally for that matter.
Not even on the cover of some magazine.

But Nora claimed she did see who she thought was Sally once.
A year or more had passed, since the aborted trip to 'Old Mexico'.
She came home one night after working at the restaurant and was looking very upset.

'What's wrong now, Nora?' I sighed.

'You know that Sally? The one who used to run around with Johnnie? I think I saw her tonight. I'm not sure. It looked like Sally, but if it was, she had dyed her hair. Her face was really puffy too. I think she put on a lot of weight. But I would recognize that goofy giggling of hers anywhere. She was so drunk in the restaurant bar and the Barfly Casanovas were crawling all over her. It was awful! How can anyone let themselves get into such a state?'

'I suppose the bottle can do that to you, Nora,' I said.

But whether Nora saw Sally that night or not, I never saw her again.

I first told this story to Nora, of course. And I've told it on more than one occasion since. Like the time I told it to Charlie when he was in London on business.

Now I've told it to you too.

And if you ever find yourself in Pecos, Texas, don't stay at the Pecos Plaza.

And that's the truth, the whole truth, and nothing but the truth.

STORY CHAPTER EIGHT

'THE SECURITY GUARD'

This is a story, a parable in parts, about poverty.
It is not glamorous. Poverty is not glamorous.
It doesn't take place in some exotic or war-ravaged land.
It doesn't need to take place there.
Poverty can take place anywhere. And it can happen to anyone no matter their situation.
All it takes is a lack of opportunity or a patch of carelessness or irresponsibility or naiveté and you are there. There, in the world of poverty.
And once there, it can be notoriously hard to escape.
People say poverty is a trap.
And they are right.

This is a poverty trap tale. It takes place in North London in the early 80's.
But poverty can show its many faces at any time and in any place.
Poverty is not particular about where or when it roosts.

Suddenly, Nora and I found ourselves with no money. We were poor in the truest sense of the word. Potless and penniless. Skinned, depleted, and broke.
We had gone to London, because a dance company, The Dallas Ballet, with which I was involved, was performing there.
It was the very first time Nora and I had been to London. We stayed in a rented house with the other dancers.

After the performances were over, the rest of the dance company went back to Texas, but Nora and I decided to stay in London.
The lease on the rental didn't end until the end of that month, so we could stay there until then.

We couldn't work. My visa only allowed me to work with that dance company. I was forbidden to take any other work 'paid or unpaid' as the visa read.

Nora and I were officially in Britain as 'tourists', but we wanted to live there and see what London life was all about.

If we found work, it would have to be 'off the books'. We had no working papers. No right to work. We had no National Insurance Number required of all British workers.
But we had no choice but to work. We could not last long on the meagre savings we had left. It was a stressful and uncomfortable time.

Nora would ask at pubs if she could clean their toilets. I would ask 'blokes' working on a building site if I could do a day's labor.
The lease on the place where the ballet company had housed us was coming to an end. We certainly could not afford to continue staying there.
Something had to be done.

It was about a week before we were due to leave the dance company's London rental. We would then be homeless.
We got up very early every day, as usual, to try to find work. We'd walk the streets together and try our luck. Mainly, we were luckless.
And then, one day, we came across a dilapidated café on a side street in North London.

A garish rainbow had been painted across the front window. When we went inside, we saw the café was called 'Rainbow'. The walls were all covered in the various painted shades of a rainbow.
'Rainbow Café' was painted on a board above the counter.

It was squalid and it was seedy along with it. The linoleum on the floor was stained and the serving counter was cracked and stained too. Stuffing-spilling chair cushions and bits of broken furniture just lay where they were. None of the café's tables or chairs matched.
And the clientele who ate there were much like the décor.
A rough place for a rough crew.
The North London poor.

I asked the pleasant looking woman behind the counter if there was any work. I lied that I could cook.

She looked at us and said, 'Good! I have to collect my daughter. You two stay here, serve the customers, and if you haven't burned down the place by the time I get back, the job's all yours.'

As she was running out the door, she added, 'Just put any money in that tray under the counter. There's some change in there.'

And we were left on our own.

We didn't burn down the place. We were now Rainbow Café workers.

The Rainbow Café was run by 'Sanyassins'. These were orange-robed devotees of Bhagwan Shree Rajneesh. It was one of those 'personality cults' that sprouted up throughout the 70's and 80's and beyond.

All the Sanyassin café workers lived in an 'Ashram' together nearby. Each had changed their given names to one the Bhagwan had given them. So 'Judith' became 'Sutra', 'Frank' became 'Punam', 'Kate' became 'Indiro', and so on.

Allegedly, the 'Orange People', as the locals called them, were part of some sort of sex cult. I'd overhear stories at the café about what went on at their Ashram.

But I found them harmless enough.

Nora and I were paid three Pounds each per day. We were also provided with lunch.

Amarelle, the woman who hired us, was not a Sanyassin. She simply worked there, just like we now did.

'You two can open up tomorrow,' she informed us. 'I'm going to be late. There's a shop just down the road, if you need to buy butter or bread or something for the café. Just take the money from the tray under the counter.'

It was a strange place. Once you were involved there, you were just thrown into the swamp. There was no training. There was no supervision. You were there and you just got on with it.

The following morning, Nora asked Amarelle, once she finally arrived, about places to rent. We were due to be out of the dance company rental in just a few more days now. She told her we had very little money.

'A lot of people around here have no money!' Amarelle laughed.
'But I know a place where you could stay. It won't be expensive. It won't be very nice either. But, if it's still available, it's somewhere to hang your hat.'
She wrote down an address.
'It's my ex-husband's friend who owns it,' she added. 'But please don't mention me to him!'

After our shift at the Rainbow, we went straight over to the place Amarelle had suggested.
We rapped on the door and a little balding fellow in a bathrobe answered. He was smoking a cigarette.
'Are you the landlord?' Nora asked. 'We're looking for a place to rent.'

The balding man told us that he was just a tenant. He ran back into his room and emerged with the landlord's telephone number.
'Call him. I'm Trevor. He only lives down the street. Are you Americans? Yes, call him,' he said.
And Trevor shut the door.
We were just about to go to a phone booth to make the call, when the front door flew back open.
'Don't tell the landlord I'm here!' Trevor pleaded.

Once we had called him, the landlord came right over. He let us in and we followed.
A stench greeted us as we did so.
The entrance hall was stinking with damp mold and old cigarette smoke. The wallpaper was a stained unseemly atrocity.

We saw that there were two flats off the hall. The landlord pointed to one of the doors to indicate that was the flat for rent. He had to lean his body against the flat's door after he used his key. Even unlocked, it was still stuck and needed a firm shove to open.

The flat itself was in the basement and very damp. There was little light coming through the flat's sole window.
It was dingy and dirty and smelly.
'How much is the rent?' Nora asked him.
'Sixteen pounds a week,' he said in reply. 'You pay for your own gas and electricity by that meter.'
He pointed to a contraption fixed to a wall.

'It takes fifty pence pieces.'

There was no lease or anything formal like that. Luckily, there was no security deposit required either.
'We'll take it,' Nora said.
And Amarelle's ex-husband's friend said, 'Fine. Every Friday, just drop off the rent to me. Enjoy!'

And he lobbed the flat keys into my hand. He went back out into the hall and began to knock on the other flat's door.
Nora and I could hear him shouting, 'Oy! Trevor Pyle! Where's my rent?'
There was some more knocking and shouting through the door, but eventually he gave up and left.

'Home Sweet Home!' Nora sighed. 'Ralphy! We have a home!'

We took as many shifts as we could get at the café. If we were both lucky enough to work a full six day week, we would have earned thirty six pounds between us.
A full week each however was not guaranteed.
I was never the best at arithmetic, but with a sixteen pound weekly rent and utilities on top of that and food and travel and all the dance and other classes we were taking, I could see it would be a struggle to get by.

We soon learned that a fifty pence coin would give us electricity for about an hour and a half. When it grew cold and we needed heat, that fifty pence coin would last only fifteen minutes or so before it demanded a companion.
I had never been in such poverty before. Fifty pence pieces, like all money, did not bud on bushes.

Home meals consisted of the cheapest options. We might have field beans and a 'tin' of mackerel for dinner. Something like that. We'd walk miles to a 'greengrocer' whose produce was just that little bit cheaper.
We were always counting pennies.

Often, after a full shift at the café, I'd have to walk to dance class in the West End. It was a ninety minute walk in each direction. We simply did not have the bus fare.
And Nora did the same.

We had very few luxuries at the flat. It was 'furnished', but not very well. Some of the chairs were broken and the bed mattress was as hard as sheet rock. Our kitchen consisted of a two-ring hot plate and the tiniest fridge I ever saw.
We shared a bathroom with Trevor. That was out in the hall. It always smelled of cigarettes. He liked 'a fag in the bog' as he put it.

We had a cheap radio and that was our main entertainment at home. When we could afford the batteries.
Nora cut out little cardboard squares from an empty cereal box. On the side without any print, she wrote a different letter of the alphabet. We made up a 'word game' from those and played that together at night sometimes. Often by candlelight.

Mostly we took classes. Work and classes. That accounted for all our time, except on Sundays.
On Sundays, we'd usually go for long walks and explore London. But our Mondays to Saturdays were already mapped out.
Work and classes.

A few weeks after we moved in, I came home from dance class one night and found Nora and Trevor talking in our flat.
Nora was extremely social and so she made friends very readily.

'Ralphy, Trevor is a security guard at the Hilton on Park Lane,' she informed me.
She announced this as if he were as interesting as an astronaut.
'And he has a new lady in his life too! She's from Manchester, isn't she, Trev?'
'Elaine's from the good side of Manchester,' he added.
'It's so romantic, Ralphy! They speak on the phone every day, since the day they met.'
'When did you meet?' I asked Trevor.
He lit another cigarette.
'A few months ago,' he said. 'She was staying at the Hilton.'

145

We sat there talking with Trevor for another couple of minutes or so before he said, 'I better go! I have to call her!'
And without another word, he ran back to his flat, his smoke trailing behind him.

Eventually, we had grown accustomed to our routine. We'd been in our damp basement flat for a few months now. It started to feel like 'home'. Nora and I even had visitors on occasion.

We never saw anyone visit Trevor though. And he was rarely there. He seemed to be working every hour of the week. If I did see him, he'd be in his guard uniform either going to or returning from his hotel job.
'He works a lot of hours, Ralphy,' Nora said. 'I'm worried about him.'

Nora worried about everyone's welfare. It was one of the reasons, no doubt, why she made friends so easily. But there was a downside to that. Nora could let herself get 'involved' in things that weren't her business.

'Don't you hear him on the phone talking with her?' Nora asked me. 'It must be costing him a fortune!' she added. 'He told me he's always the one to call to save her money.'
'That's his business, Nora,' I replied.
'And he's on there for hours and hours every single night. Some nights, all night. He doesn't seem to say much to her though. She must be a real chatterbox!'
'Well, he's working. He can afford it,' I said dismissively.
'Ralphy! Don't you remember the landlord knocking on his door for the rent? I don't think he can afford it!'
'Not our business, Nora! Not our business!'

I guess it was about two weeks after Nora told me she was 'worried' about Trevor, when I next saw him. He was leaving to go to work as I was returning home from class.
He looked very thin to me. I remember noticing that. Trevor was a skinny, little fellow to begin with, but he looked positively emaciated now.

'Trev, have you been ill?' I asked him.
'Have I been what?' he asked as he had a drag on his 'roll-up'.

'Ill. Have you been ill? You look so thin.' I repeated.
'No, I'm not ill. I have to go. I'm doing a double shift tonight.'
And he went his way.

Although I was an utter kitchen novice, things were beginning to sink in for me at the café.
I'd watch what Amarelle or Nora did and then did my best to copy them.
I was becoming quite the little chef.
I had never really cooked before, but with Amarelle's guidance and the encouragement of Nora and some of the Orange People who worked there, I started to get the hang of it.

I'd even try new recipes and once managed to pull off a soufflé for the lunch menu.
That was a new one for our North London café regulars.
I created a new breakfast cereal too. I'd put some wheat flakes and oats and raisins and some oil and honey into a bowl and mix it thoroughly. Then I'd roll it out, bake it in the 'cooker', let it cool, and called it 'granola'.
It turned into our most popular breakfast item.

Nora was instrumental in cleaning the café. Little by little, she had turned that filthy place into a welcoming retreat for the locals. She put up a notice to ask for unwanted furniture and, over time, we were able to get rid of most of the broken tables and chairs.
She also organized poetry readings there on Friday nights.

Within half a year, Nora had become the most popular of all the people who worked at the Rainbow. All the customers knew her by name and would ask after her if she was not working.
She had become a local fixture. I was too. By proxy. I was Nora's 'geezer'.

Once, when I was working with one of the Orange People, I was asked to join in with them on one of their activities. Rupa, a very young, bubbly, and outgoing girl, tried to get me to go visit their Ashram.
'You should come, Ralphy,' she said while gazing into my eyes.
'The Bhagwan would love you! I'll show you what to do during our 'trance dance'.'

I gathered a 'trance dance' was something for which you might need instruction.

But, to be fair, the Orange People were not aggressive in their proselytizing. They didn't need to be. Just like the junkies on the streets, North London was full of Orange People in those days. They were not short on recruits. A lot of people were searching for something, anything, other than what they had. Some, I'm sure, are searching still.

I was heading out to work at the Rainbow one morning, when I saw Trevor walking on the pavement up ahead of me. He didn't notice me as I was following along behind him.
He was behaving strangely.
He'd stop suddenly and stoop down and pick something up off the pavement. He then took out a little plastic bag from his pocket and dropped it in.
Every few paces he would stop, stoop, and drop something again into the bag he carried.
As I got closer to him, I could see what he was doing.
He was picking up used cigarette butts off the ground. He'd look for one that still had some tobacco remaining and then put it into his bag.
I said nothing. He never saw me witnessing him do that.

Poverty can be very good for recycling. Even a previously smoked 'fag' has a second life. Nonetheless, seeing him do that made me shudder.
'That's a dirty way to save money on tobacco,' I thought to myself.

I once ran into Trevor as he was exiting a betting shop near where we lived.
'Hi, Trev,' I said. 'How was your luck?'
He just shook his head with that wan expression on his face.
He had an 'All Alone in the World' air about him.
'Your horse didn't come in?' I asked.
'You haven't seen the landlord hanging about, have you, mate?' he asked in reply.
I told him I hadn't.
'Ta,' he said as he wandered off.

I never told Nora about either incident. I didn't think it was important.

I had not been inside Trevor's flat before. I'd see him in the hall or out on the streets sometimes, as I say.
And sometimes too when waiting desperately in the hallway for the bathroom we all shared together.
But I'd never been in his flat. Nora had, but she was far more sociable than I could ever hope to be.
She was what they call a 'People Person'.

One night, Nora and I were in bed sleeping. Well, I was sleeping anyway, until I was disturbed by a voice in the dark.
'Listen, Ralphy! Listen! It's Trevor! He's crying!'
'Huh?'
'Listen!'
I listened. Sure enough, I could make out what sounded like male wailing. And whimpering too.

'You know what he has in his kitchen cupboards, Ralphy?'
I told her I didn't.
'Nothing. He has nothing in there. I saw him this morning. He'd left his door open. He was in his guard uniform and sitting on the edge of the bed crying.'
Resignedly, I asked, 'What did you do?'
'I looked in on him through the door. I went in and said, you know, 'Hey! Trev! What's the matter?' And I offered to make him a cup of coffee. He just sat there with his head in his hands and sobbing. So, I looked through his cupboards for some coffee, but there wasn't any. There wasn't anything at all in there.'
'Maybe he eats at work, Nora,' I grunted.

Now I was wide awake.

'You know why he had left his door open?' Nora asked, despite my lack of interest. 'Because it was freezing in his flat. He has no money for the meter. It's been really chilly too lately. He left his door open to try to get some heat from the hallway. Isn't that awful?'
'Awful, Nora,' I said.
'He had to ask me for bus fare so he could get to work. I think that was why he was crying. He didn't even have the fare to get to his job!'

I didn't say anything to that at first.

'He doesn't have a penny!' she added.

She was sounding more and more upset.

'Well, that can't be,' I finally said as I tried to calm her down.

'Don't give him bus fare. He works every hour under the sun. And under the moon too.'

'He told me he missed work before, because he didn't have the money to get there,' she replied.

'So where's all his money going?' I asked blearily.

'He didn't say,' Nora said.

There was a long silence.

Just as I thought I could drift back off back to sleep, Nora said, 'You have a talk with him, Ralphy.'

Trevor was our accidental neighbor. It's not like he was kin or anything.

But Nora could not accept people suffering around her.

Especially when she didn't know why.

I knew she wouldn't let go of this.

To be honest, it was difficult to find time to talk to Trevor.

Even if I had fancied doing so.

I was busy working to survive and going to classes. Most days I'd be gone from seven in the morning until after ten at night.

Except for Sundays.

And Nora's life was like that too.

We barely had time for one another let alone for Trevor and his problems.

One Sunday morning, Nora came racing in from the hall.

'He's in the 'loo'! Go out there! Wait for him. This is a perfect time for you to talk to him. Go! Go!' she said as she tried to push me out the door.

I went out into the hallway and waited.

When Trevor came out, enveloped in cigarette smoke, I was more than shocked.

I hadn't seen him for a couple of weeks.

He looked grey. Were it possible, I'd say he looked even thinner than before. And balder too.

150

He obviously hadn't shaved for days and days. He looked like he had been out living on the street.

'Trev, I need to have a word with you,' I began. 'Can I come in?'

He blinked at me in confusion.

'OK,' he shrugged.

I followed him into his flat. We stood there together on the floor. His flat was much larger than ours, but furnished as poorly as our flat was too.

I looked around. There, on his countertop, was a single 'tin' of baked beans. The lid hadn't been removed completely. A spoon was sticking out of the part that had.

It looked like it had been there for days.

The entire flat smelled like an ashtray.

Trevor went over to his bed where he had tossed his tobacco and rolling papers.

I wondered if that was more of his 'street tobacco' that I had seen him collecting.

He rolled one up and turned to look at me.

'I have to go to work soon,' he said. 'What's on your mind?'

I told Trevor about Nora and the bus fare. I told him I saw him collecting 'fag ends' off the street. I told him we noticed he wasn't himself lately. I asked if he was OK.

I said, 'Look, Trev, we're neighbors. Sometimes when something's not right, it helps to talk about it. Maybe some new ideas will come out of it. Who's to say?'

He looked at me as if he had the whole world bottled up within him. His eyes were shiny as if they were on the verge of tears.

Then he said, 'They cut off my phone. I can't talk to her.'

He dragged on his 'fag' like he was angry at it.

'Who can't you talk to, Trev? Why'd they cut off your phone?'

'Elaine. I can't talk to Elaine. And she needs me. She was telling me about a dolphin broach she saw at the Hilton's gift shop.'

'Slow down, Trev. Why'd they cut off your phone?'

'I can't pay the bill!'

'I thought you could pay in installments, if you fell behind.'

'No, it was for over six thousand pounds. They're taking me to court.'

151

'Six thousand pounds? Your phone bill was for over six thousand pounds?' I asked him in astonishment.
I didn't know if I was going to burst out laughing, it was so absurd.

'I haven't been able to pay it for months. I have to send my wages to Elaine. She needs it for her kids. She has two kids. She was saying they need things like band uniforms and her husband's trying to take the kids away from her, because she has no job and has no money, but how's she supposed to get a job and have money when she has two kids to look after on her own?'
'Wait. You send her your wages?' I asked him for clarity's sake.
'That way she has proof that she has a regular income and then her husband won't have a leg to stand on in court,' he explained.

'But, Trev, what about your rent?' I enquired.
'I'm six months behind. I'm trying to avoid the landlord. I came home from work a couple days ago and this came.'
Trevor went over to a cardboard box and fished out a letter.
He handed it to me.
'Trev, this is a Notice to Vacate. He's evicting you.'
'I know. I know. I don't know what to do. They're warning me at work too. I miss some of my shifts, because I can't afford to get there. And they keep telling me I have to clean myself up, but I can't afford razor blades either.'

'Trev, Elaine…are you planning to move in with her?' I asked him carefully.
'That's what we were planning on the phone. Of course she said we'd have to wait until after the custody hearing. So we wouldn't upset the kids.'
'Uh huh,' I said.

I don't know. I hope you're thinking what I was thinking.
Otherwise, there are a lot more 'Trevors' out there than I care to think about.

'When did you last see Elaine, Trev?'
'At the hotel.'
'She's been back to your hotel?'
'No, that first time. When we met.'
'You haven't seen her since you first met?'

152

'No, but we talk on the phone every night. Well, we did. I have to call her! She's depending on me!'

'How did you two meet exactly?' I asked.
'At the hotel,' he said as if I were an idiot.
'At the hotel, yes, I know. But what happened? How did you meet?'
'Well, she came down from Manchester for one of those conventions,' Trevor said as he smiled in happy memory.
'She was staying at the hotel. She'd come in and walk by security and she'd always have a friendly word to say. So, after a few days, she made a point, she told me this later, of stopping by and asking me for directions somewhere. She said she really didn't need directions at all, but she could see I had a kind face, she said, and was drawn to me,' he continued.
'And the morning before she left, she said I was nothing like her husband who'd only grunt at her and didn't care about her or the kids. But she could see I cared. And she gave me her number and begged me to call her. And that's what I did.'

'How long have you been sending your wages to her?' I asked.
'As soon as I heard about the custody thing with the kids. She told me about that the first time I called her.'

An idea suddenly came to me.

'So you know her address, Trev?' I asked casually.
'Of course. She asks me to send her little things. Things she saw when she was down in London. She wants me to send her this dolphin broach she saw in the hotel gift shop. She asked me to do that for her the last time we spoke. I said that I would. But I can't. It costs over a hundred pounds. And I can't call her. She's probably checking the post everyday for her dolphin broach. I can't call her to say that it's not there yet!'

'So you have her address? OK, Trev, here's my advice to you. Hold some of your wages back for yourself this week and go up to Manchester and see her. But, Trev, don't tell her you're coming. Let it be a surprise.'

There was a pause.
A blank look passed over Trevor's face.
And then a 'light' came on.

'I get paid next Friday,' he said almost to himself. 'I could go and see her!'
And he suddenly stood up as if all the zest in the world was coursing through him.
He was instantly rejuvenated.
'Thanks, Ralphy! Cheers, mate!'
And he started ushering me toward the door.
'I have to go to work now,' he beamed happily.

And as quickly as that, I found myself back out in the hall.
'I guess he has bus fare,' I remember thinking to myself.

Nora pounced on me like a puma as I entered our flat.
'What did he say? You were in there a while! What did you say?'
'Ssshh, Nora,' I said as I nodded toward the hallway.
'Oh!' Nora said putting her hand in front of her mouth.
And she stood there and listened hard.
We soon heard Trevor fumble with his door, walk through the hall, and then go out the front door.

'OK! He's gone. What did he say?' Nora asked expectantly.
I told her what was going on.
'What a bitch,' she said.
Then I told her the advice I had given.
'Poor, Trev,' she sighed. 'I wonder what he'll find?'

One of the many classes I was taking was a ballet class at the Urdang Academy in Covent Garden. After class that Friday, the ballet mistress made an announcement. She told us that the Royal Opera were looking for 'Supers' to fill out crowd scenes. They wanted dancers and had been asking around all the ballet schools.
Katherine, the teacher, approached me.
'Ralphy, you should go audition. They need male dancers. I'm sure they'd use you. It only pays twenty pounds per performance though.'
'Twenty pounds,' I thought to myself. 'Only twenty pounds!'
'You have working papers, haven't you?' she asked.
I told her that I did not.
'That's a pity. They won't employ you without them.'

I had to walk all the way home after that disappointment too. I had money for the class, but not the fare home.
'Twenty pounds a show! Twenty pounds a show!' I kept muttering to myself as I walked and walked.
'Poverty trap!'

I was just turning into our street, when I saw Trevor on the other side of the pavement. He had a duffle bag in his hand.
'Trev!' I called out.
He looked around in three directions before he saw me.
'Are you off to Manchester then?' I asked.
He nodded with a big smile on his face and carried on walking.
'Good luck, mate!' I shouted after him.
Good luck.

When I walked into our flat, Nora was sitting at the table and listening to the radio.
She sat there by candlelight.
'Why aren't the lights on?' I asked her.
'I just got in myself, she said. 'I didn't have any money for the meter. Do you have any fifty 'p' pieces?'
'No, I had to walk home.'

As we sat there in the light of the candle, I told Nora that I had bumped into Trevor.
'I saw him when he was leaving,' she said.
'I've never seen him so happy. He was like a little kid.'

Nora and I both had to work double shifts at the Rainbow that Saturday.
It was always a mess there on Saturday mornings.
Nora had made 'Friday Night Poetry Readings at the Rainbow' the local hotspot and the place to be.
Poetry enthusiasts can be very messy, I've discovered.

There were cups, plates, and candle wax everywhere you looked.
All the tables and chairs had been scattered in every direction.
A tempest in a tearoom.
The sink was so full of dirty dishes that filthy pots and pans were dotted around on the floor awaiting collection.

155

That morning, I even found two junkies asleep at a table and two chairs outside the café.

Al fresco dining and reclining at the Rainbow.

Amarelle arrived late, as usual. She was struggling with something heavy wrapped in a blanket. I went over to help her.

'What is this thing?' I grunted as I carried it to the counter.

'It's a telly,' Amarelle said. 'Our neighbours bought a new one and gave us theirs. This is our old one. It's Wimbledon today. The Men's Final. We can watch the tennis later.'

Many of the people who ate at the Rainbow wouldn't have owned a television.

They'd watch it in a pub maybe.

Nora and I didn't have a television.

So it was a special treat for everyone.

Although Wimbledon was in full swing, it did not rain.

For some reason, in London, if two people pick up tennis rackets and walk out on to a court, especially at Wimbledon, it will rain.

But, unusually, that Saturday, it did not rain.

In fact, it was a fine day.

After the three of us had tackled the 'Poetry Crowd' aftermath, Amarelle had me arrange the telly so it would face most of our customers.

This involved a long and windy discussion. Both Amarelle and Nora loved discussing. Absolutely loved it.

I must have shifted that television here, and then over there, and back again at least eleven times.

'That's it!' Nora exclaimed finally, after I lugged it up onto a shelf where we normally kept superfluous kitchenware.

'Yes, that's perfect, Ralphy,' Amarelle concurred.

Word spread fast that the Rainbow had a Wimbledon connection.

When people heard they could watch the tennis while being served cheese sandwiches and cups of tea, they started flocking in.

Mostly they were 'Orange People'. I suppose a lot of Orange People were tennis fans.

Amarelle, Nora, and I started cooking lunch in preparation for the tennis rush.

We had to pause to serve the 'early birds' teas and coffees and beans on toast or my bogus granola.

I can still remember most of the luncheon menu we served that Saturday.

Cauliflower Soup 35p
Adzuki Bean Pie with Salad 50p
Choice of Omelettes 40p
Scalloped Potatoes and Cheese 40p
Cheese and Pickle Sandwiches 35p

And Rhubarb Crumble with Custard 30p

Nora wrote all that down in colored chalk on the blackboard so it looked like a rainbow.

While we were preparing the lunch fare, it started getting very busy. Amarelle had switched on the set and the BBC were showing highlights from earlier matches. They were airing excerpts of how the two finalists had reached the Final.

We were already doing a brisk trade. Once lunch was ready, it was non-stop. Amarelle or Nora would catch my eye during the rush and puff out their cheeks and look up at the ceiling in resignation. I imagine I was doing the same thing back at them.

As it grew closer to the Final itself, we were jam-packed. People were standing outside trying to get in. We'd have to shout out from the counter, 'Please! No more please!'

As I served yet another table, I could see there was a lot of chatting from the tennis pundits on the screen. But I couldn't hear a word they were saying over the café din. All I could see was their mouths moving.

But when the players themselves walked on to the court, our café clientele quieted down. Everyone wanted to watch the match. There were a few more last minute scrambled food orders, but most people's attention was now firmly fixed on the screen.

When a set had been concluded and there was a short pause in the match, everyone ordered something at the same time. It was madness. We raced around while serving plates of food and drink. We had to keep cooking too as we were running out of lunch items.

When the match was over, our café crowd thinned out dramatically. A few stayed behind to listen to the commentary team waffle on some more.
Amarelle, Nora, and I sat at a table together and had our lunch while things were slow.
The BBC News came on.

None of us paid much attention to the news. We sat there exhausted as we ate.

I guess I was daydreaming a bit. I don't know what I was thinking about when my attention was grabbed by a news bulletin on the television.
I caught it midway through.

'…and Andrew Marshall, thirty two, a member of Greater Manchester Fire Service, London Road Fire Station.
Elaine Boyd, thirty four, a Manchester estate agent, allegedly knew her attacker. She had once met Mr. Pyle previously in London.'

Then a photo of a smiling Trevor in his security guard uniform appeared on the screen.
I nudged Nora to turn around and look.

A BBC correspondent then came on to interview two senior policemen.
One, a Greater Manchester Police spokesman said, 'Initial reports suggest that late on Friday night Mr. Pyle had broken through the conservatory window of the home shared by Mr. Marshall and Ms. Boyd. He then armed himself with a knife he found in their kitchen and attacked them.'

Then, the Investigating Officer said, 'This is one of the most vicious and unprovoked attacks I've ever come across at a crime scene. Mr. Pyle was rushed to hospital, but died later from his self-inflicted wounds. Mr. Marshall and Ms. Boyd were repeatedly stabbed in the frenzied attack and died at the scene.'

When the BBC reporter gave Trevor's home address, one of our customers shouted out, 'He's a local geezer! What a nutter!'

They put Trevor's photo back on the screen and the newsreader said, 'Double Murder/Suicide in Manchester. More details on *BBC News at Ten.*'

There was no mention of any 'two kids' caught up in a custody battle. There was no mention of any children at all.

Nora sat there with her hands over her mouth. Her eyes were wild and darting.
Amarelle asked her, 'Is that the bloke you've been talking to me about?'
Nora nodded slowly in shock.
'Oh My God!' Amarelle said.
I just sat there as if all the blood had been drained away from me.

Nora and I walked home together after work. I don't think we said a word along the way. Nora was so upset that she was shivering. I put my arm around her shoulders to console her as we walked.
She was trembling. I was numb.
Trevor was dead.

The next day, the Sunday tabloids had a field day. Trevor's face was splashed across every newspaper's front page. As Nora and I walked past news kiosks, there he was smiling back at us.
The headlines were gruesome.

TREVOR 'THE BUTCHER' PYLE
Guard Carves Up Two in Kitchen Frenzy

NEVER TREVOR!
Suicide Guard Murders Manchester Couple

DOUBLE HOMOCIDE IN MANCHESTER!
Security Guard Pyle Dials 'M' For Murder

MANCHESTER BLOODBATH
'Trevor' Severs Two with Kitchen Knife
Pix Inside!

And each lurid headline was accompanied by that same smiling photo of Trevor.

The hotel must have released his work photo to the press. It was the same photograph that the BBC had used.

Later that day, while we were out walking, Nora saw that someone had discarded their Sunday paper in a bin and she ran over to retrieve it. We couldn't afford to buy our own.

We sat down on a bench in Waterlow Park and read about Trevor together.

'The police stated that Mr. Pyle had an 'obsessive relationship' with Ms. Boyd,' the newspaper report began.

'A preliminary report showed that he had inundated her with unwanted letters and gifts.

A spokesman for the police suggested that many of these letters and gifts found at the premises were unopened.

Police investigators opened these items and subsequently discovered many other letters from Mr. Pyle hidden in a kitchen cabinet. They were full of banknotes.'

Nora pointed that out with her finger for me to read.

'A neighbour, Charlotte Buckland, 27, claimed that Mr. Pyle had been harassing Ms. Boyd for months.'

'Elaine told me he would call her every single night. She said she had met him once when she was in London and somehow he got her number. She told him to sling his hook, but he refused to take the hint. She was frightened of him. Elaine said that she used to hang up on him, but he would just call her back again and again. So she started to leave the receiver off the hook, walk away, and then go to bed.

She said sometimes the next morning, when she went over to the phone to hang it back up, she could still hear him breathing on the other end. He just kept the line open all through the night.'

'Ms. Buckland further stated that Ms. Boyd was planning to change her number,' it read.

'Elaine said she was sick to the gills of it and was going to change her number, but then he stopped calling a week or so ago. She was so relieved. And now this! Poor Duck!'

160

'Mr. Malcolm Armstrong, 47, security manager at the Hilton on Park Lane where Mr. Pyle was employed as a security guard, claimed Mr. Pyle had been behaving unusually for the past few months.'

'Staff at the hotel were all concerned about Trevor,' Mr. Armstrong stated. 'All he would talk about was this Elaine, Ms. Boyd rather. Trevor did tend to get fixated on things. I felt sorry for the chap. He had become the butt of jokes among certain members of staff.'

'Mr. Armstrong pointed out that Mr. Pyle's work had been suffering over the past few months.'

'I caught him several times trying to use hotel phones at reception to place long distance calls. His attendance at work and his appearance too had become a problem in recent weeks. I was considering whether to let him go.'

There were other interviews with family members of the victims and more neighbors. The paper said that Trevor had neither relatives nor friends whom they could trace.
'He was put into care as an infant,' it read.
'He appears to have been a classic 'loner'.'

When Nora and I got back home, Trevor's flat was swarming with police.
Nora and I were both interviewed.
It was tricky. We were illegal aliens. We didn't want the police sniffing around our business.
Nora told the police that Trevor was having trouble with money. She said that she knew about Trevor and Elaine, because he told her about it.

I said very little myself. I told them that I knew Trevor was having trouble paying his rent. I said he kept mainly to himself.
I did not say that I was the one who suggested he go to Manchester and see Elaine.
It was a lie of omission.

I told myself that I could live with that.

I don't give advice anymore. People sometimes ask for my advice, but I am very careful about what I say to them. I listen. I am sympathetic. But I never tell them what they should do anymore. Ever.

And if I overhear someone else giving advice about something they couldn't possibly know all about, I cringe.

I remember me, so cocksure and such a wise-guy, as I set up Trevor to confront the woman who, I was convinced, had turned his life upside down.

I was sure he was being hoodwinked and I didn't like it. I was advising him to do what I wanted him to do.

Not what he needed to do. Because I didn't really know what he needed.

My own 'poverty of understanding' made my advice poor too.

I may not be the brightest on the planet, but I thought I knew that Elaine was taking poor Trevor for a ride. I thought he should know and at least have a chance to catch her in her lie.

I should have known better. You can never predict how people will react. You can never be sure how people interpret what is happening to them.

Sometimes, it's best to leave their delusions in peace. Even if those delusions ruin them. Like Trevor's ruined him.

We like to think people will learn from their mistakes.

We like to think that we will learn from ours.

Trevor would learn to be less trusting of people perhaps.

Or learn not to read so much into so little.

But that may not be so.

People may not be capable of learning from a mistake.

There may be a 'poverty of capability'.

Maybe Trevor, when he saw Elaine and her partner together, thought she was cheating on him and shattered his fantasy and so he murdered her and her fireman.

A true crime of passion.

I don't really know. But I do know there's a reason why people don't want to get 'involved' anymore.

We can't predict what will happen if we do.

I have to live with my part in the responsibility for the death of three people. It has put me off giving advice forever.

Elaine would have soon finished with Trevor had I not interfered. And Trevor would eventually have found his level again somehow. I should never have let myself become involved.

Secretly, even to myself, I blamed Nora for insisting that I do so.

But the secrets we hold from ourselves have a habit of revealing themselves in time.
The secret 'Rebel without a Cause' pops out in midlife inappropriately.
The secret 'Free Spirit' abandons and betrays their family.
The secret 'Resentment' makes a later forgiveness impossible.
And so, such secrets sow the weeds in our lives.

Was Elaine nothing more than a cold hearted 'scamstress'?
Was Trevor delusional and simply invented his 'relationship' with her?
Trevor's endless phone calls and gifts, solicited or otherwise, do suggest that he was obsessive.
Maybe Elaine lied to her neighbors about Trevor to cover her tracks.
None of them mentioned knowing anything about how Trevor's wage packets ended up in her kitchen cabinet.
It's possible that Trevor sent his earnings, without any prompting from Elaine, in a misguided attempt to buy her affections.
Maybe Trevor just read too much into nothing and conjured up his 'relationship' with Elaine out of fantasy and wishful thinking.
Or Elaine was just a dab hand at extracting money from vulnerable 'loners' by pleading poverty.
Perhaps there is some truth in all those scenarios.

I don't think I'll ever know the real truth of 'Trevor and Elaine'.

So, yes, this is a story about poverty.
Poverty comes in many shapes and many guises.
At any time. And anywhere.
And it's not always about money.

And that's the truth too.

STORY CHAPTER NINE

'THE TIGER OF TIRUPATHI'

I should kick off this story with the 'Bad News'.
Nora and I were going through what they call 'marital difficulties'.
But don't worry. I'm not about to go all maudlin on you.

I don't know exactly why we were going through marital difficulties.
Things were going well enough. We had just gained residency status
in Britain. We were free to stay and work.
We'd sprung the poverty trap in which we were ensnared.
We were no longer struggling to survive. We moved away from the
dark and miserable flat, where we were living, into a much larger and
nicer flat.
All of these positive developments happened by the dumbest of luck.
We should have been happy, but we were not.

I was taking ballet class at 'The Pineapple' in Covent Garden one
evening and, after class, one of the novice dance students approached
me.
'Are you a professional?' she asked me in an awestruck way.
'You're really quite splendid!'
She blushed so much I couldn't suppress my smile.

I told her that I had been professional when I lived in the States.
'I was in several dance companies there,' I told her. 'And theatre too.
But I can't work here legally, so all I'm left with now is taking
classes.'

I noticed that she was wearing her leotard back to front. That made
me chuckle to myself, because I used to make the same sort of dance
attire faux pas when I first began my studies. I remembered my
fellow novice, Larry, who would wear his dance belt the wrong way
around at the start.
It's a ballet rite of passage, I suppose, eventually to figure such
things out on your own.

'They should let you perform on stage here,' she protested.
'It's a waste of talent!'

I guess about a week or so after that, she approached me again after class.
'I was telling my father about you,' she began shyly. 'I told him it wasn't right that you couldn't be in dance companies here.'
I didn't know what to say. I just nodded.
Then she gave me a business card.
'Call my father. He's an immigration solicitor. He said he'd help you.'
'That's very kind of you,' I replied. 'But I wouldn't be able to afford an immigration solicitor! I can barely afford to take class!'
And then she said, 'No, no, Daddy will help you. He's an arts patron. He'll be happy to help. Call him!'
And she smiled, nodded bashfully, and walked away.

So, I called 'Daddy' and, sure enough, he was willing to help. A few meetings and a few forms filled in by him later and 'abracadabra' I had an application for a 'Right to Remain' in at the Home Office. And a few months after that, I was legal. And because Nora and I were married, she was legal too.

But, despite this great fillip to our fortunes, Nora and I decided, well, I decided, that maybe we needed a 'Break' to see 'How we really felt about each other'.

I 'moved' into our spare room, stopped attending the jazz class we took together, ate alone, and basically kept myself to myself.
I was not sure what Nora was up to, but I'd hear her come home late at night sometimes. She'd fumble with her keys at the door and mumble under her breath as she made her way into the bathroom. I figured she was out drinking with some of her dance pals.

It was not a happy time. An easier time perhaps, but not a happier one.

And it just so happened that it was during this 'Nora and Ralphy Break', when I first came to know Ted.

I had read a notice in *The Stage* that a producer, Ted, was looking for actors to do a demo of a radio play he had written. He was looking for 'Genuine American Accents'.

I contacted him, introduced myself, and we arranged to meet at a London pub in Holborn called the 'Princess Louise'. And after talking about his radio play in more detail and sharing a few drinks, he offered me the leading role.

The recording went well. Ted was happy. And we became friends.

I discovered later that Ted was a bit of a 'Star'. You may never have heard of him, but he was a successful actor who worked at all the major theatres in Britain. Like the Royal Shakespeare Company and the National Theatre and in the main West End theatres too.

He was also a generally knowledgeable and capable guy. A 'Star' in everything, but public adulation.

While most other actors 'rested', because they could find no work, Ted found too much of it. He was always in demand. He was always on the go.

A few weeks after we recorded his radio play, Ted and I met again for a drink at the 'Princess Louise'. He was telling me that he had just been offered a year's contract on a big West End musical. But he had a problem. He was already involved with a London acting company who were rehearsing a play for a three month tour to India. And the West End mob wanted him to start now. Or never.

As he was explaining this, he suddenly stopped. It was obvious he was mulling over something. Ted glanced up at the ceiling, looked back down, had a gulp of his beer, looked at me, and said, 'Why not? You could do it.'

'Do what?' I asked him.

'You can do the Indian tour and replace me. It's a Yank play anyway. Some Neil Simon froth. You'd be perfect. Then I'm free to take the West End contract. I'll call the director of the Indian tour first thing tomorrow. I'm sure he'll be happy to have you.'

This all came as a shock of a surprise. And as Ted and I parted, he said, 'I'll let you know.'

And as ridiculously improbable as all this sounds, somehow it all worked out.

I was good to go. To India.

Now, normally, I would never do something like that. I mean something that would have taken me away from Nora for so long. A three month tour of India without Nora by my side? No, I would never consider such a thing. I had turned down countless other tours before in America, if I couldn't take Nora along with me.
Not that I ever told Nora about that.
But because I felt we needed this 'Break', I went for this one.

I went to rehearsals and everything was organized and professional. I was happily welcomed and immediately made to feel part of the team.
Everybody's happy! Everybody's going on a Five Star Tour of India! And on very good money.

The director, Marcus, treated me like an old friend.
'As soon as Ted suggested you, Ralphy, I knew you'd be perfect.'
Marcus was a 'professional's professional'. He was both liked and knew what he was doing. This is far less common in the theatre than you might think.

The Indian producer was a fabulously wealthy, Western popular-culture lover. He loved everything about it and couldn't get enough of it. He was always asking me if I knew someone famous.
'Do you know Michael Jackson? Did you ever meet Madonna when she's in London?' But, I'm afraid, I always had to disappoint him with that.

He was from a fine, old, distinguished family. I think they had a link to the old pre-British Empire 'Maharaja' system.
He was also eye-poppingly generous.

Everything was perfect. Everything was fine.
Except for me and Nora of course. That was not fine.
I never even mentioned the Indian tour to her. I just grunted casually in passing that I was 'going away' for a while.

Now, my memory is a bit fuzzy here. I cannot remember if Marcus, the director, was fired, or if he walked out over some arrangement that didn't pan out, or if he had been offered a bigger job elsewhere. All I clearly recall is that I went into rehearsal one day and he was gone.

And the next thing I knew, the Maharaja is announcing to all assembled that I am the new director.

'Tiger will lead you now.'

(He always called me 'Tiger'.)

He took me to one side and said, 'You can do it, Tiger.'

He then offered me an even better contract on better money.

So I now took on two roles, both actor and director.

I should add that part of the contract with the Maharaja stipulated that we were all to turn our Duty Free allowance over to him.

India in 1988, for that is when this all happened, made the import of certain Western luxury goods and Hi-Tech items illegal. Things like cameras and branded alcohol could only be brought in by tourists with a tourist limit. I was to bring a bottle each of Martini Extra Dry and Johnnie Walker Black.

The other actors were asked to bring in similar items for the Maharaja.

I guessed he liked to party and entertain his guests in a 'Western Style' as well.

It was nearly time to go. Rehearsals were at an end. I'd had a series of jabs and pricks to prevent me from succumbing to some awful disease. I had strange Visas put into my passport. I had anti-malarial pills. I had a copy of 'A Rough Guide to India'.

I was Third World ready.

I don't think I even saw Nora on the day we took the flight.

We flew into Delhi, ran the gauntlet of hundreds of beggars, got into several taxis, and made our way to the hotel. I remember staring out the cab window at the wondrous, new sights all around me and wishing Nora were with me to share it. I began to think I had been an idiot for suggesting we should take a 'Break'.

This was to be my first long adventure without Nora, since we married fourteen years previously.

I mention this, because my worry about us may have affected what happened later. I don't know myself for sure. It was on my mind though. I must admit.

168

It wasn't long before I started missing Nora terribly and began to write to her almost every single day. This involved finding the local post office wherever we were. These were pre-email days. I can tell you that the Indian Post Office is deserving of a story all on its own, but I won't tax you with that here.

The theatre company was being co-sponsored by the most luxurious hotels in India.
As I was the director, or 'Mr. London Director' as hotel staff insisted on addressing me, I was afforded the finest rooms wherever we went. Some of the hotel suites were larger than Nora's and my London flat. Opulence was the rule.

Our play, *Plaza Suite*, would be performed in the largest theatres in India and also in the luxury hotels where we were staying. The hotels would spend a fortune building a replica set in their large banquet rooms.

One of my responsibilities was to travel ahead of the rest of the group and inspect the state of the stage-set where we were next due to perform. I was accompanied by Sammy, the technical director. He was also Indian.
After inspecting the set, I would talk to the stagehands.
Inevitably, something would be amiss like stage doors hung at odd angles or half the back wall not yet erected. 'Little' things like that. In calm, measured tones I'd explain what needed doing and that time was of the essence.
And then Sammy would re-explain in the local dialect by screaming loudly and throwing hammers around dangerously.
And the sets always ended up just as we needed them to be.
Sammy and I. We were a team.

And so the tour went very smoothly. Delhi to Goa to Bombay to Madras and elsewhere.

Once I had completed the set inspection, my time was my own. The rest of the theatre company wouldn't arrive until the following morning. I'd look a few things up in my 'Rough Guide' and then run them past Sammy or the hotel staff to see what they thought. 'Should I go here?' I'd say, while showing them something I saw in my guidebook. 'Or what about here? Or maybe visit here?'
That was my usual patter.

And then one of my guidebook options would be seized upon. For example, 'Oh! Mr. London Director! You must go to that market! My cousin is there! You simply must go! He has the finest silks! He will treat you right! You will get a good deal!'

And I would go to that market. I would look for their cousin. Even if I had no interest in silk. I would go for the adventure. Sometimes I would go well off the tourist trail. Even the rickshaw or tuk-tuk drivers would ask if I was sure I wanted to go 'there'.

And then later, once the other actors had arrived, we'd sit in the hotel bar together and I'd tell them the things I had done. I'd show them some of the little treasures I had bought. I'd tell them the story about how I came by them.

And I think it was this that gave the Maharaja and his colleagues the idea that I was one to take risks and sally forth on my own.

'Fearless Tiger'.

On closing nights, after the run of the play in a city was over, I would go up to the hotel suite of the Maharaja and talk about how it went and what to expect in the next city on our tour.

One night, in Madras, when I went to his room for this purpose, there were about half a dozen other people there. They were all extremely wealthy Indians. I discovered that they were the hotel owners and the theatre owners. One was a big 'Bollywood' producer. The play was making them a pile of money, so they were all in an excellent mood.

'We have a smash hit on our hands, Tiger!' one of the hotel owners drunkenly teased me while mussing up my hair.

My only real worry was the actors adding more and more 'business' on stage for laughs. I shared my concern with the producers. The show was now running fifteen minutes longer than when we opened. That's rarely a good thing in the theatre, but they all laughed away my concerns.

'Tiger! It's perfect! Just enjoy! Enjoy!'

Then, quite unexpectedly, the Maharaja announced to this super-rich set that the following day was my birthday. I do not know how he found that out, but find it out he certainly did.

One of them exclaimed, 'We must do something for Tiger! His birthday! Tiger, what do you want?' And they all fell into conversation about what I should do on my birthday.

Then the youngest member of this fabulously wealthy group said, 'Tirupathi! Tiger must go to Tirupathi!' And that suggestion seemed to trump all the other suggestions.

I had to go there. 'You simply must!'

But the Maharaja said, 'No, Tiger cannot go to Tirupathi. Tirupathi is closed to Westerners. They won't let him in.'

And they started to argue, fueled as they were on the Indian version of Johnnie Walker Black, the Duty Free Johnnie Walker long since gone.

'It's Tiger! Tiger can talk himself into anywhere!' One of them insisted.

'It's been closed to Westerners for more ten years!' countered the Bollywood producer.

But finally they decided that I 'must' go to Tirupathi and that I would be allowed to enter there.

'Let us see if there are strings to be pulled,' the Maharaja said mysteriously as a final word.

I went back to my own room.

Tirupathi, by the way, is a Temple near Madras. Madras is called Chennai now, but it was still Madras when I was there. Tirupathi is the site of the Temple of Sri Balaji.

There was a tiny mention of it in my 'Rough Guide', but not much else. The guidebook also said it was closed to Westerners.

The next day was a day off. It was my birthday and I had no responsibilities until the following day when Sammy and I had to fly in advance to Bombay, now Mumbai, but still Bombay when I was there.

I awoke that morning and stumbled over to the bathroom near the front door of the hotel suite. When I looked, I saw an envelope had been shoved under my door.

It was full of cash. Lots of it. And with it were several tickets. One was for a bus coach and two others were entrance tickets to Tirupathi.

I looked at my watch. According to the bus ticket, I had half an hour to get on it. I threw my things on, ran out the door, hailed a cab, and told the driver to take me to the bus stop.

I was going to Tirupathi.

By the time I arrived, there was already a long line of pilgrims waiting to take the bus to the Temple. I was the one and only Westerner in the group.

The Maharaja and his friends seemed to know everyone and their influence was powerful. They must have sent word that I was coming. Everyone was deferring to me and offering me treats. Some wanted to take my photograph.

When the coach arrived, the bus driver took my ticket and then insisted that I sit in the front seat just behind him.
'Mr. London Director, you sit here.'
The others were simply crammed in and sat or not depending on their luck.
But I was treated like some very important special guest who deserved special concessions.
It made me feel like I was sticking out even more.

The bus journey was a long and tortuous one. We travelled on back roads in very poor condition. Tirupathi was not an easy place to reach. A true pilgrimage demands a 'Pilgrim's Progress', I suppose. Occasionally we would stop to stretch our legs at some roadside drinks stand. Some of my fellow travelers would ask me for my autograph or ask if I'd pose in yet more photographs with them. This was getting embarrassing.

As we grew closer to our destination, I saw many other pilgrims out walking on the road to get there. And then a passenger behind me said, 'Many thousands come to Tirupathi daily. Any wish made in front of the idol of Sri Balaji will be granted.'
He then handed me his business card.
'If you are looking to distribute carpets in London, we should talk.'

Our bus started to climb steeply uphill. The road seemed to ribbon around the mountain it was climbing. We must have passed thousands of pilgrims as they climbed the hill to Tirupathi on foot.

Finally, our bus arrived at our destination and I was greeted by the greatest chaos I have ever experienced.
Our bus pulled into an area where there were scores and scores of other parked buses.

Everyone was very excited. Everyone stopped speaking English too and so I had no clue what was going on. The bus driver took one of my remaining tickets from my morning envelope. He signaled for me to follow him while every other person on our coach ran off to a series of side buildings.

The driver took me toward a statue in the middle of a broad central plaza.

'You wait here,' he said.

I saw him walk over to some ticket collectors standing at the Temple entrance at the top of a long set of stairs carved into the rock. The bus driver was pointing at me and talking and gesticulating rapidly as he showed my ticket to the collectors.

'It's good, Mr. London Director,' he said when he returned. 'It's good. They will allow you to enter.' That was easy, I thought. He pointed to my wrist watch.

'We return in three hours. You must not be late.'

And then he too meandered off toward one of the side buildings where the others had gone.

I was on my own.

I looked around the plaza. Everything was carved from the mountain rock face. The statues, the paving stones, the steps, were all sculpted from the same blue-grey soapstone.

I could hear people sounding conch horns. There was the smell of incense everywhere. All around the perimeter of the wide plaza were hundreds and hundreds of stalls selling incense, incense burners, candles, and images of Sri Balaji. They were all doing a brisk business.

I looked over to the side buildings where my bus coach group had gone. Filing out from their exits were pilgrims all with their heads shaven. Men, women, and children.

Some had different colored powered dyes on their hairless heads. Everyone was starting to look like everyone else.

I discovered later that having one's head shaved was auspicious and helped in making a successful request of Sri Balaji. But I did not know that at the time.

At the time, I did not know what to think.

I could no longer tell who had been in my group or not, so I made my way over to the Temple entrance on my own. I took out my envelope. There was one ticket remaining. It read, 'Special Darsham'. I showed that to the ticket collectors and they ushered me through the entrance gate and down the steep stone stairs to the Temple below.

The Temple itself was also carved from the same mountain soapstone. Surrounding it were wire caged 'holding' areas. I noticed that everyone was walking toward these cages so I joined them, but as I tried to enter one, I was rebuffed by a custodian. He looked at my ticket and then pointed over to his left to indicate that was where I should be heading.

As I walked in that direction, I looked into the other cages. They were all crammed full with people. Every cage was packed. Pilgrims would remain in these holding areas until given the signal that their particular cage group was now free to enter the Temple proper. When I reached my 'Special Darsham' cage though, I noticed that it was not full. Not only that, but there were blue plastic seats in the cage. None of the other holding areas had seating. I gave my ticket to the custodian there and went into the wire cage and sat down.

'You are very blessed to be able to come here,' said a man sitting beside me.
'Westerners used to be able to come here, but the hippies brought their drugs and noise and disrespected the Temple. They do not know how to show reverence.'
I nodded.
'Don't forget, if you want top carpets in London, you must call me.'
It was my friend from the bus. Without his hair, I did not recognize him.

We sat there for about fifteen minutes. Another man gave me his business card. He could cater for any event. 'Even in London, Sahib.'

And then we heard the signal that it was our turn to enter. We all stood up and started filing toward an arch carved in the stone. When we walked through, the pathway was divided by a wire fence. We, perhaps fifty of us, were on one side while on the other side were pilgrims from other cages. On their side, I will try not to exaggerate, were perhaps five thousand people head-shaved and shoved together.

As we walked with plenty of arm-swinging room, I watched in amazement at the throng on the other side. People were holding up babies to avoid the crush as the infants urinated in the air. But I was with the 'elite'. It was not something I was used to.

On entering the Temple itself, I must admit to going into a state of shock. It was so incredibly beautiful. Tirupathi is one of the very richest temples in all of India. Everything was made of solid gold. The most stunning statuary, the most exquisite ornaments, and the finest jewels I ever laid my eyes upon.

Essentially the Temple is a cave carved into the rock. There is a grotto there that is the main attraction for the pilgrims. For it is at the end of this grotto where the image of Sri Balaji rests and the pilgrims' requests could be made. The grotto is accessed through a narrow pathway leading off from the main part of the Temple. Before I joined the group trying to enter the grotto, I watched as men in lungis raked huge piles of cash offerings in large cages and separated the notes.

I joined the grotto line. There were other men in lungis tending small fires on the steep stone walls of the grotto. I made my way forward step by slow step.
As I grew closer, I could see that there were two custodians standing on either side of Sri Balaji's statue. They would wait a moment, while someone looked at the statue, and then push them away. I thought that was odd, until it was my turn.

Sri Balaji's statue is stunning. In other words, if you see it, you will be stunned.
You cannot move. It is like your mind is trying to figure out what it is seeing. The god's eyes are covered with translucent gauze. The statue itself is garlanded in flowers and jewels and gleaming gold spun cloth. Row upon row of chains of precious stones are draped over the statue's shoulders. In one of his hands was perhaps the largest and most perfect emerald I ever saw.
And then I too am being shoved out of the way.

The statue is at the end of the grotto. Once I had been shoved away, I looked and saw that there was another narrow pathway leading back to the Temple.

175

I made my way along that path. From the high steep rock walls of the grotto, Temple servants came down to offer pilgrims water from a ladle.

When they offered some to me, I shook my head 'no'.

Not in a 'No, I don't want any of your contaminated water' kind of way, but more of a 'No, I am not worthy' kind of way.

I did not want to disrespect what was going on. I am not Hindu. I did not want to pretend I was something I was not. I could feel the reverence of others and I did not want to make light of that.

But when I refused the water, something very strange happened. There was much chattering from the Temple servants. An involved discussion was going on and then one of the servants picked up something and climbed down the rock face on to the path where I was standing.

I do not know what he said, but he made an announcement to the other pilgrims.

He then proceeded to place a silver crown on my head.

I could only grab a quick glance before my 'crowning'. I saw my crown was made up of what looked like, bizarrely enough, carved silver feet. I was in shock. I didn't know what to make of it.

What I did know was that suddenly everyone was running up to me and hugging and kissing me. I was mobbed. Dozens and dozens of shaven-headed pilgrims embraced me. Eventually, another of the Temple servants removed my 'crown' and I walked down the narrow path out of the grotto and back into the main Temple.

I was a confused 'King for the Day'.

I admit that I was a little shaken. I wasn't expecting anything like that. I felt moved. I felt part of a very important thing. I felt conspicuous by my presence.

I walked into the central part of the Temple. On one side were some tall canvas 'chutes' that fed into wire cages. I saw people drop money offerings down the chutes. I took out a fifty rupee note and dropped it in. And then it happened again. Pilgrims were coming up to me and hugging me. A Temple servant approached me and gave me some lentils wrapped in a leaf and tied off with stick piercings. He indicated that I should eat that. I did so, despite being warned a hundred times not to eat food prepared away from our hotel.

But it was fine.

I still have that little leaf basket to this very day.

I am not sure how long I was in the Temple. It all happened in a surreal and mystical blur. I remember walking outside and making my way back up the stone stairs. I stopped at one of the stalls and bought a few souvenirs.

There were 'wig stalls' where you could buy back your shorn locks or someone else's. Tirupathi businessmen do not miss a trick. The wig stalls were all doing a booming business.

Then it struck me that I did not know how I could find our bus again. I remember wandering around about two hundred, identical, flower festooned buses in their special parking area. It was silly of me not to have checked where we were parked before I headed off to the Temple. Luckily, our driver, now hairless, finally saw me and I got on the bus, sat down in my seat behind the driver, and we began the long journey home.

Sammy once told me, while we were inspecting the stage-set in Goa, that the Maharaja lived in Madras in a huge 'compound' with fifteen bedrooms and assorted side buildings and guest houses. There were armed guards at the entrance gate.

'It's a palace, Tiger! As wondrous as the Taj Mahal!' Sammy exclaimed excitedly.

The Raj Buckingham Palace!'

But, unlike Sammy, I had never been invited to his home.

Usually, the Maharaja stayed in the same hotel as the theatre group, even when we were in Madras where his 'compound' was located. But when I got back to the hotel, after the visit to the Temple, there was a message waiting for me at reception. It was from the Maharaja.

'Happy Birthday, my Fearless Tiger! Tonight, we celebrate!' It read. They were going to have a birthday party for me that night at his home. 'Together, we shall mark your special day!'

There was about an hour before his car would come to collect me and the other actors according to his note.

I shook myself to get a 'second wind'. A birthday party.

It was going to be a long night.

When we arrived, I could clearly see that an enormous fuss had been made on my behalf. There were dozens of important people there from business, movies, and the government.

The British and American ambassadors were there too. I was flabbergasted.

As soon as I entered what could only be described as a palace, Sammy was spot-on about that, the Maharaja and the others involved in recommending I go to Tirupathi wanted to hear the whole story.
'Tell us, Tiger! Leave out nothing!'
So, I did. I told them all about my journey there and my 'silver feet crowning' and the kissing and hugging too.
They all laughed and slapped their thighs until I thought they'd fall over in exhaustion.
'Yes, of course! The silver-footed crown!' the Maharajah said with a smile. 'I had forgotten. Whoever wears the crown, Tiger, will be forever protected by the gods. You are under the feet of the gods now!' I never saw the Maharajah laugh so hard.
'But, Tiger, you didn't shave your head!' the Bollywood producer added through his own tears of laughter.
'The next time we will send you to Ranthambhore!'
(That's a Tiger Sanctuary. Ha-Ha.)

A huge birthday cake was brought out with great ceremony. It was rendered in an elaborate tiger shape. It was very cleverly made and big enough to serve all of my birthday celebrating throng. Everyone sang to my good luck and good fortune in an Indian birthday song I had never heard before.
The Maharaja walked over with his wife. She was beautiful, articulate, and enchanting. Of course.
'This is Tiger, my darling,' he said as he kissed her cheek.
'Tiger will amuse you! Tiger, tell Anjula about your day at Tirupathi,' he laughed.
'Tiger, you went to Tirupathi?' Anjula asked me. She looked shocked. 'You were allowed to enter?'
The Maharaja's eyes were gleeful. 'Amuse her, Tiger!'
And he laughed again and went elsewhere to mix.

So, I told Anjula about Tirupathi and how it was suggested I go and how I got there and what happened when I did.
As I did so, she shook her head back and forth and smiled in disbelief. Anjula was a class act.
'Tiger,' she said, 'My husband and I are Brahmin and the Temple of Sri Balaji is very important to us. It was my family ancestors who donated the emerald that sits in his hand.'

She was very pleased that I had managed to go there.

'My husband insisted that he could gain you entrance, but I did not think it possible.' But gain me entrance, he did.

Anjula looked down and bit her lower lip. I could see she was contemplating something.

'There is something I must show you,' she finally said.

And she beseeched me to stay just where I was until she returned.

'I'll be but a moment.' And she excused herself and went off.

When she came back she was holding a fine, silver double-hinged picture frame. And on opening the frame, two exquisite paintings appeared. One on each side of the frame.

'This one is of Sri Balaji and the other is of his wife,' Anjula explained to me.

'She has her own Temple at the foot of her husband's hilltop Temple.' The little paintings looked very old.

'You should have this, Tiger,' she said and she closed the frame and thrust it into my hand. I just stood there, bowled over, with the frame in my hand. I didn't know what to say.

'Thank you,' I finally stammered.

Years later, I gave Anjula's generous gift to a Hindu friend of mine in London. He was having rotten luck with his business. I thought it might change things around for him. My only regret is that now I do not have the silver frame to help convince you that my story is true. But it is true nonetheless.

When our tour was coming to an end, the Maharaja said he had arranged a 'special treat' for me. He handed me an envelope, again stuffed with cash, and an Air India ticket to Bombay *(Mumbai)*. His friend, the Bollywood producer, was going to meet me there and give me a personal tour of Bollywood. I met all the major Indian movie stars, even though I did not know who they were.

It was a 'special treat' indeed.

And then I flew back home to London and Nora.

I imagine you have guessed what 'wish' I made at Sri Balaji's Temple. But my wish was not granted.

Nora and I did not overcome our 'marital difficulties'.

Perhaps I should have shaved my head.

STORY CHAPTER TEN

'THE MONDRIAN PROJECT'

I don't want to tell you this story.
It's a tale full of betrayal, illicit encounters, double-dealing, and kinky sex, although that depends somewhat on how you might define the adjective 'kinky'.

If you care for such fare, then by all means read on. Just remember that what you might find titillating and exciting is, to me, a sad and deeply regretted memory.
I know I am going to come off smelling like soiled nappies or diapers or baby disposables as well. Whatever you call them, they all smell the same.

I am sure I will do my best to excuse what happened, but happened it did, and no matter how much 'spin' I put on it, that will always be true.

My first excuse is that Nora and I were no longer sleeping under the same roof while much of what I will relate to you here took place.
She and I were separated and my intimate life with her was separated too. We still were in one another's constant company throughout the day, but at night we slept apart and alone.

It would be easy to say that was the reason why I went off the rails and did things I would normally never do, but even I don't believe that anymore.

I guess I better start at the beginning so you'll have a bit of background.

Nora and I were still married and living in London. We had started a theatre company there. It was a lot of responsibility and had a high stress factor too. Although we were semi-separated, we still ran the theatre together.
Nora and I were together and not together, if that makes any sense.

180

Running our theatre was a lot of hard, unrelenting work for little reward.

Raising money was always an issue. The Theatre Landlord wanted money, the Business Rates Department wanted money, and so did all the various electricians and builders and artists upon whom we relied.

But we ourselves made no money. I could say that was not our goal. I could say that having a theatre was reward in itself.

And that's true too.

Ours was an 'Alternative Theatre'. Not mainstream. A 'Fringe Venue', as they say in London. We produced new plays, dance concerts, music gigs, and experimental performances and, as a result, we took on every 'Stray Cat' that came through the door.

'Stray Cats' were what we called people who were talented, but could not find a home at which to exercise that talent.

For instance, there was the eccentric, yet wildly creative, milliner I met at a market. She created hats that you'd need the brazen exhibitionism of a Pop Star Diva to wear. She soon discovered a flair for set-design while working with us.

And then there was the 'Mad Composer' who was extremely gifted, but utterly unemployable. He had no social graces at all, but we stuck by him and he created some magnificent sound scores for us.

And too, there were the many, many actors, dancers, and musicians who just didn't fit in anywhere else, but thrived in our company.

But perhaps the 'strayest' of all the 'Stray Cats' was Silent John.

He was a self-proclaimed artist I met one day at a café. He was drawing in a sketch book and I went over to him and asked if I could have a look. His work was impressive and unique, but also strange in the 'wrong' sort of way that made it both naïve and non-commercial. I put him to work with our set painting crew.

He was known as 'Silent John', because he refused to speak aloud. He would only communicate by writing little messages on a battered black notepad he carried in his pocket.

Silent John had broken into and then squatted a condemned house overlooking a park. There was a heavy steel door over what was once the front door and the windows had all been boarded over.

Red and white Council notices on the front door and windows forbade entry.

When we needed him for work, we'd have to go over there and throw stones three times at one of the boarded windows.

Nora called them 'signaling stones'.

He'd eventually come out and, saying nothing of course, accompany us to the theatre.

So, at our theatre, if it was unusual, we tried it.

And, of course, we gained neither money nor fame for our efforts. And our efforts were considerable.

We produced a lot of shows. Nora might choreograph a dance concert. I might write and produce a new play. And the rest of the time, bands, raves, and club nights kept us on the go. Something was on every single day and night even if that something was a wedding reception for an Angolan couple or a birthday celebration for an Icelandic poet who had hired our venue.

Nora and I had no life other than that theatre.

It demanded and consumed all our energies.

Despite all this, Nora and I decided to expand. Our plan was to take a play I had just written about the Dutch painter, Mondrian, and produce it in Amsterdam.

Pan-European arts projects were all the rage in the early 90's, when this story I am relating to you here took place, and the European Union had a policy to promote such activities.

We applied for and received a bursary from the Netherlands Cultural Ministry to develop the project and fly to Amsterdam to do just that. I don't know about now, but at the time the Dutch were extremely open-minded about artistic endeavors. Even though neither Nora nor I had a Dutch connection, the Dutch Cultural Attaché still agreed to sponsor our project.

'Keep us abreast of developments,' is all the Cultural Attaché, Ton DeVries, requested.

About a week after the Dutch bursary money arrived, Nora and I flew to the Netherlands.

We had never been to Holland before. Nora, however, had once performed in London with an English dancer named Janet. She now lived and worked in Amsterdam and Nora arranged it so that we could stay with her.

Janet, I soon discovered, was an extremely disciplined dancer and quite strict on herself.
Nora and I would allow ourselves the occasional treat, the odd beer or chocolate bar, but Janet would have none of it. She carried herself with dignity and perfect posture at all times.

After we arrived and were settled, Janet took us on a walking tour and showed us the 'Melkweg', a huge Dutch club, the Van Gogh Museum, and the Amsterdam theatre district.
'All the main theatre venues are located here in the same district,' she told us. 'If your show is coming here, it's bound to be performed at one of these theatres.'
Nora jotted down the names of all the theatres we passed.
'I'm performing a dance concert next season at that one,' Janet informed us as she pointed out yet another theatre venue.

The next morning, Nora and I got up very early.
We only had three days in Amsterdam, before we had to return to London, to find an agent who would take on and produce our project.
We had brought a production portfolio with mock-up black and white photos of what the Mondrian project might look like and, of course, the play script itself.
That was about it. As I say, we knew no one there other than Janet. We had no contacts. No letter of introduction or referral.
Nothing to help 'unsqueal the wheels'.

But Nora and I were nothing, if not determined. Nora asked Janet for a telephone directory before she left for her dance class.
'We'll just cold call,' Nora told her.
'Good luck with that!' Janet laughed. She shook her head and rolled her eyes as she walked out the door.

We went through the directory and underlined every theatrical agency we saw. Then we picked up the phone and started calling. We both took turns and made it into a kind of contest to see which one of us could get an appointment first.

Nora won. On her very first agency call, she managed to get someone to agree to see us about our Mondrian project. After another two hours or so of this 'cold calling', we gained two more agency appointments. All three agency appointments were for that very day. 'The Dutch are so open-minded!' Nora beamed.

Janet had left us an Amsterdam street map, so we could find our way around town on our own.
Amsterdam is a terrific place for walking, if you're eagle-eyed enough to avoid the tramcars and the cyclists. We walked along with the mass of tourists. We wished we were tourists too, but we had a job to do and could not simply stroll around happily.

We found the address, easily enough, of the first agent who had agreed to see us.
It was located in a narrow, red-brick, terraced house. The area looked very expensive.
When it was time for our appointment, we buzzed the door.
A female voice on the intercom asked us what we wanted. We told her who we were and she buzzed us in.
A tall, thin, blond Dutch woman sat at the reception desk. We were told to wait as she called to tell her boss we were there.
A couple minutes later, an extremely tall man sporting a walrus moustache came out of his office.
'I am Hans,' he said. 'Come in! Come in!'
We followed Hans into his office.

We talked about the project and I went through the portfolio with him.
'It's the 75th anniversary this year of Mondrian and the founding of the 'De Stijl' movement,' I told him.
'We want to do the play here. Not London. We think it would be of more interest to a Dutch audience than a British one.'
'Yes, I can see that,' he agreed.

And we spoke more about the play and how we planned to employ Dutch actors and designers. Hans seemed to be very enthusiastic.
'I know people who might be interested in backing this,' he told us. However he went on to say that he wanted total control over the entire project. Nora and I would simply be 'advisors'.
'The risk is all mine, you see.'
'We'll have to think about that,' Nora said.

We thanked him and left.

As we were leaving Hans' office, I said to Nora, 'He acted like he was doing us a favor!'

'There are two more yet to see,' Nora said encouragingly.

Nora and I stopped at a cozy coffeehouse by a canal. We had a couple hours to kill before we were due to see the next agent. We ordered some coffee and pancakes. We hadn't eaten any breakfast before we set off. We just got up, started calling, and then headed out the door once we had the appointments arranged.

Nora told me that she was in 'love' with Amsterdam and she was certain that our project would be performed there.

'I like the energy here! I like the way of life!'

'Nora, we haven't even been here a day yet,' I reminded her.

'Sometimes, Ralphy, you just get a feeling for a place,' she said as she poured more syrup on her pancakes.

We finished our meal and headed off to our next appointment.

The second agent, Bettina, was not at all interested.

'We only take on established theatre artists,' she said snootily.

'What you two are suggesting you wish to do is very difficult. We simply could not be involved in such a thing.'

'Then why did you agree to see us?' Nora asked her.

'I am always interested in hearing about new projects!' she said as if scandalized.

Our final agency meeting was scheduled for the end of the day. Nora and I just took in the atmosphere until then. We stopped at a little café for cheese sandwiches and watched some very talented street performers juggling fire-sticks. Canal boats passed beneath the low bridges as a multitude of cyclists passed overhead.

'I love this place!' Nora trilled.

Piet, the last agent we were due to see, had offices near Vondelpark not far from where Janet lived.

His secretary was a very extroverted redhead with swimming pool blue eyes. She was the type of woman who would never venture forth without first spending four hours assuring herself that her make-up and hair were perfect.

'Welcome to our Dutch domain!' she said when we arrived. 'I love London theatre! It's all so sophisticated! Artists! I love all of them!' She told us her name was Alise.

I could see that Alise was not going down well with Nora. She mistrusted what she called 'luvvies' and theatre groupies too. She also did not 'connect' with glamorous women.
'Fakes and fruitcakes,' she'd call them.

Nora and I sat and waited on the office yellow leather settee until Piet appeared at his office door and beckoned us to enter.
'Come in!' he boomed.

Piet was a friendly and charismatic character. His attitude was very laid back. I talked him through the project and what we hoped to achieve. He listened while he smoked a cigarette.
'This is fabulous!' he said as he interrupted me.
'This is just what I've been looking for!' he added.
He took the portfolio and started scanning quickly through its contents.
'Fabulous! Fabulous!' he said as he flicked through its pages.
Nora and I looked at one another.
'Just leave this with me. I will arrange meetings with producers and at the top venues. Leave it with me!'

Piet did not want to control the entire project. He wanted to act as our exclusive agent in the Netherlands.
'I take a percentage! I believe in you! This is just the start of many projects for the three of us!'

We agreed that Piet would arrange the necessary meetings.
'I'll contact you in London once everything has been set. Can you come over again in about two week's time? I'll need to make certain that everyone we need to see will be free to do so,' he said in perfect English.
So we agreed to return in two week's time.

When we ran into Janet again that evening, she could not believe our good fortune.
'I've never heard of such a thing,' she said shaking her head in pleased amazement.

'The Dutch are usually so cautious when it comes to business matters. I didn't tell you that, because I didn't want to discourage you,' Janet added.

As Nora and I had accomplished what we had set out to do, we could simply be tourists ourselves for the rest of our stay.
In the evenings, we went out clubbing or to the theatre. During the days, we'd go for long walks and picnic in the beautiful parks.
I was beginning to think that Nora was right.
Amsterdam was delightful.

We flew back to London feeling very good about our Mondrian project.

Nora wouldn't stop talking about all the things she wanted to do when we returned to Amsterdam.
'Janet told me about a museum where they have a huge collection of Van Gogh paintings and there's a sculpture park too. She said they have white bicycles there that you can use for free to get around. And I want to go to Café de Jaren, because Janet said all the dancers hang out there.'
Her list of the things that she wanted to do lasted the entire return flight home.

But once back in London, and after we crunched the numbers, we realized that our Netherlands Embassy bursary would never stretch to cover the cost of both of us returning to Amsterdam.
We had given Janet the money we would otherwise have spent on a hotel room. Then there were the flights, food and drink, and nights out on the town.
No, only one of us could go back.
Nora was not happy about that.
'You go, Nora,' I said. 'You can talk them through the project as well as I can.'
'No, you have to go,' Nora said matter-of-factly.
'It's your play after all.'

So we agreed that I would return to Amsterdam alone.
'Just bring me back a souvenir,' Nora requested.
'Something Dutch.'

I called Piet from London and told him that I would be returning on my own in two weeks.

'That's perfect!' he enthused. 'I've already set up a meeting with two top producers. Bert and Classe are good friends of mine. They're the best. They're very interested in meeting with us.'

I gave Piet my flight details, we agreed where we'd meet, and I hung up.

Nora wanted to know all about 'Bert and Classe'.

'We should call Janet and ask her what she knows about them,' she suggested. 'And you should ask Ton at the Embassy too.'

This was in the days before people could be 'Googled'. That device did not yet exist.

But I brushed aside Nora's wise suggestion to contact Janet and Ton anyway.

'I don't know, Nora. Piet said he knew them. He said they were his friends.'

We spent the two weeks before my solo return to Amsterdam working on the details of the project. I called Ton at the Embassy and informed him that we had made some progress and left it at that. I made a rough budget and Nora called theatres in Amsterdam to ask about venue costs.

We had an idea that the Mondrian project would cost roughly 750,000 guilders to produce.

10% of that would go to Nora and me less Piet's commission.

When I arrived at Schiphol Airport, Piet was waiting for me.

'You're staying at my flat in Amsterdam,' he told me.

'I stay at my girlfriend's house. I insist!'

We got in his car and he drove me to his flat on the Prinsengracht. His flat was on the top floor of a black stone-cladded block and accessed by a spiral staircase. It was a bijou flat, very well-appointed, with gorgeous views overlooking the canal.

'We meet with Bert and Classe tomorrow evening,' he said.

'Let's talk about it over dinner.'

Dinner was at a nearby, noisy, trendy bar. The acoustics were dreadful. It was like a wall of noise in there. I had to shout to make myself heard.

I told Piet what Nora and I had budgeted for the project and what his commission would be.

'Good! That sounds about right!' he shouted back.

I was not sure if he had even heard what I said.

'I'll have to pick you up tomorrow evening. We must drive to the meeting. Bert and Classe live outside Amsterdam.'

We agreed a time for our rendezvous.

After dinner, Piet drove off to stay with his girlfriend and I started walking back to his flat. On the way, I noticed a late night shop was still open. There was an illuminated black, red, and white 'Penguin Shop' sign over the door. I grabbed a few necessities there and a good bottle of wine.

I planned to take that back for Nora as her 'souvenir'. It wasn't 'Dutch' as Nora had requested, but it would do.

The next day, I spent my time walking all around Amsterdam and headed back to the theatre district for another look. As evening drew near, I walked back, grabbed the portfolio, and waited for Piet outside his block of flats at the appointed time.

'We're going to Zaandam. They have their offices there,' Piet told me as I got into his car.

'It's not too far. Just be yourself. They are both very excited to be meeting you.'

And we drove off.

When we arrived in Zaandam, Piet pulled up in front of a hotel.

'We're meeting them in there,' he said as he slammed his car door shut.

As we walked into the hotel bar, Bert and Classe waved to Piet. Piet said something to them in Dutch and they all laughed.

In fact, the entire meeting took place in Dutch. Neither Bert not Classe spoke any English. That took me by surprise. It seemed to me that everyone I had met in Amsterdam spoke perfect English. Even the man behind the counter at the 'Penguin Shop'.

Piet did most of the talking and he showed them the production portfolio Nora and I had put together. There was a lot of smiling and joking going on, but it all went over my head. We ordered dinner and drinks.

At one point, both Bert and Classe got up together, I guessed, to use the toilets. And I was alone with Piet.

'I was right!' Piet whispered to me. 'They are both on board. You have your producers!'
'Did you talk them through my budget yet?' I asked him.
'Yes, of course! This is not a problem. They are both very wealthy and they've been looking for a 'prestige project' just like yours. The money is no object. You are going to be very famous!'

Bert and Classe returned to our table.
Bert handed me a bottle of jenever he must have bought at the bar. Jenever is sort of a Dutch gin.
'How do you say?.. A gift! It's good!' Bert smiled.
It was the only thing in English he had uttered throughout the entire meeting.

Piet, Bert, and Classe kept talking and they took out their diaries and agreed future dates to meet. At least that is what it looked like they were doing.
Then we all stood up to say our goodbyes.
Bert handed me his business card.
Bert Stubbins, it read, *Probleemoplosser.*
That means 'Problem solver' as I discovered later.

Piet was ecstatic as he drove us back to Amsterdam.
'This is going to be world class! They're going to line up all the top actors in the Netherlands. Top script translators, top designers! They want to make a big splash with this!'
'They told you they were drawing up a production contract?' I asked.
'Yes, certainly, a contract. That will take some time, but that will all be taken care of too. Don't look so worried! All you need to do is enjoy your new success!'

When we arrived back in Amsterdam, Piet walked up with me to his flat. He grabbed some clothes and some toiletries.
'I'll stop by in the morning. Can you leave the production portfolio with me? It will help get the others we need on board.'
I handed him the portfolio and he left.

It was late and I was exhausted. I had spent the entire day walking all over Amsterdam before heading up to Zaandam with Piet.

I sat down and thought about what had just happened at the meeting.
I decided that Piet was right. I should just relax and enjoy my good
fortune.
I got myself ready for bed.

I don't know what time it was when Piet's intercom buzzed, but it
was certainly in the middle of the night.
I staggered half-asleep over to the intercom phone.
'Yes?' I asked.
A woman's voice replied.
'I here for Mr. Stubbins,' she said.
Eventually it dawned on me that she was asking for Bert.
'No, Mr. Stubbins isn't here,' I sleepily said.
'You American Guy? Yes?' she asked. 'Mr. Stubbins say to come
here. Flat D.'
I buzzed her in.

A few moments later, there was a knock at the door.
When I opened it, I was greeted by the sight of a young Asian
woman wearing a very short, shiny, red plastic raincoat over black
fishnet stockings and red high heels.
'Come in,' I stammered.

She minced toward me in tiny high-heeled steps and threw her arms
around my neck.
'Mr.Stubbins say I give good time,' she whispered in my ear.
Then she giggled and pushed herself away and smiled broadly.
She was either born with the perfect smile with the most perfectly
white, perfect teeth or her handlers knew a good dentist.

'Hi! American Guy!'
'You call me Koli,' she announced imperiously.
And as she said 'Koli', she threw her arms up over her head like a
cheerleader and shook herself about in a private little dance.
'I, Thai Girl.'
She flashed that perfect smile and removed her raincoat.

Underneath was a pulsating set of frilly, red lingerie. It was certainly
not something you might wear while out and about.
It left, well, nothing to the imagination.

191

I was still half-asleep, as I say, and this all came as somewhat of a surprise. I just stood there in my boxer shorts trying to take this all in. I didn't know what to do, but I had a good idea that Koli did. Finally, I asked her if she'd like some wine.

'Good wine?' she scowled.

'I think so.'

I opened the wine, which I was saving for Nora, and poured two glasses.

We sat together on Piet's small, blue settee.

'You tell Mr. Stubbins, Koli best girl. Number One Sexy.'

'OK,' I said. 'I'll tell him.'

She lifted my hand holding my wine glass up to hers as if she wanted me to make a toast.

'You say, Koli the best, Mr. Stubbins.'

I looked at her.

'You say!'

'OK. Koli is the best, Mr. Stubbins.' I repeated.

And with that, she immediately grabbed both wine glasses and placed them on the coffee table in front of us. The next thing I knew Koli is sitting on my lap and playing with my nose.

'Let's have a bit of wine first,' I suggested feebly.

I managed to slide her off my lap so she was sitting again beside me. Koli looked confused. 'You no like Koli, American Guy?'

I assured her that I liked her just fine.

So there I was in the wee hours of the morning, sitting on Piet's settee, and splitting a bottle of wine with this overtly sexual and dizzyingly sexy, young Thai woman. But all I was doing was feeling awkward about it all. Surprises have that effect on me sometimes.

We just sat there together and talked for a while.

If, while we were talking, I said something that made Koli laugh, she'd giggle and her hands would lunge straight for me.

This scenario repeated itself several times. She laughed at nearly everything I said.

She'd coyly slither up to a full embrace and we'd end up face to face, she with her perfect smile and me with my look, no doubt, of uncertain surprise.

She'd pout disapprovingly every time I would extricate myself from her clutches.

But she was not put off from trying again and again.

Telling her that I was married made not a jot of difference.
'Nobody here, but Koli… and you,' she cooed truthfully as she
wormed her way into my arms yet again.

After we finished the wine, I rifled through my wallet and gave her a
hundred guilders.
(Why not? Why should she be out of pocket, just because I wouldn't
sample her wares?)
Once I gave her the money, she gave me a quick kiss and a wink.
She grabbed her coat.
'You say Koli best girl! Yes?' She reminded me.
I nodded reassuringly.
And out the door she went.

I know all of you red-blooded types out there are thinking, 'What an
idiot!'
Or worse.
I know how you feel. I often agree with you.
But Koli, as irresistible as she was, had enough of her own problems,
no doubt, without my adding to them.
And, believe me, she was truly irresistible. I am sure I damaged some
vital internal organs by resisting her bounty.
But perhaps, because nothing did 'happen', I can remember our
encounter far more vividly than if something had.
And as far as Bert was concerned, I just thought that was how they
did business in Amsterdam to 'clinch the deal'.

Piet stopped by the next morning as promised. I did not tell him
about the delightful Koli's late night visit.
We went through all the production details and he told me about
people he had in mind for the set-design and other jobs.
'But won't Bert and Classe want some input on that?' I asked him.
'I'm sure they are thinking about the same people,' he assured me.

When I was back in London, I told Nora everything that had
happened, except about Koli of course.
She grilled me on every detail.
'When will the contract be finished? What did Piet say? When did
they say we'd go into production?'

She was very excited. Perhaps, at last, all our hard work was going to pay off.

I gave Nora the bottle of jenever that Bert had given to me.
'I got this for you,' I said. 'It's your souvenir.'
'What is it?'
'It's Dutch gin.'
'Gin? We don't drink gin! Why did you buy gin?'
'Well, it's Dutch, isn't it?'
'I suppose so,' she said dubiously.
Of course Koli and I had consumed the wine that Nora would have preferred.

A few days later, Nora got up early and left on her own to go to work at our theatre.
I decided to stay home and try to remove some of the major debris from our flat.

Our flat was always a mess. We'd come home from a long exhausting day and just collapse in a heap. As a consequence, household chores were regularly missed.
Our mess would pile up and up until the entire flat looked like a sink full of dirty dishes with dirty laundry scattered everywhere. Nora and I would put up with that for weeks and weeks until one or the other of us became so fed up with coming home to a rubbish barge that we did something about it.
On this occasion, I was fed up with it first and started tackling the chaos.

Now, I don't know why this happened. I admit it was very unusual, but for some reason, while I was doing this 'blitz' cleaning, I was looking for something in Nora's sock drawer in our red-painted wardrobe. To this day, I can't remember what it was. But, anyway, while I was looking for that something, I found something else.
A neat pile of letters to Nora bound in blue ribbon.
The letters were not from me.
I flicked through them, but they were unsigned.
Unsigned love letters.

I confronted Nora about this when she got back from the theatre.

194

She looked embarrassed. She didn't try to turn the tables on me and question why I was nosing around in her sock drawer.

'They're all from Silent John,' she finally admitted.
'Silent John! You're getting love letters from Silent John?!'
'He's been putting them in my bag at the theatre for weeks,' she explained. 'Ever since people noticed the two of us haven't been getting along.'
'But why are you saving them?' I fumed.
'I don't know,' Nora said.
She meant she didn't know what to say.
I gave her both barrels.
'You can't encourage someone like that, Nora! You have to talk to him! You don't save his ridiculous love letters!'
And there were tears and overly heated words that never can be taken back. I was too angry and upset to be reasonable.

It was after that when I moved out of the flat we shared and started sleeping on the theatre office floor.

A few days after the 'sock drawer incident', I had a phone call from Alise, Piet's assistant.
She said she was in London and wanted to meet with me to return the portfolio.
'We made copies now and Piet said to give you back the original,' she said.

We agreed to meet for a drink that evening in a fashionable, overly priced wine bar in the West End.
Alise arrived dressed in a Thierry Mugler blue mini dress like she was on a fashion shoot. She was always well-dressed whenever I saw her, but she had made a real effort this time.
'Alise, you look like Cindy Crawford's more beautiful younger sister,' I flattered her.

She returned the portfolio and we sat and had a few drinks.
'Everyone is talking about you in Amsterdam,' she said with her eyes as big as saucers.
'Everyone wants to be part of the project. The phone's been ringing off the hook at the office.'

The more Alise drank, the more star-struck she became.

'Piet wants to know when you are coming back for a visit,' she said in a tipsy.

'But this time you must stay at my friend's house. It's much nicer than Piet's flat!'

I told her I hoped to return soon.

'Then it's settled! You will stay with me at my friend's house!'

I said nothing to that.

A couple of days after Alise's visit, Piet called.

'We need you in Amsterdam,' he said. 'The publicity has already started. I didn't have to do a thing. It's all word of mouth. Everyone wants to know about the Mondrian project! The press are asking me to arrange interviews and I need your biography now!'

I didn't have the money to go back right away. It was embarrassing to admit to that.

'Piet, the Embassy bursary is gone. I'll have to find some travelling money from somewhere first.'

Piet just scoffed at me.

'That's not a worry! I'll get Bert and Classe to front you the money. They want you here as badly as I do!'

And, sure enough, a few days later I was wired the money to travel. Even though there was more than enough for the two of us to go, I didn't even try to include Nora this time.

After the travel money arrived, I called Piet to arrange things for my next visit, but he sounded very strange on the phone. He was always joking and laid back, but this time he sounded all business.

'Piet, what's the matter?' I asked him. 'You don't sound like yourself. Is there a problem with the project?'

He assured me that there was not.

'Then what's the matter?'

And then he said, 'I am really disappointed in you, Ralphy. I sent my assistant over to return your portfolio and then you start an affair with her.'

'Say what?'

196

'Yes, she's been telling everyone about how you took her out and got her drunk and took her back to the theatre late at night and had kinky sex that she wasn't really sure she wanted, but now she thinks she's in love with you! This is not how I thought you behaved! It's unprofessional!'

It was one of those situations when you want to laugh, but you can't laugh, because someone is seriously angry with you over the nothing that you want to laugh about.
So I just calmly explained to Piet that nothing had happened between the two of us.
'Piet, we met for a couple of drinks and that was it.'
'She says much more happened than that!'
I suggested he ask Alise about my theatre, since she claimed we had 'kinky sex' there.
'She's never seen our theatre. She's never been there. Why she's making up this fairy tale, I don't know. Go ahead and ask her and you'll see I'm being straight with you.' I said a trifle fed up.
'I will do just that,' he said unconvinced.

The very next day Piet rang again. He sounded very sheepish down the phone.
'I don't know what to say other than to apologize,' he said. 'Alise admitted that she didn't really go back to your theatre with you. I think it was all some fantasy. She can get carried away like that sometimes, when she's been drinking. Especially around artistic people.'
'It sounds like it,' I replied.

What I didn't realize however was how clever and scheming Alise really was. But that discovery soon came when I next returned to Amsterdam.

As before, Piet collected me at Schiphol airport. And, as before, he gave me the run of his flat. I certainly had no plans to stay at Alise's 'friend's house'.
We sat together and he went through some publicity interviews I needed to do while I was there. He said that the contract was still not finished.
'It's becoming such a huge thing now that Bert and Classe need to rethink the contract and production costs. They see the project as even more elaborate than we do.'

I spent the entire day talking with journalists and arts forums. I felt like I was some kid's show-and-tell exhibit. Piet even managed to get me a television interview on an arts program.
I kept asking him if we'd be meeting with Bert and Classe, but he was vague about that.
I suppose he was more interested in me feeding the publicity machine while I was in town.

The world famous Holland Festival was in full flow while I was in Amsterdam that time.
Artists from all over the world congregate in Holland. Many world premiers of plays and operas and dance concerts take place during the Festival.
And there are lots of opening night parties for the art patrons and the performers.

After a long day of being interviewed, I went back to Piet's flat. As soon as I walked through the door, the phone rang.
It was Alise. She acted as if the 'kinky sex' fantasy affair, she had lied about happening, never happened. I said nothing about it either.

'Phillip Morris is sponsoring the 'After Party' tonight for Netherlands Dance Theatre. I have tickets. It would be good for you to make an appearance and meet some people face to face. Piet thinks so too.'
I had some doubts about joining Alise for that, but decided I'd go anyway.

The 'After Party' was being held in the Muziektheatre, the premier dance venue in the Netherlands. I made my way there on foot and found Alise in the theatre bar. It was packed with revelers. They were all dressed in costume. Everyone except for me, that is. Alise had neglected to mention to me that it was a costume party.
I was the odd one out.

Alise was wearing a yellow flamenco outfit with red detail.
She was seated at a table with about eight other people. All of them were dressed as if it were Halloween, but with an arts theme. Janet was there too and dressed as a ballerina with white tutu.

'Where's Nora, Ralphy?' Janet asked me. I lied and said she was busy with our London theatre. 'You will give her my love, won't you?' she added.
'Tell her your Mondrian thing is the talk of the town!'

Alise introduced me to those I didn't already know and everyone wanted to know about our play project. The drinks flowed endlessly. I was having a good time. Free drinks and interesting company. It was fun and just what I needed after a long day of interview grillings.

I was enjoying myself, laughing, and drinking when I noticed Alise was staring at me. When she saw that she had caught my eye, she whispered in my ear, 'Ralphy, have you seen, *Basic Instinct*?'
It was 1992 and *Basic Instinct* had just made its way to our screens. I told her that I had not.
'You're just like Michael Douglas in that,' she smiled.
I guessed that was some sort of compliment.
'I thought you'd like that story I made up about us in London,' she giggled.
'Now no one believes that anything happened between us, so now of course it can, and no one will ever believe it did. You are safe.'
Yes, Alise was a very clever woman.

I suppose here I could explain away what happened next by pointing out the sock drawer letters and my theatre office floor self-banishment. I could do that easily enough.
But even I no longer find that convincing.
When Alise suggested I go with her to her friend's house, I said, 'OK.'

I waited until I saw Janet go off to the toilets and stood up.
Alise grabbed me by the arm and led me straight outside. She hailed the first taxi she saw and we made our way to her friend's house.

The Netherlands, as you probably know, is short on space. As a result, the Dutch build tall and narrow buildings relative to the rest of Europe.
Alise's 'friend's house' was of this type.

When we entered, there was a staircase just opposite the front door and I followed Alise's yellow flamenco dress trail as she ascended. The staircase was so narrow and steep that I could put my hands on the steps above as I made my way up them.

Alise led me all the way to the top of the house. And when we reached that point, she pulled open a trapdoor in the ceiling. That revealed yet more stairs and they terminated in an opening in the flooring above. We both climbed through and I found myself in a very luxurious love nest.
'I told you it was nicer than Piet's flat,' Alise reminded me.

It was tiny, but self-contained. Francis Bacon's *Study for a Portrait of Van Gogh* hung above a red love seat in the lounge.
Whoever really owned that house had created the perfect place for illicit encounters. Any intruders would have been heard tramping up that staircase long before they could gain entrance. Privacy was assured.
'Just give me a moment,' Alise said as she disappeared into a bathroom.
Her flamenco dress swished behind her as she did so.

I looked at the Francis Bacon painting and other modern art and sculptures that made up the décor. I could see a king-sized four poster bed through the bedroom door. I imagined it must have been a hell of a job getting that up the stairs.
There was a small kitchenette through an archway beside the bedroom.
I went in and poured myself a glass of water.

When I returned to the lounge, Alise was emerging from the bathroom. There was no sign of her flamenco dress.
'Now let me tell you all about '*Basic Instinct*',' she purred.

Yes, I know. Soiled diapers, nappies, and baby disposables. That's the smell of a love rat and that was just what I was.

Piet and I had agreed to meet at his office the following morning before my return to London. I made my way there. Alise was behind her desk and behaved as if nothing had happened at all. She joked with me as always, while I waited to go into Piet's office, and made small talk. No one would ever have guessed that the two of us had just spent the night together. The only sign she made that something had indeed gone on between us was a little wink as I left her in reception and walked into Piet's office.

'I received this letter by courier this morning,' Piet said as I entered his office and sat down.
He looked unhappy.
'It's from Bert and Classe. They feel the project costs are too high. They are saying that they cannot see where their profit will come from, if we proceed on this basis.'
I was shocked.
'I thought you talked them through the budget and said it was no problem.'
'Yes, but that was before the project grew so large. You don't understand how things work here. All the venues will raise their hiring costs, because they know it is a big project. So will the designers. Bert and Classe think costs will spiral.'

I asked to read the letter for myself.
'It's in Dutch, of course,'' Piet said as he shrugged his shoulders gloomily.
'What do you suggest?' I asked him.
'I don't know what to say,' he replied.
'I just don't know.'
Piet said he would contact Bert and Classe later to discuss it.
'But it looks to me like it is dead in the water according to what they've written in their letter.'
I was more than surprised that Piet would give up so easily after having been so enthusiastic from the start.
'Call me in a week and maybe I'll have more news,' he said while shaking his head.

I flew back to London not knowing what to think. In just two brief days, I had betrayed Nora and I had lost the project too. They say that bad things come in threes and two of them had already happened. I felt a failure.

I should only have been focusing on our project and not flamenco dresses.

When I got back to London, I went straight to our flat to tell Nora the news about the project, but there was no sign of her. I headed down to the theatre to see if she was there, but she wasn't.
'No one has seen her for a couple days,' one of the set-builders told me. 'We need to buy some more timber, nails, and wood screws too.'
I sorted out the set-builders' needs and went back home.

But Nora did not return. I was getting worried, but trying to invent some believable reason why she was nowhere to be found. Perhaps she saw an old friend and was away with them, I thought. I wasn't ready to panic yet even though, as I was getting ready for bed, there was still no sign of her.
It was the first night I had spent at our flat in weeks.

The next morning, I heard the post plop through the door slot on to the floor. Among the junk and bills was a fat padded manila envelope. The return address was from Piet's office.
'Maybe it's the contract after all,' I hoped to myself.
But it was not a contract. In fact, it had nothing to do with the project at all.
It was from Alise.

Her letter must have been forty pages long. It was entirely sexual in nature. Mainly it consisted of future fantasies she had in mind whenever I was back in her 'Dutch domain', as she called it.
I read the first few pages and gave up and skipped ahead to the ending.
On the last page, she had taped a matchstick to the stationery, drawn with red crayon a graphic image of us 'coupling', and then finished with the words, *'YOU ARE HOT STUFF!'*
I was thinking that it was lucky Nora wasn't there when that arrived.

And then I noticed something else at the bottom of the manila envelope. It was a smaller sealed envelope marked, *'For Your Eyes Only'*.
I thought it would be yet more of her sex mad ravings, but when I opened that envelope I was stunned by what I found.
It was a copy of the letter in Dutch from Bert and Classe.

'You should have this translated.' Alise had written in English in the top margin. She added something else in Dutch, in yet more rubric writing, across the bottom of the letter.
I went outside and threw Alise's 'love letter' down a storm drain. But I kept the copy of Bert and Classe's letter.

By evening, Nora was still nowhere to be found and I did start to panic. I called all our friends. Even those we hadn't been in touch with for a long time. I called the dance studio where Nora took classes.
No one had seen her.

I was tormenting myself whether I should call her family or not. I didn't want to do that. I didn't want to worry them, when there was nothing they could do anyway.
I was actually pacing up and down on the floor trying to think what to do. Should I call the police? Should I arrange a search party? Maybe it was the guilt of my recent affair, but I felt responsible for her disappearance. I had been ignoring her ever since the sock drawer letters were discovered and left her alone while I was off in Holland. Maybe she did something stupid, because of my moody, distant behavior.

Finally, a thought crossed my mind. The only one who I hadn't spoken to about Nora was Silent John. I hadn't seen him either since my return to London. I decided to go over to his place.

I threw the three 'signaling stones' at his window, but there was no response. But I knew he had to be in there. The only places he would go were the little café where I had met him and the theatre when we came to collect him. I hadn't seen him at the theatre or that café.
So why wasn't he answering?

I decided to walk around to the back of his house. I was going to throw stones at the boarded-up back windows, when I noticed it. Smoke.
Black, curly plumes of smoke were pouring out of the holes in the back of the roof.
'John! John!' I shouted.
'John!'
But there was not a sign of life.

And then a terrifying thought hit me and fear raced through me.
'Nora!!! Nora!!! Are you in there?! Nora!'
But the only response was more black smoke billowing from the roof.

I called the Fire Brigade and waited in front of Silent John's 'house squat' for their arrival. Eventually, about six different fire engines with sirens blaring pulled up. All the neighbors came out to see what was going on. I led the firemen to the back of the house and pointed at the smoke. One of them pushed me away firmly while two others took fire-axes and began bashing away at the boards on the windows.
'My wife could be in there!' I pleaded.
'You get out front and away from this,' a no-nonsense fireman told me.

I remember holding my head in despair, just like that figure in Edvard Munch's *The Scream*, as I walked to the front of the house to wait with the nosey neighbors.
I wanted to punch some of them for making stupid small talk about fires and gossiping about the condemned house ablaze on their street. It was like a fireworks display to them.

After about half an hour of waiting like that, I saw an ambulance crew take a stretcher around the back of the house. Soon after, another ambulance crew ran to the back with another stretcher. And about fifteen minutes after that, they both came back with someone in their care.
I could see one of them was Nora.
I ran toward the ambulance crew, but someone held me back.
'Nora!' I cried. 'Nora!'
I got close enough to see that she was alive. Her face was covered in soot and she looked weak. They put her in the back of the ambulance.
I saw that the other crew of paramedics were drawing a sheet over the head of the other person. I caught a glimpse before they did so. It was Silent John.

'I'm her husband!' I told the paramedics as they tried to shut the ambulance door. 'I'm going with her!' And I did.

At the hospital, I was told to wait while she was taken into 'Accident and Emergency'.

A kindly nurse brought me a cup of tea while I was waiting, but I didn't even react when she placed the cup in my hand.
I was horrified.

I waited there for over an hour before a doctor finally came out to talk with me.
'It's only minor smoke inhalation,' he calmly explained. 'We're lucky she's such a strong young lady. It doesn't appear that there will be any lasting damage.'
I was so relieved that I felt like I was floating off the ground.
'She'll stay the night for observation and you come collect her in the morning, if all is well.'
I know it sounds sappy, mawkish, whatever, but I hugged him in sheer relief.

I called the hospital as soon as I arose the next morning. They told me Nora could come home. I just dropped the phone and ran straight to the hospital.
They brought Nora out in a wheelchair, but she didn't really need one. As soon as I saw her, I picked her up in my arms while struggling to choke back my tears.
'Let's go home, Nora,' I said soothingly.
'Let's go home.'
I carried her all the way back to our flat.

I'd never seen Nora so utterly exhausted.
'I'll tell you what happened later, Ralphy,' she sighed. 'I'm so tired.'
I helped her get ready for bed and we both lay down together for the first time in weeks.
Nora fell straight asleep. I held her in my arms for a while before getting back up.
She slept the entire day.

Very early the next morning, I was greeted with the words, 'I'm starving!', and Nora jumped out of bed and ran straight to the kitchen. When I walked in, she was already eating.
'I haven't eaten for two days,' she ravenously explained.

And then Nora told me the story about what had happened.

'I wanted to make things right between us,' she began. 'I don't like you sleeping at the theatre. I went over to see Silent John. I wanted to talk to him about his letters and fix all of that before you came back from Amsterdam.

I went over there the night before you were due back and he let me in,' Nora continued with a piece of buttered toast in her hand.

'I told him that he had to stop writing me letters, although it was very flattering, because I am married and you are his friend. And I told him I only loved you.'

I just felt like the rotten no-good skunk that I was.

Don't worry. I don't expect any sympathy. Nor deserve any.

'And he started acting very strangely and wrote me a note saying that I would not have come to see him on my own unless I had feelings for him too. He wrote that I was scared of his love for me. But I told him that wasn't it. I told him I could never love him, because I love you.'

I tried my best not to get weepy.

'And then, quick as a cat, he ran at me and slapped me. He overpowered me and pushed and dragged me up the stairs into a back room. He tied me with plastic cables to a broken chair he'd fixed to a radiator. And left me there. I listened for when he might go out, so I could shout for help, but even when he did, no one could hear me. I didn't have anything to eat or drink, except for some rainwater that was dripping on me through the roof. John never came back into the room. I think he left me there to die.'

'Good God, Nora! That damn flipped-out loony! But, wait, how did the fire start?' I asked.

'I don't know,' she said sadly. 'I guess John started it. I could smell the smoke and it was starting to fill the room. I could see the flames tickling under the locked door. I was praying you'd come save me, Ralphy. That's all I could do. And you did! You did!'

I can't remember ever fighting back tears any harder in all my life.

I spent the day nursing Nora and making her favorite foods for her. The latest news on the Mondrian Project could wait.

When Nora was up to it, I told her about the letter and that Bert and Classe were withdrawing from the project.

'That doesn't make any sense,' Nora said dismissively. 'They're the ones who wanted to expand the project! Why are they saying it has grown 'too big' now?'

And I told Nora that I had a copy of the letter and had arranged to meet with Ton, the Netherlands Embassy Cultural Attaché, to translate it.

'Maybe he can give us some more insight into this than Piet did,' I suggested. 'I told him it was urgent.'

A couple days later, I made my way to the Netherlands Embassy in London. I had reception buzz Ton to let him know I had arrived. He came down to meet me and we sat and had coffee in the magnificently vaulted Embassy atrium.

I told him what had happened during my last visit to Amsterdam. He also thought it was odd that they had pulled their backing in such a way.

Then, I showed Ton the copy of the letter that Alise had sent me.

'Would you mind translating aloud?' I asked him.

And this is what he said:

'It says here that they are withdrawing their financial support, because they cannot agree to give your agent 25% of the net profit on the project.'

My eyes widened.

'They say that you at first agreed that your agent would receive a commission from your fee directly, but then you had insisted, according to your agent, that he have a major producing role and given the profit percentage from their end.'

I couldn't believe my ears. I never insisted on that. It was all lies. Piet's lies.

Ton continued, 'They go on here to say that they are extremely disappointed, because they were confident they could have made a successful production in the Netherlands.'

Then Ton looked at me.

'I am sure you are not aware of this,' he said carefully. 'At least, I hope not. I see one of these producers is named 'Stubbins'. Stubbins is a very well known pornographer in my country and runs many of the legal window booths for prostitution in Amsterdam. He has been trying to use his wealth, over the past few years, to gain an air of respectability. But I am not sure if it is wise to be doing business with him. Your name would be tainted with his.'

I was stunned. I was shocked. I was angry at myself. How could I still be so overly trusting?

I thought I had learned the lesson about being wary long ago. I was furious and frustrated to find out that I was wrong.

Maybe you are not as naïve as I obviously am, but when you trust someone, like I did Piet, and then find out that he is just a self-serving scoundrel, it is soul destroying.

How dare he say false things to those producers and then pass it off as if it were my wish?! And then tie our production into producers who make money from abusing women.

I never spoke with Piet again.

But before I left the embassy, I asked Ton to translate the cryptic Dutch message Alise had written in red crayon across the bottom of the letter. As he looked at it, his face blossomed to a blush and he laughed nervously. He wouldn't tell me what she had written.

All he said was, 'You better be careful. It looks like one of our Dutch girls wants to eat you alive!' Then I too went scarlet.

Although Piet was crossed off from my life forever, I still had to deal with Alise and her unwanted letter of passion.

I called her and thanked her for sending me the copy of the Dutch producers' letter.

And before she could respond, I let her know, in no uncertain terms, that I did not appreciate her 'love letter' and wouldn't welcome another one.

'That wasn't too clever, was it, Alise?' I said devoid of any feeling.

'You are angry?' she said in surprise.

'I never want to hear from you again.'

'And I thought you were a gentleman!' she said acidly.

I hung up.

(Yes, I know. More soiled diapers.)

Nora and I never produced our Mondrian Project in Amsterdam or anywhere else. But if you go to 'You Tube' and search 'Mondrian Project' you will see a short video clip of the making of the production portfolio. I think you can still find it there.

Hopefully, that will be enough to convince you that my story is true.

And, perhaps, it was indeed my dalliance with Alise that led to yet more of Nora and my 'marital difficulties' and ultimately led to our parting.

That's true too. But that's a story too far for now.

208

STORY CHAPTER ELEVEN

'HEART BREAK'

This is a confusing and disturbing story, because it's about a
confusing and disturbing time.
Nora and I were over.
Finished. Yesterday's newspaper. A sad memory. Another looming
divorce statistic.

We'd been together ever since we were kids. We grew up together
really. We met when we were only nineteen years old and had spent
all our adult life together as a couple.

I wish I could give you a clear, reasonable understanding of how we
came to be shipwrecked, but I cannot. Perhaps it was the stress of
working together. Maybe it was realizing that our ambitious dreams
would never come to pass. It could even have been a mid-life
madness or hidden resentment. Perhaps it was that which led to Nora
retreating to the bottle and to me growing so cold and distant inside
and out. I don't know.

I do know that when things finally died between us, it felt like it was
happening to someone else. I know that may sound strange, but I felt
as if it were all some awful nightmare that someone else had
suffered. That it was not really happening to us at all, but some
horror conjured up from the dark. The light of day would make it all
disappear. But daylight brought no relief. It took me many months
before I could accept it was true.
We were no more.

I remember, at the end, coming home after spending Christmas with
my family. Nora hadn't been home for three days before I left. These
unexplained absences had been going on for many months and
months, if not longer. And when I did see her, after one of these
binge escapades, she was invariably drunk or hung-over.
When I'd clean our flat, I started finding empty vodka bottles and the
like that Nora had discarded and forgotten about.

So we just spent Christmas apart.

And then, after returning home from that Christmas without Nora, I was letting myself back into our flat. As I tried my key in the mortise lock, I could see it was already unlocked.
Suddenly the door pulled open.
'Welcome back!'
It was Nora.

And she started acting just like the old Nora, asking me about my stay and what gifts I had received. She wasn't the missing or silent woman she'd become over the past year or so.
And she was sober.

'I've cleaned the whole flat!' she said with a broad smile.
'And there's homemade soup. I thought you might be hungry.'
I was jet-lagged, yes, but jet-lagged or not, I still would not have known what to say.
I said nothing. I just stood in the doorway, one hand clutching a luggage trolley.
'Here! Sit down! I got a Christmas present for you!' Nora said full of excitement.

A hollow, empty feeling washed through me.
'Nora,' I said, as I walked through the door, 'We can't be together anymore.'
I heard those words escaping from my mouth.

'You can't just come and go as you please,' I said without any emotion. 'You won't talk to me. You don't even try to explain. And I've no idea where you are. I think you are at our theatre, but people tell me that you aren't. I'm sorry, Nora. We can't be together anymore.'

And Nora, for her part, said nothing.
She simply put the Christmas gift she'd bought for me down on the coffee table. Then she went into the bedroom and got her small canvass backpack. She went to her sock drawer and shoved some underwear into the backpack. She took a couple of her favorite T-shirts too. She grabbed a few things from the bathroom and I heard her make her way to the door.

I just sat on the couch and stared at the gift on the table. I was feeling so hollow it was like I was invisible. As if everything were on hold.

Then, I felt Nora's presence standing over me. When I looked up at her, she wore a resigned look on her face. Like she knew this might happen. Her eyes were glassy with tears.
She gave me the most loving, kind smile. The kind two lovers might make knowing one is off to their doom and they cannot make a proper goodbye.
And then she turned and left.
She left with a piece of my heart that would be lost forever.
Cynics be damned. If you still do have a heart, then you still can be heartbroken.

I opened Nora's Christmas gift. It was a photo frame. The photo inside showed the two of us together when we first met at college. I still have no idea where she found that photograph.

And as time passed and our associations together, like the theatre and divorce proceedings, ended, I never saw Nora again.
No, I lie. I did see her again. But it was not my Nora. Not the Nora who magically reappeared for that final time with the homemade soup.
The bottle had seen to that.
I don't want to remember that Nora. I don't want to recall the dreadful things that other people told me about that Nora.
I don't want people to know her horror. All I can tell you is that some of the things I heard then were far worse than the lies I've told you now.

I forced myself to call Nora's family and tell them about their daughter's drinking, her 'disappearances', and why I didn't see them at Christmas.
But my news did not surprise them. They told me they knew she was drinking from their phone conversations with her. 'She hasn't been my daughter on the phone for months, Ralphy,' her dad told me. 'Her mother is in pieces. We called and called over Christmas, but no one answered.'

I think I told him Nora and I were finished, but I am not sure. I was in a surreal state as if someone else were speaking on the phone.
I can't remember what he said in reply.

I can't even remember hanging up the phone.

I stayed in that surreal state off and on for months and beyond.
For the first time in my adult life, I was trying not to think of Nora.
Not to think about the person who was part of me and I her.

There was much fall out from our demise. Mutual friends took sides.
Some with Nora. Others with me. And as anyone who has gone
through such a thing will know, other things began to fall apart along
with it.

Our London theatre closed. I lost heart in keeping it going without
Nora. Strange disruptive influences began to manifest themselves in
my life. An insane actress began stalking me and harassing me so
persistently that I had to bring in the police. Burglars broke into the
theatre twice in one week. The goodwill that kept things afloat
floated away.
I had no choice but to close our theatre business.
My life with Nora was over and the life we had created together was
over with it.

I was on my own. I now had no job or place to go to anymore.
Nor did I have my soul mate.

Nora continued drinking heavily and I'd hear reports, from people
who had worked with us at our theatre, of the terrible things that she
was up to or that had happened to her as a result of the bottle.
But these are the horrors that I can't bear to share with you.

So, as I say, it was a confusing and disturbing time. Not only had I
lost Nora, but I couldn't stomach hearing what she was doing now.
I was in that awful emotional situation when you feel two conflicting
things at the same time. I was heartbroken and I was angry. I had the
stuffing knocked out of me and wanted to knock the stuffing out of
something else.
Nora was gone and so was my peace of mind and purpose for living.

Don't worry. I know that is all very depressing, but I had to tell you
what was going on so you might better understand what happened
afterward.

I really didn't know what to do. Nora had moved out of our flat and gone elsewhere. I heard she was living with a group of drunks in a condemned building. I spent all my energy trying not to think about her, but that's all my mind wanted to think about.

I started spending a lot of time on my own. For over ten years, Nora and I ran our London theatre and I was constantly in the company of others. I went from social gadfly to recluse in a month.
I just wanted to lick my wounds in peace.

If you've ever been like that, then you will surely know what I mean. You can't see a way forward. There are too many things to do to change anything.
And would it really change anything, if you did do them?
You feel trapped.
You don't feel you're up to 'moving on'.
It's a bad place to be.
You can take pills from a doctor or drink too much in an attempt to cope.
But it doesn't help.
You might feel better briefly.
But the cage you are stuck in is still locked shut.
In the end, only your own efforts will make the difference.
Even if you do get outside help.
But when your heart is broken, it can be hard to see that.

But I knew I could not go on in this way. I had to force myself to reengage with the world.
I know myself.
I, Ralph E. Waldo, cannot survive without the company of others.
To whom would I tell my stories? Without others, from where would my future stories come? I had to do something to 'move on'.
Otherwise I would shrivel up and die.
And, to be honest, I sometimes felt like that would be the easier option.

I arranged to meet my old friend, Ted, at the 'Princess Louise'. I used to work with him and had several incredible working adventures as a result of knowing him.
Ted was a good source of no-nonsense advice. And that was what I sorely needed.

213

'Think about what you want,' Ted said over his drink. 'Think about what you need to do to get yourself up and running again.'
'Everything, Ted,' I replied. 'I need everything to get going again.'

And then Ted told me about how his wife had run off with his best friend and took their two children.
'I was the last to know, Ralphy. She abandoned me without a word and took the kids. It took me eighteen months to get some semblance of normal visitation rights,' he explained. 'I knew that was what I needed to do. See my kids again. And that's what I did.'
And then he said, 'I lost my work too when she ran off. I took my eye off the ball and lost everything, Ralphy. I know what you're going through.'
We ordered some more beers.

'Ralphy, put yourself back out there,' Ted advised. 'Date again. Concentrate on one area you can make better and then do it. Things have a way of taking care of themselves, if you give them a chance.'
'Date? No one 'dates' anymore, Ted,' I laughed.
'Well, 'go out' then. Whatever they call it these days,' he replied.

As for me, I never give advice anymore. There's a good story behind why I don't, but I don't need to go into all that here.
If someone comes to me with a personal problem, I listen. I sympathize. And that's it. I never offer advice.
However, I've no problem with taking advice.
I lapped up Ted's words readily enough.

I returned home to my empty flat. I sat down at the kitchen table and cried. (Yes, men can do that. We just don't like talking about it.)
I sat there and wept and wept. I remember crying until my sinuses blocked and blubbered aloud, 'Let this world end and not we two.'

But Ted's words did help. He was right. If I could concentrate on making one thing better, as he suggested, then perhaps I'd feel more like my old self again.
But concentrate on what? 'Dating' as Ted recommended? That sounded truly daunting. I hadn't been on a date for over twenty years. And I was primed with the 'loyalty bug' to block off any attraction to other women. Well, most of the time anyway.
Twenty plus years of marriage does that to you. And, if it doesn't, you won't make it to twenty plus years together in the first place.

214

And then, suddenly, it dawned on me. It was one of those 'Eureka!' moments. Right out of nowhere.

I couldn't face going out with other women, but I could tell myself that I was doing it to research a new play I was writing.

I decided that was what I would do. I'd 'date', but I'd do it under the pretext of research into 'dating rituals' for a new play.

'At least it will get me out of the flat,' I thought.

I remember feeling so much better when I put it to myself like that.

Of course, I had a huge advantage over most men. I had run a theatre. I knew hundreds of women and had worked closely with dozens of them there.

Not that I'm Gable or Pitt or Clooney or any 'Babe Magnet' like that. But I knew young, single women. I knew 'thirty somethings' who had never settled down. I knew exotic actresses and dancers who repeatedly changed partners and loved new 'romantic adventures'. I knew lovely single mothers who made poor choices with the men in their lives. I knew divorced women. Wronged women. Mad postmodern feminist man-eaters.

I knew them all.

Dating would be no problem. I had no desire to do so, but I could do so.

'It's just research, Ralphy,' I told myself to remove all the pressure.

And so it began. I would 'date' and then go home and write about the experience in my diary. Then, later, I would collate those experiences and create a new stage play that would reveal everything about modern dating rituals.

I had no title for it yet, but, as is my wont, I was determined now to see it through.

A couple of weeks after my 'Eureka' moment, I had a phone call from an Irish actress who used to take my classes at the theatre. Nina was lovely, attractive, giving, and very keen on acting and her career. She called to see if I was still offering classes now that the theatre had closed.

'We were all making such good progress, Ralphy. I really liked the group. Are you going to keep the classes going?' She asked me.

'Not for the time being, Nina,' I told her.

She sounded very disappointed.

And then words left my mouth the like of which had not left them for many a summer's season.

'Nina, there's a new production by Peter Hall at the National. I want to see it. You want to come with me?'

'When?' she asked.

'Whenever you're free,' I said casually.

And Nina agreed to be my first 'date', although she did not know she was my first date of course.

She sounded very nervous when she agreed, I should say. I don't think she was expecting me to ask her out when she rang.

She became very 'skittish' and excited on the phone.

We set the date.

Nina was a lovely woman, as I say. We had a splendid time together at the National and I cleverly kept turning the conversation around so she could talk about herself and the things she wanted from life. For the most part, I listened to her and said little myself.

She was very romantic. I mean in the sense of her outlook on things. She believed very strongly in a 'Mister Right' who would appear from a puff of smoke and make all her dreams come true.

After the play, she took me to a wine bar she frequented. The regulars all knew her by name. The barman didn't need to ask her what she wanted. He already knew.

'This is my bar,' Nina said. 'I don't mean I own it! I mean this is my watering hole. My haven. I come here to write. It's a romantic adventure of sorts. It's all about love.'

I didn't know that Nina was a writer.

'What are you going to call it?' I asked her.

'Heartbreak,' she said.

After a few glasses of wine, Nina started to open up even more. I must say, it was all rather much to handle.

'You see, I'm mad about love! I could fall in love anytime! I am in love with the idea of being in love. This is why I'm so cautious. I know how susceptible I am. People tell me to forget about love. You know, 'Use them before they use you'. But I won't settle for that.'

Her eyes glowed as she looked at me. She continued her love monologue without a pause and grew more animated as she did so. She'd lean in with a hungry look as she slurred on about her passion.

I was starting to feel very uncomfortable.

And yet, I felt sorry for Nina too. If she ever did meet her 'Mister Right', she'd scare the polka dots off him and he'd sprint off without so much as a by your leave.
I made up some excuse about a 'busy day tomorrow' and left.

Back at my flat, I grabbed my diary and started making my first entry in my 'dating ritual' study. It was about 'Romantic Types'. Then I slumped into my bed alone.
I didn't ask Nina out again.

A few days after my 'date' with Nina, I ran into Jillian, an actress who had done some performing at our theatre. It was always rewarding to see her, because she lived with a sunny smile on her face. Her happy presence made everyone around her happy too. Jillian got around quite a lot socially and was full of strange tales of the experiences she'd had.
She told me about all the auditions she'd been attending and famous people she'd seen at parties and clubs. 'I saw Madonna at 'China White'- *a London club*- one night, Ralphy. It was right after she divorced. You should have seen all the boys lining up for their chance!'

I didn't know much about Jillian's personal life. I tried to steer clear of that sort of thing when working at the theatre. I always aimed at keeping things 'professional'.
But this was the new Ralphy now and so I purposefully turned our conversation to personal matters.

She told me that she heard about Nora and my break-up.
'It's so sad, Ralphy. It's one of life's tragedies,' she said ruefully.
And I asked her about how her own affairs of the heart were going.
'Oh! Men! Bad Boys! They're all the same. I just take things as they come.'
'And is anything coming along right now?' I asked her.
'What do you mean?'
'I mean if you're not seeing anyone…'
'Ralphy! Are you asking me out?' she laughed in surprise.
'There's a food festival down at Battersea Park this Saturday. I'm going. Maybe you want to come along with me.'

Jillian stared at me for a moment like she was trying to figure me out. 'OK,' she smiled. 'It's a date.'

We had a fabulously fun time together. Jillian seemed to know every other person who crossed our path. She even knew some of the staff serving the food. She was a social animal just like I am. Or was. I was thinking this was a good sign.

We laid out a blanket, which I had brought along, and ate our food while sitting on the grass. There were hundreds of other picnickers sitting around us.

Several of them knew Jillian too.

We were laughing and joking and sharing our food. I think I was feeling happy again for the first time in far too long.

And then out of somewhere, Jillian asked me the strangest question. 'Ralphy, what do you think of Elvis?'

'Elvis?'

'Elvis Presley, yes, what do you think of him?'

I told her what I thought. 'He's the King of Rock and Roll.'

'No,' she said as she shook her head. 'He's overrated, don't you think?'

'No, Jill, I don't think so. I think he's the King all right.'

And she flashed that most beautiful smile of hers at me.

'You don't know how rare a person you are!' she laughed. 'Usually when I give my 'Elvis Test' to a man I might be interested in, they fail miserably! As soon as I disagree with them, they change their opinion right on the spot to agree with me. Then I know what they're really after.'

(Hmmm. Jillian thought I was 'a man she might be interested in', I mused to myself.)

'What are they really after?' I asked her.

'Sex, Ralphy! Sex! You're one in a million-million, you are!' she said in a burst of laughter.

And it suddenly dawned on me that Jillian was completely out of my league and was a battle-hardened warrior of the dating scene. Why, she even had a test to check her dates' intentions. And as clever as that was, the thought of that had never crossed my mind.

Jillian asked me to come over for drinks that weekend, but I claimed to be busy. I liked her, but this was only a 'research project' I reminded myself. I didn't want a follow-up date.

And, like with Nina, when I returned home, I made my next diary entry and included Jillian's 'Elvis Test' in my summary.

I know this may all sound rather poor form on my part. Using women to be date research test dummies. But, in my defense, I would have felt too awkward to go out with a woman otherwise.
I wasn't trying to bed them or abuse or lie to them. I was just taking Ted's advice to 'put myself out there again.' I needed a break from all my heartache. A 'Heart Break', if you will.
That's my excuse anyway.

I continued taking dating opportunities whenever they presented themselves. That happened maybe six times a month.
If one of them called me back after a date, I'd make up some reason why I was not free to see them again. If I happened to be on a date with a 'man-eater' and she made it clear that she wanted to go 'back to my place', I'd have a ready made get-out clause to deflect that.
I wasn't ready to date yet, let alone sleep with someone new.
And after every interaction, I would continue adding insights into my diary.

I was starting to accumulate a lot of dating information and was quickly learning the ins-and-outs of contemporary dating.

My personal 'Dating Research' experience had now taught me, for instance, to keep well away from single women who lived with a tomcat. To them, the tomcat is more human than you are. Listening to the adventures of Mister Tiggles does not a pleasant evening make.
I learned too to keep my distance from the extremely shy, yet beautiful. They are shy for a reason. An often unspeakable, horrific reason.

Such examples I came across several times in my 'research'.

Look out too for women who tell you far too much too soon about themselves on a first date. You won't be able to get to know them any better than you did the very first time you met them.

Discovering your date's dining habits can also be very revealing. I've seen things done in fine restaurants that wouldn't be acceptable at a wayward kids' birthday party.

Not that I am a candidate for the 'Sophisticated Diner Olympic Team' myself.

But do make sure your date won't swish her finger around in the remainder of her pasta sauce and declare, loudly, 'This is finger lickin' good!'

And then proceed to show you.

There are other dining establishments for dates such as these.

My dating ritual study also highlighted my own dating flaws. I was so rusty that I am sure I squeaked as I walked during some of my dates. Sometimes my conversational skills dried and multiple awkward moments ensued. A lot of my dating disasters were a result of my taking the wrong date to the wrong place or going somewhere out of their 'comfort zone' or mine.

I am sure too that some of my dates thought my behavior was 'peculiar' and would warn other women about 'types' like me.

I tried to keep to my plan of never dating someone more than once. I just kept telling myself 'It's research' and avoided getting involved. I wasn't always successful. Sometimes I liked my date so much that it just naturally came about that we set another time to meet.

But it wasn't right. I was not over Nora. I knew nothing could happen that had any substance. I'd always mention I wasn't really ready for anything more at some point.

No matter the woman I was dating, I always tried to remember that behind all the masks and poses dwells a human being-frail and vulnerable.

Then I'd 'move on' and keep up my research.

Maybe you can't understand my dilemma.

I still loved Nora. The thought of being intimate with someone else was repellent to me. I had made a mistake with someone in Holland once and regretted it immediately.

I knew Nora was my desire. But she was gone.

What can I tell you? My heart was broken and not yet repaired.

If such things are ever really 'repaired'.

So, while others would have simply gone with the flow and let the mess fall where it may, I could not exercise that option.

Perhaps you like to play the field and taste all the sweets offered to you. Or you could be lonely and would love to go on any date at all and cry your prayers at night that you might 'meet someone'.
But I was in neither of those camps.

I took no advantage of any offers for a quick fumble or more. I enjoyed the company of my dates, for the most part, and that was it. And I can only tell you, if you are a predator and relish the game, that even the mad postmodern feminist man-eaters end up hurt by your casualness.
I have mopped up their tears many times myself over the years.
I listened to all the fallout.
All the heartbreak. But that's your business.

And if you are lonely and desperate, try telling yourself that you are not. Lonely and desperate reads just like a plane skywriting. It only guarantees that you will remain lonely and desperate.

Trust me, most of the real information you pick up from your date is not spoken. It is in the attitude and the eye contact. Look for the kind of person with whom you hope to be.
'I want to be with anyone!' is the best way to guarantee that you won't be.
And be sure to figure out the kind of person you are yourself too before you start out.
If you don't know what you are looking for, you have no chance in finding it.

And for all who have given up on dating, reduce it to soulless, nihilistic groping, and turn it into a sex hunt instead, or as Nina put it, 'Use them before they use you', you might find my reticence to take advantage of my situation 'repressed' or 'old school'.
That's your business too.
But if you are divorced, when you didn't hope to be, or have lost a long term partner to illness or misfortune, then I think you will understand my predicament quite clearly.

I am no 'dating guru'. That's for certain. But I share with you what I came to know.

221

I guess I was about six months into my research project when I met Margarita.

I took one of my dates to a comedy club where a series of stand-ups were performing.
At one point, an excessively tall, blond woman walked up to the microphone.
She had to adjust the mike up another foot from where the previous comic had left it. She was a giantess. Her mere presence grabbed the room's attention before she even opened her mouth.
She spoke with a Swedish accent as she introduced herself.

'Hello, boys! Hello, girls! My name is Margarita. I'm Swedish, meatballs!' she began.

Her comedy act was basically a deconstruction of men who had dated her.
'Men are emotional zeroes. Go with a man and you are already babysitting!'

Her entire set ran in that vein.

'And men just can't take a hint. I tell one of them to 'Hop off that way, Little Bunny,' and he says, *'Ah! I like it when women play hard to get!'*
'Idiot!'
'I go back to my flat and there he is holding flowers and a cheap bottle of sparkling pink 'plonk'.'
'I say, 'What's this?' and he says, *'It's a sign of my undying love and affection for you.'*
'He doesn't even know me!' she exclaimed with her eyes wide.
'It's a sign of your major lunatic dysfunction, I told him!
And he just stood there smiling like the village idiot!'

I must say her stuff was going down very well with the women in the audience. My date was laughing her head off. Margarita's Swedish accent only served to make it all that much funnier. The men in the audience were laughing too, but I think that was more motivated by their leering at the comic Swedish titan.

I went back to the comedy club on my own the next night. Margarita would be perfect for my dating ritual research project. It was obvious that she had a lot of experience in that arena.

And, unlike Nina or Jillian, she was not an old acquaintance who might read too much into my interest. Plus it was a challenge. I didn't know her. I'd have to break the ice on my own.

I hadn't the need for that so far. I was simply dating women who were somehow associated with my former social/theatre circle. Margarita was different.

After she finished her set, she walked over to the club bar for a drink. She was a popular addition there. Audience members would walk up to her and tell her how funny she was. I saw three different men chat her up and press slips of paper with their phone numbers into her hand. After they'd leave, she'd crumble up their phone numbers and throw them behind the bar. 'Another fake agent who says he'll make me a star,' she yawned to the barman.

When I saw my chance, I walked up to her and introduced myself.

'I am researching a play about dating from the man's perspective. You seem to have a good handle on how women view it,' I ventured as an ice breaker.

'You're a playwright?' she asked while trying to size me up.

I explained what I was in the midst of writing.

'I haven't a title for it yet,' I told her.

Our conversation was punctuated every now and then by interruptions as strange men drunkenly tried their luck with her. She gave them all short shrift.

'If you've the time, maybe we can meet for coffee and share our stories,' I asked her.

She gazed down at me. In her high heels, she must have been at least a foot taller than I was. She was what, I guess, people call an 'Amazon'. She towered over the entire room.

'OK. Maybe we can have your coffee,' she said with suspicion.

We agreed on a place and time to meet.

When we met for our coffee and chat, I discovered that Margarita was not always in comic mode, despite her comedy background. I figured that much out right away. She could be gloomy, in fact.

She'd laugh and be silly when a topic was light and breezy, but that quickly faded away when we began to discuss 'dating'.

'Men are pigs,' she declared over her coffee. 'I trust none of them. Even nice guys like you are pigs, but you just don't know it.'
I didn't disagree. I know plenty of men who are 'pigs'. I guess they were all that she had come across. There are enough of them.

I told Margarita about my experience with 'Tomcat-owning' women and 'Elvis Test' women and 'Mister Right' women and the rest. She just shook her head.
'That all may be so, but it is you men who make us so crazy!' She insisted.
'Everything that comes out of your mouths is a lie in some sense. I mean, are you really even writing a play at all?'

I don't know why I did this. Maybe her question took me by surprise. I didn't really know Margarita. But for some reason, she was the first person I told what had really happened to Nora and me.
I must have laid it on pretty thick. I could see she was becoming tearful.

'My father did the same thing to my mother and me. He didn't love us. He loved vodka and his spirit mistress killed him. I haven't trusted men ever since. They are emotional zeroes!'
That was the first line in her stand-up routine, I remembered.
'My ex-husband didn't even rate a zero!' she laughed.
'And still you make a joke of it,' I said.
'Laughter is the only medicine, Sir,' she informed me.

Like Jillian, Margarita was entirely out of my league.
Maybe more so.
Again, as in the comedy club bar, strange men would just walk up to our table at the coffee bar and try their luck with her. She shot them all down as coldly as you like.
It was easy to see that she was well-practiced in dealing with unwanted admirers.

Margarita quizzed me some more about my 'research'.
'Some women, I've learned, will do an entire web search about you before your date,' I told her.

'They tell you all about your virtual self. Watch out for them. Their insatiable curiosity about you will not end there. I caught two of that sort snooping through my diary. And another one poking through my coat pockets after I excused myself to go to the restroom!'
'Beware the men who swear the 'little movie' they're taking of you on their mobile is 'just for them',' Margarita countered.

We ordered another coffee. When it arrived, I took out the little leather diary where I kept my notes and showed it to her.
She flicked through it, looked at me, and said, 'I suppose you slept with all of them as well. Where's the scorecard on that smorgasbord?'
I told her it was strictly research and there was no 'smorgasbord'.
'Therapeutic research,' I said.
She rolled her eyes, smiling as she did so.

'This is fun,' I remember thinking to myself.
I guess she was thinking the same thing.
'So, when are you going to ask me out to dinner?' she asked to my surprise.
'Monday's good,' she added.

And so, that Monday, I took her to a Swedish restaurant in North London called 'Anna's Place'. 'It's like a little Sweden in London, Ralphy,' a friend told me by way of recommendation.
It had a very Scandinavian look. I mean, it was very clean in design without ruffles or bows. Lots of wood. Plenty of window light.

We walked up together to the reservation desk.
'Table for two for Mr. Waldo,' I said.
Margarita found that hilarious. I realized that she had never heard my surname before.
'Mr. Valdo!' she said in mock imitation as we made our way to our table.
'I'll call you Mr. Volvo! It reminds me of home!'
She was very funny, as I say, when the mood struck her.
Which was often.

It couldn't have been easy being Margarita. She must have been well over six feet tall in her stocking feet, I imagine. And on all the occasions at which I had seen her, she seemed to be wearing ever higher and higher heels.

I know I didn't reach her shoulder blades as we walked together to our table. I bet she was nearly seven feet tall in the high heeled boots she was wearing.

Believe me, every eye swayed her way, male or female.

We ordered some drinks before looking at the menu.

'I wonder what you'll write in your little diary tonight?' she teased me.

And then it dawned on me that Margarita was the first 'date' I had been on who knew I was doing 'research'.

I changed the subject.

'Margarita, you see any weather-balloons up there? Do you have to duck from the ducks?' I asked her as our drinks arrived.

'I'm getting a crick in my neck trying to look you in the eye. Why do always wear such high heels?'

'Oh! Mr. Volvo!' she responded with a sigh. 'They stare at me in flip-flops. They stare at me in running shoes. People stare at me. May as well give them something to stare at.'

Her voice had the resigned tone of someone who had surrendered to their fate long ago.

Then she looked at me and said, 'But you, Mr. Volvo, you don't stare at me. You see me.'

I could see that the thought of that pleased her.

Margarita looked at her menu.

'They serve 'Flygande Jacob' here! I haven't had that for ages!'

I looked at the dish she desired. It was an odd sounding chicken, bacon, and banana combo. When it was time to place our order, I went for the meatballs with warm potato salad.

After we ordered, I told Margarita about a few of the 'Date Dining Disasters' I had suffered or caused myself during my research project.

It was the perfect topic.

Margarita's own dining disaster stories put mine to shame.

'I once went with a Greco-Roman Olympic wrestling champion,' she began bitter-sweetly.

'He was Ukrainian. I couldn't eat with him in public. Every time, after he ate, he used to pound his chest hard three times and then see how long his belch could last,' she continued with perfect comic timing.

'I used to call him 'He-Man'. His antics would have fit in perfectly around a Neanderthal's campfire.'

'Or a Viking's,' I added.

'Well, this Viking Woman would have none of it! He had his uses, but as a dining companion, no.'

There was no doubt about it. Margarita's was the most pleasurable 'date' I had yet been on.

And when our food arrived, she was blissfully ecstatic.

'I haven't had this since I was a little girl!' She sighed happily.

I think the best way I could describe our dinner conversation is to liken it to a comedy boxing match.

Margarita would have a dig at the male of the species, often with devastating effect. And I'd respond with jabs and left hooks as I tore into the female dating psyche.

A battle of mordent wits or, in my case, mordant half-wit.

'About a month ago,' she said. 'I was doing a gig and this bloke kept throwing condoms up on the stage, the idiot. I stopped what I was saying and started to blow them up and pretend I was making balloon sculptures!'

'Yeah?' I replied. 'Well, I once went out with a woman who ripped off one of my shirt buttons, told me she knew 'Black Magic', and said she was going to put a love spell on me!'

We shared a horselaugh over that one.

Margarita was so much fun. OK, I did have to stare down two different men, who couldn't keep their eyes off Margarita. Even though their own wives or girlfriends were sitting right there with them. I wasn't convinced they were stealing a look, because they were fans of Margarita's stand-up work.

That was annoying. But she herself was witty, very funny, and didn't stick her finger in her sauce. Not even once.

She played no 'Elvis Test' games either. And neither did I.

Our conversation created its own momentum. Neither of us needed to waste a moment's thought on what we might say next.

There was a relaxing flow between us. An effortless flow.

'Here's one from the archives, Margarita,' I said chuckling to myself.

'One of my 'research-dates' told me she called some stranger who'd given her his number on the 'Tube'.
She said, *'So, I said to myself, why not? And I called him! A woman answered. I think it was his wife. He seemed so nice too!'*
'While she's telling me this, I'm thinking, *'If you don't know why it's unwise to call some strange guy who presses their phone number into your hand, because they saw you on a public conveyance, I don't know what to say!'* I laughed.
Margarita shook her head sadly at the insanity of that.
'Synade blått,' she said.
'What did you say?' I asked in confusion.
'Synade blått,' she repeated slowly. ''Blue-eyed' as we say in Sweden. Someone who welcomes the wolf in the door, because they cannot see it is the wolf.'
'I'll be stealing that expression for myself!' I laughed.

Ours was the best conversation I'd had, since Nora began her drinking.

Our waitress cleared our plates and brought over dessert menus.
'Mr. Volvo, this place is wonderful! Look! They have Mandelflarn! And Morotskaka and Jordgubbskram too!! It's a Swedish heaven here!'
Yes, these strange sounding concoctions were all on the dessert menu.
'So which do you fancy?' I asked her.
She stopped and put down her menu. She cocked her head to one side and pondered me for a few seconds.
Then she said, 'I think, Mr. Volvo, we can make a better dessert than any of these.'
There had been a few post-dinner 'dessert cliché overtures' on other dates, such as Margarita's, but hers was undoubtedly the best of the lot.
I had considered none of these offers before, but threw my research overboard after considering Margarita's dessert offer.
'Your kitchen or mine?' she added.
'Yours,' I said. 'A Swedish kitchen will be better equipped.'
We paid the bill and left.

I tried hailing a Black Cab in front of the restaurant, but they were all occupied as they drove by. I knew there was a 'mini-cab' office just a short walk away and suggested we get a cab there.

228

And just as we were making our way there, I saw her.
It was Nora.

She was seated with three men on a street bench just ahead of us.
Two of them were West Indians and the other one was a rough
looking white guy covered in tattoos.
Nora seemed to be in a drunken stupor. I don't think she even
noticed me.
The two West Indians were sharing something hidden in a paper bag.
The Tattooed guy was openly drinking from a large plastic cider
bottle.

I looked at Nora as Margarita and I moved closer to where she was
seated. Her left eye was a sore-looking, nasty, black-and-blue slit.
Her right cheek was badly swollen and distorted.
She clearly had been beaten repeatedly.

As the two of us passed the bench, the three drunken men took turns
shouting abuse at Margarita.
'Hey! Blondie! Blondie! We got a drink for you, Gorgeous! Oy!
Blondie! Look at 'em long legs!'
And then one of them, the rough-looking tattooed character, walked
up to her and put his arm around her waist.
'Say, Blondie! I got what you want! Sit yourself down!'

Before I had a chance to react, Margarita shot an elbow hard and low
into his ribs. It looked like a well practiced self-defense move.
'A fighter!' Tattooed guy slurred as he winced and stumbled back
over to his companions on the bench. They were all full of deranged
laughter. Except for Nora.
She just remained in her stupor. She did glance up while her drinking
buddies were harassing my date, but there was not a flicker of
recognition in her eyes.

We made it to the mini-cab office and, when a cab was free, headed
off to Margarita's flat. I didn't tell her that Nora was the woman on
the bench with those drunks. In fact, she was one of the drunks
herself.

I was a mess in that cab. Here I was going home for the night with
quite a Swedish dish. A dish I really liked. That excited me and was
new to me.

But I also hated myself for leaving Nora there with those street rats.

Even if you are divorced that doesn't end your emotional attachment to your former partner. Legally, maybe, I had no responsibility for Nora anymore, but that didn't make me feel any better about it.

I didn't want to tell Margarita that Nora was the female part of that drunken crew who had harassed her. It would only have put a dampener on things.
And I liked Margarita. She was more than just good company. I could imagine us working out well together. There was something there between us.
But seeing Nora like that was too much. I hardly spoke a word in that cab.

'Mr. Volvo, you are as silent as a Finn,' Margarita pointed out as we left the cab and made our way to her door.
'You don't have room for Swedish dessert?'
I regretted saying, 'I better get back to mine,' as soon as I said it.
Margarita gave me a peck on the cheek.
'You are a funny one, Mr. Volvo!' she laughed.
And I made my way home. Alone.

I felt like going back to that bench to slaughter Nora's drinking thugs. I felt like going back to Margarita's place. I felt like crawling into a dark hole and dying. I was a mess of contradictions. I had just been feeling the best I had felt for many months and then felt the worst I've ever felt. I felt stupid and guilty. I felt helpless and hopeless. I felt all those things. All together and all at the same time.

That night, after I got home, I decided that my dating research was over. Margarita's date was my last and final entry.
I didn't see Margarita again and she wasn't the type to call.

But I didn't lose contact with her.
I heard she moved back to Sweden. I know she met someone, married, and had two kids with him. I know that she continued with her stand-up work too.

I know all this, because we're linked together on a social networking site where you can keep tabs on those who once crossed your path.
No interaction is like two ships passing in the night anymore.

These days, I suppose, you can peak into the various lives you might have lived had you made other choices.
As an example, I could imagine, if I had wished, what life may have ensued had I partaken of my Swedish dessert.
Virtual, virtual lives.

And as for Nora, I would occasionally see her on the street in the company of other local drunks. But I never spoke with her.

Then, a few months after the drunken street bench incident, there was the sound of someone fiddling with the lock on my front door. It was the middle of the night. I bolted out of bed, grabbed a baseball bat, and flung the door open.

It was Nora. Her clothes were torn and her left breast was exposed. She was stinking drunk. She had forgotten that we no longer lived together. She just stood there tottering and said nothing.
I let her in and she promptly passed out on the couch.
The next morning, when I got up, she was gone.

The memory of that night is burned into me forever.

Eventually, I did write a play based on my dating diary research.
It was the most painful writing I had ever done.
Even if I did try to slip in some comic moments to lighten the mood.
I called it '*Heart Break*'.

My apologies to Nina for stealing (well, sort of stealing) the title for her book on love and using it for my own play's title.

Heart Break won an international online drama competition of no particular acclaim, but it was never produced.
However, if you must hunt on the web, you might find it under 'British New Plays Competition Winners'.
At least, I think you'll find it there.
And you can read it for yourself.

Then you'll know my tale of 'Heart Break' is true.

STORY CHAPTER TWELVE

'THE FINAL SCENARIO'

I needed to find a new identity. I had to find my place again in this world. I didn't know who I was anymore. Where did I fit in?
Before, I was one half of 'Nora and Ralphy'.
Now, I was just 'Ralphy'. But who was he? Where was he?

It was during this search to answer those questions, when I first became a 'professional role-player'.
It was the start of my new life after Nora and I were no more.
It is also my first 'Post-Nora' story.

This tale I am about to tell eventually became a scene in a play I penned called *The Men In Black*. Not the Hollywood movie of that name. The play is nothing like the movie and was written long before the movie's release.
I've told it as a story many times before it became a scene in a play too.

Sometimes, I would tell this story while in the midst of my research on dating rituals for a new play I was writing. It would depend on the date of course. Not all my 'research dates' would respond well to my 'Alistair Story'.
If they mentioned they were into horror or sci-fi though, I might burn this offering:

I once met a psychiatrist. We were working together. He was examining student 'shrinks' during their final assessments before they qualified as psychiatrists in their own right.
I was there working as a 'simulated patient'. Students would interview me in front of the examiner who would mark down how well, or not, they did.

I'd ask student after student three questions about drug side-effects. The same exact three questions in precisely the same manner all day long. It was tediously repetitive work.

I was just recently divorced and had given up on the theater my 'ex' and I had run together. I had to earn my living anyway I could.

After the students finished interviewing me, the examining psychiatrist would then ask them some more questions and further mark their forms.
We were working together all day long.

After the exam, we went out for a beer together.
Michael, the psychiatrist, told me he was the current President of the British Psychiatric Association.
I was in need of extra money at the time, as I say. Nora and I were finished and both she and my previous work were gone.
And I stumbled upon an idea.

'Michael, have you ever thought about using simulated patients to train practicing psychiatrists? Not just students?'
He blinked at me.
'Say you wrote some scenarios about real patients, we wouldn't use their real names, and then you and other psychiatrists could observe one another interviewing me.'
He didn't look skeptical.
'And you could use any test cases you liked. For instance, you might have one about a violent patient and then you can all talk among yourselves, after I've been interviewed, to see if what you saw and heard in the interview was the best way to go.'
I was thinking on my feet.

Now, I really must tell you this. Since that first meeting with Michael, I have worked with psychiatrists for many years now and they are as slippery as you can get. Michael certainly was. He was irredeemably emotionless. I could never tell what he was really thinking or feeling.
Detached, I suppose, is the word that most nearly best describes him. No offence to psychiatrists, but you know many of you are just that. Detached.
The form has been franked many times.
But I did not have that accumulated wisdom then.

And Michael said, 'That's a very intriguing idea. We've never used role-play in such a way before. We've a seminar coming up about 'suicide watch' in consultations.'

'OK,' I encouraged him.
(That was the first time I had ever heard the word 'role-play'. Outside the bedroom, at any rate.)
'And perhaps we could bring you along and try what you suggest,' he said while nodding his head.

So we rapidly agreed a fee. It was a lot more money than the 'simulated patient' agency work paid.
Michael explained that he would send me five test case scenarios to learn and I would memorize these and portray them at the seminar. The seminar was a month away.

But Michael did not send the scenarios. He promised and promised. 'You'll have them first thing in the morning,' he'd say when I rang to remind him.
But still they did not appear.
It was going to take me some considerable time to learn five scenarios.

The seminar was now a week away.

And then midweek in that final week, a courier knocked on my door. I opened the courier pack. At last. It was the scenarios. And a note. *'Better late than never. Michael.'*

I made a pot of coffee and sat myself down with Michael's materials.

Michael and I had agreed that he would not include any information on the outcome of the test case scenarios so as to avoid any bias in my portrayal. We didn't want the psychiatrists doing the interviews with me to read any 'tells' on my part. If I knew, for example, that the patient went on to self-harm after therapy, I might be too tempted to 'over-egg' my role.
So I was in the dark as much as they were about what actually happened to the real patients after they had been evaluated and received treatment.

All the scenarios were similar. They were all about people who had self-harmed in some way and were a danger to themselves.
Some were just 'fed up' and didn't care about anyone or anything. Not even themselves.

234

Others were about people so overwhelmed by guilt or grief that they could see no way back. They all just wanted to 'end it all'.
It was not easy reading.

Like I say, they were all of that ilk. Until, that is, I read the fifth and final scenario.
And it is here where my story really begins.

The first four scenarios were of similar length with about the same amount of background information, but the fifth scenario was much longer. There were pages and pages of consultation notes. These included interviews and follow-up sessions and suggested diagnoses as well. There was more background on the fifth scenario alone than in all the others put together.

Let me be honest. The fifth scenario was truly off the wall. I had never heard of such a thing before.

According to the notes in the courier pack, the patient was a man who was terrified of mirrors or in seeing any reflection of himself at all.
He was convinced that his life would change forever, if he ever saw his own reflection.
I thought Michael sent so much information on this patient, because he was intrigued by him too.

The fifth scenario went on to reveal that this unfortunate fellow had been picked up by the police who had stopped him from jumping off an overpass on a highway. This is how he first came under the radar of mental health services.
The police obtained a court order that this man be forced to undergo psychological evaluation as he was a threat to his own safety.

Let's call the patient, Alistair, even if that is not his real name.
Anyway, 'Alistair' immediately claimed at the start of his psychological evaluation that he was not the person the psychiatrist was talking to at present.

'I am not the tall, thin man you see sitting in front of you!' he insisted.
'I am much shorter! With male pattern baldness! I have two kids!'

235

The consultation notes mentioned that Alistair was extremely 'agitated' and 'desperate' throughout his initial evaluation.
Other case notes stated that there was no record of his having any children or any family at all for that matter. Furthermore, the physical description of Alistair at his evaluation described him as an extremely tall and emaciated man. Not this short, bald guy he kept vehemently insisting he 'really' was.
'This isn't me!' he bellowed. 'This isn't me!'

Fascinated, I read on.

The psychiatric notes mentioned that the consultant evaluating Alistair attempted to calm him down, but with little success. He acknowledged, in the hope of gaining his trust, that he understood Alistair thought he was other than the person he appeared to be.
The notes went on to say that Alistair would always look down when he spoke and focus on the ground when up and moving.
He would never look anyone in the eye.

'When you say that this is not you, what do you mean by that?' the psychiatrist asked him. 'Why do you think you are not as you appear?'
And Alistair said, 'I mean before this. Before this now. Then. Then I looked different. Then I … my children!' He sobbed.
But finally the psychiatrist did manage to calm down the agitated Alistair enough for him to tell his story. Well, at least some of it.

Michael had included the original transcript of that initial interview.
The real name of 'Alistair' had been blacked out.
I am paraphrasing, but the gist of that interview went something like this:

Alistair
'And so you see, Doctor, I finally decided to listen to her and come to see you.'

Doctor
'Listen to whom?'

Alistair
'My daughter, Janet. She could tell her daddy was suffering.'

236

Doctor
'Your daughter told you to come here?'

Alistair
'Yes, I was afraid no one would believe me. But she insisted.'

Doctor
'Janet did?'

Alistair
'Yes, Janet. She's only fourteen, but she really runs the show at our house.'

Doctor
'I am afraid, Alistair, that it was the police who were responsible for my seeing you.'

Alistair
'The police?'

Doctor
'Yes, the police said that you tried to jump from an overpass. You don't recall that?'

Alistair
'Yes! The overpass! But that was after Janet told me to come and see you.'

Doctor
'According to police documents, you do not have any children, Alistair. Is that incorrect?'

Alistair
'Janet! She's gone now! But she did exist. And Toby too! He's my son! And they're both gone now!'

Doctor
'They died?'

Alistair
'No! I died to them.'

Doctor
'I don't understand. You died?'

Alistair
'Yes! I disappeared.'

Doctor
'You abandoned them?'

Alistair
'No, I disappeared and then they disappeared too.'

And 'Alistair' grew so distraught at his 'loss' that he could not carry on.

The psychiatrist stated in his notes that Alistair was utterly convinced that parts of his life were 'disappearing' and that no one would believe him, because he could not prove what he knew in his heart to be true. The psychiatrist recommended that Alistair receive further counseling and be hospitalized for his own protection. He was to be placed on 'suicide watch' as he was clearly at risk.

Alistair was then sent to a mental health institution for further evaluation and therapy.

I read through the admission notes of senior staff while Alistair was in hospital.
As soon as he was shown to his room, he immediately shattered a mirror above the wash basin. He grew hysterical and held his hands firmly over his eyes until every single piece of the mirror was removed by hospital staff. He placed papers and any object he could find on any reflective surfaces. He would sit for hours at a time staring at the walls. If anyone came into his room, he would never look up or into their eyes. Despite several attempts at medicating him, he grew worse. He was in a perpetual state of anxiety and fear.

I happened across an interview a few weeks after he was sent to the institution.

As Alistair was not responding to drug therapy nor capable of calmly explaining what his problems were during consultations, he was offered hypnotherapy to see if that might help him to talk about his anxieties.

During this hypnotherapy session, Alistair explained when he first noticed his 'disappearing'.

Alistair
'I am not here right now.'

Doctor
'What do you mean by 'right now? '

Alistair
'I mean who I am right now is not who I was before!'

Doctor
'Please, just remain calm and relaxed as you are. Speak slowly. You are doing well. I am here to help you.'

Alistair
'Yes, forgive me.'

Doctor
'Could you tell me exactly when you first noticed this all happening?'

Alistair
'Do you believe me?'

Doctor
'I believe that you believe this to be true. Just relax and know you are safe. Tell me when it all began. Then perhaps I can better understand your circumstance.'

And this is what Alistair said:

Alistair

'All right. I was sleeping. Or at least I suspect I was sleeping. And I
didn't look anything like this! I was shorter! I ..'

Doctor

'Try not to let yourself be sidetracked.'

Alistair

'Yes. Anyway, I woke up. I guess I can say I woke up. And there
standing at the end of my bed were three men.'

Doctor

'You saw three men? What were they doing?'

Alistair

'They were like in silhouette. They wore black fedora hats. All three
of them. They were wearing capes too. Black capes.'

Doctor

'What were they doing there? Did you recognize them?'

Alistair

'They looked like they walked out of some old movie.'

Doctor

'Yes?'

Alistair

'I did not know them. I didn't know why they were there. But they
stood there staring at me.'

Doctor

'Could you see their faces?'

Alistair

'No, I ...wait! Yes! I could see they were smiling. They were smiling
and staring at me.'

Doctor

'They were smiling?'

Alistair

'Yes! And they all started nodding together.'

Doctor

'Nodding? You mean as if to indicate 'yes'?'

Alistair

'That's what I thought.'

Doctor

'Did they speak?'

Alistair

'No. Not a word. They were as silent as death.'

Doctor

'I see. And then?'

Alistair

'I thought I must be dreaming. I looked away and pinched my arm, but when I looked back up they were still there.'

Doctor

'So you weren't dreaming?'

Alistair

'How I wish I were! How I wish it were all a dream!'

Doctor

'You are safe here. Remain calm. This is very helpful. Please try to continue.'

Alistair

'They...they placed something at the foot of my bed. Some objects. And then they just walked away.'

Doctor

'So you saw them go?'

Alistair

'It was like figures disappearing into a shadow. And they were gone.'

Doctor
'And you got up?'

Alistair
'Yes. I got up. I switched on the light and got up to take a look.'

Doctor
'And what did you see?'

Alistair
'The objects. They were there all right.'

Doctor
'Objects of what sort?'

Alistair
'They were oddly shaped ceramic pieces. Yes, I can see them now.
One, I remember, was shaped like a crescent moon. Another, almost
like a star. I couldn't make out the other shapes.'

Doctor
'You are doing well. So these other shapes were nothing you could
recognize?'

Alistair
'No. Oddly shaped.'

Doctor
'And what did you do when you saw these objects?'

Alistair
'I bent down. How I wish I hadn't!'

Doctor
'You bent down?'

Alistair
'Yes. If I hadn't touched them!'

Doctor
'You are safe. Go on. So you touched them?'

Alistair
'Yes'

Doctor
'And what happened then?'

Alistair
'It's so peculiar. The instant I touched them they changed.'

Doctor
'Changed? In what way?'

Alistair
'I touched the crescent moon and it became a bunch of paper flowers.'

Doctor
'Paper flowers?'

Alistair
'I touched the star and it became a silken scarf.'

Doctor
'All the objects changed as you touched them?'

Alistair
'Yes. They changed like I was a magician performing parlour tricks.'

Doctor
'You felt you were a magician?'

Alistair
'They all became like cheap magic store trinkets.'

Doctor
'And where are these items now?'

Alistair
'In my bedroom.'

Doctor
'But you are homeless. Where is your bedroom?'

Alistair

'Not now. The bedroom in my house where I used to live. Before all this.'

Doctor

'OK. Before 'all this'. What happened after the change to the objects?'

Alistair

'I was stunned. I was spooked. That's the only word for it.'

Doctor

'You were in shock?'

Alistair

'Yes, shock. I went over to the sink. I threw cold water in my face…'

Doctor

'You splashed your face with water?'

Alistair

'I thought it would clear my head.'

Doctor

'Yes?'

Alistair

'But when I looked back up into the mirror, it wasn't me staring back!'

Doctor

'It wasn't you?'

Alistair

'I ran out the door. I ran outside. I was gasping for air. I had to be dreaming. But when I tried to go back to my house it was different.'

Doctor

'How was it different?'

Alistair

'It wasn't my house anymore. It was painted a different colour. My keys wouldn't work in the lock!'

Doctor

'Please try to remain calm.'

Alistair

'This isn't me! Those men! They took my home from me. They stole my identity. They took my children from me. Every time I see my reflection now I become someone else!'

Doctor

'I understand.'

Alistair

'No, you don't understand! I've changed dozens of times, since that night! Anytime I'd catch my reflection, it was someone else staring back at me!
I look in a mirror and my children are gone! I see myself in the reflection of a window and I am a woman! Or obese! Or a teenager! Or an old man!
I know who I am! I am not this me!'

He went on to say that after he suffered these 'changes', he'd often find himself 'transported' to unfamiliar surroundings as well.

Alistair

'Sometimes I don't know who I am or where I am!'

The hypnotherapist reported that Alistair became so agitated that he had to end the session and bring Alistair out of his trance state. And once he had, Alistair jumped up and immediately began to beat his own head repeatedly against the interview room wall. Security staff rushed in to restrain him.
'You won't remember me!' he wailed as they took him away.

Eventually, he had to be physically restrained even in his own room. He could not be allowed to continue harming himself.

In his notes, the therapist wrote that Alistair was in serious danger and may have developed 'multiple personalities'. He felt that Alistair may be repressing these personalities.

I put down Alistair's story. I wasn't sure how best to portray him at the seminar. There were so many different 'theories and opinions' about his condition that I didn't know where to start.

And finally it was the day of the seminar itself.

The first part of the day covered some discussions of personal experiences with 'suicide watch' patients. It was tragic listening.

There were perhaps a hundred psychiatrists in attendance. I had hoped to have a quick word with Michael about 'Alistair', but he was so busy with his colleagues that there was no opportunity.

And then it was time for me to do the five scenarios. I would do all five scenarios on the trot and there would be discussion and feedback after each scenario. That was the plan.

The first four test cases went very smoothly.

I did the one about the mathematics teacher who was convinced that the rest of the school staff were laughing at him behind his back and how they blamed him for the school's poor performance. He just wanted to die, because 'It would be better for everyone'.
I portrayed a drug-addicted patient who was thrown out of his halfway house for having sex with another patient. He'd prefer to die rather than to go back to living on the streets.
I 'role-played' a man who was raped when returning from a pub. He lived with his mother and was so ashamed that she might find out that he attempted to hang himself. Another scenario was about a schizophrenic man who kept telling the doctors that 'All will be revealed' when they'd ask him what the TV 'voices' he was hearing were telling him to do.

I was interviewed by one of the psychiatrists in front of the entire group and the doctors all would then offer suggestions about how they might have handled things differently. They'd tell each other how things were done in their own practices.

And after all the discussion and feedback, Michael would tell the rest of the group what actually happened with that patient.

'He was managed with drug therapy and counseling. He did not go on to self-harm.'

Or

'This patient's risk assessment was evaluated improperly. He went on to hang himself while still in hospital.'

Michael did this for each of the first four scenarios.

Michael looked very pleased with how everything was going. Well, 'very pleased' for Michael anyway. As I told you, he was impossible to read. Perhaps he was just pleased with himself.

But Michael's pleasure, whatever the source, would be short-lived.

After someone volunteered to do the final scenario with me, I prepared myself to become 'Alistair'.

The interview itself went very well. I did my best 'tormented soul' impersonation. I tried to convey a sense that Alistair truly believed in what he was saying. The interviewing doctor did an excellent job. She was calming and non-judgmental and 'Alistair' was able to open up to her.

And then Michael called 'time' and it was over.

Just as with the other test cases, Michael asked for feedback on the interview.

And, as before, the observing psychiatrists gave their input.

I was feeling very good and quite satisfied about a job well done, when a man stood up.

He had long white hair that would not have been out of place on the head of a fairy tale warlock and he clearly held himself in some regard.

He mumbled his name, Dr. Werner, before launching into a tirade directed at Michael.

'This is simply..,' he sputtered, 'This is simply an outrage! This is nothing short of fraud! Our esteemed President Michael is using this seminar to validate his own research and crackpot theories!

I understand you are now writing a sequel to your *The Men In Black Syndrome*?' he asked sneeringly.

I learned later that Dr Werner was a rival of Michael's. He resented Michael's Presidency of the Association. They did not get along and that's an understatement.

'Your behaviour is transparently unprofessional!' He ranted.
'Our President should not be writing spurious psychobabble for the masses! *The Men In Black Syndrome*! It's beneath contempt!'

I hadn't a clue what *The Men In Black Syndrome* was about. I tried to read it later. It's mainly a theory Michael had about patients who claimed to have been abducted by aliens or spirits. His research showed that a significant proportion of these patients subsequently claimed to have been visited by three men dressed in black. Michael's conjecture was that these patients 'humanized' their perceived alien abductors by changing what was unfathomable to them into these more human 'Men In Black'.
It goes on to discuss the symbolism of 'groupings of three' and how 'black descriptive terms' are significant in assessing a patient's mood.
But I don't need to go into all that here.

'I know this case particularly well,' Dr Werner crowed as he tossed his mane.
'In fact, I was the doctor the hospital requested review this case. There was no evidence that 'Alistair' claimed to have been visited or taken by aliens. How dare you present this case to seminar to lend credence to your own dubious research!'

And then two other psychiatrists tried feebly to intervene, 'I don't feel this is the appropriate forum.' and 'I feel this is unhelpful language in facilitating discussion.' Michael, meanwhile, just stood there as emotionless as a snake.
But Dr Werner would not be silenced.
'This will be taken up at Council!' He roared.
And shaking that ash-white clown wig of his in rage, he flounced out of the room.

There was an uneasy silence. And then, in his detached and dismissive way, Michael just carried on as if nothing had happened. As with all the other scenarios, he facilitated more feedback and informed the rest of the group of Alistair's fate. He spoke in exactly the same measured tones as before Dr Werner's outburst.

'We do not know, with any certainty, what happened with Alistair,' Michael explained. 'We suspect he somehow left hospital without staff noticing. It's an enigmatic situation by general consensus. Hospital staff notes record that Alistair was fed, medicated, and then restrained for the night. But there was no sign of him at morning inspection. Somehow he had escaped during the night.'

That couldn't have been easy, I thought. To get out of restraints, exit a locked and alarmed door, go through corridors and other locked and alarmed doors without anyone noticing? No, that couldn't have been easy.

'An investigation into his escape looked for any changes to normal hospital practices that may have led to security lapses,' Michael continued. 'Their investigation noted that the only change to routine at the time of Alistair's disappearance was a change in the patients' serving trays. The blue plastic trays, formerly in use, were replaced with aluminium trays for hygienic purposes. Staff indicated that some of the patients were upset by this change to their daily routine.'

I was taking all this in, when Dr Werner suddenly burst back into the room. He was still foaming in his fury.
'So what lies have you been telling them now? Fraud!'
He looked at the rest of the group and said, 'Has he convinced you that we lost a patient through alien abduction?!'
And with that he charged at Michael and grabbed his shoulders trying to pull him down to the floor.
'Fraud!'

I ran over to separate them. Michael was struggling like a sumo wrestler trying to keep his feet.
'Dr Werner!' I shouted, as I tried to pull him off. 'Dr Werner!' and finally he relented.
Dr Werner was huffing and puffing. His face was all rosy red.

You can see why this story ended up as a scene in a play. Unseemly grappling by professional psychiatrists? Alien abduction? You couldn't ask for more.

But real life is stranger sometimes than any play could ever hope to be.

Dr Werner caught his breath and then said, 'Let me tell you the truth! Alistair's disappearance was thoroughly investigated. They concluded that he must have had assistance in making his escape. He was not whisked away by aliens! In fact, closed-circuit cameras clearly showed an unknown, short, balding man in the hospital corridor on the night of his disappearance. Admittedly, the absence of any image of Alistair himself on security cameras remains a mystery. Perhaps this unknown man hid Alistair in a laundry trolley. That is the most likely explanation.'

A creepy chill crawled up my spine. I had to give myself a little shuddering shake to get rid of it. I know it is impossible, but maybe Alistair 'disappeared', because he was telling the truth all along. I sat there for the remainder of the seminar thinking just that.

Michael's sequel to *The Men in Black Syndrome* was published a year or so after the seminar. Alistair's case was central to this sequel. Michael claimed that Alistair's case was typical of 'Identity Crisis Abductees'.
He called his new book *The Alien Within*.

I started seeing Michael plugging his book on the daytime TV Talk Show circuit. He must have been making a fortune.
But my invoice to him for the seminar work went unpaid for months. Despite his many promises to the contrary. 'You'll have it first thing tomorrow morning,' he promised.
And that's the truth too.

Now I know a lot of people may have some trouble believing this story. But it is true. It happened just like it happened.
Sometimes things are so strange that you couldn't possibly make them up.
Alistair's story is one of those cases.
I am sure I have Alistair's case notes around somewhere, if you still don't believe me.

So here you have the strange tale of how I first became a 'professional role-player' and began a new chapter in my life.
My first 'Post-Nora' chapter.
The first story of the rest of my life.

STORY CHAPTER THIRTEEN

'THE SOUND OF MUSIC'

I was doing a week long 'role-play' job for Nokia in Budapest. They were holding staff training sessions there.
I was working for another actor, Ted, an old friend, who in turn was working for corporate 'trainers'. These are 'business consultants' who come in and talk about 'Leadership' and 'Change Culture' etc. Sorry about all the 'quotation marks', but anything they do needs putting in quotes. Things rarely are what they say they are.

Some of these business consultants are psychologists. We had one of those with us- the 'Fake Nice' Frank. He was Australian.
Some are business trainers with an MBA. We had one of those with us too- the 'Permafrosted' Marcia. She was Czech.
Others are specialists in a particular business area. They always charge a fortune and even the business people themselves are often unconvinced in the merit of what they have to say.

Ted and I had little to do during that week's training in Hungary. We might lead some warm-up exercises in the morning for the group and contribute to discussions, if asked. One of our roles was to do little vignettes intermittently to illustrate key points the trainers were hoping to get across to the group.
Later in the day, we'd do some role-play scenarios with the Nokia people themselves, so they could practice mentoring and coaching difficult or struggling employees. That was our main task.

Ted had designed these role-play situations. That was his business and main source of income. He was paid top money for creating role-play designs for business trainers.

Ted and I had rehearsed them for weeks before we flew out from London.

Our Czech and Australian would talk and talk throughout the training day. They also had an avalanche of slides with pie-charts and bar-charts and statistical tables and 'little sayings' that they imagined would reinforce their points. Ted and I would break up the monotony for the Nokia group with our vignettes and role-plays.

Ted, who once got me a great job touring India on a theatrical tour, was, as I say, an old friend. He was a big help to me too while I was going through my divorce.
He'd been through some bad years himself, after a bright start, and that can be a tough thing to overcome. But Ted came out the other end and made a good business out of designing dramatic interventions in corporate training.

We stayed at the Corinthia, the finest hotel in Budapest.
Business trainers always demand the very best of travel and accommodation. For instance, our trainers flew First Class while Ted and I flew Economy. We each had a perfectly adequate room, but the trainers had a 'better' room, more expensive room, two floors up from ours. In fact, it soon became a 'Budapest bone of contention' when Marcia, our Czech MBA, discovered that my room (or 'non-penthouse accommodation' as Marcia termed it) proved to have the best views overlooking Budapest in the entire hotel.

None of this mattered to me, but Ted was grumbling about it.
'We're supposed to be working as a team,' he said. 'And they treat us like underlings.'

But Ted was nothing but professional in the trainers' presence. He would arrange 'post-mortems' after each day's session to discuss how the training went. We'd all sit and talk about it.
Then we'd go out for drinks and talk some more about it. And then dinner. There might even be some planned evening excursion to partake with the Nokia people. We'd be in one another's company for up to eighteen hours a day.

The two trainers and Ted would talk incessantly about the Nokia people and who was good and who not. When the Nokia people weren't around of course. And after the drinks kicked in, they'd talk about anything else.

That was Ted's way. He was conscientious. He needed the trainers on board so he could get future work. He stuck to them like a new puppy.

I was just along for the ride.

We were about to face the third day of that week's training, when I joined Ted at breakfast. He looked distressed.

'What's the matter?' I asked him.

I could see that he was not himself.

He pushed a cocktail napkin across the table.

'What's this?'

'Read it,' Ted said.

'Frank and I feel your role-play designs are not working,' it read.
'We're going to cut them as of today.'

The 'I' on the napkin note was the frosty Marcia, of course.

'What the hell, Ted?! When did this make an appearance?' I asked him.

'It was under my door when I got up this morning,' he said still shocked.

'They inform you of this on a cocktail napkin?'

'I know! I don't understand. I designed the role-plays with them. We had dozens of phone calls and meetings and emails discussing this. This will ruin my business!'

I should tell you that the trainers came from 'Ashmount', one of the leading management consultant facilities in Europe. It's located in a Gothic Manor with lush gardens once used as an English royal residence in the 16th century.

Ashmount had many of the world's top trainers on its books and would distribute work to them according to whatever specialized area a client, like Nokia, might want to consider in the training of their staff.

Our two trainers were forever talking about their work in Chile or India or wherever else that Ashmount had sent their way.

I guess Ted feared that once word got back to Ashmount, he'd never work for any of their trainers again.

'And they didn't even talk to me about it!' he despaired. 'We spent all last evening with them and then this! I can't believe this is happening!'

I saw our two trainers coming down to breakfast together. I nudged toward Ted to turn around.

'I'm going over there!' He said with conviction. 'They can't do this!' And Ted left me there at the table.

I was not happy. Ted was a hard-working, capable, dedicated fellow. He'd been through a hostile divorce. He had lost his home and his kids as a result. Even if he did now have visitation rights.

When I first met Ted, he was a well known actor, but the fall-out from his divorce shattered his confidence. He lost his zip for living too.

Finally, he had pulled himself out of the muck and was successful again. But he was still a little fragile. His self-confidence had taken some severe body blows.

Ted was more than a work colleague. He was my friend.

I wasn't thinking too kindly of our trainers.

Ted came back a beaten man.

'They've pulled them, Ralphy.'

We went to that day's session, but didn't do very much. I mean, even less than before. At the point when we would have done Ted's role-plays, Frank just kept talking and showing slides. The Nokia people were getting fidgety, so Frank veered away from his chirpy chatter and endless slides.

'And now one of our thespians,' he said as he flourished a hand at me, 'will demonstrate the 'Four Stages of Change'.

This information came straight from Outer Space.

I looked at Ted. He just stared at the floor.

And then Frank went through the 'Four Stages' with accompanying slides of course. He used Maria in *The Sound of Music* as an example.

'First, there is the period known as 'Denial',' he began. 'Maria at first denied her change in feelings for Captain Von Trapp.'

I had to get up in front of the group and demonstrate 'Denial'.

He then proceeded to talk about 'Resistance'.

'Maria then resists her changed feelings. She goes to such lengths to resist them that she leaves the Von Trapp home and goes back to the convent.'

I had to get up and portray that too.

'Eventually, the person will begin the stage of 'Exploration'. In Maria's case, it was the advice of her Mother Abbess that brought her to the point where she could explore these changed feelings. Sometimes this stage of exploration requires the help of a mentor,' he added.

And I got back up and 'Explored.'

'And finally there is 'Acceptance'. Maria returns to the Von Trapp home and grows to accept her change in feelings for the Captain,' Frank concluded.

And I got to my feet and 'Accepted' too.

I got laughter and a round of applause for demonstrating 'Exploration' while pretending to be Maria doing her famous spinning with arms upraised on the mountain.

None of this was even discussed beforehand.

'This could be bad,' I thought. 'Now they're treating us like performing monkeys.'

At lunch, Frank made a point of saying how well I had done and how useful my 'demonstrations' had been. He was trying to ease the tension among us. Marcia just sat there in an expressionless way. She was the steely strong, but unfeeling type. Marcia was not one to waste time on the sensitivities of other people.

Ted said not a single word. The whole thing was awkward.

We finished the day and started again with the post-training discussions and the drinks and dinner. It was hard going and Ted was only half there.

His spirit had been broken.

After we finished that evening's post-mortem gab fest, I went for a walk alone.

Budapest is a beautiful old city of collapsing, dilapidated grandeur. To be honest, it had never fully recovered from the after-effects of two World Wars. It wasn't so much that it had been destroyed, but more that it seemed to have lost its way. The ordinary person's life was a struggle there. Money was hard to come by. I didn't see much wealth evident anyway. People had a look in their eyes like they were desperate to get away. This was in pre-European Union days. They were still in the fallout of the collapse of Communism.

There were 'Club Girls' everywhere I walked. They'd approach in pairs and ask me to go to their club with them.
'Do you like girls? We have so much fun! We show you how we dance to the music!' they'd beam in broken English as they'd sway and giggle.
Hungarian women can be very beautiful, I quickly discovered, but most of these Club Girls looked like teenagers to me.

As I approached our hotel, another pair of Club Girls approached me.
'You stay here?' one of them asked.
I said that I did.
'You get Big Discount! Look! Our Club's just across the street!'
And they gestured toward a neon sign and a large black door surrounded in Christmas lights. Loud techno music was throbbing from inside.
'Please! Please! You come!' they pleaded.
'Another time maybe,' I said as I pushed my way through the revolving door into our lobby.

As I walked past the reception desk, I saw Frank was still in the hotel bar. When he noticed me, he waved me over to join him.
'Let me get you one,' Frank said. 'What you drinking, mate?'

My beer eventually appeared. Something seemed to be on Frank's mind. I was hoping he wanted to talk about how to deal with the awkwardness that had crept into our working situation. But instead he asked me, 'Did some girls talk to you while you came in just now?'
I told him what happened.
'Yeah, mate, me too.' He said. 'Me too.' He took a gulp of the whisky he was drinking.
'I wouldn't go there on my own,' he said.
'Not on my own.'

I changed the subject. I asked him about the problem with his passport.

He had a work visa, but Hungarian officialdom had some issue with him.

'They don't like us Aussies,' he joked.

He was delayed at the airport upon arrival and had to surrender his passport.

'No,' he said unconcerned. 'They haven't returned my passport yet. It's just some stupid, bureaucratic mix-up.'

And then he asked, 'What do you think goes on in there?'

I wasn't sure what he was talking about.

'In where, Frank?' I asked him.

'In that club,' he replied.

Now, I was divorced at the time and a free spirit, but Frank was not. In the past few days he spoke often of his wife, another psychologist, and his two young boys.

'I don't know, Frank,' I finally said. 'But I do know those two girls out front were young enough to be our daughters.'

'So you wouldn't go there?'

'No, Frank.'

'Right,' he said almost to himself. He had another gulp of his drink and then his mood suddenly changed.

'I thought you actors were supposed to be wild and always wanting to party?'

He was acting like he was annoyed with me. It was as if he were challenging me.

Maybe he was just drunk.

'You only live once,' he lectured.

I finished my beer.

'I'll see you at breakfast, Frank.'

And I went back to my room.

But, that next morning, I didn't see Frank at breakfast. Marcia was not pleased.

'We are meant to review the day ahead. I agreed we could do it at breakfast and he's not here.'

'Maybe he's getting his passport problem fixed,' I suggested.

Just then Ted came in and joined us. He looked like he hadn't slept.

'I've designed some new role-plays,' he announced in a sleep-deprived gush.

'I think I know how to make them work better.'

And he went through his new ideas with Marcia. But she was not convinced.

'It's just not working,' she moaned in her customary way.

'We've moved on now.'

When we entered the training room, everyone was already waiting for us. And then Frank rushed in a few minutes after we did. He said nothing by way of apology to Marcia, who was looking at him with disapproval. And he neither looked at nor said anything to me.

During the mid-morning break, Ted came up to me. He had finally accepted the situation. 'They're not interested in trying to make it work,' he said.

I agreed.

'It's just not working!' he mocked. 'We've moved on!' He said with a 'Marcia-like' dismissive shake of his head.

Ted's Marcia impersonation was uncanny. If you closed your eyes, you'd swear it was her.

That night, the chief Nokia representative took the four of us out to dinner. He was from Finland. We went to a traditional Hungarian restaurant located in some former castle. He seemed happy with how things were going. And he grew happier as the wine began to flow.

I once went with a Finnish woman. Their language is impossible, but I did retain the odd phrase or two from my time with her. When our meal arrived, I said to Marko, the Nokia Rep, 'Hyvaa Ruokahalua.' He laughed. That means, I hope, Bon appétit.

But our dinner conversation left me less than impressed. Words fail me when I try to describe the shameless, sycophantic manner of Frank and Marcia. Their noses picked up the scent of future work from a top company and they both went in for the kill.

'Isn't that fascinating?' Marcia drooled. 'To think that Nokia started out by making rubber boots! Amazing!' she said in reply to some comment Marco had made.

And Frank might even have been worse. He got himself very worked up over the fact that the legend of 'Kris Kringle' came from Lapland in Finland and not Germany like so many people think.
'Finland really should promote that fact about its culture. They're missing a trick there,' he said with great seriousness.
Nokia, of course, is headquartered in Finland.

This was all starting to get to me. I'm all in favor of people trying to get work when the opportunity arises. I do it myself all the time. But the two of them were so transparently trying to butter up this Nokia guy that it set me off.

I don't remember how it all got started, but I do recall feeling particularly nauseous, when Marcia started acting so bubbly with Marko about how much she loved *The Sound of Music*. I'd never seen this animated side to her before. Her fake smile was like a coffin lid opening.
Perhaps Marko mentioned that he liked Julie Andrews, when I was daydreaming away from their brazen pandering.
And then it just came out.

'I was in that. I was one of the kids in that,' I said.
Marcia looked stunned. Ted coughed a surprised warning at me.

'Oh yeah, there were lots of kids in that. We'd take turns being in place when they set up the cameras. In fact, I did a lot of the singing in that. They dubbed some of our voices over the movie kids' voices. I didn't think it was such a big deal at the time, but nowadays everyone thinks it's interesting. In those days, we didn't even get a screen credit.'

Ted kicked me from under the table as he stared down at his plate.
Frank claimed that he thought my voice sounded familiar when we first met.
Yes, Frank was that cloyingly patronizing.

Marcia began to grill me. She was, I discovered, an expert on *The Sound of Music.*
I guess she really did like it.
'So you were in Austria as a child?' She asked me snootily. She was trying to trip me up.

And I said, 'No, no, a lot of it was done in Hollywood Studios. I didn't go on location.' And no matter how hard she tried to expose me, I just kept batting her doubts away.

Marko was totally convinced and well impressed.

'You can't have kids doing everything on location,' I said.

'I also appeared in the stage version with Debbie Reynolds. What a dame,' I added for extra effect.

When Marko dropped us off at our hotel, I said to him, 'hauska tutustua' which means 'nice to meet you'. At least I hope it means that.

Marko laughed like I had just told the best joke ever.

Ted and I went for a drink together in the hotel bar.

'Why did you do that, Ralphy?' he asked me as he shook his head.

We had a good laugh.

'Debbie Reynolds!' Ted said with tears in his eyes.

And we laughed some more.

While we were drinking our beers, I said, 'That's the trouble with people like those two, who disrespect others, Ted. They end up disrespected themselves by those in the know.'

I made further outrageous claims for the remainder of the week. I'd let Marcia and Frank build up a head of steam on a topic and then drop in a whopper to undermine them. So if, for example, they started talking about London, I might say:

'Well, of course, if you really want to know London you have to know the history of the storage areas underneath the Piazza in Covent Garden. There's a whole clandestine history of London there. Churchill used it as a secret command center during the war. He held peace talks there with Nazi envoys, so the stories go. It was all very hush-hush. Even now, the British government doesn't talk about the 'Hidden Bunker'. They don't want people knowing about it.'

Or if they were talking about the Eiffel Tower, I might venture, 'Of course, everyone wanted it pulled down as soon as they saw it. They found it hideous. Many Parisians have told me this. The only reason it is still there is that the French were so preoccupied with the social unrest at the time that they used it as a radio tower for communications. If it wasn't for Marconi and his wireless, the Eiffel tower would have been on the scrapheap ages ago.'

Yes, I know. I was behaving like an ass. But if you have an itch, don't ask someone else to scratch it for you.

It wasn't my proudest moment, I admit, but it did make the rest of the week much more bearable.

It was the final day of our stay. As usual, we hadn't much to do, but had to stay sharp as we could be called upon at any moment to 'act'.

In the afternoon, Marcia had the Nokia delegates fill in three different feedback forms.

Frank meanwhile led the 'Final Roundup', as he called it. He got them all to talk about the most valuable thing that they'd take away from the training course. And after that, he began to acknowledge all the people who had made the Budapest training possible.

Marko was there on that final day, so he received particular attention.

'None of this would have been possible without Marko,' he said in faux admiration.

'I want to thank him for giving us this time together.'

Marcia sat there with a fixed smile. And then Frank led a round of applause for Marko. Ted and I looked at one another as we clapped.

'And of course Marcia too!' Frank enthused.

And there was a smattering of some more applause.

'And Ashmount Management Group as well.'

Ted and I were not mentioned. We were the Invisible Men.

As the session broke up, several of the Nokia people came up to me and Ted to thank us. Marko did too. 'I tell my children that I had dinner with a Movie Star!' he said with a big smile.

'Kiitos,' I said to him.

Thank you.

As Ted and I continued saying our goodbyes to the group, Marcia and Frank corralled Marko. I could see them both jabbering away at the same time and handing him their business cards. After a while, he excused himself to join the departing Nokia group.

We didn't fly out until later the next day, so our evening was free.

'Meet in the bar in fifteen minutes?' Frank asked the rest of us.

We found a table and sat down. Once we ordered drinks, Marcia led the final debriefing. 'I think actors can be very useful in training,' she began. 'But I am not convinced they should be designing exercises for the group. It's something I'll have to discuss back at Ashmount.'

Ted had given up. He didn't seem bothered. He just drank his beer and took it all in. Resigned to his fate.

Frank said, 'What I enjoyed so much was how we all worked together as a team. Even after all the changes forced upon us. Job well done everyone!'

And he raised his drink in a toast.

Just then, two tough looking, broad shouldered, guys wearing leather jackets and flat caps walked into the bar. They looked around, saw where we were sitting, and one of them said something to the other. They came over.

'Mister, you owe us money,' one of them said to Frank.

The other man just stood there with his arms folded across his chest. He stared at Frank.

Frank looked as shocked as the rest of us.

'You give it now,' he insisted.

Frank looked over at me like he expected help. He tried not to look at the man who was talking to him or the one staring at him either.

'You come outside. You pay us.'

'What's this all about? Marcia demanded. She was indignant. She was good at that. 'Frank, do you know these men?'

The man who was talking nodded to the guy who was staring at Frank. He unfolded his arms, walked around the table behind where Frank was sitting, and put his big hands on Frank's shoulders.

Frank was squirming.

I thought things might get ugly. Ted just looked away like he wasn't even there.

I saw the bar manager and signaled for him to come over.

He did. But before I could open my mouth, the talking guy started speaking in Hungarian to the bar manager. The other guy just kept his hands on Frank's shoulders.

'Will someone please tell us what is going on?' Marcia broke in.

And the manager said to Frank, 'Sir, these men claim that you failed to pay Entertainment Tax the other night at their club.'

He said something else in Hungarian to the two men. The one who had been doing all the talking said something back.
And then the manager added, 'And in Private Clubs in Budapest, sir, there is an additional tax on alcoholic beverages above the normal government levy. They claim you owe them for that as well.'
Some more Hungarian was bandied about.
'You could have purchased a temporary Club membership at hotel reception, Sir. That would have avoided this problem.'
Frank looked like a burglar caught holding a bag of loot.
'They're demanding you pay them 300,000 Forints. Otherwise they will involve the police.'
300,000 Forints was about a thousand British Pounds at the time.

Frank tried to stand up, but the big guy standing behind him wouldn't let him.
'I'm going to reception. I'll get the money. I need to put it on my credit card,' Frank pleaded. The bar manager translated that into Hungarian and Frank was then allowed to leave his chair.
The two Club guys escorted Frank to the lobby and reception.

Marcia looked secretly pleased and disapproving at the same time.
She was looking away when Frank left with his two new friends, but, I swear, I could see a little smile on her face.
Something else for her to report back to Ashmount.

'Is there anything else, sir?' the bar manager asked me.
'I'll have another beer,' Ted interjected.

The morning of our departure, I got up very early to take one last walk through Budapest. I joined in with the early morning crowd on their way to work. I just followed along with them and took in the scenery. I saw some very exhausted looking young women in revealing clothes. They were not on their way to work.
They were on their way home from it.

When I walked into our hotel breakfast room, it was a good hour earlier than when we had all met there through the week. But Frank was already there. He was sitting on his own.

I went over to him.

'Frank, what about your passport?' I asked him.

He explained that when he went to reception last night, they had it there for him.

'That was lucky,' I said.

I didn't say anything about his Entertainment Tax trouble.

'Yes, lucky,' he shrugged.

Ted and I arrived at Ferihegyi Airport before Marcia and Frank. They were travelling First Class and so were allowed to check-in later than we were.

There was only one staff member at the British Airways check-in desk.

'Ted, that fellow at the BA desk, that's the guy at our hotel reception, isn't it?' I asked as we awaited our turn.

Ted had a look.

'I think so, Ralphy. Yes, you're right. It is, isn't it?'

When we reached the desk, we handed the guy our tickets and passports. I asked him if he was 'moonlighting.'

'Moonlighting? What is moonlighting?' he asked uncertainly.

So, I explained what moonlighting was and he started laughing. In fact, he was laughing so hard he had to stop and wipe his eyes.

'That's Cseke! I'm Elek. We're twins.'

Ted said, 'People must confuse the two of you all the time.'

'Yes, but no one ever accused us of moonlighting before!'

We all shared a good laugh over that.

And then Elek said, 'You know, we have some seats free in First Class. Do you want to take a couple of them off our hands?'

Ted and I said that we did.

An upgrade. One of life's little victories.

We ran into Marcia and Frank at our gate. When it was time to board, we all rose as one as they asked for 'Passengers Travelling First Class'.

Marcia made her disapproving face.

'Where do you two think you're going?'

'It's an upgrade,' I told her.

She looked relieved.

She had enough to feed back to Ashmount already without saying the 'actors' had abused their expenses.

Frank though seemed happy about our good fortune.

'Try the duck, Ralphy, if they have it.'

We got ourselves settled on board. I went to check the toilet. Frank insisted that it was worth a look.

'There's even a shoe shine machine in there!'

There was a drape divider at the toilet that separated it from Business Class. When I got there, I heard a voice behind it that sounded very familiar.

A menacing voice.

I pulled back the drape a tad to see what it was.

There, right in the first row, were Frank's two Club Thugs from the bar. They had two very young girls with them. The talking thug was growling something at the pair of them. Both girls were dressed like they were going to an Oscar ceremony.

Expensively revealing.

They both looked scared. Terrified really.

I could see the tracks of black mascara that had teared down their faces.

I let the drape go and leaned back against the bulkhead.

Sometimes something doesn't seem right, but you don't know the back-story. Your instinct tells you to intervene, but your brain reminds you that you've no proof of anything. And then there's the fear to intervene too in the mix.

I just froze there for a moment struggling with my own thoughts and feelings.

I was reminded of Nora, after we'd fallen apart, being abused by drunken thugs in her company. I couldn't do a thing about that either.

I felt helpless to intervene in the face of obvious abuse.

And I did not like it.

I did not like it one little bit.

I will not stomach bullies. Bullies, I cannot abide. I will not suffer them. Once in High School, I saw off three of them for picking on John Bogarde for being a 'Freak.'

I have form for intervening with bullies. Not necessarily to fight, but more to tell them what they are. Mostly it ends with profanities back and forth before they skulk off.

But this was different. These two were professional bullies. And I wasn't sure of my ground. But my gut wasn't happy.

I went back and sat next to Ted.

'What's the matter with you?' he laughed. 'What are you scowling at? Wipe your face! You've got spittle on it!'

I was so frustrated that I was grunting aloud and grinding my teeth. I was absolutely seething.

I told Ted what I saw.

'Don't jump to conclusions, Ralphy. That doesn't mean anything,' he said.

'Yes, it does, Ted,' I insisted. 'You know it does.'

'Don't start trouble. We don't know anything for sure.'

'Don't rock the boat, you mean?'

'Don't rock the plane.'

But I was sure I was right. I was sure that those two girls were in over their heads and in the hands of some very abusive people.

I thought it best not to tell Frank that his two chums were on board. I thought I'd spare him that knowledge. He'd be of no help anyway. Not that I was helping the situation much myself.

We took off.

British Airways treat their First Class passengers as if they were royalty. I have never seen the British give such good service before. It's like a spa meets cocktail bar meets Michelin Star restaurant in the sky.

I was kicking myself for not enjoying it more. Part of me though was sitting in Business Class with the thugs.

And then, as amazing as this hi-tech world can be, the pilot emerged from the cockpit to greet us.

'Who's flying the plane?' some wag joked.

'It's all under control,' he reassured us charmingly.

He personally walked up and introduced himself to each of us in 'First Class'.

The Pilot, Captain Harbor, eventually arrived at where Ted and I were sitting.
Ted told him about what we'd been doing in Budapest.
'Ah! So you were working with Marcia and Frank?' he asked.
He even remembered their names.
'Funny. They didn't mention that,' he said.
'Funny,' Ted said.
I said nothing other than 'hello'. I was feeling too ashamed of myself. I was 'living it up' while back in Business Class some serious badness was going on.

Captain Harbor spoke to all the rest of the First Class passengers and then he made his way up the gangway back to the cockpit door.
He turned and said, 'If anything is not to your satisfaction, please do let me know of it.'
So I raised my hand.
I think this took him by surprise, so I started waving my hand around.
Ted looked away in embarrassment as Captain Harbour came right over.

Despite Ted's throat-clearing warnings, I told Captain Harbor about our run-in with the Club Thugs at the hotel. I told him what I saw on the plane.
'The Head Steward has already informed me of his concerns,' he said.
'We've radioed ahead to inform the authorities.'
He thanked me.
'I will let them know what you told me.'

When my duck arrived, it was as good as Frank said.

At Heathrow, I made a point of looking out for the Club Thugs and their 'girlfriends'. I made Ted stay behind to help me spot them.

We watched as the Talking Man and his Silent Friend went up to the same immigration desk. The two girls were standing right behind them. The talking one handed over all the passports. The woman official looked through their documents. She said something to them and then she signaled for two guards to come over.

We watched as the four of them were all led away to a side room. 'For further questioning,' Ted said as if he were imitating a TV cop. 'Yeah, Ted, there are all kinds of terrorists,' I replied.

Sometimes life plays fairer than we expect. A few months later, Ted was contacted directly by Marko, the Nokia Rep, and was asked to design role-play scenarios for Nokia's entire sales force.

Ted took me with him to do those jobs. For two years, we travelled and worked together in the 'World of Nokia', which was a very big world indeed.

And unlike my claim to *The Sound of Music* stardom, that's completely true.
Or as the Finnish might say, 'Se on Tosi.'
(It's true.)

STORY CHAPTER FOURTEEN

'THE GENUINE PAPYRUS'

It was nearing Halloween in London. Always a gloomy time of year.
The sun sets by 4pm and the misty, chilling rain soaks bone deep.
You rarely see a smile on the faces of the pedestrians. All their eyes
are downcast. Everyone is anxious to get somewhere warm and dry.
Everyone yearns for a little bit of sunshine.
If anyone is prone to the blues, they will find themselves blue.
All you can do is endure.

And one day, during this dreadful season, as I returned from work,
looked at the post, and slumped myself in exhaustion on the sofa, the
phone rang.
It was my 'role-play' agent.

'Ralphy Boy! What are you doing the last two weeks of November?'
she asked me.
I could hear a little pleased giggle in her voice.
'Nothing I can't rearrange,' I told her.
'How would you like to go to Cairo with the Royal College of
Surgeons? How would you like two weeks of work there and staying
at luxury hotels?'
Now she was audibly giggling.
'Money is no problem. They told me to name my price for booking
you.'
'How can I say no?' I replied.
'Don't I treat you well?' she teased me.

I should tell you that I had worked for the Royal College of Surgeons
of England and Wales once before. It was for their prestigious
membership exams in London. I had to learn several medical
scenarios and candidates would have to find out what was wrong
with the patient I was portraying.
It was hard work, but it was a lot of fun too. I'd go out with the
surgeons after work and we'd always have a good laugh. As a result,
I became good friends with several of them.

I guess they were the ones who requested my services in Cairo.
'You'll need to get a travel visa. I'll send you details as soon as I get them,' my agent explained.

I was going to the Land of the Pyramids! Sun! No rain! No more 4pm sunsets! No more downcast eyes and gloomy faces on the street! Heaven.

All the travel details, such as work visa matters, were being handled by a Colonel Mistrata. He was the representative for the Egyptian military who were hosting the Royal College in Cairo.
I met him at the Egyptian Embassy in London. He was a dead ringer for Omar Sharif. I was taken to a side room, as soon as I arrived, and my passport was quickly stamped with the required visa. That meant, luckily, I could bypass the hundreds of Egyptians impatiently awaiting their turn to resolve some issue at the Embassy.

'Show your stamp at passport control in Cairo. There is no need for you to queue. They will simply wave you through,' the Colonel informed me stiffly.

After the contracts and visa and inoculations were negotiated, I was all set.
Two weeks in Cairo. Just the sunshine prescription I needed.

My agent told me that I would be accompanied by another actor. She said that the Egyptian military would not find an actress acceptable and my agent booked this other actor to do the female roles in Cairo. Yes, I found that somewhat odd too.

The other actor, Sergio, was very effeminate, but a terrific actor too as I later discovered. He was as close as you could get to the real thing without acting like some drag queen.
But it still seemed strange to me that they banned women, but not men acting like women.

Odd to a Western eye anyway.

Sergio and I flew to Cairo together. The surgeons themselves had flown out the week before, because part of their membership exam did not involve the use of actors portraying patients.
Sergio and I were only needed for the second and third weeks of the three weeks of exams.

The flight itself was perfectly fine, but problems started as soon as we landed. It was nearly 11pm by the time our plane touched down. When we tried to get through Egyptian immigration control, we were stopped and told that we had the wrong visa.
Colonel Mistrata's assurance of easy passage proved to be more than erroneous.

We were told to go to a tiny, drab waiting room. We were in there for over an hour before some official came to talk to us. He knew absolutely nothing about what we were to do in Cairo.
'Your visa stamp lacks a valid signature,' he said full of suspicion. Finally, I was able to retrieve some documents from my carry-on bag and explained why we were there. Once the official was convinced that we were there on behalf of the surgeons and the Egyptian military, everything changed immediately and we were ushered through without further incident.

'I knew we'd be delayed here!' Sergio moaned. 'Didn't I say that on the plane, Ralphy? Now we won't be able to get a cab and check into the hotel, because it's so late. And I bet the hotel is like the airport and they won't know why we're here either!'

I should tell you that Sergio was a friendly and pleasant enough guy, but he surely looked on the dark side of every issue. His main conversation was about how things could and would go wrong and how things wouldn't work out.
'We'll be sleeping on the streets!'
He needed constant reassurance. He was like that old *L'il Abner* cartoon character, 'Joe Btfsplk', a hard-luck 'jinx', who walked around with a rain cloud over his head.
He always assumed the worst.

Sergio and I did get a cab to the hotel. There was meant to be one booked for us, but we couldn't find it, if there was one booked. Sergio whined and whined about that too.
But he was spot on with his hotel ill-fortune forecast.

We were not booked into the same hotel as the surgeons. Their hotel, the Nile Hilton, was on the opposite side of the Nile from our hotel, the Cairo Sheraton.

When we went to reception, the hotel staff had no idea who we were or why we were there.

The Surgical Exam Coordinator, Angela, who was staying with the surgeons at the Hilton, had left no message at reception. It was far too late to try and ring her for assistance.

It was a mess and a mess after a ten hour flight, airport delays, and a long cab ride is a major mess.

'What did I say in the cab, Ralphy? I told you our hotel reservation would go missing!' Sergio added helpfully.

It was 1:30 in the wee hours and there was no one to contact at the surgeons' hotel until the following morning. I asked for the Sheraton's hotel manager.

He was a well-dressed, educated, older man. He seemed urbane and worldly.

I told him our story and I showed him letters from the Royal Surgeons' coordinator and Colonel Mistrata. It was the same information that I showed to the official at the airport when our passport stamps failed to impress him.

That did the trick again.

'Give each of them suites on the penthouse level,' he instructed the reception staff.

He pointed at two porters who quickly grabbed our luggage.

'Please bring us the proper paperwork to confirm your stay with us, Mr. Waldo, after you've seen the surgeons tomorrow.'

We were then taken to our separate luxurious suites and I don't know about Sergio, but I just flopped on the bed and fell straight asleep.

Early the next day, Sergio and I went to find the surgeons and to speak with Angela about our hotel issue.

We walked over the Kubri el-Gamia Bridge and made our way to their hotel.

I had to stop Sergio from going up and petting the many feral cats we kept encountering along the way.

'They're so cute!' he'd squeal as he reached for yet another one.

'They have bubonic plague, Serge!' I repeatedly warned him.

Cairo is, what I'd call, a 'catty' city. Cats are everywhere. They're a bit like our squirrels, only they're cats and they have the plague.
In fact, I find Ancient Egypt a 'catty' culture too. Lots of cat imagery. And talk about trying to take it with you! I mean, really.
Sorry. I went off on one there.
Back to our story.

There was a massive security operation going on outside the surgeons' hotel. It was just like the airport with scanners and soldiers with automatic weapons.
We had to go through that wringer before we could enter the hotel.

A hotel guest waiting with us at security said there was a terrorist attack at the Khan el-Khalil bazaar, the largest market in Cairo, the day before we arrived. Many were killed or injured and tourists were targeted particularly. 'It's all over the news,' she said.
'I knew it! Just our luck to arrive in Egypt right when they decide to start killing tourists,' Sergio whined.

This attack threw the entire Egyptian military into action and they were determined that the Royal College of Surgeons for England and Wales would not fall victim to terrorism.
I suppose that's why their hotel ended up looking more like a military bunker than the Five Star luxury accommodation it was.

We found Angela and the surgeons' exam staff coordinators in the breakfast bar. We were told that the surgeons themselves had the day off and had gone on a day trip to Alexandria.
Our 'role-playing as patients' work would start tomorrow.

We asked Angela about this 'proper paperwork' that the hotel manager requested, but no one seemed to know anything about it.
'Just say you're with the surgeons,' Angela scowled dismissively.
'These Egyptians! Obsessed with their paperwork! It's probably there and they just can't see it.'

We were told to meet back at the surgeons' hotel later that evening when we'd all meet for dinner. One of Angela's assistants gave us our role-play schedule for the week, so we would know when to portray which 'patient' on which day.

Sergio and I used the rest of the day to explore Cairo. He was superb at telling me what things we should see. He had obviously done a lot of homework looking through travel guidebooks. I am useless at that, so I was happy to have Sergio with me, despite his constant concerns of 'impending doom.'

We walked the streets of Cairo. Many young men and boys approached us to buy souvenirs from them.
'You! English? American? You come with me! My shop is just down this street! It is not far! The finest antiquities. My family has had them for many generations. You come see.'
We spent the day avoiding their pleas to buy.
'I have authentic papyrus! Real Egyptian hieroglyphs!'

Sergio gave me a running commentary on the historical significance of some of the Cairo districts where we walked. He was better than a tour guide.

When we returned that evening to the Hilton, the surgeons were all in the bar. They quickly bought Sergio and me a drink. They seemed very happy to have had the day off.

'We have been doing these clinical exams since the day we arrived. It's been starting at eight in the morning and we haven't been finishing until nearly 10pm! I thought this was meant to be a break from work!' One of the surgeons joked.
'This is a break from work. It's an 'NHS' break. You know, you work until you break!' another doctor-wit added.
I asked them if they had been doing any sightseeing and they all said they had been doing nothing, but work, until today when they visited Alexandria.
'It gets easy now! You joined us right after the hard graft is over!' one of the surgeons teased us.
'Typical actors,' a sour-faced surgeon added.

We were called into dinner and had to walk through the lobby to get to the hotel restaurant. In the lobby were two Egyptian military officers. It was clear that the surgeons already knew them well. They joined us at dinner.

One of them, Major Mohammed, spoke to all of us about 'security issues'.

'Each of you will be given your own 'personal minder'. Please do not venture forth on your own without them. If you wish to go somewhere or visit a market, you must travel with your minder. Please!' The Major was very insistent.

'Tomorrow afternoon, after the day's examinations are over, we have arranged a private tour for you at the Egyptian Antiquities Museum. There will be coaches waiting for you at the examination site.'

We discovered that the 'examination site' was at a military hospital on the outskirts of Cairo. Very early every morning, Sergio and I would walk to the surgeons' hotel to catch a coach that would take us all to that exam site. Once we were on the coach, we could then ask any questions we might have about that day's 'role-play' with the surgeons, who would be examining the candidates for membership.

The first day went very smoothly. I had to portray someone rather dim who needed stomach surgery. The candidate had to figure out that I did not understand what he wanted to do and then explain again in far simpler terms.

Sergio meanwhile portrayed a woman who became hysterical when she heard her husband died in surgery. I could hear him weeping uncontrollably in the examination room next to mine.

He was very convincing.

At the end of each day of exams, the surgeons would meet with the successful candidates and there would be a ceremony at which they'd receive their 'Membership of the Royal College of Surgeons' certificates. This is a major rite of passage for doctors who hope to train as surgeons and a significant leg-up to their careers.

There were many speeches and many proud parents beaming at their successful offspring.

All the candidates were Egyptian military doctors.

But on that first day at this 'Membership' ceremony, something unexpected happened.

The certificates were being awarded when, much to our amazement, what seemed to be the entire Egyptian military entered the ceremony room.

All the soldiers were dressed in fine white uniforms.

They were followed in by, what I guessed were, Egyptian politicians in expensive looking suits.

As they entered, I could see the military hospital staff craning their necks outside in the corridor to have a look.

'Do you know who that is?!' Sergio asked me. He was pointing at one of the well-dressed politicians. He looked very excited.

'It's the President!'

This was the very first 'foreign exam' the Royal College had ever offered. It was very flattering to the Egyptian military that they had been chosen for this milestone. Usually foreign doctors would have to travel to London or Edinburgh to take these exams.

President Mubarak gave a short speech in Egyptian, which of course I could not understand, but he could still communicate in his style of delivery how pleased he was for his countrymen.

He continued in English, 'I welcome the surgeons of England. May you think of Egypt as your second home.'

He then quickly took his leave and the rest of us stayed and had glasses of sparkling apple juice to celebrate with the new members.

We went out to wait for the coach to take us to our promised 'private tour' of the Egyptian Museum. When it arrived, we could see that there were some people already on it. Major Mohammed told us that these were our 'minders'.

Each surgeon was given one minder in turn. But not Sergio and me. We were given one minder for the pair of us.

Our 'minder' was Khaled. He was very tall and, I guess, in his early twenties. He said he worked at the 'Intelligence Ministry', but had requested this duty.

'Khaled, later this week we want to visit that bazaar that was attacked. Is that possible?' I asked him.

He looked sadly at me. I guess he thought it was not a good idea.

'Yes, it is possible. I will speak to the Major about it,' he said formally.

When we arrived at the Egyptian Museum, it was closed to the public at that hour, but we were ushered in without delay. We were then given a personal tour of all the incredible treasures there by the Head of the Museum himself.

We were taken to the King Tutankhamen area and allowed to get close enough to touch some of the artifacts there had we wished.

It was a life enhancing experience.

Instead of waiting among hoards of visitors just to catch a glimpse of Tutankhamen's gold, we were shown every piece in exquisite detail with expert commentary.

Nora and I once gave a miss to the Dallas-Pittsburg Super Bowl when King Tutankhamen's treasures were on loan at the Dallas Museum. I was a dancer at the Dallas Ballet at the time. It was the only day we could get an entry ticket. Texans miss their football for nothing and no one.

But this Cairo visit to see 'King Tut' was much the superior one.

After every day of exams, we would be taken to visit another ancient site that truly took the breath away. One afternoon we were taken to the Sphinx and all our minders, armed with semi-automatic weapons, chased everyone else away so we could gaze upon it at our leisure.

We were taken on camel treks in the desert. Three of the surgeons and I had a bet on who could get to a designated spot quickest via camel.

Take it from me. Camel racing is a very bumpy business.

And even bumpier when you lose the race.

I was a distant second.

'Sand got in my eyes,' I explained to the victor.

We were even taken into a pyramid itself which is unheard of for tourists.

But that reminded me of 'caving' and a bad experience I once had in Kentucky. Since then, I always tried to avoid claustrophobic situations.

That, I could not enjoy as much as the surgeons clearly did.

Nonetheless, no one could have asked for any greater hospitality than we received and no one could have had such exclusive access to so many wonders of the world.

During our private tour of the Egyptian Museum, Major Mohammed approached me.

'Are you happy, my friend? Are we making you feel welcome?' he asked with a smile.

I assured him I felt more than 'welcome' and thanked him for arranging such an incredible experience.

'Everyday here will be a wonder,' I told him. 'This is the City of Wonders.' He laughed loudly.

'You are as polite as an Egyptian!' he laughed again.

Major Mohammed told me that on the same day as the terror attack at the bazaar, the Egyptian Museum had been burgled.

'Mainly, they stole ancient scripts and writings. A few pieces of statuary and some amulets were also taken. They were unable to access the Tutankhamen area or other parts of the museum where the greatest of our treasures are on display.'

'But everyone will know what they took is stolen,' I said. 'How can they ever sell it?'

'There are private collectors the world over who seek to hoard treasures for themselves,' he explained. 'It's a game for them to acquire such things.'

'A selfish game,' I replied.

'Oh yes! Selfish certainly, my friend,' he said. 'But such people, for an example, would pay a great deal for a genuine papyrus from the time of the Pharaohs.'

And then he added, 'But certainly the culprits will be apprehended. The hidden eyes of the surveillance cameras will see to that.'

At the end of the first week of exams, Khaled approached me.

'The Major says that if you discover the surgeons also want to visit the bazaar, we may all go there.'

That spurred me into instant action and I quickly asked as many surgeons as I could. Nearly all of them were more than happy to go. Most surgeons tend to like adventure. I guess that's why I get on with them so famously.

Only one acted as if he wasn't interested.

'No, I don't want to see tourist trinkets. When I travel, I always purchase something of lasting value as a keepsake,' he said haughtily.

'I won't find that there!' he scoffed. 'I'll find something much more genuine right here in the hotel gift shop, thank you very much.'
It was the sour-faced surgeon who had called Sergio and me 'typical actors' when we first met him at the hotel bar.

And so it was agreed, despite Sourpuss's lack of interest, that we'd visit the bazaar the following morning.
It would be our first exam-free day since we arrived.

After breakfast, we all gathered in the surgeons' hotel lobby. All the minders had brought their cars and Sergio and I went to join Khaled. 'We must all stay together. No one must wander from the group,' he instructed us with great seriousness.

Before we left, the Major took me aside. 'The surgeons are inordinately fond of you, my friend,' he said. 'They will do whatever you ask of them. Your enthusiasm in convincing them to visit the bazaar was most impressive!' he laughed. 'You are inhabited by an ancient Egyptian soul within you.'

Khaled and the rest of our convoy were driving to the bazaar very quickly. I felt like I was in a police car chasing the bad guys.
I could see Sergio digging his fingers into his seat behind me.

During the drive, Khaled told us he was engaged to be married.
Sergio asked him if they had set the date.
'Soon! Allah be praised, may it be soon!' he said.
I was surprised how anxious he was about it.
'May her recovery be swift,' he added.
'Recovery? Is she ill?' Sergio asked him.
'She was injured in the blast at the Khan el-Khalili bazaar. Her family has a large carpet business there. It was ill-fated. She was just there to see her family when tragedy struck.'
I started feeling uneasy about being the one who had encouraged this visit there.
'There is hope that she will not lose her sight,' he added hopefully.
'She is in the care of our finest military doctors. May Allah be praised and protect her!'

This was all said while we zoomed along in and out of traffic jams and trying to keep up with the rest of our convoy.

If negotiating traffic jams were an Olympic event, Egyptians would get on the podium for Gold, Silver, and Bronze every time. And why there are no Egyptian Grand Prix drivers, I'll never understand. They'd win every race.

Eventually, we pulled up at a police barrier near the bazaar where the other minders' cars had stopped. Major Mohammed walked to each of our cars in turn. 'We will enter the bazaar here,' he said.
'Just leave anything you don't need with you in the car. It will be safe.'
He then walked up to the police barrier and the police moved the barricade aside so we could all pass. They chased away other shoppers from trying to get in the same way.

We all stayed together as a single group. All our minders walked alongside us and each had their semi-automatic weapons in their hands.
Major Mohammed acted as tour guide as he led the way.
'Tell me what you desire and I will show you where such items may be purchased.'
We must have made quite an impression. Although the bazaar was crammed full of shoppers, they would all clear off in a hurry when they saw us approach.

The Khan el-Khalili bazaar is a 'haggling' market and it's absolutely enormous. It's almost a city within a city.
Nothing has a fixed price and everything is open to bargaining.
Some of the surgeons were looking for little gifts for their families back home. They'd point out to their minder what they wanted and the minder did the 'haggling'.
The shopkeepers were forced to offer us all very good deals.

Khaled did the same thing for Sergio and me. If we wanted exotic musk oils, for instance, he'd listen to the shopkeeper's 'price' and then tell the shopkeeper what 'price' to give us.

By the time we left, all of us were laden down with our own personal bazaar treasures,

On the ride back to the hotel, Khaled's mobile rang.
He pulled over. I could not understand what was being said, but I could tell it was not good news.

Khaled covered his face and lowered his head to the steering wheel. He was whimpering to himself and shaking.

Sergio and I did not know what to say.

Slowly, he uncovered his face and leaned back on the seat.

'They say she needs a special operation,' he finally said. 'The military hospitals here do not have the facilities to carry it out. She needs a European or American hospital for this, they say. Otherwise she will lose her sight!'

And with that, Sergio blurted out 'Then we'll have to speak to the surgeons! They have to help!'

'No, it will cost many thousands,' Khaled said sadly. 'There is no hope in raising it,' he lamented.

'There is no hope now!'

We drove back to our Sheraton base in silence.

Sergio and I walked quickly past reception, as our 'paperwork' situation was as yet unresolved, and we went for a drink together in our hotel bar.

'Ralphy, the surgeons have to help Khaled's fiancé,' Sergio insisted. 'We have to do something. We can't just leave him in tears and hopeless like that. We can at least talk to the surgeons and tell them what's going on,' he suggested.

'They have to help!'

Sergio's reaction reminded me of Nora in her prime. She also could not bear to see others suffer. Like hers, Sergio's instinct was to help others in trouble and need. He had no hesitation about getting 'involved' in someone else's woes.

I, on the other hand, had come to be extremely wary of joining in such causes. I'd learned the hard way, from previous experience, that getting 'involved' can have dire consequences.

Even fatal ones.

I'd intervene with bullies when necessary, but I was leery about attempts to assist others out of the messes that life threw their way. But, all the same, I admired Sergio's sense of compassion for Khaled and his fiancé.

Perhaps it was his solicitous nature that rekindled my own, long lost one.

'All right, Serge,' I said in surrender. 'Let's see if we can get the surgeons to help.'

And, true to form, Sergio being Sergio immediately moaned, 'I bet they won't though!'

Later, Sergio and I walked over to the surgeons' hotel. They were all in the bar and feeling merry and showing off the things they had bought at the bazaar.
'I bought this for the wife!' one of them said as he held up a skimpy, sequined harem outfit.
'You mean you bought that for you!' another surgeon laughed.

Sergio went from one surgeon to the next and told them what had happened to Khaled's fiancé. His determination was impressive.
'Is there nothing you can do for her? Surely, you can!' he'd ask them.
'Back home perhaps,' one of the surgeons said. 'But not here.'
'It's not my area of expertise,' another said.
'Talk to Mr. Patterson about it. He's the eye guy,' he suggested.
He pointed out a man deep in discussion with the manager of the hotel gift shop.
'That's Patterson,' he said helpfully.

You should know that British consultant surgeons become 'Misters' after they have qualified as consultants. They are not referred to as 'doctors' anymore. A 'Doctor' is not as highly placed medically as a 'Mister'. Or as experienced.

Sergio and I saw immediately that Mr. Patterson was the 'sour-faced' surgeon who did not want to visit the bazaar.
He was one of the world's leading Ophthalmologists, the helpful surgeon had told us. He had published many articles about current advances in eye surgery.
All his colleagues respected him a great deal.
The helpful surgeon certainly thought highly of him.
'He's the top man,' he said. 'The 'eye go to guy',' he laughed.

Sergio accosted Mr. Patterson, as he left the gift shop, and told him about Khaled and his fiancé.
'What do you want me to do about it?' he asked dismissively.
'Third World people have Third World problems.'
'But you could save her sight!' Sergio protested.
'Only if she's in the care of the NHS,' he responded.
'And she isn't.'

'I knew he wouldn't help, Ralphy!' Sergio fumed as we rejoined the other surgeons.

We were in the last week of our stay. The exams were going well and it was always pleasant to see the successful candidates' joy at passing the exam.
But Khaled's misery tempered our pleasure.

Midweek in that final week, Major Mohammed made an announcement.
'The President has invited all of us for dinner and festivities on the Presidential yacht tomorrow evening. I have informed your minders and they will be taking you to the yacht in their own cars. Please do not be late.'

Sergio had to portray a pregnant woman during the exam on the day of our visit to the President's yacht. He had to bring a lot of costume pieces and props to do the role. These included borrowed hotel pillows and bed linen to create his 'baby bump'.
He asked Khaled, after the exam, if he could stop by our hotel before we headed off to the yacht.
'I want to get rid of all this stuff!' he moaned.
I did not see the 'pregnant' Sergio perform, since I was doing my own role, but from all reports he was brilliant.

But our detour back to the hotel caused problems. As we tried to make headway to the yacht, we hit a very tangled traffic jam.
We were making progress at about a foot every other minute.
Khaled was getting concerned. He kept calling Major Mohammed to let him know of our predicament. When there was a chance to make some time, Khaled drove like a madman until we hit the next traffic jam. It was like that all the way to the yacht.
They delayed sailing until we got there.

When we finally arrived, Major Mohammed was extremely polite to us, but he was not so pleasant to Khaled.

I spoke to the Major after his dressing down of Khaled.
'That was not his fault,' I told him. 'He did everything he could do to get us here on time. I would not be happy to hear that he is in trouble for this.'

And Major Mohammed smiled his smile.

'Are you certain you do not have Egyptian blood?' he teased me.

When I pressed him again not to blame Khaled for our tardiness, he would only say, 'We shall see.'

President Mubarak was seated at the head table with various dignitaries and the most senior surgeons from the Royal College. Major Mohammed was seated at his right hand.

Sergio and I were seated at a table with all the chiefs of staff of the Egyptian military.

Other dignitaries like the Head of the Antiquities Museum were seated at other tables.

It was all white linen tablecloths with servants everywhere and quite a formal State function at which I found myself.

The Egyptian military people at my table were a very serious group. Our conversation focused on American interventions in the Middle East. My American accent played a part, no doubt, in encouraging such a topic.

I had the impression that they did not like Americans very much. Or rather American foreign policy.

'Your country knows nothing about the Middle East,' the Chief of Staff of the Army told me. 'Their blindness cannot be cured.'

The President gave a short speech in English in which he thanked the surgeons and all those who had helped to coordinate their stay.

'May this be the start of a new tradition. May this day always be remembered. The British surgeons have at last come to our Homeland.'

There was much applause.

After dinner, we were treated to a performance of classic Egyptian dance and music. It was absolutely fascinating. The talented performers sang traditional songs and danced traditional dances. All of this was going on while we sailed down the Nile.

Then suddenly Sergio nudged me.

'Look, Ralphy,' he said, as he furtively pointed at another table.

When I glanced across, I saw Mr. Patterson was talking with Khaled. They were deep in conversation together.

'Maybe Sourpuss had a change of heart!' Sergio said in happy amazement.

After our Nile cruise, Khaled said very little as he drove us back to the hotel.
We said nothing about noticing his conversation with Mr. Patterson.

At one point during the drive, Sergio asked Khaled about 'burkas' and if he knew women who wore them.
'My fiancé wears one,' he told us.
'She says it deflects unwanted attention and makes her feel free to be out on her own. It's only your perspective that makes it seem oppressive. That's how you see it. She chooses to wear it. I don't tell her to do so.'
'But how can she even see all covered up like that?' Sergio asked.
And then he realized his gaff.
We travelled back the rest of the way in utter silence.

When Sergio and I arrived back at our hotel, the hotel manager called us over.
'We have yet to receive the paperwork covering your stay with us,' he informed us.
'As you are scheduled to leave us in two days time, we need to address this matter.'
Sergio told him, in anxiety-ridden panic, that the surgeons were taking care of everything and that we were just actors working on a job for them. 'This doesn't have anything to do with us!' he exclaimed.
'Let me call the surgeons' administrator,' I said trying to calm the situation down. I am sure it is all just an oversight.'

So I called Angela and told her that her idea that we simply say, 'We're with the surgeons', wasn't working.
She was very annoyed.
'Put the manager on the phone,' she said in exasperation.
I handed over the phone.
'I knew this would happen!' Sergio squealed at me in dismay.
'I can't afford to front the money for a two week stay here!'

The hotel manager and Angela spoke for quite a while. The manager kept saying that the hotel voucher to guarantee payment for our stay had not been sent by the travel agency engaged by the surgeons.

'We have not seen it. I personally checked the fax machine and there has been nothing from the London agency.'

There was a pause.

Angela did not like loose ends. Even though she and I were chummy enough, she could be quite surly to people when things did not go to plan. I could not hear what she was saying to the manager, but from the look on his face, she was giving him an earful.

'I will check again, madam, and call you back.'

He hung up.

'I am sure this is simply a mistake,' he said to us.

'I will check our incoming correspondence again to see if we have mislaid the payment voucher.'

He walked back over to the reception desk and said something to the three employees there. One of them started doing something on the computer.

Sergio and I walked through the lobby to the hotel bar and ordered a couple drinks, but before they arrived the hotel manager came up to our table.

'I am very sorry. It seems the payment voucher was sent via an e-mail attachment and not by fax as we had expected. This is entirely our error. It was overlooked and we should have checked. Please do forgive us for troubling you.'

And he bowed and walked away.

'Ralphy, how could they miss seeing that?' Sergio said as he shook his head.

'It was right in front of their eyes the entire time!'

There was a minor disruption during the next day's exams. The candidate doctors were under so much pressure to pass the exam that they sometimes forgot that they were at an exam and failed to act accordingly.

They'd talk to one another about the examination station they had just completed and how they thought they did and what they should have done while they waited in the corridor to go into the next station.

Angela caught three of them nervously talking together in this way. She promptly stopped the exam and had all three removed from the building.

We all paused for about ten minutes or so, while this was happening, before we could restart the exam.

I left the little room that served as my station and went out into the corridor.
Much to my surprise, I saw that Khaled was already there. He usually just arrived at the end of the exams to collect us.
I don't think he saw me.
He was walking down the corridor and looking in each station in turn. Finally, he looked in one room and went in.

I walked down the hall and glanced into the room he had entered. Mr. Patterson was in there.
I didn't listen in on their conversation, but I could see they were talking about something serious.
When I saw Sergio, I told him about seeing Khaled with Mr. Patterson.
'Maybe we had Sourpuss all wrong,' he said.

At the completion of the day's exams, Major Mohammed approached me.
'I will be driving you back to your hotel this evening. Khaled has to attend to some urgent family business.'
The Major was graciousness itself, but I could tell he was not happy with Khaled.

There was a 'special event' at the surgeons' hotel that evening. After dinner, the surgeons were going to put on their own entertainment. Sergio and I made our way over to join them.
It was a rip-roaring, no-holds-barred, and hilarious evening. The surgeons were all in fine form and one of their number played a wicked ukulele in the manner of George Formby. I'd have to describe the entertainment as 'bawdy' at best.
That skimpy, sequined harem outfit, one of the surgeons bought at the bazaar, even made an appearance.
They did a cross-dressing sketch in which they teased poor Sergio mercilessly. And they mocked me too by imitating my 'style' in corralling them all to go to that market.
They did this in a terrible American accent.
'But 'youse' guys! You gotta go! It'll be like so much fun!'
I took it all in good cheer.
I had to. No one escaped unscathed. Not even Angela.

Later, we all retired to the bar and continued our mayhem there.

After a short while, I left on my own. Sergio stayed and kept up with the surgeons' drinking.

I was no match for them. And, to be honest, after losing my wife, Nora, to the bottle, I also lost a lot of my ability to laugh at drunken antics too.

Drunken talk and drunken over-familiarity held little appeal to me anymore.

I walked the long distance back to our hotel on my own. It was, as always, a lovely and balmy night. The moon was full and a breeze brought out the crowds.

When I reached the Kubri el-Gamia bridge, it was full of people talking and young couples laughing as I made my way across it.

It was the local spot at which to 'hang out'.

Young kids would sit on the bridge railings. Had they fallen off, the long drop into the Nile would have been fatal.

Of course there was the inevitable, noisy, traffic jam on the bridge too.

Horns, hooted to no effect, are the sound track of Cairo.

I was making my way past all that chaos, when I spotted Khaled's car up ahead in the bridge gridlock.

As I approached his unmoving car, I saw he was not alone.

'Maybe it's his fiancé,' I thought.

But as I walked by, I could see it was not his fiancé.

It was Mr. Patterson.

I tried to lose myself in the throng so they'd not notice I had seen them.

I started thinking that maybe Sergio was right and we had been more than unfair to Mr. Patterson. Perhaps he did care about Khaled's problems.

'You can't be a world famous surgeon and not care about people,' I concluded to myself.

It was the final day of the exams. We were all due to fly back to London tomorrow.

Yesterday's exam 'scandal' had made the Egyptian news. In one of their 'English language' newspapers, they showed photos of the three young doctors who were escorted from the exam and called them 'cheats and scoundrels' and 'a disgrace to the good name of Egypt,'

It was harsh treatment.

We finished the exams, held the membership ceremony, drank some more sparkling apple juice in way of welcome, and then headed back to our hotel.
It was our final evening in Cairo.

Sergio and I had a drink together at the Sheraton bar and then we headed off to see the surgeons.
'I wonder what they have planned for this evening?' I asked.
'Ralphy, just promise me you'll keep me out of that bar over there!' Sergio pleaded.
'My liver can't take it!'

When we reached their hotel, we saw there was a delay at the security gate outside.
It always took a few minutes to get through hotel security, but that evening it was an utter fiasco. Expensive looking women in cocktail dresses and their husbands were looking exasperated.
I asked a woman tourist in the security 'queue' what was going on.
'We don't know! Apparently they found something on the x-ray machine earlier,' the woman said. 'We've been trying to get back to our room for half an hour, haven't we, darling?' she asked whom I guessed was her husband.

We waited and waited for our turn to maneuver past the newly improved security gauntlet.
Finally, we were allowed to enter, but not before security staff had gone through everything in our pockets. Sergio had a little backpack that he always carried with him and he was forced to empty all its contents and put them on the x-ray conveyor.
We had to show our passports even though the security staff knew us well by then.
'What's this all about?' Sergio asked me.

We went into the lobby. It was full of military police.
Some of the surgeons were in the bar. We made our way over to them.
I saw the surgeon who had played the ukulele the evening before and joked with him, but he was not his usual humorous self.
'What's happening?' I asked him.
'What's not?' he responded cryptically.

'What do you mean?'

'The police have been here ever since we got back from today's exam,' he said. 'They were making enquiries about some robbery at the Egyptian Antiquities Museum. They took Patterson away for questioning.'

'Mr. Patterson?' I asked. 'What do the police want with Mr. Patterson?'

'They received a tip off, or so they claimed, that some of the stolen museum goods were here at our hotel. When Patterson and I went through security, he was pulled aside. They claim that he had one of the stolen items in his possession.'

'That's unbelievable,' I said.

'I said the same thing too.'

'What did they say he had?' I asked him.

'It's bonkers. They say he had a genuine Pharaonic papyrus.'

'Really! Come on! That's all you hear!' I laughed. 'Everyone is selling an 'authentic genuine papyrus'! I've been offered ten of them a day myself!'

'The police say that this one is genuine,' he replied thoroughly fed up.

Later, I saw the Major enter the hotel. He was accompanied by about half a dozen soldiers in uniform. He gave some curt orders to them and they dispersed themselves throughout the hotel. They were clearly hunting for something.

I saw two of them interrogating the hotel gift shop manager.

Major Mohammed was always very giving of his time and polite to me, but as I approached him to ask what was going on, he did not seem like the same man.

'I cannot discuss this matter with you,' he said tersely.

And he turned and walked away.

When we boarded our plane to London the next morning, Mr. Patterson was not with us.

I also never had the chance to say goodbye to Khaled.

On the morning of our departure, all the other minders were at the hotel to wish us well and say their goodbyes.

But Khaled was not among their number.

'He probably has more pressing matters on his mind than saying fare thee well to us,' Sergio suggested. I guessed that was true.

It was only after returning to London, when I finally found out what had happened.

I had Major Mohammed's e-mail address and wrote to thank him and asked him to stay in touch.

'When you come to London,' I wrote, 'I hope to show you the same hospitality as you showed to us.'

To my surprise, he replied by letter. I have no notion as to how he knew my home address.

What he wrote in response shocked me.

'My dear friend, it is with sadness that I must tell you that your Mr. Patterson has been arrested and will stand trial for receiving stolen goods.

His accomplice, Khaled, works in our Military Intelligence Division. Through his contacts there, he was able to discover who was responsible for the theft from the Antiquities Museum.

He used this knowledge to obtain a stolen item which he then gave to Mr. Patterson.

This item is priceless and we have now recovered it.

Khaled will stand trial in a military court.

He claims, in his defence, that Mr. Patterson had forced him to obtain the item on his behalf.

Khaled stated under interview that Mr. Patterson had offered to pay for his fiancé's flight to London and would carry out necessary eye surgery on her there.

This he would do in exchange for the antiquity that Khaled had in his possession. We are now investigating this claim.

We are all very sad that such a thing has occurred.

Our hope is that the Royal College will continue, in future, to hold their exams in Cairo. I would be grateful for any assistance you might offer in making this so.

It saddens us to think that such an honour could be jeopardized by greed and stupidity.

We sincerely hope this will not be the case.'

Yours faithfully,
Major Tewfiq al-Mohammed

There was no return address.

I was more than bemused. Did the Major imagine that I exercised some clout with the Royal College? How did he expect me to be of 'assistance'?

I emailed the Major to keep me informed, but he did not reply.

What ultimately happened to Khaled I do not know. Nor do I know the fate of his fiancé. I cannot tell you if her vision was saved or not.

A few months after our return from Cairo, I was booked to work for the surgeons again. This time in London.

But when I arrived, none of the surgeons, who were in Cairo, spoke about the 'Papyrus Affair'.

Then, to my surprise, I saw that Mr. Patterson was one of the examiners there.

Somehow he must have escaped a prison sentence.

I don't imagine that Khaled was as fortunate.

I thought better than to raise the topic with Mr. Patterson himself.

I did speak with Angela, the surgeons' administrator, but all she told me was that we would be going back to Cairo to hold future exams there.

She mentioned nothing at all about Mr. Patterson or Khaled.

Everyone acted as if nothing really had happened.

They just all turned a blind eye to it.

But this did all happen and it happened just as I related it to you here.

If you don't believe me, contact the Royal College of Surgeons of England and Wales and ask them about it yourself.

Well, OK, maybe they won't want to discuss it.

But that doesn't make my story of 'The Genuine Papyrus' any less genuine itself.

STORY CHAPTER FIFTEEN

'OTTO'

Brace yourselves. This is one weird story, full of coincidences, and I find it hard to believe that it happened myself. And that is true despite the fact that it happened to me.

I had just finished getting my life back in order after a painful 'recovery and renewal' period following the loss of Nora and our theatre. I was doing a lot of freelance 'role-play' work for a while, until an entirely new career opened up before me. It was by the ficklest finger of fine fortune.
Suddenly, by this unearned good luck, I accidentally became a 'Speech Doctor' in great demand.

My old friend, Ted, decided to run for election to be a Member of the European Union Parliament and he asked me to help him in his campaign to become an 'MEP'. I served as his test audience guinea pig before he made his speeches. I'd give him feedback on what was working well and what wasn't. His public speeches started to go down well and one thing then led to another.
Ted won his seat and he kept directing other politicians my way for speech work.

I don't know what would have become of me, if it were not for Ted. I owe him much. He kept getting me work, when I was at my lowest ebb. He helped me, when my marriage had sunk to the seabed. He was a good source of practical advice. And he was my friend, above all, and a valued one at that.
And now he was a politician.

Years before, Ted had been through a nasty divorce. When Nora and I broke down, we just went our own way and our divorce was straightforward, if a divorce can be straightforward. But Ted and his wife had a long, drawn-out fight with armies of lawyers aligned to each side. It was an expensive and awful 'mess', as Ted termed it. It took Ted months and months to gain access to his own kids.

I don't know how he survived it. I didn't know his former wife and I don't know the ins-and-outs of their fall out, but I do know it knocked the guts out of Ted.

But he did survive. At first, he had to stop doing his successful acting work. He had lost all his self-confidence. And after he recovered from that loss, he started writing business training courses. He did well at that too. Ted always did well at whatever he set his mind and efforts.
And now he was 'MEP' for his home town in Norfolk.

Not only was I now a 'Speech Doctor', thanks to Ted, but it led to other work. Business leaders would contact me and ask for my assistance prior to giving some keynote speech or conference talk. I was particularly good, so others claim, at 'drawing people out of themselves'. The business people kept spreading the word that I could get them to connect better with their audiences.
I started meeting a lot of famous and powerful people. They all had to speak at some public event. And, all of a sudden, I didn't need to worry about money anymore.
That was new to me.
A good new. An unknown new.

Ted would commute to Brussels or Strasbourg depending on where his Parliamentary duties took him. He was still able to keep his home in London though.
I was happy about that. It meant I could still see my friend. Or at least that was my thought. In fact, he was so busy now that I hardly ever saw him.

I guess it was about a year after Ted was elected, when he finally rang me and asked to meet. He was so swept up in his new responsibilities and his commuting that he had no time for anyone. We spoke on the phone, of course, and exchanged e-mails, but we hadn't seen one another, face to face, for far too long.
'I have a surprise for you, Ralphy,' Ted said intriguingly over the phone.
We set a time to meet.

Ted and I always met, whenever we could meet, at the 'Princess Louise' in Holborn. It was the pub where we first made our acquaintance. Years ago, I had an audition there for a radio drama Ted had written. He hired me and it was our preferred watering hole thereafter.

When I arrived on the allotted day, I could see that Ted was not alone.
'Ralphy,' he announced proudly. 'This is Susan.'

I could see that 'Susan' was his new lady. But, and this is hard to believe, I saw much more than that.
'Sue!' I shouted. 'Wow!'
And we both gave each other a bear hug of a greeting.
'Ralphy Waldo! Waldo the Wildman!' she shrieked. 'Ted told me it was you we were meeting, but I didn't let on that I knew you!'
Ted looked shocked.
'Ted! Sue and I moved with the same crowd together in the States!' I laughed. 'How the daisy did you two meet?'

The look on Ted's face!
I hadn't had a belly laugh like that for many years. I mean, like when your sides hurt. I'm talking about a real rib-tickler.
'You know each other?' Ted asked uncertainly.
'Yes!' I said as I wiped my eyes. 'We haven't seen one another since our college days!'

'Susan' was an ex-flame of my old college friend, Charlie. We once all shared a harrowing adventure together in the New Hampshire mountains. In those days, she was simply 'Sue', but now she had transfigured, obviously, into the much more formidable 'Susan'.
I didn't mention the 'Charlie and Sue' past to Ted.

Susan said that she moved to London years ago with her now ex-husband.
'I hadn't a clue that you were living in London too, Ralphy! I wish I had!'
'Ted and I met in Brussels,' she continued. 'I'm a lobbyist for the fishing industry.'
'I caught her in the fishnet of my charm,' Ted said while batting his eyes.

'We just moved in together last week,' Susan explained. 'And what fishnet?' she said to Ted. 'You'd scare all the fish away!'

'He snores!' she informed me with a teasing laugh.

Susan told me all about her ex-husband and how he was a rat and a liar.

'We met in the States. It was a few months after Charlie and I broke up. He told me he came from this fine, old English family. Wow! I can't believe I fell for that baloney! When we had our boy, he insisted we move back to Britain. But he didn't come from a 'fine' family-surprise surprise. Not that it really matters. Nothing he told me turned out to be true. But what did matter was that he couldn't keep it in his pants. I don't put up with that, so I left his sorry ass.'

'Well, it worked out all right!' I said. 'It's always good to see another Yank in London.'

I did remember from our college days that 'Susan' was not one to treat disrespectfully. I once saw her punch a frat boy right in the mouth for being 'overly familiar'. I also remember her being very clever.

'Did you say you have a boy?' I asked her.

'Yes, Otto. He's ten now. He's the only good thing that the rat ever did for me.'

We had a great night reminiscing. Susan didn't ask about Nora. She didn't know that we eventually married and divorced. And I didn't mention Nora either.

Ted, Susan, and I met up whenever we could after that. It was such a strange coincidence that I knew Ted's new love. They say three's a crowd, but that's not always true.

After a few nights on the town together, I was invited to Ted and Susan's flat for dinner. It was going to be my first opportunity to meet Otto.

I was looking forward to that.

The day before my dinner invitation, Ted called me.

'I better tell you something, Ralphy,' he began.

'Otto has a few 'problems'.'

'What do you mean 'problems'?' I asked him.

'The doctors say he has something called 'Asperger's Syndrome'. He can be 'funny' socially. He gets fixated on one activity too sometimes. Susan and I found a good school for him where they know about his condition. Don't worry! I'm sure he'll be fine with you though.'

I had heard of Asperger's Syndrome, but I didn't know much about it.

The next evening, I got myself ready and headed off for my dinner with Ted, Susan, and Otto. I rang their bell and waited for them to buzz me in.
'Do you like dinosaurs?' a tiny voice asked through the intercom.
'Yes, I do,' I replied.
'Then you may enter!' And, who I imagined was Otto, buzzed me in.

As soon as I went through their door, Otto ran straight at me. I didn't have a chance to say hello to Ted and Susan before Otto had grabbed me by the hand and led me to his bedroom.

'I have models of all the dinosaurs and I know each one by name and I know they come from the Jurassic Age and I've seen '*Jurassic Park*' five times now and I can see it on the newest online service anytime I want, but the original one is the only good one. The other ones are 'poopy scoopy'!'
Ted and Susan were standing at Otto's bedroom door observing all this.
'Language, Young Man,' Susan said to him.
'But they are! They are all 'poopy scoopy'!' He shouted and ran out the door.
'You see what I mean?' Ted whispered to me.

I guess some people would have been thrown by Otto's boundless energy, but I can honestly say that it did not bother me in the slightest. He was a lovely, handsome, clever boy. Perhaps he was a bit 'inappropriate' sometimes. He did play with his dinner more than eat it. He interrupted our conversations mid-sentence several times, but lots of kids would do that.
If you engaged his attention, he was a lot of fun.

After dinner and coffee, Susan told Otto it was time for bed. That set him off in a flurry of running around the flat and saying, 'No! No! No!'

But lots of kids act that way too when you tell them it's lights out.

I heard a lot of giggling and screaming from Otto's room as Susan tried to get him to settle down for the night.

'He's a great kid really, Ted,' I said.

'He's a handful when he puts his mind to it,' Ted replied.

Susan eventually succeeded in getting Otto into bed.

'Phew!' she said as she returned and sat back at the table.

'Did he ask you about it again?' Ted asked her.

'Yes, he asked me again,' Susan sighed.

'Ask you what?' I said.

'Oh, he wants to know all about 'God' now and 'religion',' Ted told me. 'It's his new 'thing'.'

'He's been like a broken record for weeks, Ralphy,' Susan said as she shook her head.

'Is God really there? Where does he live? Is he in the church down our street?' she said imitating Otto.

'He won't stop. I guess one of the kids at school said something about 'God' and Otto can be like a dog with a bone when he wants to know about something.'

'So why don't you take him to church?' I enquired.

I had no idea what Ted or Susan thought about 'God'. But I found out soon enough.

'Absolutely not!' Susan told me firmly. 'He has enough problems without religion confusing him.'

Ted nodded in agreement. 'If we indulge all his whims, that's all we'll end up doing.'

Later, as I headed back to my place, I thought about Otto. It must be difficult for parents to cope with an illness like that. I have no children myself. Nora and I couldn't have any. But I know parents, worthy of the name, always worry about their kids and their welfare. I've lived, briefly, with 'Hells Angels' in the past and they worried about their kids too.

It's what parents do, I suppose.

And that's true whether the child has a 'problem' or not.

A week or so later, Ted called me.

'Ralphy, Susan and I were wondering if maybe you were right.'

'Right? Right about what, Ted?'

'About taking Otto to church.'

I didn't suggest that to them. Well, OK, maybe I did. But I really just meant to ask why they didn't do it. I felt very uncomfortable that they had taken my question and turned it into 'advice'.

'He's still going on about that stuff, is he?' I finally asked.

'You've no idea. His school contacted us and said that Otto is interrupting lessons by asking all these questions about 'God'. They suggest that we try to encourage his interest and perhaps then he can move on from it.'

'That sounds like a plan,' I said.

'But there's no way Susan is going to take him to church. She and I are alike in this. I can't see me sitting there in some pew while people are singing *Amazing Grace*. I'd burst out laughing!'

'Maybe they won't sing *Amazing Grace*, Ted,' I suggested.

'Any hymn, Ralphy! Any hymn and I'm going to get the giggles. And anyway, I'm too busy. I don't have the time.'

'And Susan won't budge either?' I asked him.

'Susan! I think Susan would stand up and start shouting at the congregation!' he laughed.

'She calls church-goers, 'God-dies', and insists they all probably believe in Father Christmas too! No, Susan would never agree to do it.'

'So what are you going to do?'

'My friend,' he said. 'This brings me to the point of my call.'

My tingling senses told me that a 'Big Ask' was coming.

'You have a point, Ted?' I teased him.

'Yes, I do. I do. Susan and I were talking,' he began, 'and we thought the only person we'd really trust taking Otto to church was you.'

'Uh huh,' I grunted vaguely.

'Well, what do you say?' Ted asked reluctantly.

Now, I don't know what moved me to say 'OK', but that's what popped out of my mouth.

'Ralphy, you're a mate!' a relieved Ted said. 'Thank you, mate.'

If I told you that I was religious, I'd be telling you I was a liar.
I went to church services when I was a kid, but I flew the nest and
hadn't done much in that area since.
I knew more about being Jewish than anything else. I had been to so
many Bar Mitzvahs. I even tried to help my childhood friend, Fish,
learn the Hebrew for his.

I didn't think about 'God' or religion really.
Trust me, when you face a matinee and evening performance of
Grease or *Coppélia* on a Sunday, like I used to do, the last thing you
think about upon rising is 'God'.
So, really, I was closer to Ted's position than I cared to admit. I
feared I might find it all faintly ridiculous too and start laughing.
I wasn't worried about me shouting out at the congregation, as Susan
might.
No, it was the potential silliness that made me fret.

But Ted's my good friend and, amazingly, he'd hooked up with an
old college classmate of mine.
I could do this for them.
And, besides, I liked Otto.

The 'Sunday Plan' involved Ted or Susan dropping Otto off at my
flat. Then Otto and I would take a short walk to St. Joseph's,
Highgate.
After the service, Ted or Susan would then collect Otto.

'Holy Joe's', as the locals called the church, was just at the end of
my block. I'd never been inside it though.
And that Sunday, as arranged, Ted dropped off Otto and the pair of
us walked off together to church.

There was a bakery on the way to 'Holy Joe's'.
It reminded me of the time when I was a kid and went to church with
my family. We'd always stop at Silber's, the local bakery, afterward.
'Otto, we'll get a treat there after the service,' I said.
Otto nodded fiercely. But he said nothing to me as we walked. He
had a determined look as he marched alongside me.

We went up to the church doors. They were badly weather-beaten and worse for wear. I could see though that they must have been magnificent years ago before their current distress.

Otto pushed through the doors and I followed.

We found a pew, although the church was crowded. Then someone rang a bell and the service started.

It was not ridiculous. People were singing, but it was pleasant enough. I didn't feel like laughing at all. That was a relief.

The Reverend seemed a good guy. But I bet he was nearly ninety years old.

He moved slowly and carefully.

I looked around the interior of the church more than take in the service.

Paint was peeling from the walls. What was once a beautiful and ornate, gold-leafed décor had fallen into neglect. There were cracks and stains on all the pillars. And one section of pews was blocked off with 'hazard' tape.

But the church was nearly full. That was good. It made it easier to blend in.

Otto was transfixed. There were some prayer books and hymnals in a rack on our pew. Otto was speed-reading those and looking up to follow the service at the same time.

A few people turned around and smiled at Otto benignly.

After the service, Otto grilled me relentlessly. Even at the bakery.

'Ralphy, is 'God' and 'The Father' the same bloke?'

'Ralphy, what's the 'Spirit'?'

'Ralphy, does 'God' start plagues?'

I replied to his inquisition with a mixture of 'Don't know', 'Not sure', and 'I used to know that.'

Otto was not impressed.

It was our turn at the bakery counter.

'What'll it be, Otto?'

He didn't even look.

'Jam donut,' he said as if I should know.

And he carried on with his non-stop questioning, with jam on his face, as we made the short walk back to my flat.

301

Ted was already waiting.

'How was that, Ots?'

'It was interesting, Ted, very interesting. There's a lot of stuff to know.'

Then he said, as he was getting into Ted's car, 'Ralphy, you don't know much about 'God', do you?'

And he shook his little head and slammed the door.

He was an astute one that Otto.

Other than that first Sunday, it was always Susan who dropped off Otto and collected him.

Ted had two kids from his first marriage and he was desperate to see them on a Sunday or he was on the Eurostar coming back from Belgium or somewhere. He was always busy with something.

But that gave me a chance to roll back the years with Susan.

We'd have good 'catch up' sessions after Otto and I returned from church.

Susan told me that 'Colin', her ex-husband, was tied up in a land speculation fraud in Florida.

'I tell you, Ralphy, the guy was a total liar,' she whispered so Otto wouldn't hear.

'He used to pretend he was some sort of royalty or something to make money off of stupid Yanks. Even I fell for his lies about his 'historic family'. He said he wanted to raise Otto in the 'Land of his Fathers', but really he was on the run from the Securities and Exchange Commission. I didn't know a thing about it. We come over here and the next thing I know I'm seeing texts from women he's been messing with. What a deadbeat!'

'It's for the best, Sue. Now you have Ted.'

'And Otto,' she added.

Susan never asked Otto about church or whether he enjoyed it or anything about it at all. She was conflicted about it. That's for sure.

On the one hand, the last thing she would have wished for was Otto 'Getting God', as she called it. But on the other, she knew that he had this strange passion for it and to prevent him from it would only cause misery.

She tried her best to suffer Otto's 'church thing' in silence.

But six months down the line from that first church Sunday, Otto had not lost his passion. Both Ted and Susan told me that Otto could get 'fixated' on a single thing and I guess that is what this was.

He was always silent when we walked to church. He had this hungry look in his eyes. It was as if he were drawn there.
And he was like a sponge. He seemed to recall every single word at every service.
But I was hopeless and nothing was sticking with me. Otto gave up on asking me questions about 'God' and started lecturing me about Him instead.

'Ralphy, 'God' is a bush on fire. 'God' is a voice in the clouds. 'God' is on the mountain. You should really follow his commandments.'
And then he'd rattle them all off.
There were one or two I had forgotten about myself.

Otto was always multi-tasking during the service. The church had this pamphlet display case as you entered. Otto would grab about four of the pamphlets and walk off. They weren't free. I'd quickly tabulate how many he had grabbed and put some money in the coin slot.
And, by the end of the service, he would have read all the pamphlets and also be able to tell me about the sermon and the readings too.
He was quite a guy our Otto.

The only thing he might do at church that caused some anxiety was speaking too loud. If he missed a word in the sermon or couldn't understand some word or phrase in one of his little pamphlets, he would ask me aloud. Loud enough for even the Reverend to hear.
Susan told me to tell him to use his 'school voice', when he started doing that.
He knew what that meant and he'd nod and be quiet.
Until after the service, of course, when he could ask me again.

I admit it. I liked my Sundays with Otto. I never had children of my own and being in his company was a real treat for me.
Even if it did mean I had to sit through a church service.

During one of Susan and my 'catch up' sessions after church, she told me that Otto was having trouble at school.

'He's been calling out again during lessons, Ralphy,' she said.
'I thought we had that licked, but apparently not. The Headmaster told me that he has been interrupting lessons again by asking 'inappropriate' questions.'
'Inappropriate?' I asked puzzled.
'Yes, he keeps asking the teachers about 'God'. It's getting worse. He'll interrupt them in the middle of class. One of his teachers told me he was trying to explain how seeds grow and Otto shouted out, 'Some of the seed fell among weeds and others among thorns. Does 'God' know where the seeds will fall?'
My heart went out to her. I could see she was drained in despair and worry.

'And he's stuck like molasses to this 'God' malarkey,' she continued. 'The doctors told us his obsessions might tail off as he grew up, but this 'God' thing is lasting even longer than his dinosaur obsession. Ted and I are thinking we should stop letting him go to church.'
'How do you think he'd take that?' I asked.
'Badly, Ralphy. Very badly. But the most frustrating thing is that it was the school's idea to let him go there in the first place. He was shouting out about 'God' during class before he went to church and he's still doing it now. It's worse, if anything. And now the school is acting as if Ted and I need to do something about it.'
'The school doesn't have any ideas?' I wondered.
'They just act like it's our problem. I don't think they have a clue what to do about it themselves.'

Ted called me that Wednesday. I was expecting him to tell me that Otto wasn't going to church anymore. I would miss him, but it's right that his schooling came first.
But Ted did not say what I expected.

'Has Otto been saying anything to you about saving people, Ralphy?' Ted asked.
His question took me aback.
'I don't think so, Ted. No, I can't recall anything about saving,' I eventually said. 'Why?'
'He came home from school on Monday and started saying that he 'saved' someone. He can go into fantasies about things like that, but this was different. He wouldn't let up. We had to give him a 'time out', because he wouldn't stop banging on about it.'

'Poor little guy,' I said.

'We had a call from the school on Tuesday,' Ted continued. 'It was the Headmaster. He said that one of Otto's classmates is visually impaired.

Apparently, this girl wears specially designed lenses and has real difficulty with close-up work.

Anyway, she goes to school on Tuesday and isn't wearing her glasses. So one of the school administrators called her parents to bring them in for her.

And when the mother of the girl answered she said, 'No, she doesn't need them any more!'

'I don't understand. What's that got to do with Otto?' I asked.

'Well, the girl came home from school on Monday, her mother said, and claimed she didn't need them to see anymore. She sat right down and started reading the comics in the paper. Without her glasses. Her mother couldn't believe it.

'She would always need her glasses and a magnifier to read the comics,' she told the school.

'It's some sort of miracle!' she insisted.

'Hmmm... That's pretty weird, Ted.' I said.

'Yes, more than weird,' he agreed. 'And then the girl told her mother that it was Otto who did it. The Headmaster told us that the girl claims Otto put a mud pie on her eyes after school on Monday and said, 'You were blind, but now you can see!'

And when she washed off the mud, she could see.'

Ted went on to tell me that the Headmaster said Otto was becoming too difficult to manage at school.

'Come on, Ted! A mud pie! Kids do that sort of stuff all over the world,' I laughed.

'Surely, the school knows that,' I went on. 'Why don't they wait and see if the girl starts wearing her glasses again? It sounds crazy to me.'

'No, he is telling all his classmates that he can 'save' them. He's been preaching about 'God' to them at lunchtime. And he's been shouting again and the kids are getting all wound up about it. Some of the bigger boys are shouting back and there's been pushing. It's a mess.'

'He's a good little preacher, Ted,' I joked. 'You should hear him laying down the law to me after church!'
But I knew this was not a laughing matter.

Of course, there was a rational explanation for 'Otto's Mud Pie Miracle'.

A few days later, Ted called me back and said that it turned out that the girl had read that comic earlier. With her glasses.
'She had just remembered the words from before. A lot of the kids at Otto's school are very suggestible,' Ted said. 'If someone puts a notion into their heads, they will believe it.'

But that did not stop Otto from performing 'miracles' at home or at school.
'We couldn't find the remote one evening,' Ted told me.
'Otto made us all hold hands while he said a prayer to find the remote. When he was done, he ran into the sitting room, reached under the cushions on our couch, and there was the remote. He held it up in both his hands and said to the ceiling, 'We thank you for this, Father.' Susan's sure he hid it there himself.'

Susan and Ted tried to end Otto's Sunday ritual. They held out for two Sundays, but finally had to cave in.

'We have no choice,' Susan said to me on the phone.
'He's so self-absorbed about it. It's all he'll talk about. He takes everything so literally. It scares me. He reads or hears something at church and it's just 'fact' to him.
I caught him, a few days ago, standing on his bed with his arms upraised, and his eyes screwed shut.'
'What you doing, Ots?' I asked him.
He didn't answer. He just froze in that position for minutes.
I stayed there staring at him.
And then he turns and glares at me and says, 'Get away from me woman! Can't you see I am about my Father's business?'
'Father's business?' I asked, You mean Colin? Ted?'
'No,' she sighed. 'The 'Father' father.'
'Oh! Right,' I said.

'We went to see the school counselor again. He thinks if he goes back to church, his 'God' obsession may pass more quickly. We hope so anyway. Not letting him go hasn't been working. That's for certain.'

So, we restarted the 'Sunday Plan'.
Otto was going back to church.
And so was I.

But Otto's school troubles were growing worse. The school agreed to allow him to stay, but he was getting a lot of 'time outs' and sessions with the school counselor.

Once after the Sunday Church-Bakery Run, Susan told me that Otto was scaring the other kids.
'I've got parents ringing me!' she moaned. 'Your Otto told our daughter that she was damned, because she wouldn't share her chocolate bar with him! And she's very upset!'
'That's the kind of thing I've been putting up with lately. I worry every time the phone rings now,' she explained. 'He told one boy he didn't need to take his insulin anymore, because he had 'healed' him.'
I thought Susan was going to start crying. She was so upset with worry.

'And he does it with me too,' she said. 'He told me that I'd be 'wailing and gnashing my teeth', if I didn't let him go back to church.'

I didn't know what to say. I could see Susan was exhausted by all this 'mess', as Ted called it.
I felt for Otto too.
'The counselor says that Otto doesn't grasp the concept of religion,' Susan told me.
'To him, it's all facts to learn. He takes everything at face value. He just apes what he sees and hears.'

That Sunday, Susan dropped off Otto as usual. We made our short trek to church and, as was his practice, Otto said nothing along the way.
Nothing out of the ordinary happened in church. At first.

Otto grabbed some more pamphlets, as we entered, and I put some money in the coin slot to pay for them. He sat in the pew and read and looked and listened as before.

But then, as the ancient Reverend made his way to the pulpit for his sermon, Otto suddenly stood up and ran straight towards him.

'Otto!' I scream-whispered. 'Otto!'

I tried to catch him, but he was too quick for me.

The poor preacher didn't know what to do. Otto just brushed past him as if he weren't there. Then he walked to the center of the church and raised his arms to heaven.

The entire congregation just glanced around at one another.

'I will abolish your carved images,' Otto thundered. 'And the sacred pillars from your midst. You shall no longer adore the work of your hands. I will tear out the sacred pillars from your midst, and destroy cities. I will wreak vengeance in anger and wrath upon the nations that have not harkened! Hear, then, what the Lord says!'

And then he froze there with his arms raised.

Trembling.

There was total silence. Awkward silence. It was as if everyone were mystified.

Which they had every right to be.

The overall effect may sound amusing, but I promise you it wasn't.

I went over to where he was standing. I tried not to make any eye contact with the rest of the congregation. I am sure I gave a little sheepish smile in mitigation as I lifted Otto up and carried him bodily back to the pew.

He was as stiff as a board.

If I told you it was embarrassing, you wouldn't know the half of it.

And Otto remained frozen like that throughout the rest of the service. He just stood there immobile. I had to hold my hand against his back so he wouldn't fall over.

So much for my plan in keeping a low profile.

I remember once, when I was just a kid myself, that a younger brother of a friend of mine was 'frozen' like that.

But that was because he had scared himself stiff over some silliness.

Otto's 'deep freeze' was not a 'scared stiff' one.

It was more like he had posed himself into an heroic, frozen statue.
Maybe he saw a Charlton Heston Bible movie. I don't know.
Maybe that's what he copied. I couldn't say.
But there I was propping him up with one hand and trying to be discreet about it.
Otto. The ten year old Moses.

When it was time to go, I had to carry Otto out of the church like he was a cardboard cut-out. It was as if he were 'joint-less'.
Several people approached me as I did so.
'Your little boy is so sweet! What verse was he quoting?' one of the old ladies asked.
(As if I'd know.)
'Guess he heard it somewhere,' I said mortified.
'You got yourself a little televangelist there, don't you?' one kind looking man teased me.

Finally, we made it back outside. When we got to the bakery, Otto started 'de-stiffening'.
'Jam Donut,' he said.
I imagine preaching is hunger-inducing work.

When we got back to my flat, Susan was waiting, but I said nothing about what had happened. Perhaps I should have told her, but I didn't want to worry her. She was worried enough about Otto as it was.

Someone at the church must have known a reporter. There was a tiny mention of the incident in *The Sun* the following day.

'Boy Preacher Spits Fire and Brimstone,' read the headline.
'St. Joseph's Church, Highgate, had an unexpected guest speaker yesterday when a young boy suddenly raced up and gave the Sunday sermon.'
'He had the Spirit in him!' Mary Forsythe of the Parish Council said. 'I think his father was as surprised as the rest of us.'
His father!
Luckily, neither Ted nor Susan saw it.

I didn't know what to do. I was going to have to go back to Holy Joe's next Sunday with Otto and now I didn't trust him. Who knows what he might do next?

I had figured out that once Otto had read something, he could immediately recall it. His passionate 'sermonette' had proven that. And he was not much good at determining what was and was not appropriate behavior in a social situation. He was clever like Susan too.

All that, I knew. But I couldn't take him back to that church, if he was going to be disruptive.

I worried about what I should do all that week.
And I worried alone without troubling Ted or Susan about it.

On Saturday, Susan rang.
'Ralphy, Otto won't be going to church this Sunday,' she announced.
I tried not to sound relieved.
'No?' I asked casually.
'Ted bought him one of those 'Guitar Hero' game things for the computer this week. He hasn't put it down since he opened it. That's all he wants he do now. I asked him this morning if he still wanted to go to church tomorrow.
'No, that's OK, Mommy mum-mum,' he said. 'I'm playing guitar. There's a lot to learn.'

'I think out little man has finally finished with 'God',' Susan said.
'I suspect you're pleased about that,' I told her.
'Thank God,' she replied.

And so that was the end of our 'Sunday Plan'.

I do go back myself to 'Holy Joe's' once in a while. I'm not a regular there or anything. I just find it peaceful. It's peaceful being among peace-minded people, I guess.

I still see Otto too. I mean, if he ever leaves his room.
His 'Guitar Hero' phase is intense. Once, when I was over there for dinner, he refused to leave his room to eat. He'd stay in there playing his computer 'guitar' the entire time I was there.
But a lot of kids do that.
Kids and music.
It's a popular combo.
As far as I know, Otto's still at it.

Things had settled down for Otto at school too.
'We haven't had any irate parents ring us for weeks,' a relieved Ted told me.

I helped Ted on a speech he was presenting in Europe. His aim was to assist charities working on 'Asperger's Syndrome'.
He was seeking funding for a European-wide Forum of such charities.
Allegedly, there's no cure.
Ted thought if charities could network about their experiences, attend seminars, that sort of thing, they might get closer to finding one.
He also campaigned for more funds for medical research in that area.

I went over to Ted's one evening to act as his 'test audience' for that speech.
I told him what I thought.
Afterward, Susan, Ted, and I sat around their kitchen table and had some coffee.
I could hear Otto in his room. He was huffing and puffing as he tried to keep up with the computer game music. He was determined to be a 'Guitar Hero' now.
His 'Moses' days were behind him.

Then Susan said to me, 'Hey, Ralphy! Whatever happened to that girl you used to run with at college? What was her name? You know, the one you were with when we all went to that hunting shack together?'
'Nora,' I said.
'Nora! Yes, Nora. Whatever happened to her?'
'Oh, that's a long story, Susan,' I said.
'We'll need all night for that one.'

And so I told Susan the story about Nora and my 'Heartbreak'. I told her the story about our theatre and projects we had done. Susan kept the coffee coming as I did so.
'Waldo, you do like your stories, don't you?' she laughed.

'Susan, get him to tell you the story about when the two of us were working together in Budapest!' Ted suggested.
And as Otto played 'Guitar Hero' in his bedroom, Ted, Susan, and I sat in the kitchen swapping stories.

'Ralphy, tell Ted about the time when we were nearly blown to smithereens at Fred's Hunting Lodge!' Sue begged me. 'You won't believe this one, Ted!'

And Ted countered, 'Did Ralphy ever tell you about the time when he was once crowned king in some Hindu Temple? Tell her that one, Ralphy,' he laughed.

I didn't leave until after dawn.

STORY CHAPTER SIXTEEN

'AFTERWORD'

I had to retire from all my role-playing, acting, and directing work.
And from my work as a 'Speech Doctor' too.
Not that most actors and directors and speech doctors can actually
plan a retirement.
My retirement certainly wasn't planned.

I had some preparation for it. I had to 'retire' from dancing in my late
thirties, but that comes with the territory.
This enforced retirement was entirely different.

I was diagnosed with something called 'COPD'. It's a problem with
my lungs.
I was shocked when the doctor told me. I never touched a cigarette in
my life.
I hadn't even heard of 'COPD' until they told me that I had it myself.

I went to see several specialist consultants once I was diagnosed.
I was telling one of them that one summer I worked at a factory that
made cardboard boxes.
I told him that I used to come home caked in dust.
'I'd have to gargle with salt water to get the taste of dust out of my
mouth,' I said.
'In those days, people didn't think to wear a face mask.'
'Cardboard dust contains some particles that are quite toxic,' he told
me.

My friend, Ted, saved a newspaper article for me. It was about this
COPD thing. The article stated that exposure to 'rising damp' and
'dry rot' can cause lung problems.
When Nora and I were first living in London, our flat was riddled
with damp.
It was a dingy basement flat with mold all over the walls.
It couldn't have done me any good. Nor Nora.

Another consultant asked me if I had ever been exposed to agricultural pesticides.

I told her about a summer when Nora and I were living in California. We stayed at a farmhouse surrounded by vineyards.

'The locals said the pesticides they used on the grapes were dangerous,' I recalled.

'Before spraying, the farmers would put up signs with a 'skull and crossbones' on them around the perimeter of the vineyard,' I told her.

'Current research is showing a possible connection with certain pesticides and lung disease,' she said.

I told my GP that the back wall of the theatre, which Nora and I used to run, was covered in blue asbestos. I had forgotten to mention that to the consultants who were treating me.

The GP thought that exposure to asbestos could well be the culprit that made me ill.

But he couldn't say, for certain, it was that either.

No one really seems to know and, I guess, it does not really matter now.

I have 'COPD' and that is my reality.

There's an NHS District Nurse, Ruby, who comes and checks on me once a week.

She's originally from St. Kitts. We always talk about her son who is training to be a doctor. I told her about the 'role-play patient' acting work I used to do in Cairo.

'I'll be sure to tell my Anthony about that, Mr. Ralphy!'

If I am having a bad week, Ruby might be the only person I see and hers the only conversation that I have.

She'll ask how I am managing and if I need help with transport or shopping. That sort of thing.

I have grown to become dependent on her.

I can still get around, but I move slowly now.

There's an oxygen tank and mask in my bedroom.

And another by my settee.

I have good and bad days just as before, but now my good days are ones when I can breathe easily and my bad days are ones when I cannot.

My good friend, Ted, gives me work when he can. He's an elected member of the European Union Parliament. I do online research for him on issues that the 'EU' is considering. That is, I do that when I am feeling up to it.
Ted will come over to visit me too when he has a big speech coming up and wants me to have a listen. I always tell him exactly what I think.
He pays me for that now, even though I never would have considered taking money from him until this 'COPD' thing came along.
It makes me feel like a charity case sometimes.

Otherwise, I have to make do with my tiny 'disability allowance' from the Council.
It's not a lot.

But money worries are not what trouble me most.
It's the limitations to my social life that I find hardest to accept.
Often, I have days when I don't have the strength to venture outdoors.
There's so much to do in London and I cannot take part.
I suppose that is what affects me more than anything.

And when I do feel up to going out with friends, it's not the same.
I still have the urge to tell a story, but I find it difficult saying my stories aloud like I used to do. I might get halfway through and, the next thing I know, my face has gone red as a beet and I am gasping for air.

So I thought I better write my stories down while I still have the 'puff'.

Coaxing from friends and loved ones too encouraged me to write them down.
'Save them for posterity, Ralphy!' my brother told me.
'Otherwise no one will ever know what bull-flannel you used to weave!'

And then too there are the immortal words of Nora.

'Ralphy, when you bite the bullet, there won't be anyone around to tell them. You better write them down. But don't use my real name!'

She told me that long, long ago.

What seems now a different lifetime ago.

So, I've written them down at last.

They're sure to have changed in the telling here.

Just as they always do.

But I know too, as soon as I write them down, they are easy pickings for the scavengers.

It's why I say the Internet has ruined everything.

There's no problem when I tell my stories aloud to friends or acquaintances, but now that I've put them to paper, they can be checked for accuracy.

I can be exposed as a fraud.

A braggart.

A liar.

A fabricator.

So I've been extra careful in the telling here.

Despite any unintended exaggerations on my part, they're all still as true as I can tell them.

I've tried my best too to defy the 'Internet Snoops'.

I believe that I've covered my tracks, although it is possible that a few 'clangors' did still sneak past my detections.

And then they'll find me out.

Truly.

R.E.W.

ABOUT CHARLES SERIO

Charles Serio is artistic director for Serio Ensemble. The Ensemble focuses on new writing and performance. Six of his published plays have been produced and performed in America and the United Kingdom.

He is a former finalist in the London Writers' Competition-poetry division and a former prize winner of the South London New Plays Competition. He works as a professional actor, teacher, director, and general 'man for all seasons' in the performing arts.

He is a previous winner of an Emmy award for his scriptwriting on the CBS television series, *'In Our Lives'*.

Charles also leads corporate workshops internationally in presentation skills and sales technique.

He lives in London.

This is his first novel.